The Tale of the Angel

by

J R Moss

J R Moss is hereby identified as author of this
work in accordance with Section 77 of the Copyright, Designs
and Patents Act 1988

Cover photograph © Inmagine Ltd.

This book is published by
Grosvenor House Publishing Ltd
28–30 High Street, Guildford, Surrey, GU1 3HY.
www.grosvenorhousepublishing.co.uk

A CIP record for this book
is available from the British Library

ISBN 1-905529-45-7

Chapter 1: It wasn't curiosity

Arthur Smollett was, or more accurately had been, a man of limited horizons. Until the recent regular deposits of dead cats in Waterton, Smollett had little interest in the outside world beyond the routine of the animal centre and his own family. It was not fully possible to ignore the unexplained arrival of pairs of dead cats in the Watertons, not least because Eric Pinker was noisily puzzled by it. Every time another cat killing occurred he would talk through with Joyce not just what colour schemes should be chosen for the burials but also why his business had taken this unexpected upturn. He had a variety of theories, each more outlandish than the previous one. And none of it mattered at all to Arthur Smollett. That is, until the day when his own ginger tabby went missing. Joyce had noticed that Lazy had not reappeared on the second day of her absence, but she thought little of it: cats were notorious for cultivating different owners and stringing them all along. But when Eric rang from the shop she half expected the worst. Arthur had been told. What made him do it Joyce never knew but Arthur decided that, instead of asking the Pinkers to bury Lazy like all the others, he would collect the cat and conduct a standard post mortem as to what the cause of death had been. Whatever he had expected, it was not what he found: heroin overdose. His amazement was such that he re-did the test. The result was both astonishing and highly illegal. And so he decided to report it, in person, with specimens.

Bristol main police station was a surviving duty station for the area that included both Waterton and Little Waterton. Smollett, having successfully demanded to see an inspector, was shown into a small tobacco-stained office to the rear of the first floor of the somewhat depressing 1960s building. Out of the grimy windows he could see the back of another office building, its dark granite face

3

streaked with rain. The inspector was tired and Smollett could tell from the crumbs on his desk and the piled up paper in his waste-basket that DI Jesmond had been at work for many hours. On the wall were pinned four maps that together showed the police catch-ment area. Below the maps was a table containing small boxes with an assortment of display aids – ribbons, oversized pins, plain stick-ers. The elderly computer in the corner appeared to be discon-nected and every square inch of the back part of the room was piled deep with cardboard files of assorted colours.

'Yes?' said Jesmond as Smollett was shown in by a weary-looking police sergeant. 'What can I do for you, Mr. er,' Jesmond looked at his notepad, 'Smollett? I see you are a vet over in Little Waterton. Is it about the police dogs?'

'No,' said Smollett. 'I want you to read this.'

He held out a thin typed report bound between two transparent plastic sheets.

'What is it?'

'It's my report.'

'Mr. Smollett, I'm a busy man. Could you perhaps tell me, so that I don't have to read it all, what the report says?'

'Certainly,' replied Smollett. This was just the interest he had been looking for. 'It's about my cat. It died of a heroin overdose!'

It is unclear what reaction Smollett had hoped to elicit. Inspector Jesmond stared incredulously at his visitor.

'I'm sorry?' he said.

'A heroin overdose. I conducted the tests myself. The specimens are here for you to check. Would you like to take a statement from me before you begin to investigate?'

Jesmond looked closely at Smollett and noted his agitated man-ner.

'Investigate?' the policeman repeated.

'It's not the only dead cat. They have been found in pairs, quite regularly, deposited in Waterton and twice in Little Waterton.'

Smollett continued with a meaningful nod towards the file he had handed over.

'All full of heroin?' Jesmond's face was expressionless.

'Possibly. I haven't been able to secure any others, but you could.'

Jesmond sighed. He went over the corner and got out a paper cup. 'Coffee?'

'No, thanks.'

Jesmond returned to his desk carrying a cup of black coffee and three biscuits. 'Mmm,' he munched. 'Are you sure?'

'Inspector Jesmond, I can guarantee you my full co-operation.'

Jesmond said nothing but continued eating biscuits, looking thoughtful. 'Well, Mr. Smollett, it was very nice meeting you. If you find anything else interesting about the cats, do write to us. My desk sergeant will read anything you send, should I be...er...otherwise engaged.'

He reached out towards the telephone, fairly obviously to recall the sergeant.

'Aren't you going to investigate then?' A pause.

'No, Mr. Smollett.'

'But this is a scandal, a crime, probably lots of crimes. These cats must have been seized, as ours was, and murdered using hard drugs.'

Another pause.

Jesmond got up and, with his back towards Smollett, looked out of the window. 'Bristol, Mr. Smollett, is a busy place. You know, I have officers in every area. They deal with rape, and killings, and muggings. They attend threatened domestic assaults, traffic accidents, etc. etc. They are very, very stretched. Mr. Smollett, even if I was inclined to search out the murderer of your cat and allocate police resources to stamping out a gang seizing cats and for no apparent reason killing them, I would have to take men and resources away from other, pressing, investigations. I intend no disrespect, Mr. Smollett, but the police would be criticised if they prioritised cats over people.'

Smollett's face was a picture of disbelief. 'You mean the police aren't interested?'

'We are interested, Mr. Smollett, of course we are. It is just that for the foreseeable future the cost of such an investigation could not possibly be justified.'

'But this is appalling. How can we sleep easily in our beds when people, possibly gangs of people, are rounding up animals, killing them and visiting them upon innocent communities. This could be anything, a vendetta or even a weird cult springing up in our midst. I've read about such things. The West Country is full of strange people who will stop at nothing.'

It was at this point that Jesmond took his eyes off his depressing

5

pile of unanswered post and looked closely at his visitor. He knew that vets, like all professionals, lived under the constant strain of professional practice, unreasonable hours and client demand and he had once had to deal with a doctor who had been reported missing Friday night, only for his secretary to find him Monday morning asleep in the company of two empty whisky bottles in a cupboard in the surgery. Was this man having a stress-induced fantasy? Who on earth would kill even one cat with an expensive drug like heroin? Had one of the police vets become obsessed with crime and projected a mystery into his own sphere of expertise, hoping to dazzle the police with his crime-solving skills? Jesmond was no expert in mental health but he had plenty of experience of litigants in person who plagued his office with imaginary tales of being spied on by M15 and of cases they were bringing to the attention of the European Court of Human Rights if the police didn't arrest the Head of M15. These individuals were usually accompanied by plastic carrier bags full of unsorted documents, mostly written by themselves (come to think of it) and they would never be parted from their 'evidence' for a second in case 'they' got hold of it. Would Smollett be parted from his 'proof'?

'Mr Smollett, I cannot justify commencing an investigation for the reasons previously stated but if you wish I can file your evidence should it ever be required. Perhaps you would like the police to take safe custody of your ....er.... specimens?'

'Certainly not.' Smollett hastily gathered his report and specimens back into his briefcase. 'Why should I want the police to file my research, do nothing with it, and possibly lose it somewhere in a filing cabinet? This is a serious matter. I have come here all the way from Little Waterton. You do know how far that is, don't you?'

This was too much for Jesmond.

'Well, Mr. Smollett...'

'I insist that you take this matter seriously. I have not come here to be fobbed off without your even troubling to read what I have written. This is a disgrace. You do realize that I play golf with the Chief Constable?'

'Then your contacts are certainly more elevated than mine and I suggest you mention it next time you tee off.'

Jesmond opened the door pointedly and called down the corridor for his sergeant before his visitor could launch forth again.

'I feel I should warn you, inspector, that...'

'Goodbye, Mr Smollett, and I will be in touch if anything similar comes to our notice.'

He closed the door the second Smollett went through without waiting for his sergeant to appear. Then he went back to the mess on his desk and stared once more at the photo of a three-year-old boy who had been reported by his parents that morning as missing. He sighed and tried to forget the earnest vision of insistence that had just burst in upon him.

Smollett left the police station in a daze. His sense of what was right and proper had been severely shaken: he determined to investigate himself.

Naturally enough he could hardly expect Joyce to be remotely sympathetic to any plan involving the amount of detailed work, and vigilance, which this one did. Smollett was not a fan of detective fiction but as an intelligent man he realised that the genesis of any crime is the confluence of motive, means and opportunity. Opportunity was easy: if you were a sadistic moron it was far less trouble to get hold of a cat than a dog or, for that matter, any other animal of a reasonable size. Dogs tended to be noisy and resist whereas cats were for the most part happy to be petted by strangers. Means was a more difficult issue. He could not necessarily assume that every murdered cat would have died of an overdose. Was there a cat strangler about? Were any of the animals drowned? Were any poisoned by carbon monoxide? But at least means was something that could be tested by getting hold of another corpse and performing a second post mortem. Motive, however, was absolutely mysterious. Why would anyone do such a thing? Do it once, let alone repeatedly? Why do these animals come from all over the county to Waterton and Little Waterton? Was it a single demented killer or a gang? Was it a form of revenge upon the two villages for some unknown offence? The possibilities were legion and he brooded on them carefully whenever he could, instead of wasting time reading newspapers or choosing the trivia of his life, which Joyce was perfectly capable of doing for him. After all, did it matter what he ate for breakfast or which tie or socks he wore? Every spare moment had to be utilised by a man so hemmed in by client appointments. Sensible possibilities all deserved consideration and in a spirit of open-mindedness he even attended a sermon by the fulminating Reverend Hollis in St. George's Church in Waterton whose congregation for once was swollen with villagers all anxious to hear his views on why the Lord was visiting their parish with a surfeit of dead felines. But a theory of divine wrath did not commend itself to Smollett nor did the vicar's proposed solution to hold an unbroken prayer vigil, or as the vicar put it, a Prayathon, over the first week-end in July.

In fact, so engaged with this problem did Arthur Smollett become that his wife began to be rather troubled about his state of mind. This was not the Arthur Smollett she had known for all these years. Instead of confiding in her and looking for her guidance and, certainly, sympathy, the new Arthur Smollett was a man fired with an inner passion, which he refused to explain. Joyce thought it most unlikely that his disappearances for the long hours between the close of the surgery and his return home were connected with another woman but she did suspect that he was under some kind of stress that must be very deep-seated. He had steadfastly refused to explain where he went and for periods of several days at a time he was not seen between closing the office at six o'clock and midnight the same evening. She could hardly ask around so small a rural community as to whether anyone else knew what he was up to so she simply waited, hoping to deduce from the contents of his pockets what he was up to.

In any investigation, the quality of one's hypothesis is in direct proportion to the quality of one's information. And certain types of information are not readily available. Take the last couple of months, for example, and the things Smollett thought he understood. To resolve the conundrum, he finally concluded, one had to find a likely suspect and then wait until a corpse, that is to say a cat corpse, appeared again. In that Waterton had its own resident heroin addict in the form of Carlton Corshall, Smollett thought it perfectly reasonable to keep the man under surveillance. Most evenings the pathetic figure of Corshall was to be seen lying in an old fur coat in the alcove in front of the butcher's shop. This was about three doors away from the Black Horse pub so it was easy enough for Smollett to park his car outside the pub and simply sit with a book and read in the summer evening light or by torch until something happened. And for about ten days nothing did.

Chapter 2: A walk in the woods.

As a first attempt it had not been bad but murder is a difficult business. Robert Thornhill was annoyed: with himself for calling the vet the previous day; with his stupid wife for not opening the door when the vet turned up; and, most of all, with the vet for wandering off. He was told where to wait. What the hell was he up to? Thornhill angrily kicked the entrance gate to the woods. The metal catch, which was already loose, sheared off. In the dawn light he opened the gate one-handed, and cut himself. For Christ's sake. Putting the shotgun on the ground for a moment, he wound a handkerchief round his hand, and grimly watched his blood soak into the soil. Another time, another day. Children were no problem. You couldn't watch them all the time, and farms were dangerous places. But murdering a woman you hardly knew was not so easy, and now he would be a suspect. The idea was to do it but not be a suspect.

'A life's work for nothing, Tess. That's what I've given him. I was like a son to him, better. It should be mine, all of it. But I know what's coming now. He'll change his will, that's what.'

Tess stank of rotted meat and her pointed face hung to one side. She limped along beside him and stopped to look trustingly into his weather-beaten face. His frame was powerful, that of a man who had spent decades in physical exertion. Thornhill shifted the gun over to his right arm, taking care that she did not taste his blood. She was sick and old. He stepped back a few paces, pointed the gun at her, and pulled the trigger. A tremendous roar shook the woods and the remnants of the big dog's corpse hit the ground. Her head had disappeared entirely, leaving the ground and nearby trees spattered with bone, fluid and blood.

Thornhill turned back to the gate, opened it slowly this time, and closed it behind him, barely hearing the squawking of the birds escaping from their perches above. This wood was private land, part of Blue Grace Farm, and no strangers would be coming this way. He began to feel better, as though her death repaired his mistake in calling the vet to do it the previous day. There had to be another chance, another way to stop this. He strode back along the farm track towards his cottage half a mile or so along it. By now the farm boys would be having breakfast in the cottage kitchen, waiting for him for their orders.

And they were. Four men sat round the big pine table in Blue Grace cottage, wondering where Thornhill could possibly be but knowing he was most likely in a foul mood. Not one of them would want to give him cause for anger, especially not his two cousins, Joe and William, whose father was the tenant of the farm. They lived in small labourers' cottages on the farm but neither of them really did much on the land. Just a bit of fetching and carrying in their cars, the cost of which came off the farm business. Joe spent most of his time indoors, claiming his back was too bad for him to do any serious work. His brother William was not much better. Despite their easy lives, these men looked far older than Robert Thornhill. Each of them had inherited the fair hair and ruddy square face of their own father but none of his cunning or presence. Neither had any interest in the fact that their sixty-six year old father had yesterday been blessed by the birth of a fifth child by his weird new wife.

'More tea, Ralph?' said Joe amiably as he refilled his own generous striped blue and white mug.

'Thanks,' the younger man replied through a mouth full of buttered toast and bacon. 'Where's the boss? Has he heard?'

'He has,' volunteered the man on Ralph's left. Trevor Pickering supervised Ralph and was supposed to be teaching him about the insides of machinery and how to lay bricks but it was not an easy task when Ralph spent most of his time listening to music through headphones. Trevor had two teenage sons and knew better than to make an issue of it. He was a bit taken that Ralph had any curiosity about events in the boss's family since he showed so little interest in the jobs under his nose.

'Funny thing a vet delivering a baby,' said Ralph, slowly.

'None of your business,' observed Trevor in a warning tone.

'But lucky he came along when he did,' persisted the other.

No one said anything further because, at that moment, a fresh pot of tea and more scrambled eggs in a frying pan appeared on the table. The woman bringing these extra items looked irritably around the room.

'Thanks,' said Joe amiably. 'Always good breakfasts in this house.'

His sister Kathleen said nothing but returned to the back part of the kitchen to refill the kettle. Shortly afterwards, Robert Thornhill arrived at the cottage. He took off his boots in the porch and headed for the warm kitchen.

'Morning, all,' Thornhill said evenly. The men greeted him in return as he picked up bread and a mug of tea. He drank down a mouthful of hot liquid and turned to Trevor. 'Dog's dead,' Thornhill continued, without expression. 'You'll find it woodside of the gate. Bury it by the big tree farmside of the gate, away from the mess. And mark the grave properly. Mrs. Thornhill will want to see it, maybe put some flowers there this afternoon.'

'Right.' said Trevor, getting up. He paused, knowing from the mess on Thornhill's coat that the boss had used the shotgun. He did not comment. 'Come on, Ralph. Get to it, lad.' He then turned to Thornhill but discreetly looked at the table: 'Missus said your uncle wants to see you after breakfast. At the house.'

'Let me know when you've finished.' Robert Thornhill smiled into Trevor's face, but it was a smile as cold as a hospital freezer. 'I shan't be gone long.'

*

The blast of the shotgun had reverberated loudly at the southern end of the woods. In a clump of fern and bluebells, half a dozen paces from the track, the dishevelled form of a plump middle-aged woman could be discerned sitting bolt upright, both heavily braceletted hands holding back her hair. First, unobserved, she consulted a silver pocket watch hanging on a chain round her neck: there were things to do. Then, for fun, she stared in a wild, exaggerated fashion around.

'Oh my God! Oh my God, we'll all be killed as we lie here. It's him, he's back. It's Little Mickey with the gun. Get up! Get up!' So saying, she prodded the nearest sleeping form vigorously with her right foot. 'Christ, move or we'll be killed. Get your clothes on, wake up. Oh God! He'll be nearly here.'

A third figure sprang nervously to his feet and began pulling on his clothes, shakily adjusting his tie and smoothing his hair back. Maddie Shallcombe expertly stuffed her large person back into the sheepskin coat she had been lying on and addressed Eric Pinker in a loud whisper:

'Eric, you look tidy. Walk up the path the other way and we'll get back to the car. Take your time. Say you're out for a walk. You haven't seen me, OK? And put your specs on. Freddie! Freddie!'

The second figure rolled over and heaved himself to his feet.

'Alright, Maddie. Just a minute.' Realising he was now the only one fully exposed to the fresh air, Freddie Pinker also began clumsily to dress. 'What's the time, Eric?'

'Quarter past seven,' his brother answered. 'See you back at the shop by nine. You open up and get the car ready. We're due to collect the body at ten fifteen.'

'Right,' said Freddie.

The by now perfectly besuited Eric Pinker pushed his spectacles up his nose and set off up the long path, leaving Mrs. Shallcombe and Freddie to sneak back to the parked hearse and drive into the village by the back road. Eric walked slowly, trying to look casual rather than brave. He definitely did not want to imagine the face of Little Mickey and tried in vain to empty his head of scenes from the previous night, scenes that clamoured for attention. The smoke in the pub, the taste of Special, various parts of various bodies – how on earth did they get down to the woods and who had done the driving? And what if the two Michaels found out? Eric stopped and tried to breathe more slowly. He felt terrible: worse than the day he found out he'd failed his accountancy exam, worse than before meeting his first trustee in bankruptcy, even worse than during Freddie's embalming lesson when he'd thrown up all over the late Mrs. Dennison. That bad.

What I need, thought Eric, summoning his courage, is to think about ways to improve the business. That'll calm me down. It didn't, but it did provide a distraction.

Pinkers' funeral business was the oldest in the area but it was in serious trouble. Not that people weren't dying, of course they were. It was the competition from Mrs. Lightfoot up in Little Waterton, a mile north of Waterton itself. Ever since she'd joined a chain and redone her place, everyone wanted her. The Pinkers' business was virtually at a standstill and debts were mounting up. If you couldn't pay for the fancy extras, you couldn't offer them to the family. Mrs. Lightfoot, however, could. What's more, she had befriended most of the over-seventies at the Church socials and the WGA meetings. He suspected her of cornering the market with the meals-on-wheels ladies by supplying homemade fruitcakes for their old people. Yes, Mrs. Lightfoot was an all-round disaster and he had spent weeks racking his brains for ways to compete. There simply wasn't one. Everyone liked her. But the truth was much worse: if Little Mickey did do him in, he would rather Mrs. Lightfoot put the pieces together than his brother Freddie. Eric frowned as he thought of his business partner. Probably not surprising Freddie looks like a butcher, Eric thought. After all, he's had twenty years in the trade. It was an advantage for the really messy bits but a lot of people are put off by his manner. Being part-time undertakers is ruining us. We need more work, more ideas. He stopped and stood still as he spied two men in the distance at the top end of the path. He knew immediately they weren't Little Mickey O'Dare and Michael Riley: they were far too small. Eric had spent a lot of time observing them from next door during the long months of plotting to lure the siren Mrs. Shallcombe away from the beds of the two Michaels and into the beds of himself and Freddie. But he didn't recognise the men either. One of them was stooping over something on the path. Somewhat heartened by this turn of events, Eric proceeded briskly towards them.

'Morning,' he said, drawing level. Ordinarily the men would have challenged him as to what he was up to on private land, but they were distracted by the remains of the Alsatian. Trevor and Ralph were stood by the torso, Trevor with his hands on his hips and carrying a large plastic bag in one hand. Ralph looked pretty green and retreated a few yards to be sick, leaving Eric staring at the dog, and at Trevor.

Something akin to a state of bliss descended on Eric when he had an idea. The fact that this happened on a fairly frequent basis never lessened the impact of the experience or the optimism it generated. It was the first of May 2002, the beginning of a new, blissful, era.

Trevor was not much given to idle conversation and was waiting for Ralph to recover himself. There was no special hurry. Mrs. Thornhill was never up in the mornings, and all they needed to do now was to decide how big a hole should be dug and where.

'Your dog?' said Eric solicitously, as though the headless creature had passed away peacefully in its kennel. What an opportunity to get started!

'No', said Trevor shortly. He did not know Eric but he could tell he was a man with soft hands who spent his time sat down all day.

'Only, I was wondering if the owner might like a proper funeral for a lost companion. For free, of course. I mean flowers, and a coffin, proper setting down and everything.' Trevor looked suspicious and eyed Eric up and down: he had seen him before. Ralph was kneeling by the path, making gagging noises. 'You see,' continued Eric, 'I'm in the funeral business and, well, I'd like to do it to promote a new aspect of the service we provide.'

'You from Lightfoot's?' Trevor asked. Eric winced.

'No. Pinkers' in Waterton. Here's my card.' Eric rummaged in a pocket and handed over a small black-edged business card. Trevor read 'Pinker & Pinker, Funeral Directors. 22A Blackhorse Lane, Waterton.'

'Is that near the Black Horse?'

'Yes, next door.'

'I don't recall seeing a parlour.'

'Ah well, we're upstairs, on top of where the florist used to be.'

Trevor scratched his head. The dog belonged to the Missus and there was no doubt she would be upset. A decent bit of fuss might ease matters along. On the other hand, he was not a man to ignore a direct order from Robert Thornhill.

'Just a minute.' Trevor reached into his jacket pocket and pulled out a mobile phone. He pressed a button in the memory and waited. Thornhill was still at the cottage. 'Hello, Trevor here. Boss, we're up at the gate with a chap called Mr. Pinker, funeral director from Waterton, says he'd do a proper funeral for Tess for free. What shall I tell him?'

'He wants to do what?'

'Do a funeral for Tess. He says it's to promote his business.'

Five seconds' awkward silence followed, presumably whilst Thornhill digested this proposal. Eric, by now no newcomer to appalling smells, was not feeling so bright this close to the dog.

'Eric or Freddie?' a distant voice said in Trevor's ear.

'You Eric or Freddie?' asked Trevor.

'Eric,' replied Eric.

'Eric,' repeated Trevor down the phone.

'Alright,' heard Trevor. 'Let him take the dog and tell him to ring me this afternoon at three o'clock. Give him the number.' The line went dead.

'Got a pencil?' Trevor put the phone back into his pocket and took the ballpoint that Eric was holding out. He turned over the Pinkers' card and wrote:

'DOG TESS. RING ROBERT THORNHILL AT 3.'

He paused, briefly chewed the end of the ballpoint, and wrote out a series of numbers. 'You can take the dog now.' He handed the card back to Eric and thrust the plastic bag into Eric's other hand. 'Get up, lad. Get a grip,' he shouted in Ralph's direction.

Eric's eyes narrowed and his nostrils flared. He fervently wished that Freddie were with him at that very minute. But there was no alternative, so he took a deep breath and got on with what had to be done. Ten minutes later, with a heavy black bin liner over his shoulder, he went through the gate and marched towards the road. Hopefully it wouldn't leak. He was not looking forward to the bus ride back into the village, but he'd probably have a seat to himself.

Chapter 3: In the study

Robert Thornhill decided to wait until nine before setting off for his Uncle Joshua's house across the fields. It gave him a bit longer to evaluate his alibi, in case it was needed.

The cottage by now was quiet. His drunken wife was asleep upstairs and his cousin Kathleen had tidied up after breakfast and washed down the flagged floor before driving off in her husband's battered red Ford Fiesta to do the shopping. He quite liked Kathleen being around, not just because Cathy couldn't do anything round the house nowadays but also because Kathleen was up to completing the farm ledgers and discussing them with him in exact detail. That was on the plus side. On the minus side, she was always on about how she should be better paid, worked her fingers to the bone and ought to get a share in the farm business when her father officially retired – not that there was any sign of that. It was a hopeless expectation and she knew it. She had no more chance of that than did her older sister, Lillian, who had married a Texan plumber and moved away years ago. Joe and William were easy-going but dense. The farms, a thousand acres tenanted and five hundred freehold, the dairy, the processing plant, the pick-your-own operation, the artists' village and the holiday cottages were all controlled and run by Robert, who was supposedly the farm foreman and was paid as such. Old Joshua would no more break up the empire than he would name his successor and heir. Laying aside treacherous hints on family occasions, Joshua's policy of saying nothing precluded any in-fighting and preserved everyone's hopes of something on his death. In practice everyone had assumed for at least a decade that Robert would inherit the lot: without him the enterprise would collapse.

The grandfather clock in the hallway chimed nine. This cottage was really two cottages knocked into one. Robert walked into the room adjoining the second porch and reached for his mobile phone to take with him. Then he remembered his uncle didn't like them so he left it by the door on his way out.

It was a sunny morning and the walk across was sufficient for him to clear his mind of his botched attempt to help nature along and rid them of all Jennifer, or whatever else she called herself nowadays. The main farmhouse was a sizeable building and was kept in immaculate repair. The exact age of it was hard to tell but it was probably originally an eighteenth century construction of brick with, unusually, a stone front. The best part of three hundred years' prosperity had caused many enlargements and embellishments to be made. Although the front of the house retained a square and somewhat forbidding appearance, the backward extensions had been used so as to produce a courtyard effect, bringing light to both wings of the house and creating in the centre a sunny patio and a kitchen garden. Joshua's first wife, Margaret (or Meg, as she was known in the family) had been given a free hand not just in decorating but also in integrating the design. Joshua never interfered in domestic matters partly, it is true, because he felt that the home was a woman's business, and, partly, because his first wife was largely spending her own money. It would be wrong to think that Joshua had married her because of the money, but it was certainly welcome. She had inherited from her father, over half a million pounds, most of which represented the proceeds of an insurance policy that he had taken out eighteen months or so before his death. It had all been investigated in the early 1980s by the company and they found no grounds to refuse payment. Yes, it did look suspicious that her fifty-year-old father, average in every way, should take out the policy, suddenly gain fifteen stone and then die of a heart attack. Could it fairly be described as suicide by knife and fork, let alone a breach of the insurance policy? Meg did not live with her father at the time and she was the only beneficiary. The company had decided that payment was unavoidable.

The front exterior of the house still looked much as it had two years ago when Meg had died unexpectedly of a stroke. Her rare white rose bushes remained planted either side of the stone pillars flanking the front door and either side of the front garden path the strip borders were a riot of early spring flowers, white and yellow. Robert walked up to the heavy white-painted door and knocked loudly using the brass pig on the knocker, the only item of domestic decoration, apart from the furniture in his den, that Joshua had chosen himself. A moment or two later Joshua opened the door.

'Come in,' he said.

Robert walked through the airy living room towards the study door. The house had been transformed since his last visit. And not for the better, he thought. Two plastic rainbows now stuck to the windowpanes and the walls had been painted mauve. In the middle of the floor a half-finished abstract canvass, entirely executed in shades of green, stood on an easel, with paint pots and dustsheets around it. The shelves either side of the fireplace had been removed and replaced by glass cabinets. One of these contained a foot-high red candle in the shape of lovers embracing. The other had a giant pregnant figurine made of clay and was decorated with dead flowers. The room reeked of incense. How could his uncle stand it?

Joshua beckoned his guest into the study, which was exactly as Robert had last seen it three months previously. Charles Dickens himself would have felt fully at home in this sombre masculine space. Joshua moved to sit behind his mahogany desk and pulled open a drawer on one side. He reached down and, with both hands, brought up a black leather-bound book, held shut by a sizeable brass clasp. Robert's heart began to sink. He looked calmly at his uncle, a tall thick set man with white, once blond, hair, a high-coloured face and exceedingly sharp blue eyes.

'Congratulations,' said Robert. 'How's Jennifer?'

'Rhiannon,' his uncle corrected him. 'Well. The vet did a good job'.

'And the baby?'

'Well. They'll be in Gloucester Infirmary for a couple of days.'

'Got a name for him yet?'

'His name will be Neville.'

'I thought it was going to be Kerounnos, if it was a boy.'

'Neville,' his uncle repeated, 'after my grandfather, your great-grandfather and his.'

Bad, thought Robert to himself, very bad. He was still standing in the middle of the room.

'Sit down,' said Joshua. 'I need to ask you a few things.'

'Business is good. It looks as though we could do very well going into turf.'

'Not those things.' The old man picked his wooden pipe from the rack on the desk and took a few minutes to light it. They sat in silence. Robert's eyes strayed over a handwritten letter lying open on the desk. 'Look into the shaving mirror at your lazy face, you son of a coward...' he read all in a familiar spidery hand. It was the usual missive from the landlord, the 4th Lord Errington. His butler, Mr. Dancer, delivered such a letter by hand on the first of every month and had done so for as long as Robert could remember. With equal ceremony the tenant invariably read it and hung it on the nail provided for that purpose by the toilet.

'Now,' said Joshua coolly. 'They tell me the shed door was locked behind her all day yesterday. Your man Trevor had to break the lock.' He paused, waiting for his nephew to say something.

'So he said.'

'She'd been in there all day trying to get out or call someone.'

'No one had cause to be there after breakfast yesterday. Dave Merchant had a couple of days off.'

'She was setting up an easel, you remember. And matching paint colours. Weren't you supposed to be helping her move in her stuff?'

So saying, the old man slowly scrutinised every inch of his nephew's face.

'I had to go to Bristol; I rang her and told her so on Monday night. She could have waited.'

There was a pause before his uncle continued.

'Might have died, the doctor at the hospital said. Blood loss, infections.' Joshua puffed at the pipe.

Was his uncle going to question him, hand on the family bible? What proof could he possibly have? Another pause. The room was now heavy with the smell of warm tobacco and Robert's eyes were beginning to sting. Eventually, very quietly, Joshua Thornhill continued:

'You won't know, of course, how concerned your grandfather was when you were born. In case,' he drew in again from the pipe and frowned, 'anything, shall we say anything untoward, should happen to you on the farm. But, of course, being as I am your godfather, I made sure nothing did. So now,' another pause, 'I want you to be Neville's godfather.'

In one move, the old man had outsmarted him. Joshua unclasped the family bible and pointed to an entry six or so pages in. At the bottom he had already written: '2002 Neville Thornhill, Godfather Robert Thornhill.' He handed an old-fashioned ink pen and the precious book to his nephew. 'You'll need to sign here.'

Robert hesitated, shocked. A refusal was unthinkable.

'With pleasure.' He signed very slowly, blowing on the ink. The child was safe.

*

It was 2.15pm and Arthur Smollett was feeling rough. He sat supporting his balding head using one hand, his elbow propped up on his melamine table. The lighting in his office, or study, as he liked to call it because clients and their pets were not allowed in there at all, was too bright. He dragged himself up, switched off the fluorescent strip and returned to the table and his previous position. He closed his eyes and began to breathe deeply. He couldn't sleep like this. Joyce, his wife and also his secretary, tapped on the glass panel in the door from the corridor, checking whether he had nodded off.

'Fancy a cup of tea, dear,' she said, softly putting her arm around his shoulder. 'Head still bad?'

'Thanks, love. Who else is there this afternoon?'

'Well, Mrs. Rossett has cancelled the 2.30. She says the parrot is eating again. And at 4.15 I've arranged for you to talk to Dr. Welling about the X-rays for Scarlet Flash. His secretary says he's operating until four. So I'm assuming you'll be here until then but I have rung round to cancel those two farm visits and put them over to eight o'clock and nine o'clock tomorrow morning, Fowler then Greentop. Nobody minded. You're something of a hero to farmers at the moment.'

'I'll sign autographs if I survive until tomorrow.'

'You will, don't worry. I'll go and get that tea.' She bustled out, taking care to close the door quietly. Arthur needed to go to bed. He really shouldn't have come in today but it wasn't possible, at such short notice, to cancel the operation on the Great Dane. Mr. Patel, its owner, had insisted on having his chosen anaesthetist come over from Cardiff. Smollett sat motionless until his wife returned. 'Oh, and by the way, Eric Pinker rang and said he wanted to have a word and would it be OK to drop round sometime after three for a chat. He said he wasn't after treatment for anything.'

'Do I know him?'

'I do. He lives in Waterton. You know his brother Freddie, the butcher.'

'What does he want?'

'He said it was private. I didn't really ask because the other phone was ringing so I just said yes. I can always tell him not to bother, if you like.'

'It doesn't matter. It'll keep me from falling asleep. Thanks for the tea.'

Mrs. Smollett left the room, taking with her a tray of papers and a dead coffee cup. Arthur Smollett stared at his tea. The events of the previous day had acquired an unreal quality as he ran it through his mind again. When Mrs. Thornhill hadn't opened the door at six, he'd driven up to the farm buildings along the road, in case Tess was still in her kennel by the yard. Though she belonged to Cathy Thornhill, David Merchant spent a lot of his time looking after her. But there was no sign of Dave. Instead, he had heard a woman screaming and shouting from the implement shed. He had known immediately what was going on, but getting the door open was impossible. In the end Trevor Pickering opened up, and not before time.

Smollett had not previously met the new Mrs. Joshua Thornhill, though he'd heard plenty about her from his wife. No woman with purple hair can hope to pass unnoticed in a rural community. His travelling box in the car had all the essentials – sterilising kit, sharp instruments, sutures, surgical thread, and needles – even if they had been put to use mostly on horses. By the time they got in, it was far too late to move the woman so he'd washed his hands at the little sink and introduced himself. In this intimate situation he had felt the need to say something, anything. So he talked about himself. Oh dear. He had then probably run through his whole life story by 3am when the child was finally out. Everyone else, including Joshua Thornhill, had been banned from the scene by the cursing mother, so it was her and him on their own.

What curses they were. Delivering horses was in a different league altogether. He'd known Rhiannon, as she now called herself, was an American but what dreadful language! Excrement, profanity, body parts and food, together with threats towards her husband's privates of a kind that put old Joshua in a totally new light. And the noise! A lot of her rantings made no sense to him. He assumed mid-wives just got used to it. At one point Rhiannon had begun to chant over and over again 'Sheila Levine, Sheila Levine.' Smollett had enquired if she wanted him to ring a friend but this hadn't gone down at all well. 'Sheila's a construct, you sadistic moron!' More screams and more invective. Smollett had shaken his head and quietly droned on again with his monologue. It was precisely the kind of scene he'd decided never to encounter. That's why he was a vet not a doctor. If she'd been a horse making this much fuss, he'd have knocked her out.

So today he was not at his best. It was 4am before he'd cleaned up and Kathleen Thornhill had persuaded Rhiannon to get in the ambulance, and 5.30am before he'd finished telling his wife what had happened. Joyce seemed able to carry on without sleep, he assumed because she'd always attended in the night to the girls when they were babies. Well Joyce was driving home today.

Tap, tap. It was Joyce again.

'Arthur, are you up to seeing Eric Pinker or not, do you think? He's in reception now.'

Smollett's wristwatch showed ten past three. 'Give me five minutes to tidy up then show him in. No need to ring through.'

Joyce returned to reception where the seated Eric Pinker was eating a chocolate biscuit and drinking coffee from a white mug with the words 'I belong to Wendy' enamelled in black across it. Eric was impressed. He'd been past the animal centre many times but never had cause to go in, though he'd known Joyce Smollett for years, long before she'd met Arthur. Joyce beamed at the visitor.

'Quite a place you've got here, Joyce.'

'Thanks. It wasn't always this big, you know, but we decided to expand into operations more, about five years ago, and one thing led to another. So now there are four vets in the practice and I run the office for them.'

Eric thought it was a miracle that they had got planning permission to erect a steel frame building in the middle of Little Waterton at all. The architect, he'd heard, had pulled strings as well as giving the front façade of the project a 'rural' appearance complete with flower boxes and whitewashed pebbledash exterior. Inside was something different altogether. It was cool, high-tech and very pleasant.

'This is a fantastic set up, Joyce. I hardly dare ask you now.'

'Ask what?'

'Well, I'm hoping to rent a corner from you, even a desk would do. I want to set up a bereavement counselling service for pet owners. You know, help them to cope with their loss. I've had a lot of experience with that sort of thing. Well, similar.'

'I thought you were an accountant.'

'Only part-time. Freddie and I had to take over Dad's business. We'd like to tailor the services we offer so as to specialise in what the market needs. We're expanding too.' Eric reached into his pocket and pulled out a small transparent plastic box containing business cards. 'Here, have one. You never know, one of your clients might find it useful.'

Joyce looked curiously at the card. It was brilliant white and printed upon it in powder-puff pink were, on one side, a pair of smiling teddy bears and, on the other, still in pink, the firm's name and contact details. 'Pinker & Pinker. Paradise for Pets. Ceremonies of Passage Arranged,' read Joyce aloud.

'What a nice idea. Do you get much business?'

'Well, we've only just started this side of it but we intend to invest in a pets' chapel and do the whole thing properly. Of course one of the reasons we'd like to team up here is to meet the local pet community so we can personalise things for when they are called on to a Higher Sphere.'

'Oh, Eric, that is very nice. And it's true, we do find the owners can get quite distressed sometimes.'

Arthur Smollett, who had meanwhile become impatient, appeared in the reception. Joyce looked up.

'Oh, Arthur, this is Eric Pinker. Eric, Arthur.'

The two men shook hands.

'This way,' said Smollett heavily, retracing his steps towards the study. Eric shot Joyce his very best smile, and followed.

Chapter 4: New dispositions

The second Tuesday in May was exactly a week after the birth of Neville Thornhill. It was a fine but cloudy day, fine enough for the firm of Dale, Dale & Ogden, Solicitors, to be out and about visiting clients.

Mr. Clifford Dale and Mr. Douglas Dale each slammed a car door shut as they settled down into their firm's brown Bristol motorcar. A car like this would never have been chosen by either of them for personal use, but this was different and it hit just the right note of expense, understatement and superiority that they needed for the type of visits that were planned for this particular morning. In the normal way the brothers preferred to interview clients in their comfortable offices. The building itself had been occupied by members of the Dale family, always attorneys at law, for at least two hundred years, the business passing from father to son or nephew through the generations.

The offices had originally been the home of Samuel Dale, the founder of the firm about whom there were many legends. His specially created wood and leather armchair, of impressive dimensions, still sat the waiting room and many of the law reports lining the wooden bookshelves around it had been bought by him and carried his name in faded brown ink. A woodcut depicting his smiling face hung behind the receptionist's chair, together with two framed photographs each of a guide dog trained for the blind at the expense of the firm in more recent times. it was a family firm in the old-fashioned sense. Between them Mr. Clifford Dale and Mr. Douglas Dale knew every secret of every resident within a fifteen mile radius, or so they thought. One might have thought it sad that this generation of Dales had no blood successors, but these were not sad people. Their daughters were not interested in continuing the legal tradition and, in any case, they had recruited young Mr. Ogden as a trainee and were more than pleased with his decision to remain on as the junior partner. As the car drove out along the gravel driveway onto the road joining Waterton and Little Waterton the brothers were looking forward to completing a familiar ritual.

This morning's double appointment, respectively at 11 and 11.10am had been repeated regularly twice a year, in May and in early September, for at least twenty years. It was a remarkable curiosity that, although the 4th Lord Errington and old Joshua Thornhill hated each other, each of them insisted on imparting their secrets to the same firm of solicitors. Neither was prepared to cede defeat and allow the other to enjoy the services of the firm and so a workable compromise had to be devised. Consequently, with precise timing and great solemnity, Mr. Clifford Dale visited Lord Errington and Mr. Douglas Dale visited Mr. Joshua Thornhill on the very same day, for the same amount of time, on each occasion. They never discussed with each other what transpired and made sure that their records were kept separately in locked drawers. Mr. Clifford was dropped off at Hamset Manor at 11am whilst Mr. Douglas drove on to the farmhouse at Blue Grace Farm. Naturally neither of them could have known that each of their clients was grappling with the same problem at the same time.

As the oversized car came to a halt at the entrance to Hamset Manor, the eccentric Mr. Dancer opened the door for the somewhat bulky Mr. Clifford Dale to climb out.

'Good morning, Mr. Clifford, sir.'

'Good morning, Dancer.'

'His Lordship is ready to receive you, sir.'

'Excellent.'

'May I carry your briefcase, sir?'

'No thank you, Dancer.'

Dancer bowed by way of assent, slowly, as he was now a hindered by his rheumatism. He shuffled forwards to lead the way, moving very slowly indeed. Following behind, Clifford Dale remarked to himself, as he usually did at this point, how curious it was that Mr. Dancer always seemed to radiate the smell of kippers. What, of course, Clifford Dale did not know was that Lord Errington existed largely on a diet of kippers and Burgundy. He claimed that his own grandfather had recommended it as a most invigorating diet for any man over sixty-five. As the 3rd Lord Errington had lived to be a hundred and three, his grandson saw no reason to ignore his example. Only Mrs. Allott, the cook, found it rather tedious to be constantly presenting kippers to Lord Errington whilst the rest of the household's needs allowed her more creative side to shine.

Hamset Manor was a truly magnificent brick-built Elizabethan house. At the front lay a single courtyard, neatly trimmed lawns on either side of the entrance road. The entrance hall had little to recommend it to modern taste, although it was much loved by the present Lord Errington whose hunting trophies hung at high level round the walls. Up to twenty glassy-eyed stags peered over the heads of Dancer and Dale as they neared the oak door into the main hall. Dancer lifted the heavy iron latch and held open the door for the visitor. He then moved ahead again, bowed deeply towards the centre of the room and made his announcement.

'Mr. Clifford Dale, my Lord, of the firm Dale, Dale & Ogden of Waterton.'

'Cliff, old man, do come in. Thank you, Dancer, that'll do.'

'Would your Lordship prefer to take coffee here or in the library?'

'Here. Thank you.'

'Morning, Corky, how are you keeping?'

Despite the best part of thirty years difference in their ages, Lord Errington always insisted on being addressed socially by the name he had acquired at prep school owing to a series of rather dubious tricks he was able to perform with the cork of a wine bottle.

'Not so bad, not so bad. Firm busy?'

'We can't complain.'

'Is your brother down with that lazy tenant of mine?'

'Of course. The usual arrangements are in place.'

There was a restrained knocking at the door, which Clifford Dale noticed but Lord Errington clearly had not. The latter walked over to the glass-paned south wall of the house, peered through the magnificent Jacobean window, and glared down the hill in the direction of Blue Grace Farm. The knocking at the door was getting louder.

'Damn lazy tenant, that Thornhill chap. I shot his uncle personally, you know, damn coward.' Clifford Dale did know, because the story was regularly repeated in full with great relish. 'Deserting Monty, damn cheek. I volunteered, you know, to be one of the marksman. Owe it to the Regiment, you know. Fellow orf of my Estate.' Dancer by now was hammering on the door with his metal-topped stick. 'Do come in, Dancer, no need to make such a row. I'm not deaf, you know.'

Dancer appeared, laboriously wheeling in front of him a trolley with a flowery porcelain coffee set and two cups upon it. On the lower shelf of the trolley lay a wicker basket containing four perfect peaches, two plates, a pair of small silver knives and a glass of Burgundy.

'Will that be all?' Dancer discreetly gathered up Lord Errington's hearing aid and put it in his pocket. He did not wait for an answer but bowed and left.

'Got a problem, Cliff, need your advice. Not now, in writing, later. Tell you all about it. Need a way through, cast iron way through. Help yourself. Coffee, and so on.'

Errington took the glass of Burgundy and frowned at the sight of the peaches. He supposed that they were yet another effort on Mrs. Allott's part to wean him off his excellent diet of kippers. He continued to stare out of the window, barely noticing the sheep grazing the hill on which the house stood. Possibly Clifford Dale had said something but without his hearing aid it would not disturb the train of Lord Errington's thoughts. It was always his practice to see his lawyers without being able to hear them. It had the great benefit that they had to listen to him without interrupting with their tedious questions and objections. If there were a serious problem, he expected them to write to him afterwards. After three or four minutes, during which he assumed that Mr. Clifford Dale had taken up whatever refreshment he required, Lord Errington commenced his monologue.

'Need help now, Cliff. Bad show all round. Grandson of mine no good, you know. Won't go into the Army, won't go to Cirencester, won't even go to Cambridge. Mother's boy. Always thought he was no good. Lies about all day. Unconscious. Goes down the village, buys some more of that rubbish. Knocks himself out again. Can't go on. Not an heir I want. Get rid of him. Cut him out. Granddaughter's alright but won't marry, damn it. What do you say, Cliff? Have a biscuit.'

At this Lord Errington rang a bell in the kitchen by pulling a sash hanging by the window. Dancer, who had been expecting this, appeared almost as by magic a few seconds later carrying a tray with Mrs. Allott's homemade biscuits upon it. Whatever Clifford Dale had responded to Lord Errington, the latter continued unruffled.

'Not that I'm entirely agin it. For the right reasons. But not all the time. Pa used a bit of laudanum himself. After his leg went. But this is a young fella. Spent his own money. Takes his mother's money. Even borrows from the servants. Chap can't run the Estate, can't do anything most of the time. Shame Roddy ain't here. Boy needs a father, firm hand. He's not having a penny of my money. House has been in the family since 1588, all the charter lands, everything. Give it to young Carlton, there'll be nothing left in a year. Blood's not everything. Boy won't starve, he's got the Swiss money coming anyway.'

All this time Errington had been staring across the home park, the eighteenth century landscape entirely created under the hand of Capability Brown. In the distance Blue Grace Farmhouse resembled a perfect tiny toy. By it was a perfect tiny toy car. Errington's eyes narrowed again. He had never believed Joshua Thornhill's claim that his startling Roddy's horse with the rifle was an accident. Roddy's death had undoubtedly caused the present crisis. In the middle distance he could see his daughter-in-law walking the dogs. A capable woman but not up to controlling her son. He clasped his hands behind his back and wondered whether he would live to see his granddaughter Sophia produce an heir in the next generation. Although he was a remarkably agile eighty-two, the odds were not such he would care to bet on them himself. However there seemed little else to do. Therefore he walked smartly back to the middle of the room where his solicitor appeared to be saying something. The younger man was sat on a slender antique upholstered chair and was reaching into his briefcase for something.

'Don't bother, Cliff. Mind's made up. Just paper it up, would you? I die, everything goes to Sophie. I'll send Dancer over Friday. For the documents.'

He then walked over to Clifford Dale and shook his hand vigorously.

'Dancer will see you out and, er, Mrs. Roberts wants a word.'

Dancer appeared without the bell being rung.

'May I assist you, sir?' Dancer said, having bowed politely in the direction of his master. Clifford Dale shook his head and smiled.

'Very well,' Dale was addressing Errington, 'but bear in mind what I said about the risks of doing this.' He turned and followed the elderly butler out of the room. By the front door Mrs. Roberts, the housekeeper, was already waiting, a large bunch of spring flowers in her hand.

'Mr. Dale, please do take these for your office. My husband's very proud of his blooms and we have plenty in the house here.'

Mrs. Roberts was a tall, dark-haired Scot in her forties. Her face somehow always seemed to carry a freshly scrubbed look. She was the very soul of politeness, unlike her grumpy god-fearing husband, the gardener.

'Why, thank you, Mrs. Roberts. That's very kind of you and, of course, his Lordship.'

Douglas Dale was already waiting in the car by the entrance.

Fifteen minutes later the Bristol swung round the corner into High Street, Waterton on the way back to the office. As it did so, Clifford Dale, out of the corner of his eye, caught sight of a crumpled, filthy, figure asleep on the pavement outside the butcher's shop. Clifford Dale sighed. What a headache the man was: Carlton Corshall, heir apparent to the Hamset Estate.

*

Freddie Pinker was a worried man. He sat on a bright pink sofa in the middle of the ground floor shop window of what had been the florists below their undertakers' office. It was an alien scene: the entire shop front was filled with what Eric had described as an absolute bargain, that is to say, two thousand pink teddies, many of which hung from the ceiling by pink ribbon. Freddie pulled a rude face in the general direction of the glass: as usual there were about six or seven small children with their faces pressed against it. He barely felt like an undertaker at all any more, despite the fact that that very morning they had buried, or as Eric would have it, assisted on her passage to the next world, Cathy Thornhill's dog.

Freddie was beginning to think that Eric had completely lost the plot. Mrs. Thornhill had wanted the dog buried behind the cottage, rather than up by the farm path. Eric had planned the occasion to coincide with the mens' lunch break and somehow managed to dragoon them all into standing in a circle around the flower-festooned grave whilst he, Eric, read a long poem (god knows from where) about the loss of one's best four-footed friend. Mrs. Thornhill attended dressed completely in black and more or less propped up by Kathleen Thornhill, whose sour expression never varied until the point where Eric announced that he was going to say a prayer for the dearly departed soul of the dog. At this Kathleen was heard loudly to remark that he was an accountant not a vicar and enough was enough. The men were also quite keen to go, having spent over half their lunchbreak listening to a eulogy for the dead dog when they would rather be eating their sandwiches. Eric's enthusiasms were something that Freddie over the years had got used to. But this one had really taken hold. All in all, although they were not receiving a penny for it, Tess had probably received a far better funeral service, decorations and attention than Pinker & Pinker had ever lavished on any human being. Even the hearse had been gaudily decked out in pink and white flowers (pink for girls, you understand) and a small square headstone was duly laid in advance at the designated spot. On it was a small but beautifully crafted bass-relief of an Alsatian dog and next to it the words: 'Tess, a trusted friend. Mother of Noddy and Nipper'.

It was not so much Eric's enthusiasm that worried Freddie as the fact that he was spending money hand over fist. Take the florist's old shop, for instance. The place had been gutted, cleaned and painted entirely pink and white in the space of four days. What kind of money did you have to spend to get that done? And the extra coffins stored in the basement that had been ordered on urgent delivery, they were expensive too. Freddie had no idea whether they would ever need a coffin big enough to take a racehorse but somehow he doubted whether Eric in ordering three of them (each in a different wood) had much more of an idea than he did. The ground floor had been dressed in soft furnishings and could be internally partitioned by curtains so as to allow a private waiting room and a lying-in chapel to be made. There was even a new sound system so that soothing music was available when needed. Freddie could see very easily how it might be an advantage to open a bereavement counselling desk at the animal centre, which Eric by now had done. At least in his periods of manning the desk at the animal centre Eric was learning something about animals, a subject which hitherto had entirely eluded him. But the problem was that none of the animals seemed to be sufficiently sick for their owners to have expressed any interest in receiving bereavement counselling. No, what really worried Freddie was the feeling that things had got out of control. He walked behind the sofa and picked up from the new white fake Louis XVI table a box of business cards. This time Eric had had them printed in blue. To be sure, they looked quite smart but they carried the legend:

'Pinker & Pinker Flowers Limited. Fab flowers for all occasions, sad or gay.'

Did this mean that Eric was going to start up a florists' business? Could it really be intended, as Eric claimed, to deceive the planning officer into thinking that a florists business was being run there when the front window displayed two thousand soft toys? And most of all where was the money coming from?

Eric had not exactly consulted with Freddie about any of these changes. But if he had, it would have made no difference. Eric was capable of talking Freddie into almost anything – witness the fact that he and Eric were now apparently caught in a steamy pentagonal relationship with Mrs. Shallcombe. Did he mean pentagonal or two triangular relationships? It was all a mess, a very worrying mess. The two Michaels had been back from Ireland since Thursday night and Freddie hadn't slept a wink since then. Somehow the repercussions of Eric's recent activities, Freddie instinctively felt, would catch up with him and on that day Freddie knew he would say, as he always did on these occasions: why do I ever listen to you?

The other problem was Eric's insistence that with three businesses on the go (well, two if you like and possibly a third) it was essential to have a secretary to take telephone calls and organise their lives for them. The simple life he had enjoyed up until a week ago appeared to be gone forever: instead of just going down to the butcher's shop in the morning and in the afternoon reporting upstairs to the undertaker's office in case there was something to do (Eric was supposed to be looking after the business in the morning), Freddie now had no idea how his time would be spent. There had been a lot of telephone calls, it was true, and most of them seemed to be connected with Eric's spending spree (or if you prefer investment). But did they need a secretary? And could they pay for one?

Freddie wandered back to the window and pulled a face at a particularly loathsome small boy who was eating an ice cream alternately with licking the window. There was also something wrong with the advert for the secretary. He had certainly read it before Eric put it in the papers and he had not noticed anything wrong with it himself but he supposed that it must have been altered in some way. The most peculiar people had turned up to request an interview. Four ladies had appeared for the vacancy and there was something unusual about each of them. For a start not one of them was under five foot eleven and they all seemed to have remarkably deep masculine voices. Two of them were dressed in skin-tight cocktail frocks and large quantities of jewellery. Two of them had come together, requesting a job share, each of them clad in a pink lame trouser suit and each carrying a foot-long cigarette holder. These women all seemed to have enormous feet: Freddie noticed these things after so many years in the undertakers' business. He thought they seemed a bit too cheerful for the line of work and definitely overdressed. However he was not the person in charge of staff recruitment. The trouser suit ladies had been early for their appointment with Eric, and Freddie had spent a most uncomfortable quarter of an hour at their insistence sandwiched between them on the sofa in the shop front during which time Cindy had placed her enormous arm around Freddie's shoulder and Lucille had endeavoured to caress his left knee with her bejewelled red-taloned fingers. The toddler audience found this a most entertaining spectacle but Freddie was afraid he would be arrested for indecency and waited in increasing desperation for Eric to get back.

There was a tap on the window. Eric grinned at his brother and gave him a cheery wave. Freddie awoke from his daydream and walked over to the door to greet Eric.

'Eric, I need to talk to you.'

'Great idea. I've got lots to tell you and I think we might have a customer up at the animal centre. There is a really serious operation going on in a couple of days time on Mrs. Alexander's cat. Have we got any cat-shaped coffins or do you think we should order some in? Where's the brochure from the wholesaler? You know, it's much cheaper to buy more than one at a time.'

'Eric, can we please sit down and talk before we buy any more stuff?'

'Of course. Not a problem. Anything at all you want to know, just ask. Isn't this place great? Doesn't it look absolutely amazing? I feel really good every time I come in here. And by the way, have there been any more phone calls about the advert?'

'Eric, I'm worried.'

'What about? We have the best idea ever for earning some money and a really great location for it. Mrs. Lightfoot isn't even in this game. Pets must be dropping dead round the County all the time, and what do people do with them? Bury them in the garden? Put them in with the rubbish? Flush the goldfish down the toilet? We have a unique opportunity...'

'Eric,' interrupted his brother, 'how much have we spent?'

'Spent? Well, spent is only part of the picture: contracted for is what matters. A lot of this stuff is not paid for as such yet. Some of the things are on loan or sale or return and....'

'How much, Eric?'

'At this point we've probably spent as such no more than £20,000 allowing for...'

'£20,000!!!'

'Well, obviously up front. And then there's...'

'Eric, we haven't got that much.'

'Oh yes we have.'

'How? The bank said they wouldn't lend us any more.'

'You have a genius for a brother, Freddie, you know that? I have got us sponsors. You know, investors.'

'Sponsors? Investors? Here?'

'The very best and they handed over cash on request. See,' said Eric, triumphantly, 'here is the receipt.'

Freddie took from his brother's hand a crumpled single sheet of paper. He read it. All the blood in his body rushed to his feet and then immediately rushed back up to the top of his head. His face went purple and his hands began to shake.

'They'll kill us,' gasped Freddie hoarsely.

'Not a bit of it,' said Eric with a beam upon his face. 'The two Michaels can't afford to kill us now, no matter what we get up to.'

Chapter 5: Ladies' business

Some people in life have developed a set of strict rules by which to live: Maddie Shallcombe was such a person. Dressed in her brown woollen suit and pale blue silk blouse, she looked for once both prim and respectable. Mr. Clifford Dale took her arm and led her from his office back into reception. It was late on a Friday afternoon and his receptionist was keen to go home.

'Goodbye, my dear. And please give my best regards to Rachel. I'm sure that Douglas will be very sorry to have missed your visit. You know we are always both delighted to see you whenever you drop by.'

Clifford Dale smiled his secret smile, as was his habit whenever he thought of Maddie Shallcombe and the hot summer of 1976. He was a newly qualified lawyer and his brother was only a student when she had first decided to entertain them in various interesting ways. What he had never figured out was why it all ended as suddenly as it had begun, and no more than a year later. Alas for the brothers, Maddie Shallcombe had discovered their legal excellence and decided to kick them out of bed. They had occasionally heard her mother remark 'never mix business with pleasure' but did not associate the maxim with themselves. The receptionist, who was new, was somewhat surprised to see the senior partner escort his client not simply to reception but out of the building altogether.

'Take care, Cliff. I'll be coming back soon to sort out everything for Rachel. And thanks for this.'

She patted a fat envelope poking out of her suit pocket. So saying, she opened the rear door of her car, parked in the road directly opposite the offices. Clifford Dale watched her get in and they exchanged waves as the car disappeared down the street. He had often wondered why a woman of Maddie Shallcombe's extraordinary wealth would own such an unprepossessing vehicle. But there it was, one could never predict the fancies of the rich. Who on earth would want to be seen in a K registration red Ford Mondeo? Apart from the windows, the car never seemed to be clean even though it was housed in a garage by the side entrance of the Black Horse. Come to think of it he'd never seen Maddie drive the car either. In recent years the two Michaels were always to be seen in the front seats whenever she used it. But then, perhaps she simply didn't like to drive. He turned back to the porch of the house that had been converted to hold the firm's offices, and gave it no further thought. He certainly did not know enough about cars to tell that the outer shell of the vehicle had been fitted onto something quite different underneath it nor had he ever had cause to suspect that the two Michaels were in truth her bodyguards. Her long-standing preference for double portions of everything was their perfect cover.

By six the car was parked outside the maternity wing of the hospital in Gloucester. Inside, in a private room, Maddie Shallcombe was deep in conversation with Rhiannon Thornhill. The room was full of flowers and cards but little Neville was nowhere to be seen: he had been taken by the nurses for treatment for his jaundice and would not be coming back for almost an hour. Mrs. Shallcombe's offerings of flowers and a blue baby outfit lay on the side table. The purple-haired occupant of the bed lay propped up on one elbow drinking orange juice.

'Aunt Mad, I already told you I don't care about the money. I don't want that hassle any more, that's why I came here in the first place. What don't kill me makes me stronger.'

'I agree, dear, but you need to understand the situation. You need to look more carefully at the farmhouse. Kathleen Thornhill goes into the cold store directly under Joshua's study and hears everything. She's already told Robert that the will has been altered. You could be in danger again.'

'That's insane. Whoever heard of a Mafia princess scaring that easy? I can look after myself if I have to. He can have the money, I don't want it. I'm an artist now, to hell with it all.'

'The baby's safe. Joshua will see to that, he has his ways. But Robert's a determined man. He'll not be shaken off so easily.'

'Leave it, Aunt Mad. Tell Mom Neville has Poppa's eyes and his big fat belly. Want a juice?'

'No thanks, dear. But you can do one thing for me, when you're up and about. I've just bought four horses and I want you to take a look at them. No one knows horses as well as you.'

'Well, I wouldn't do it now except for you. But I owe you a lot of favours, Aunt Mad. You got me out of that hellhole New York, and out of it all. I don't know how you did it but they took it from you. Even Poppa hasn't come looking for me. So OK, just give me a few days to get Neville settled at home and I'll give you a ring.'

'Good girl, Rhiannon. You know, I have visitors planned soon, difficult visitors. I'd like to take them out for a breath of fresh air but only to see someone I can trust.'

'Would you by any chance be wanting them to see the horses as well as the baby?'

'Only if that were agreeable to you.'

'Sure, why not? If they're with you they're in their best Sunday clothes. Sometimes I miss that whole world, it can be kinda fun. But let me tell ya, I'm glad to be away from it. Just tell me when and I'll put on my Southern Belle accent.'

'I don't know about that, dear, but a little hospitality could save a lot of lives. Anyway, I believe one of the horses is a beauty but you tell me what you think.'

'Did Mom send a message?'

'She did. She said she's glad one of her grandsons is out of the business. I never thought I'd hear it.'

There was a knock at the door and a nurse returned with what looked like a parcel of white blankets out of which Neville's tiny face peeked. His puffy red eyelids were closed in sleep. Rhiannon sat up and pointed at a small basket in the corner of the room.

'Over there is fine for now.' The nurse simply nodded and put Neville carefully down in the basket. She left. Maddie Shallcombe rose from her seat.

'Better be off now, dear. Rachel is on duty on her own tonight. You take care, now.'

'See you later, Aunt Mad. I gotta get some sleep here. Little bastard is never out for long.'

Maddie carefully opened the door and closed it behind her.

*

Back at the Black Horse, Friday night was warming up well. Rachel Shallcombe, a stunning dark haired girl in her mid-twenties was working hard behind the bar. Friday was always busy, particularly since they had started the Karaoke club on the first floor. From the outside one would not have thought that one floor of a seventeenth century building could have absorbed the entire noise of a Karaoke operation.

The look of the building was misleading. Its appearance was designed to replicate that of the old Black Horse that burned down in 1970. Maddie Shallcombe's mother had cut the pink ribbon on the opening of the new building. And what a lengthy construction period it had been. The villagers were beginning to think that the pub would never be finished. The project took almost three years to complete and the builders were busy literally day and night seven days a week to get it done. The local Council was beginning to get edgy at the procession of heavy vehicles delivering materials onto the site and the constant blockages on the High Street in Waterton. But nobody complained directly. Grace Shallcombe was a favourite with all of them. And, what's more, she had done everything humanly possible to screen the building works from the street and to contain the noise and dirt. From the pavement right next to the temporary wall that had been erected, nothing of the inside could be seen. In the end, just as the village had got used to the German and Scandinavian technicians who always seemed to be doing something over on the site, works were over. Grace Shallcombe advertised in the local paper that there would be free drinks for the opening night and that business was back to normal.

The returning locals were amazed to see that everything was more or less exactly as it had been before. The old oak bar tables had been replaced. The red chairs were back again. The horse brasses hanging behind the counter, the racks and racks of bottles, even the fairy lights round the mirrors in the ladies' toilets, everything was the same. The only difference was that the new place was easier to clean and the windows did not stick in the wintertime. It was almost as though they had imagined the previous three years' works. If anyone ever asked Grace what the technicians had been up to, her answer was always the same: they were putting in proper pressurised equipment for the beer and there would never be a disappointing pint again.

Rachel knew all about her grandma, although she had been little when Grace passed away. Even despite her four years at Harvard, Rachel had no doubt that she should be coming back. Four years passes quickly in a place like Waterton. Some people had never even noticed that she had been away.

By quarter past seven Maddie Shallcombe herself was back behind the bar and the two Michaels were as usual in the corner table by the window. It was invariably their habit at about this time on Tuesday and Friday evenings to play a game of chess. Their special table was a round oak table, dark and heavy, with three legs. There were several chess sets in the box seat under the window but the one they liked to use had big silver-gilt figurines respectively cops and robbers. The cops were wearing late nineteenth century policemen's uniforms and the robbers were dressed in pyjamas with arrows across them and were carrying bags marked 'swag'. It was always the same: when one of the Michaels was plotting his move, the other would warily sweep the public bar watching what the clientele was up to. Nobody ever bothered them on chess nights and certainly nobody would think to comment on the fact that each of them drank only glasses of milk in pint pots. It was not that they were tea-total but they were never seen to drink when Mrs. Shallcombe herself was about.

All around them was the kind of noise one associated with a jolly evening in the pub. The Black Horse was popular locally for its excellent food, its warm atmosphere and above all the quality of the beer. It had always been a free house, that is to say, the owner could bring in whatever beers she liked. Maddie Shallcombe, like her mother before her, used this to the fullest advantage. There were one or two beers that no one had seen anywhere else, most famously the pub's 'Special,' which generations of Shallcombes brewed themselves. Real ales were obtainable locally in a number of houses but Special was only available at the Black Horse and only then when Mrs. Shallcombe herself considered the occasion to merit it. Eric Pinker, once he had tasted Special, lived and breathed for the day when he might see it again.

Eric had earlier persuaded Arthur and Joyce Smollett to come down to the Black Horse for a drink earlier in the evening as a means of getting them to have a looked at the refurbished shop next door. They had gone home and Eric had since fallen into conversation with a man sitting at the next table, a Great Dane at his feet. It was partly the sorry state of the dog that attracted Eric's macabre attention in the first place. It had recently been operated on and had an enormous bandage over one eye and a protective cone about its neck so that it could not scratch the wound. It lay disconsolately by the feet of its owner, a sharp-suited Indian called Tommy Patel.

Eric was intrigued by Tommy Patel. It was not so much his rather formally-dressed appearance as the fact that Eric had frequently seen him inside the pub, but had never seen him go inside or for that matter come out again. Eric was in the way of watching the comings and goings next door in some detail. Partly he wanted to keep an eye on the two Michaels and partly he was keen to find out what the board on the front door really meant. The inscription upon it designated certain hours as "open" and certain other hours as "special appointments only". Though he had grown up in the village and stared at this same board (or its predecessor) since he was a small boy, Eric had never understood what a "special appointment" could possibly be. As far as he could tell, during the times so designated the pub had always been closed, the lights out and no signs of activity could be detected. He had, of course, tried asking Maddie Shallcombe directly but he only got the same answer that he had had from old Grace Shallcombe herself. 'If ever you need to know, you'll know.' On the far side of the room, sitting right up at the bar, Eric saw Freddie's archenemy, Howard Morgan. Morgan, in Eric's opinion, was a narrow-minded git, miserable as sin and dead from the knees up. As misfortune would have it, their mothers had been great friends and almost since primary school Freddie and Howard had been forced into each other's company. Their mutual loathing was only enhanced by the fact that Howard Morgan ran a fleet of hearses for Mrs. Lightfoot, over whose success he never stopped crowing. Indeed, that very evening as he had walked in, he had sneeringly wished Eric a good evening and enquired as to whether Freddie had found any dead canaries recently. Eric ignored him as usual but he was glad that his brother had not been there because Freddie had trouble controlling his temper.

It was a warm evening and by nine o'clock was beginning to go dark. Mrs. Shallcombe was on splendid form. She particularly liked Friday evenings. She wore her most flamboyant red and gold low-cut blouse and a long black skirt. Her hands always carried the same two bracelets, heavy charms on a double curb chain in matching grey metal. And on her fingers she wore the same collection of strangely shaped rings, also in the grey metal. Rachel was having a little rest and had wandered over to the two Michaels to watch their game. She also was dressed in the low-cut flamboyant style of her mother but she wore no bracelets, only a pair of grey rings, like her mother's. It was obvious to Eric that Tommy Patel never took his eyes off her.

'Beautiful girl, ain't she, our Rachel?' Eric observed to his neighbour.

'Yeah,' the Indian said in a strong north London accent, 'Beautiful, unobtainable, everything you want and everything you don't want.'

'You know Rachel, then?'

'No, not really. I have some business with her mother.'

'Haven't I seen your dog down at the animal centre? I'm Eric Pinker, Pinker &....'

'From next door, yeah, I know. I heard you got a desk at the centre. Buy you a drink, mate?'

'Cheers. I'll have a lager, please, any kind.'

A few minutes later Patel returned with two bottles and two lager glasses. Each of them poured a little out and toasted the other: 'Your health!'

Eric was full of curiosity. 'You're not from these parts, are you?'

'Just here on business, maybe stay a few days, who knows?'

'So what's your line of work?'

'Well, I'm waiting for something to come through right now. It sometimes takes a while for things to get going. My name's Tommy, Tommy Patel. I expect you already know, seeing as how you work at the centre.'

'Oh yes,' said Eric cheerily. 'So where are you from?'

'London, the wicked city. But I've recently come back off my holidays and I've a few things to sort out.' Eric, who was not familiar with prison slang, stared around the bar. Most of the customers had gone upstairs to watch the singing.

'Well I'm waiting for my brother, Freddie but he seems to have disappeared. Short chap, chunky. You can't see him in the other bar can you?'

'I ain't seen him.'

Almost on cue, Eric spotted Paulette in the distance, coming through the other bar. Paulette was Eric's new secretary, recruited as of Wednesday morning. Already she had made herself invaluable. She could type, knew how to use the computer, was good on the telephone and was extremely pleasant. She arrived in a smart blue suit and flat black leather slippers and her nails, though polished, were not painted. Even better, she had her own shining blue Golf, which meant that, when business lunches were unavoidable, Eric had a driver. What a stroke of luck! Even Freddie, who was normally hostile to women over six foot tall, was in favour. After conducting so many interviews Eric was getting used to the fact that women of this height often had deep voices so Paulette's voice, which a week ago would have made him suspicious, seemed entirely normal. Eric waited impatiently for Paulette to make her way over but she hadn't seen him and had disappeared again out of sight.

Eric just could not figure out where Freddie could possibly be. He had last seen him in the early afternoon when they had had a wonderful frolic with Maddie Shallcombe in the two racehorse coffins in the basement. Eric grinned to himself. It had been Freddie who was complaining about how hard the coffins were so Maddie had rushed upstairs, stark naked, shouting 'Come on, boys, grab some teddies!' So they had. Freddie hadn't seemed very keen on the pink teddy idea but may be it was the kids staring in through the window all the time that bothered him. Paulette was away for the afternoon interviewing vicars about attitudes to pet burial. Eric dared not look at Mrs. Shallcombe, not when the Michaels were present, so he grinned again into his drink. Not like Freddie to disappear, though, especially when he had not had anything to eat. The idea had been that they would come down here for one of Mrs. Shallcombe's pies.

In fact, the answer to Eric's conundrum was almost beyond his imagining: Freddie had spent the late afternoon and early evening having a succession of cups of tea with Paulette confessing to her how out of his depth he felt with Eric's various projects, including Mrs. Shallcombe. Paulette had listened, very sympathetically, for almost four hours in the shop. By the time it was dark Freddie finally suggested that she come with them for something to eat, but then he had lost his nerve at the thought of going into the bar where the two Michaels were sat at the back, stone cold sober and in full view of Mrs. Shallcombe.

'Ah, here he is,' Eric muttered to Tommy Patel, waving in the direction of the opening behind the figure of Howard Morgan. Freddie, with Paulette on his arm, headed towards them.

Quite what happened next remains a matter of open discussion. Paulette appeared to be saying something to Freddie as they passed by but no one knew if Morgan had heard it. What did happen was quite unexpected: Howard Morgan, who had been drinking steadily all night, got unsteadily off his stool by the bar and blocked Freddie's way. Maddie Shallcombe, who had a sixth sense for trouble, moved closer to them.

'Got an assignation then, you little creep?'

'Step aside, Morgan.'

'Shave his legs for him, do you, Pinker?'

Freddie moved to the bar, picked up Morgan's drink, and threw it in his face. In a second Morgan had reached to the bar for a beer mug, smashing it against the side, the handle clutched firmly with the jagged edges of broken glass threatening Freddie. Freddie instinctively moved behind the nearest table and threw it against Morgan's legs. There were very few people in the bar at this point and Freddie saw only the Michaels in the corner and Eric and Tommy on the other side. Eric went white as a sheet but the others did not seem concerned. Quick as a flash, Rachel and Mrs. Shallcombe reached the protagonists. Mrs. Shallcombe slapped Morgan on the back and he fell to the floor: Rachel did the same to Freddie who also fell to the floor. Paulette looked absolutely horrified and stood rooted to the spot, watching Mrs. Shallcombe turn the diamond shaped ring on her right hand back into its normal position. Mrs. Shallcombe then took Paulette aside and said quietly:

'Would you like to take Freddie home now? I think he may need to sleep for a while. Michael here will give you a hand.'

At this Little Mickey strode forward, picked up Freddie by the shoulders and carried him effortlessly to the back door. Mrs. Shallcombe went quickly over to Eric and put her arm round his shoulder.

'Nothing to worry about, Eric. He's off for a rest. Would you like a little glass of Special, calm your nerves? You too, Tommy?'

The white-faced Eric simply nodded. Patel seemed to be enjoying the excitement.

'Very nice, thanks. And nicely done.'

Patel stroked his sleepy dog. Soon Rachel had cleared away the mess and both Howard Morgan's prostrate body and Michael Riley had disappeared.

Eric's evening from that point on took on a surreal quality. He felt immensely happy and at the same time immensely lazy. He felt as though he were floating above the table. He laughed endlessly at jokes that he couldn't quite remember. That Tommy Patel was a real wit. But best of all, when he finally wandered off to walk home, he saw that Howard Morgan's hearse was still parked in front of the pub. On closer inspection, he discovered that Howard Morgan was lying on the roof of it, presumably left there for safe keeping by Michael Riley. Eric felt happy, so happy. He went next door into the shop and pulled out of a box a large circular pink funeral wreath made of fragrant silk flowers. He returned and placed it on the chest of the unconscious Howard Morgan. He then sat down and laughed for about ten minutes before staggering off home.

Freddie was not at home but Eric decided to think about it later, when he had slept on it. Although Eric did not know it, there was no cause for concern. Freddie was also fast asleep still, lying peacefully in the centre of Madame Seraglio's disco floor in Bristol. Around him gyrated the magnificent figures of the dancers and the pink and blue spots of the lights played over him. But he knew nothing of it and only woke at five o'clock that morning when Paulette decided it was time to go home.

Chapter 6: Cutting in

On the eastern side of Hamset Manor House a high stone wall could easily be seen by people driving along the road from Little Waterton towards the junction with the main road to Gloucester. Any one who consulted an AA guide of the area would know that for one morning only, on Good Friday, the infamous Hamset rose garden was open to visitors. From the wrong side of the wall, nothing could be seen of what lay beyond it, for the rose garden was a very private place.

Surprisingly few visitors ever came, even from the local area, but for tax and legal reasons the opportunity had to be available. In the year 2002, no one had come, perhaps because it had been pouring with rain. Lady Vivienne Wilhelmina Corshall (nee Meyrick), known in the family as Viv, was in charge directly of the rose garden. It was a big area by the standards of the early seventeenth century, when it had originally been laid, and at certain times of year resembled an outdoor room complete with alcoves and furniture. The Estate gardener, Mr. Roberts, spent many hours labouring to her direction, often complaining to his wife that he did not see how the house could be supplied with homegrown vegetables if he was never allowed to work in peace in the greenhouses. Yet he had to admit that the result of his work was extraordinary. A high beech hedge formed an encircling inner wall around the inner area which was divided into four, each quarter separated from the others by a five-foot high privet hedge. At the central point of the design a similar hedge had been used to create a circle in which a magnificent white marble Greek maiden stood, around her ankles an octagonal pool fed by water flowing from a pitcher she carried. Each quarter of the garden had its own seating, one side covered and one side open. The covered areas were made up of a dense canopy of roses.

Generations of owners had learned when each plant was likely to flower and the display had been selected so that there were always several batches of roses flowering in the garden. Winter visitors were genuinely puzzled as to how the sheltered garden continued to bloom. But the many tricks required to achieve this would never be disclosed: these tricks were only ever passed by word of mouth to the next owner who invariably added more to the repertoire. Viv herself had added a new group of single petalled white roses that flowered in January. She it was who discovered that, by adding a certain type of plant juice to the soil around the roots, one could create from the matt and unremarkable flowers a pink and white petal mix resembling raspberry ripple ice cream. She spent many summer hours in this garden planning, pruning, and collecting petals for crushing. She was also engaged on a project that could not be finished in her lifetime, but which she expected her successor to continue, of stripping from every rose-tree every thorn it carried. This was slow and potentially painful work but the little areas where she had completed the operation made it possible for the old trees to be caressed and admired for their intricate forms and beautiful colour. She came here to think troublesome thoughts when neces-sary.

The original builder of the house was one Sir Cleverley Corshall who in the late sixteenth century decided that he had made enough money from his modest brick-manufacturing operation in Gloucester to build a new family home on the hill. The old manor house, now known as Cleverley Hall, was an ancient building of no identifiable foundation. It lay next-door to the church in Waterton and when the new building was completed Sir Cleverley donated it to the vicar of Waterton for his own enjoyment. In exchange, char-acteristically, Sir Cleverley extracted from the Vicar on behalf of himself and all his successors a promise that on the great feast days of Christmas, Easter and Michaelmas Day the parish would furnish sufficient flowers to deck the interior of the private chapel built in the new manor house. With only a brief interruption during the English Civil War, when the Corshalls had sided with Parliament and the Parish of Waterton with the King, the tradition had been main-tained to the present day. Lady Vivienne was moving steadily around the lower layers of the roses in the quarter closest to the entrance door to the house. She never worked with gloves, prefer-ring the intimacy of direct contact and putting up with the inevitable bleeding. Had anyone asked about it, she would undoubtedly have responded that all the owners of the rose garden had shed their blood in it. And she would have been right, although none of the owners had done so quite as spectacularly as Sir Isaac Corshall, whose wife had run him through with his own sword because he intended to volunteer a surrender of the house and garden to be used as a munitions depot for Cromwell's troops. It was not that Lady Elizabeth was a Royalist but rather she would not tolerate the destruction of the garden. At the time she had claimed that a Royalist assassin attacked Sir Isaac in the garden but on her deathbed she had confessed the truth. The vicar who heard this confession officially expressed the view that her advanced age had caused her recollection to falter, but all later owners of the rose garden knew perfectly well that they would have done exactly the same as Lady Elizabeth in face of a similar threat.

However none of this was in the forefront of Lady Vivienne's mind as she worked her way along the roses. She moved deliberately, pruning here, dead- heading there. The bark went into one basket, the dead bloom into another. Her implement was very sharp and no mistakes could be tolerated. What she did have on her mind was what to do with her son Carlton on the occasion of the forthcoming Tenants' Dinner. Last year he had simply failed to appear but word came back to her later that some of the departing guests had spotted him lying over the steps of the side kitchen entrance. She had long since given up the hope that he would accept methadone treatment and the need to protect the Estate from her son was becoming pressing. Since Roddy's death only Errington himself had represented the Estate at the annual Dinner but this year he had sent out an instruction that his granddaughter Sophie was to attend and sit next to him. The implication was unmistakable but Viv was worried as to how far her father-in-law would go in his rescue plans. She knew he had it in his power to disinherit Carlton if he wished. But what he could not do was to transfer the descent of the title. Unless Carlton died before his grandfather the land and the title would be separated and she knew that this was a state of affairs the old man would never tolerate. The separation was only possible because no land grant had been made by Queen Victoria in conferring upon Sir Randall Corshall the title Lord Errington. It was very much a case of a special honour in recognition of Sir Randall's role in organising the Queen's official celebrations in India to coincide with the Great

46

Jubilee in England. By then the Corshalls were fabulously wealthy and a further gift would not have been appropriate.

Lady Vivienne knew perfectly well that time was running out for Carlton. For so long as Roddy had been alive what Carlton got up to really made no difference. At the rate he had been going, there had been every chance that Roddy would have survived him and the title have been inherited through Sophie's line. Lady Vivienne paused in her work and painfully straightened up. With the back of her left hand she wiped the sweat from her face and took a deep breath. Today was Friday the seventeenth of May. That gave just over six weeks before the dinner on the twenty-fifth of June, the summer quarter day. The afternoon was unseasonably warm and, though a storm had been promised for the evening, there were no signs of it yet. She walked slowly over to the benches and table in the Lion Quarter of the garden. A brass hand-bell lay on the table and she rang it loudly three times. This was the signal for Mrs. Roberts in the kitchen to bring out a jug of ice-cold lemonade. It was now four o'clock and time for a break in any case. She sat down and waited. Five minutes passed in this way.

'Shall I lay the table here, Lady Vivienne?' Lady Vivienne approved very much of Mrs. Roberts and her generally obliging manner. As the housekeeper, she made every effort to befriend and support Mrs. Allott the cook, whilst at the same time making sure that the kitchen expenditure was kept within bounds and was properly documented. How Roberts had managed to find himself such an intelligent and even-tempered partner was often the subject of comment.

'Not necessary, thank you, Mrs. Roberts. The tray will be adequate. Tell me, have you any thoughts about the menu for the Tenants' Dinner?'

'Well, I have been talking with Mrs. Allott about it a little bit. We were thinking of a choice between beef and salmon this year as we had chicken and veal on offer last year. Mrs. Allott has proposed a cold soup to start and wants to try her hand at small fancy breads instead of the big plaited loaves we usually do.'

'I think you can be fairly adventurous on the menu side. The food is about the only part of the whole evening that isn't part of some tradition or other. We must reckon up the guests this year. There are usually some changes. Who have we got?'

'Sam Thornhill and his wife from Barnhill, the MacGregor brothers from Topham, Mr. and Mrs. Fowler from Pig Home. That's six.

What shall we do about Blue Grace? Mr. Thornhill senior always comes but never brings his wife. The new one's just had a baby anyway. What about Robert Thornhill?'

'Not this year, Mrs. Roberts. I will have a word with his Lordship about it. You see, he's intending that Sophie should go along this time but she's so much younger than everyone else. I think we ought to invite the next generation, as it were. There are quite a few younger possibilities. Dennis Fowler has a surgery in Little Waterton: he was at college when Sophie was. And then there's young Billy Thornhill, Robert's son. He can't be much younger than Sophie and I hear he's down from Oxford this summer. I think we should plan on the basis that those two should come along as well. After all, it's time Sophie widened her set down here.'

'Very good, Lady Vivienne.' Mrs. Roberts saw nothing controversial in any of this and she was quite confident Lady Vivienne would get it all past Lord Errington.

Lady Vivienne drank a long glass of lemonade before pouring a second. If tradition were to be broken by inviting Sophie, they might as well introduce a couple of eligible chaps into the framework as well. The dinner would be excruciating for Sophie: Viv knew perfectly well what went on, having heard blow by blow accounts every year from Roddy in the past. It was always the same. The visitors were announced and welcomed personally one by one by Lord Errington at the door of the main hall. Mr. Dancer served elderflower drinks to the women and gin and tonic to the men. A single long table was laid at the far end of the hall, with Lord Errington presiding in the centre, and Dancer, aided for the occasion by Mrs. Roberts, served a great feast, very slowly. There was a speech of welcome and a speech by each of the Estate tenants between the courses. They were supposed to be explaining to Lord Errington what had been going on on the farm in the previous year but by long tradition, having briefly mentioned truthful basics, each tenant then told the tallest story he could think of. At the conclusion of the dinner but before the ladies retired to the blue drawing room Lord Errington announced the winner and presented a prize for the tallest story. Last year Reggie Fowler had won with a tale about the finding of a bag of gold nuggets in the intestines of one of his sows. The dinner in some form or other was thought to have been held from at least Norman times. It was the only meal of the year where Lord Errington could be guaranteed not to insist on his favourite kippers being served up. But the modern form of the proceeding was very much as prescribed by Sir Placet Corshall who moved the occasion from Cleverley Hall across to the main house largely because he wanted the tenants to admire his recently-acquired French furniture and Spanish needlework, all part of the booty with which George III paid him for his excellent service in the Peninsular War. Sir Placet, despite his name, was a most hated and feared landlord, whose enthusiasm for mantraps round the Estate, and in particular in what was now known as Blue Grace Woods, had caused the death of more than a few of the local children. The point about the dinner, in Sir Placet's day, was to demonstrate that no matter what differences there were between landlord and tenants during the year, they each recognised that the others had the right to be there and enjoy the respect of that small community of long-standing owners and users of the land. In Sir Placet's time it was an especial point of honour amongst the tenants that they would not steal his deer on the day of the Tenants' Dinner.

Lady Vivienne was ready to take the flower heads indoors to the drying-room. She held, very carefully, in the palm of her right hand a single neatly severed rosehead and conjured before her the features of her wasted son. Though she knew others had done so, she had never herself feared her father-in-law. She instinctively knew how his mind would be working but she had no grounds for accusation. The house was resplendent in the glow of the late afternoon sun: she knew that the old man's priorities were right.

*

By early evening the clouds had begun to darken. The sticky heat irritated Freddie Pinker, particularly as he had taken such care to put on his new blue suit that afternoon. At last Mrs. Alexander's cat had died and Eric had buried it in the bottom corner of Colonel Alexander's garden, with full military honours. Apparently that was what you did with a retired regimental cat. Freddie still had the idea that Eric's business proposals were risky but he was becoming more used to it now that Paulette was there to calm him down. She had a remarkable calming influence over even Eric. It was a good two weeks since Freddie had seen his brother frantically turning out filing cabinets in the office trying to find something that he had mislaid only that minute. Paulette knew where everything was and had really brought the whole operation up to a professional standard. Even the way she answered the telephone excited admiration in Freddie, and Eric sometimes rang up on a pretext in order to hear a deep, efficient, voice on the other end of the line say:

'The Pinker Establishment: Flowers, Funerals and Faithful Friends' Resting Place. Paulette speaking. How can I help you?'

She had managed to persuade Eric that he should pay for Freddie's new suit and both of them had been advised by the secretary to get a better haircut. Eric, as a result, acquired the slick look of an estate agent. Freddie, on the other hand, looked rather well in the '50s hairstyle that Paulette chose for him although his stocky muscular frame looked somewhat ill at ease in the confines of the sharp blue jacket of his new outfit.

Tonight Paulette was sitting in the passenger seat of the hearse. They had dropped Eric in the village on the way and Freddie had promised to drive Paulette over to Bristol to a friend's house because her car would not be ready from its service until Saturday morning. As they drove out of the village Freddie realised he needed to get some petrol. He was not prepared to pay motorway prices for it so he pulled into the petrol station at King Stanley off the A419 shortly before he would get onto the M5 to Bristol. He filled the vehicle rather absent-mindedly wondering how bad the Friday night traffic would be. Paulette was reading a copy of Cosmopolitan and Freddie's eyes were on the litreage counter at the petrol pump. Consequently he failed to notice that at the far side of the station a second hearse had pulled up for a refill. Howard Morgan, who now lived slightly south of Bristol, was in the habit of taking his vehicle home at the weekend for a thorough cleaning. It was a labour of love and he always did it personally on a Sunday morning. Friday evenings he always stopped here to buy new waxing cloths and polish.

Freddie stood in the queue to pay, and Paulette began gesticulating at him through the glass wall of the shop, hoping that he would pick up a newspaper on his way through past the till. Freddie stared at her but could not make out what she wanted. So she got out of the car and walked into the shop, picked up a copy of the Western Mail and handed it to him with a smile. Freddie paid the girl behind the counter, pocketed the change and turned to leave. At that precise moment the familiar figure of Howard Morgan advanced towards them bearing a wire shopping basket and an assortment of cleaning materials. The sickly smell of the pink wreath had haunted him for days.

'Still shagging sheep, Pinker, or is it mutton in lamb's dress now?' Morgan leered at Paulette.

'Shut your fat mouth, Morgan, and mind your manners.'

'Is there a problem, gentlemen?' The garage operator walked inside, followed by a big black mongrel dog wearing a muzzle.

'Come on, Paulette, let's go,' said Freddie. Morgan turned to join the back of the checkout queue. He said nothing but looked sour. The garage man was irritated. He didn't like two hearses on his forecourt at once, thinking it might put superstitious customers off.

Paulette got back into the car and strapped herself in. She found it very gratifying how protective Freddie had become towards her. Freddie swung the hearse back onto the A419 and headed sedately towards junction 13. The motorway was crowded and it now looked as though it was going to rain.

Paulette didn't see what Freddie next saw in his rear mirror: almost out of nowhere the other hearse, its lights on full dazzle, had speeded virtually into his rear and looked as though it was going to overtake him at the last minute. But it didn't.

Morgan pulled out to overtake in the middle lane but instead of doing so made a rude gesture with his fingers as the car pulled level. Then he shot ahead, cut in in front of Freddie's vehicle and slammed his brakes on. Freddie swerved into the right hand lane and tried to escape with a burst of speed. Morgan accelerated in the slow lane and pulled out in front of him, cut in then braked sharply again, forcing Freddie into the fast lane. Freddie knew what was coming next and decided to pre-empt it by outrunning the other vehicle. Paulette caught her breath as she looked at the speedometer. They were doing ninety miles an hour and Morgan was keeping pace with them in the middle lane. If he overtook them now and slammed his brakes on again they would all be killed.

Freddie put his foot down on the accelerator: the hearse was doing a rattling hundred and ten but Morgan would not drop back. In front of them cars were diving into the slow lane and forcing others off onto the hard shoulder. Four vehicles collided in the rush to get out of the way. One overturned and minutes later burst into flames. People were fleeing their cars and running into the hedges and bushes on the outer edge of the hard shoulder. Clouds of blue and black smoke spiralled into the air. A milk tanker ploughed into the line of cars on the hard shoulder and overturned. Milk spilled in all directions sending the traffic behind skidding. The squeal of brakes and the sound of banging metal followed the hearses along. They screamed past the service station exit at Michael Wood faster and faster leaving behind them a trail of devastation. Paulette was sick with fear, unable to take her eyes off Freddie, terrified to say anything that might distract him. Morgan is mad, she thought, mad, mad. Water lashed down against the windscreen, where the wipers went at full belt. Freddie stared furiously out over the steering wheel, his red, sweating face taut with concentration. He could barely see a hundred yards ahead in these conditions. It was life or death for him and Paulette. Morgan was insane with hatred, bent on overtaking and cutting in for one last time. He had to keep going.

The police had been alerted by dozens of mobile phones and two helicopters were heading north over the M5 towards junction 14, flying low over the traffic as a warning. The southbound carriage-way was ablaze with the blue lights of police cars trying to catch up and in the far distance a dozen emergency vehicles were rushing to the scene behind. Experienced firemen had never seen anything like this on their section of the motorway and they were already calling out for extra help from as far away as Birmingham and Cardiff. Standby medical teams had been alerted in ten hospitals and the army had been contacted for heavy lifting gear to be brought in. The Chief Constable of Avon was personally directing the police co-ordination on his mobile phone from a golf course on the other side of the county, trying to supervise the chaotic rescue services and barking out orders for his second in command to stop the hearses at the front.

Freddie's hearse was empty but Morgan's had Monday's coffin in the back. When the dials hit a hundred and twenty, the coffin blasted through the rear window spreading itself over the fast and middle lanes. In a matter of moments eight cars had slewed into it. Paulette heard it hit the road then the first of the crashes into it before she shot out of range, almost pinned to her seat by the force of the speed they were doing. Still Morgan kept pace, now trying to push his hearse closer and closer to the side of the other without losing control. The rear windows were steaming up and she could feel the tyres no longer had full grip on the road surface. How much faster could they go before the engine or the tyres blew?

The southbound carriageway was a picture from hell. Drivers

heading north on the opposite carriageway slowed to watch the excitement. But not enough. It only took one driver to watch for one second too long to start a second chain of disasters as the traffic on this side began to concertina into the rear of the first car. It was impossible to avoid the impact for the northbound section as all three lanes and the hard shoulder were involved at once and the cars approaching impact had virtually no warning before having to brake fiercely and swerve. A second pall of smoke rose over the other side of the central reservation. People were abandoning their cars in the middle of the road, afraid of being crushed by traffic from behind running into wrecks in the middle of the lanes. Pedestrians were taking refuge by running onto the barrier separating the carriageways and lines of them could be seen in the half light, some huddled under raincoats, others talking on mobile phones.

Eventually the hearses were forced to a stop by the combined action of six police cars that joined the motorway at junction 15. As soon as Freddie realised that the police were roaring up in the slow lane, he felt it was safe to slow and pull in. Morgan believed he could outrun them but was quite mistaken. The cars in front positioned themselves so that to avoid head-on collision Morgan had to slow and stay clean in the middle lane. Then they closed in on all sides now that the fast lane was free. Three cars ahead dropped metal stinger boards, their upturned nails waiting for the tyres of the hearse. In seconds the sickening sound of the tyres bursting preceded a massive lurch by Morgan's vehicle across towards the hard shoulder, turning round three times as it went. Police motorcycles swarmed round, watching the hearse finally come to rest in a thicket of gorse bushes. The lead officer found Morgan partially concussed by the impact of the airbag bursting into life in his face. Morgan informed the second officer, who forced open the door of the driver's side, that he was going to murder that fucking bastard Pinker, and promptly passed out.

By this time twenty-five miles of the northbound carriageway had been brought to a halt by a five thousand-car pile-up on which the rain now poured. The size of the tailback on the southbound side could not be much less and the problem was showing no signs of reducing as more cars joined from junctions further away with no prospect of getting off again. Traffic from the M4 was being prevented by the police from joining the M5 and it was being re-diverted northwards along a parallel A road. All arterial routes were at a standstill. Officers from three Counties were taking witnesses' names and statements. It was not even known whether anybody had been killed. In these road conditions it took two hours for the arresting officers driving in front of the main logjam to get the drivers and Paulette over to the principal police station in the middle of Bristol.

Last orders at the Black Horse on a Friday night always left Eric with the hope that he might somehow persuade Mrs. Shallcombe to return with him next door. Once again, it was not to be. In his coat pocket the piercing sound of his telephone playing 'Dixie' made him visibly jump. He fumbled for the phone then held it to his ear, grimacing regretfully at Maddie Shallcombe who had come to collect the redundant glasses on the table occupied by Eric and Tommy Patel.

'Hello. Who is it?' There was a pause. 'Yes, Paulette, what can I do for you?' Another pause, this time a long one. 'You what? You're joking, surely?' Then an even longer pause. '£100,000? But....'

Tommy Patel looked up from his drink to see Eric's face drain of colour. Mrs. Shallcombe made no move away from the table and stopped wiping it in order to listen to what was going on.

'Madam who? I've never heard of her. Why would she put that much money up for Freddie?'

Mrs. Shallcombe looked thoughtful signalled with one hand for Little Mickey to come over from the chessboard.

'May I?' Mrs. Shallcombe held out her hand for the telephone. Eric nodded and handed it over. 'Paulette, this is Maddie Shallcombe. Is there anything I can do to help? Tell me where you are and Little Mickey will come round and drop you and Freddie home if you like.' She waited whilst Paulette spoke for several minutes. Mrs. Shallcombe made intermittent listening noises before a final 'OK'. Then she cut off the line. 'Freddie's been charged with careless driving. Paulette made a statement to the police that Howard Morgan tried to kill them on the motorway and they're doing him for dangerous driving. Freddie's got police bail and someone's come up with the money. Mickey, they're in the main police station in Bristol.'

Mickey nodded and headed out into the rain to find the car. It was only when he turned the radio on a few minutes later that he realised what a long night it was going to be.

'How long has Freddie known Madame Seraglio?' Mrs. Shallcombe asked.

Eric shrugged his shoulders and for once in his life looked completely blank. He was badly shaken.

'It ain't like her,' Patel said quietly so only Maddie Shallcombe heard him 'It ain't like her to risk that much cash. Not unless she's recruiting.'

Mrs. Shallcombe nodded at her daughter behind the bar.

'Time, gentlemen, please.'

Chapter 7: Gifts

The following day was wet. That Saturday morning Waterton was unusually quiet. The shops were open, but few people were about and after the events of the previous evening nobody felt very much like driving. Eric, who sometimes on a Saturday morning tried to peer through the windows of the Black Horse to see what was going on during special appointment hours, was fast asleep. So, for that matter, was Freddie. The only difference was that Eric was upstairs in bed whereas Freddie had crashed out on the sofa in the shop window. An element of modesty was preserved because Little Mickey had drawn the pink chapel curtains for privacy. The drive to Bristol had been a nightmare for him and by the time he got to the main police station it was only to discover that Freddie had been released into the company of Madame Seraglio over three hours previously.

Mickey O'Dare did not like going to Madame Seraglio's club even on business: he definitely did not like it during opening hours. He had not enjoyed being looked up and down by the enormous lady greeter standing under the entrance canopy. She had blocked the entrance to the basement door, fluttered her long false eyelashes at him and insisted on frisking him in public in a fashion which, were he not on Mrs. Shallcombe's business, would have resulted in the greeter getting a broken jaw. Furthermore he did not like the room in which Madame Seraglio kept him waiting: he did not like the collection of Elizabeth Taylor photographs framed on the wall, nor the whips hanging from it, nor the four large heart-shaped mirrors screwed onto the floor nor the rumpled black and red bedspread on the bed in the middle of the room. He did not like Madame Seraglio, when she finally did appear, and he did not like the way Madame Seraglio stroked his arm, breathed perfume into his face and cooed: 'Freddie, oh Freddie Pinker! Such a brave man, so courteous, so strong, so sweet.' For the second time in two weeks Little Mickey had picked up the unconscious body of Freddie Pinker, this time dumping it into the back of Mrs. Shallcombe's car. He could tell from the empty champagne bottles in Madame Seraglio's personal studio, to say nothing of the broken glasses, pink ribbons and fake police helmets that Pinker had not been drinking alone.

Inside the Black Horse that morning it was warm and cosy. The two Michaels were upstairs. Only Rachel and Tommy Patel were in the bar area. They were having coffee at Patel's favourite table.

'What time did Mickey get in last night?' Rachel poured herself a second cup of coffee.

'About six this morning. He was in a foul mood.'

'Trouble?'

'No, not really,' said Patel. 'The old tart likes to wind him up. You've seen it when we go there on business. He hates it down there.'

'Yeah. Funny how it bothers him. It's only a club. After all, its not that much different from the normal ones. Did he see any signs of, you know, changes?'

'Not a thing. Madame Seraglio claims she's still with the Wings. She's just taken a shine to Freddie Pinker. God knows why.'

'Oh, I don't know. He looks kind of rough and he is very hot tempered but really quite a gentleman. I can see how it might work. But he and Eric don't seem to notice anything.'

'You can say that again. How long have they been friendly with your mum?'

'Not my business, not yours. Anyway, Tommy, how long are you staying here?'

'It's taken a while to call the money back in. But there's a meeting fixed with my Uncle Dev down here on Thursday. I reckon he'll go for it. Anyway I done four years inside for him. It's only right I get my share.'

'So what did you do with yourself, then?'

'Open prison is not so bad. You meet a lot of people, the right sort of people. Solicitors, civil servants, all kinds of people that know how to do things. I've got a lot of new contacts, I can tell you.'

'Whose idea was it then, anyway?'

'Both of us really. Simple ideas work best. He was working for the tax office and loads of cheques were coming in. He just waited to collect up a few big ones and I opened the account in my name. Once we had six million he went back to India to lie low for a bit.'

'So what name did you use?'

'Easy. Inlandi Revendi!'

Rachel laughed. 'Good one, Tommy! Pity they got you.'

'Part of the plan, darling. Six million tax-free. Four-year law degree external from the Open University, all expenses paid by Her Majesty's Government. Free board and lodging. Money invested with your mum. What more do you want?'

Rachel grinned. She liked Tommy Patel's style.

'Rachel, why don't you take a break, come away with me for a bit. I got plenty of time and money now. We could have a good time.'

'I'm done travelling, Tommy. I was out while you were in.'

'Come on, Rachel. You come out to South Africa, meet my mum. You'll like her. We could do all sorts of stuff. I'm not so bad, you know. OK, I should have told you maybe before I got picked up. But with us we don't tell the women and you was young.'

'Don't start. I got over you at Harvard and I'm not turning the clock back. No thanks. I'm staying here. I've got a lot to do.'

So saying, she tidied the coffee cups onto a little tray, smiled at Patel and walked over to the bar. Patel picked up his raincoat from the chair next to him and hung it over his arm.

'Come on, girl,' he said to the sleepy-looking dog at his feet. 'See you later, then, Rachel. I reckon its safe to go out now that the meeting is fixed. Any chance you could let me out?'

Rachel reached under the bar counter and pressed a series of numbers into a control pad. 'All you need to do is turn the big key in the bottom lock. Ring when you want to come back in.'

As the door closed behind Tommy Patel, Maddie Shallcombe reached the top of the steps from the cellar. Rachel turned round.

'Hi, Mum. Not seen much of you lately.'

'What do you mean? We see each other every night.'

'You're up to something. So what's going on in Russia?'

'Who told you? I'll have to have a word with Michael Riley, that I will.'

'It's not his fault. I tricked it out of him.'

If Mrs. Shallcombe went visiting, it was normally on a Wednesday and always there and back in a day. The pub was closed Wednesdays even to special appointments. It was Michael Riley's job to wait at Heathrow for her. On the shelf underneath the main counter lay a little basket made of woven plastic. On the front was stitched a bright design of flowers. She picked up the basket and put her arm round Rachel's waist.

'Come on, favourite girl, come to the little room with me.'

The little room was the smaller of the two bars. Maddie Shallcombe lifted the bar counter and looked around. Against each of the walls lay a large green leather sofa, each with a couple of small round tables in front of it. Rachel followed her mother through and the pair of them sat on the sofa on the left side of the room.

'I've got something for you, Rachel. Brought it back.' So saying, she reached into the little turquoise basket and brought out a parcel eight inches long and about three inches thick. It was loosely wrapped in yellow tissue paper. Rachel gave her mother an enquiring look. 'Come on then, open it.'

'But it's not my birthday yet.'

'Don't you want to open it? You don't have to, if you don't want to.'

Rachel shook the box inside, very carefully. Then she lifted the lid and stared silently at the contents.

'That's right,' her mother said, 'cupboards.'

Rachel put the package on the sofa and hugged her mother. It was the proudest moment of her life. 'Thanks, Mum. I promise you won't regret it.'

'Well, put them on then. Shall I help you?'

Rachel held both arms towards her mother who fastened first one and then the other bracelet into place. They were identical to the pair worn by Maddie Shallcombe herself. The same thick curb chains out of the same grey metal, the same charms on them. It was impossible to tell what the metal was. It did not seem to be precious but it was not steel either. There were no jewels at all. The bracelets looked cheap, but were not. Her mother continued happily:

'You already know almost as much as I did when I took over from my mother. You know the bank accounts and the props and all our special recipes. See, try and remember a few of the charms. This one, the little star, is your grandmother's jewels and photos. This one here, the Christmas tree, is the special ingredients. The dancing shoe is the address book and the accounts. The little hat is the resting cupboard and I expect you know what this one is.' She pointed at a heart-shaped charm. 'But you don't know where it is.' Rachel was moving her left arm up and down, feeling the unaccustomed weight. 'You'll soon get used to them.'

'You're not going away, are you?'

'No. This Wednesday I need to get Dev Patel's briefcase ready. And Thursday afternoon the Wings are due in. But listen, Rachel, I'm expecting another very delicate operation this summer. If anything happens to me, the business is yours and I need to show you where everything is.'

'Be careful, Mum.'

'I always am, except when I'm having fun. And then only a little bit. I follow the most important rule of all: never mix business and pleasure.'

'Tommy's going back to South Africa. On his own.'

Her mother seemed satisfied.

'Plenty of good-looking young fellows around these here parts. Let's go down to the cellars. The main cellar's still mine but your keys open everything too. The second cellar is yours and all the cupboards in it.' Rachel gasped.

'Is it done already?'

'Yes it is, but I want to show you something in the strong room first.'

So saying she returned to the area behind the bar, Rachel following and bringing with her the turquoise basket. They both ignored the steps down into the pub cellar. On the wall next to the steps was a rack of hooks with coats on them.

'Let's go the quick way, shall we?'

Rachel nodded and they both stood close to the coats. Maddie reached behind one of the coats and found a small opening in a metal panel about six inches square. She picked out a charm from the bracelet on her left hand and pushed it into the hole. Immediately three steel panels dropped from the ceiling, forming the three outer sides of a rectangular enclosure. There was only a slight click as the walls of the lift shaft fell into place.

*

Saturday lunchtime was always pretty quiet at Blue Grace Cottage. Sometimes if the weather was good there were things to do but when it rained, as it had that morning, the farm men usually decided to catch up with their morning work in the following week. The people at the processing plant could carry on but there is not a lot that can comfortably be done on a farm when it is pouring with rain and the big animals all are indoors. There was always paperwork, of course, but Kathleen was doing all that over at the main farmhouse. Robert sometimes had lunch on Saturdays at the Green Man in Little Waterton as the Black Horse was usually shut. But for some reason today he decided to go straight back to the cottage and make a quick cheese sandwich. He had already dropped Rhiannon off at the farmhouse by one o'clock. The baby was waiting and she was ready to feed it. As he put the heavy key in the bottom lock, he remembered that only the mortice would be on because his son Billy was over for a few days. He opened the door and closed it as quietly as he could so as not to wake his wife. He took off his wet shoes and coat and pulled on a pair of dry shoes for indoors.

As he walked into the kitchen, his heart sank.

'Enjoy your morning out with her?' Cathy Thornhill had already finished half the bottle of vodka. She was wearing a blue nightdress and a flowered nylon housecoat. She wore nothing on her feet and her hair was uncombed.

'Why don't you eat something?' Thornhill asked.

'If you touch her, I'll poison you, I swear it.'

'Touch who? All I've been doing is looking at horses.'

'You can't fool me, Robert Thornhill. I know all about you and the way that you look at that purple-haired bitch.'

'Pull yourself together, woman. I'm going down to the Green Man, if anybody wants me.'

'Don't you even want to say hello to your son? Or are you that desperate for a drink?'

'You know I don't drink.'

Billy Thornhill had started down the staircase and stopped as he heard his parents' voices. He knew from the fact that his mother was already up that something bad was going on. He would have retreated but his father had already seen him.

'You,' Robert said loudly to his son, 'carry your mother up to bed when she's finished the bottle.' He returned to the porch, pulled on his wet things and slammed the front door. All the while Mrs. Thornhill sat at the kitchen table crying noisily.

Billy Thornhill didn't really blame his mother. This was the second day his father had gone down early of a morning and taken Rhiannon to the horses on the other side of Bristol. He'd heard his father the previous evening describing in tones of astonished admiration how well Rhiannon had handled the horses, how knowledgeable she seemed and how expertly she had assessed his father's favourite horse, Bananas. This was no ordinary horse but an excellent thoroughbred with an expensive racing pedigree. He guessed that selling this horse meant something was going on but he did not know what, as his father rarely spoke to him. In fact, he had not seen his parents much at all for years. His Uncle Joshua had insisted on getting him away from home as a boy, as soon as it became apparent that his mother was not fit to look after him. So it had been a succession of boarding schools before he went to University. After he'd gone up to Oxford he had managed to find part-time work in the City and rarely came home. It was an unpleasant atmosphere there and it set him on edge to watch his mother drink. But there was nothing he could do. He was only here now because Kathleen had written to say that he ought to come back more often: she did not think his mother would last very long.

Cathy Thornhill had dried her tears. She was now sitting quietly at the kitchen table and smoking a cigarette. She was a paper-thin woman with chalk-white skin and red eyes. She always drank vodka in one of the tea mugs. The bottle was no longer on the table. Billy saw that it had been emptied and left in the bucket under the sink.

'Got to go out, Mum.' He couldn't stand it indoors any more than his father could.

'You're no better than him. Go, if you must.'

The rain was easing off as he got into his car. It was another Ford Fiesta, red like Kathleen's but much older and even more battered. Billy decided to drive into Waterton, see if he could find something to eat and possibly get a present for the baby. He didn't really know what to get but thought that a couple of the shops might have something promising. He turned first onto the Gloucester Road, which was very quiet for a Saturday, and about half a mile down the road turned right off it again onto the main road into Waterton.

Waterton was about four miles from the crossroad. From the road itself very little was to be seen apart from a signpost pointing down the village road. At the top it said "Waterton" and underneath that, hanging off it, were two metal chains bearing a painted metal sign about nine inches high depicting a black horse.

In fact quite a lot of things went on in Waterton. The Hamset brickworks were just beyond the village and about fifty people worked in the factory owned by the estate. There was a big lorry depot just out of sight behind the main shops and there was a medium sized supermarket belonging to one of the smaller chains. Between Waterton and Little Waterton lay the milk distribution and storage centre that Joshua Thornhill had had to build to accommodate the overflow business from the farm. Little Waterton also had shops but they were not as good. He wasn't interested on this particular day in browsing the DIY store or the dress shops that he knew were in Little Waterton centre. Besides, his father had gone down to the Green Man and he did not particularly want to bump into him.

So Billy parked the car in the square in the middle of Waterton, surprised to see how few other cars were there that day. He walked past the little library next to the vicar's house at Cleverley Hall and headed for the coffee shop next to the church. As he walked along, idly looking over the village green, he screwed his eyes up to stare at an unfamiliar and unexpected vision. What was all that pink? The last he had known, the shop next to the Black Horse was Mrs. Donger's, the florist. Deciding to come back for his coffee later he walked round towards the pink shop front. As he got closer he could see toys hanging in the window and he wondered whether they were for sale. But before he reached the shop itself he noticed something lying on the pavement not far from the front door. Two Siamese cats, each wearing a collar, lay flat out next to each other, apparently dead. He walked over to them. It did not look as though an accident had taken place as there was no damage to the cats and in any case they were not lying by the road. They looked almost peaceful, as though they had been arranged in the simulation of death. Billy shook his head, puzzled. Then he looked up at the shop front. In silver letters the glass had been inscribed 'Pinker & Pinker. Flowers, Funerals and Faithful Friends' Resting Place.'

It took Billy a moment to connect the teddies and the inscription and he had not quite decided whether to ring the bell and enquire if the shop might like to take in the bodies of the deceased cats and chase up the owners from the details on the collars. As it happened, his thoughts were interrupted. A short stocky middle-aged man in a blue suit drew back the pink curtain to reveal a pink sofa behind him. The man was unshaven and was wearing round his neck a colourful Hawaiian garland. As soon as he saw Billy, the man took the garland off and threw it behind the sofa. Billy decided to ring the bell.

Freddie opened the door. 'Yes?'

'Look, I'm sorry to disturb you but I was wondering if you knew anything about these? Or possibly could suggest what should be done with them.'

Freddie had a strong stomach. He was not in the least bothered by so early an introduction to the two cat corpses. Good, thought Freddie, Eric will be pleased.

'Are they yours?' Freddie enquired.

'No, they were just here when I came past.'

'Well, wait a minute and I'll get some bags.'

Freddie disappeared before Billy could say anything further. He shortly reappeared, having meanwhile removed the jacket of his suit.

'I'm Freddie Pinker. Aren't you Billy Thornhill?'

'Yes.'

'I heard you were coming back. Word gets round. I haven't seen you since you were a boy.'

Freddie meanwhile effortlessly bagged up the two cats and swung them over his shoulder, one bag in each hand. 'Any chance you could hold the door for me?'

'Yes, of course.'

They walked up the pair of steps and went through the front door. Billy automatically held open the glass-fronted door into the shop itself. Freddie went to the back part of the shop which was still curtained off from the window.

'Tina. 6 Horseshoe Crescent, Bristol. Contact if lost.' Freddie was reading a disc from the collar he had removed. 'I wonder how it got all the way from Bristol.'

Billy came to look over his shoulder.

'Do you think there is something odd about these cats being left here? When I found them they didn't even seem to be wet. Where is the other one from?'

Freddie took the other collar in his hand.

'Charles. I belong to Jeremy Brunton, 11 Marsh Drive, Bathavon.'

Freddie and Billy looked at each other.

'That's very funny,' said Billy with a shrug.

'I'm going to wake Eric up. He'll know what to do. Do you want a coffee?'

'No thanks. Are you selling those teddies?'

'No. But you can have one if you like. Mind if I borrow your newspaper?'

'Keep it by all means. Nothing much happening.'

Billy turned to go, pausing only to stuff a pink teddy down underneath his raincoat. Freddie was poised to go upstairs and get Eric when he caught sight of the headlines. 'HEARSE RACE TRAFFIC HORROR SHOCK.'

'On second thoughts,' said Freddie, handing the newspaper back to its original owner, 'I don't think I'll bother with a paper.'

Chapter 8: New faces.

In the new financial heart of London old firms are as comfortable as new ones. Canary Wharf had been destroyed by the IRA, only to rise again more splendid than ever. The buildings had a special grace because of their surroundings. More tranquil than New York and Chicago, the skyscrapers of London stood aloof by themselves in their own stretch of the ancient River Thames, almost isolated from the hustle, bustle and traffic of the older areas of London. The colour of the fast flowing river, now blue, now brown, reflected off the steep glass walls of each high-rise that had sprung up. Inside the mighty computer banks contained countless amounts of confidential information, and untold numbers of transactions hit cyber space every day from these offices. Merchant banks, finance houses, lawyers, they all had relocated from the nineteenth century buildings in the old centre of the City to these calm towers that dwarfed all earlier structures.

Three towers in particular rose above the rest and in the basement of one of them a heated debate was being conducted. On the steel exterior door in, the words 'PROTECT LIMITED' had been etched. Behind the door a large open plan office lit by a combination of natural and fluorescent light was to be seen. About ten people, roughly half of them women, were peering at computer screens or speaking on the telephone. The nearest desk had brochures stacked against it. The brochures were small but glossy, each one carrying on the front a picture of a white stretch limousine and underneath it a series of prices. Standard service was listed as £5,000 a day and deluxe service was listed as £10,000 a day. The room was clearly busy but not noisy as the telephones were all on flash not ring. To the left of the main room was the only private office. Again the door was steel in construction and etched upon this door were the words: 'Managing Director.'

In the open office nothing could be heard of the row going on in the smaller room. Harold Crane, chairman and managing director, sat patiently behind the steel and frosted-glass table, which served as his desk. It was hard to tell his age but fifty or sixty would have been equally good guesses. He had grizzled grey hair and olive skin. One of his front teeth had been broken in a fight many years ago but he had declined to get it fixed, believing (quite rightly) that perfect dentistry, whilst admired in the United States, is invariably taken in Britain as a sign of weak personality. Sitting in an easy chair to his right was another man of a similar age. The second man was of Afro-Caribbean descent and anyone could see that he was, or had been, once extremely fit. He was wearing a silver grey silk suit. There was something almost incongruous in so large a man drinking so small a cup of espresso. In the middle of the room a much younger man paced about, clearly very dissatisfied.

'Call ourselves gangsters?'

'Vince, Vince, you 'ave a lot to learn, my son,' the man behind the desk replied. Harold Crane seemed slightly amused, although why was not obvious.

'What are we doing, paying the Angel? I thought we was in the protection business, don't they pay us? I can't believe this.'

'We pay her, we protect her, that protects us.'

'I don't get it. You are seriously sending me with four solid gold ingots to deliver to that witch?'

At this the second man put down his coffee cup and eyed Vince disapprovingly.

'Language, son, language,' his father said. 'Surely you have noticed other firms where the proprietors drop like flies. You pay the Angel and you retire and die in your bed, just like your grand-dad.'

'But we must be paying fortunes. I don't see her do anything for us.'

'It is an honour, son, a great honour. We are her protectors, her Wings. No one touches our business and we don't expand unless she agrees. She looks after our money if we get in trouble, no commission. We can meet at her place safely. She is a very influential person, and a shareholder. You need to meet somebody, she can fix it. She knows how to ask questions if ever you find someone who doesn't want to talk to you. And she is very, very discreet. And very, very trusted. It's not a job. You are born to it.'

'You're safe enough, Vincent. I will be there with you.' The man in the silver suit was grinning from ear to ear.

'Very funny, Corn.'

Vincent Crane realised he was wasting his time by complaining further.

'I'll go and get my car.'

'No.' His father pointed a pen at him. 'You'll be travelling in something not so showy. Your friend Izzy Yamani is going with you. He'll meet you both on the south end of Waterloo Bridge. He'll drive you down. You don't need high security for this. The Angel's place is a fortress. All you need to be is discreet. An old car is better than one of ours.' He turned to the older man. 'I envy you both, it's nice down there.'

Vincent shrugged. 'OK, meet you by the front door, Corn.'

He walked out, closing the door noisily behind him.

'Think he'll give up the hardware?' Harold asked his old friend.

Cornwallis Jones straightened his yellow tie. 'Not a chance. I want to be there.'

Harold looked deadpan across to Corn. 'Remember our first trip to Gracie Shallcombe?'

Both men suddenly burst into uproarious laughter. Harold Crane reached into his breast pocket and pulled out a handkerchief to mop his streaming eyes. Cornwallis Jones was rocking back and forwards unable to control himself. After a couple of minutes the laughter subsided.

'Best be off.' Jones stood up, automatically patting his left breast pocket to check his equipment was with him.

'Tell her both sides have finished their investigations and gone home. I don't think we'll have to wait too long for an answer.'

'Anything else?'

'Pay my respects to them both. I hear that Rachel will be joining the business. Oh, and tell that son of mine we always take flowers to the ladies.'

Corn winked at his boss and old friend and went to catch up with Vincent.

*

The Tenants' Dinner was an occasion of considerable anxiety to the entire staff of Hamset Manor. For a start, Lord Errington expected the highest possible standards to be maintained and, as it was his only social event all year, he had the following twelve months to ponder upon any complaints he might have. Lady Vivienne, of course, was responsible for orchestrating the timing of the event and, much worse from her point of view, she was also responsible for allocating seating at the table. This year the weather had been wonderfully warm. For a change, the opening drinks were served on the lawn in the courtyard whilst the company gathered. At 7.30 precisely Dancer struck the portable gong a blow. The company then filed two by two through the entrance hall and into the main hall, led by Lord Errington with his granddaughter the Hon. Sophia Phillippa Meyrick Corshall upon his arm. Presently all were seated at the long table. Errington sat in the middle, as usual. His chair back rose above him, a dark mahogany creation of the days of Charles II. It was an uncomfortable chair and Errington had had a special cushion made to enable him to tolerate the discomfort. Despite this it was his favourite chair for these purposes because it was imposing and marked him out as being the host. The other chairs were comfortable but unremarkable early Victorian items, always with armrests. He had discovered about twenty years ago that some of his tenants were of a weight that could not be supported by chairs without arms. He sometimes still chortled at the recollection of the loud crack of splintering wood at one dinner when Sam Thornhill and his cousin Ernest had sat down at the same time on a pair of these flimsier chairs.

The table, beneath the heavy tablecloth, had been made up from separate parts that were normally kept in one of the upstairs rooms. When they were placed together it was possible to seat all of the guests with sufficient space for them to manage comfortably the several layers of cutlery, spare plates and assorted glasses. It was a rule that the very best china service and gold-plated silver cutlery was to be used. On this occasion the full-length portrait of the 2nd Lord Errington was brought up from the kitchen corridor and placed above the central fireplace. It was he who had insisted in his will that this tradition be observed by his successor and, by default, his painted presence became a part of the ritual. The 2nd Lord Errington was also known, mainly by the tenants, as the Black Lord. This was owing, according to legend, to his hot temper and propensity to flog both horses and servants from time to time. However the Black Lord had been in charge of the estate only for a very few years. He met an untimely end in the First World War not as a result of enemy action but consequent on an illegal duel using army-issue pistols after having accused a fellow officer of cheating at cards.

Despite the fact that it was still light, candles were lit at the table and by tradition burned right through the six-course meal. The hall in any case was not particularly well lit at the chimney end. Sophie sat opposite her grandfather and on either side of her were placed old Joshua Thornhill (to her right) and young Billy Thornhill (to her left). This was not to acknowledge the fact that Joshua Thornhill was the longest standing of the tenants, although no doubt that is how the other tenants took it. The real reason was that Errington wished to see the whites of Thornhill's eyes throughout the meal. It was not Lord Errington's habit to speak during the meal itself although he did put his hearing aid back in so as to hear the competition stories that were traditional. Joshua Thornhill was equally determined to enjoy the evening if only to spite his landlord. On his other side was his cousin Sam. Since they rarely saw each other, they had plenty to talk about during the meal and, given Joshua's recent acquisition of a fifth child, family reminiscences were in order. However for most of the meal Joshua, considering himself a ladies' man, made energetic conversation to Sophie Corshall, who simply could not break away to exchange a word with Billy on her other side.

The meal was outstanding and the steaming portions were huge. In the end, for once, Lady Vivienne had put her foot down and insisted on importing three experienced silver service waitresses from a catering company because Dancer was not quick enough to cope with things at his age. There would have been other staff available but it seemed better not to get anything wrong: the previous year Dancer had dropped a fork in Reggie Fowler's pudding and she had not heard the end of this from her father-in-law for the best part of six months.

The annual speeches by each tenant caused much guffawing and the occasional cheer. Sophie was to make the prize presentation. Sam Thornhill looked likely to win easily with a long-winded fantasy about betting on the contents of his I.A.C.S. forms filled in for the Intervention Board. The story took some working up but the climax of it was a conversation alleged between Sam Thornhill and a stranger he met nosing around Barnhill Farm. Sam reportedly bet the visitor his new combine harvester for the visitor's car if the visitor could guess how many sheep he had returned on the form. The visitor guessed correctly, to Sam's outrage and horror. On his enquiring how he could possibly guess correctly, the visitor replied: 'I work at the Intervention Board and you send your forms to me. I'm here inspecting whether they're correct!'

The entire company, with the exception of Sophie and Billy, thought this was highly amusing. They by chance looked at each other, Sophie raising one eyebrow but she knew immediately who had won the big picnic hamper of Harrods' fancy foods that was the prize for the best tale of the evening. The basket lay at one end of the table on a separate trolley and was much admired. All manner of exotica were inside: tinned fruitcake, biscuits, jars of caviar, pots of unusual jams, tinned pheasant, tropical fruits and goodness knows what. Reggie Fowler had his on display for two months after winning last year, and he shared the perishable items with his prize pig, reckoning she had earned it by inspiring him.

Sometime shortly after the last story, a conversation was struck up between Billy and Sophie.

'They seemed to like that!' Ventured Billy.

'Not as good as last year's, they say. But I'm not normally allowed to this social. Gramps is up to something, I expect.' Sophie Corshall's strong voice made itself heard over the general commotion. She was twenty-eight years old and had suspicions that her grandfather was planning a breeding programme to secure the succession for the Estate: a surprising number of unmarried, educated young men had mysteriously found their way into her company via her grandfather in recent weeks. This one was rather nice.

'Jolly good dinner. A lot better than the College feasts, I'd say. Did you plan it?'

'Not this year. Mother likes to do it. Keeps Gramps in order a bit. Otherwise we'd all be eating kippers!' Sophie laughed, so did Billy: the tenants had all heard of Errington's prescription for immortality. What a pretty girl she was! And what a pity his own grandfather was on such bad terms with hers.

Lord Errington, who by then had removed his hearing aid again, did not hear this conversation. He wished he had, for it was obvious to him that his granddaughter had taken a shine to young Billy, and he still had hopes of gaining a grandson speedily. Nothing wrong with an Oxford man and Robert Thornhill was hard-working enough. Mustn't get distracted, he thought. Errington put his hearing aid back on, switched it on and stood up.

'Ahem!' Errington cleared his throat and reached down to the table for the silver-cased hoof of his favourite horse on which a small bell had been soldered. He rang it energetically and the room fell silent. From his pocket he pulled a rolled up collection of papers covered in tiny writing and from this he began to read, peering closely at the text. 'Ladies and gentlemen, members of the family, welcome once more to the Tenants' Dinner and my good wishes. After another difficult decision this year the prize for the best account of his farm needs to be awarded to one of our tenants. This year instead of making the presentation myself I am going to call on someone else to do it. As you can see I am not getting any younger, although you are, and I need to have someone ready to step in to run the Estate and look after things. So I have chosen my grand-daughter, Sophie, to help me when I need it. She is as lovely as any lady in the land and has more brains in her little finger than I have anywhere else.' He put the papers down and continued: 'Come on, gel. Pick a winner. Got to be the best, what?'

He began clapping his hands and others followed suit. Sophie had suspected this might happen. She held up her hand and stood up so she could see everyone. Her grandfather had sat down and was watching closely.

'I see my grandfather is testing me this evening by giving me the most difficult task of all. How can I choose between so many excellent speeches? How can I say no to Mr Ernest Thornhill and the vanishing bucket, or to Mr Joshua Thornhill and the poisonous sausage-meat plant? What about Mr Greentop's talking lettuce or the Monster of Topham Farm that has struck terror in all our hearts, not just those of the MacGregors? And how can I forget the day Sharon stopped eating her swill and instead ate Mr Fowler's accounts? It's a close run thing this year and in the end I have decided to give the prize to the story that has caught the mood of the times. It has a monster in it and the monster eats accounts and the monster talks and one day will have you planting sausage-plants and for this year it has vanished. Ladies and gentlemen, grandfather, I choose the story about the Intervention Board, the most convincing monster of all.'

Sam Thornhill grinned triumphantly and raised both arms victoriously over his head. Everyone clapped. Sophie went over to the end of the table and presented Sam with a small rosette bearing the words 'Tallest Story 2002.' Sophie was much admired in consequence of this speech, and not just by Billy.

An hour later, when the guests were leaving, Lord Errington headed Billy off from the others and said to him, in a tone which could not be questioned:

'Come round tomorrow morning. Eleven prompt. Tell Sophie about Oxford.'

Naturally enough, he never bothered to mention the appointment to his granddaughter who the following day was compelled, though not against her will, to spend the latter part of the morning with Billy Thornhill. At around about lunchtime she decided that the appalling feuding between her grandfather and Joshua Thornhill should not be permitted to stop her and Billy enjoying each other's company. Therefore she invited him to ride with her that afternoon and it was only at ten o'clock that evening that Sophie reappeared at the Manor. Her mother, unaware of his Lordship's designs, was not at all displeased and made a mental note to encourage her daughter by all means. Though nobody up at Hamset Manor could be expected to understand why, it would not in any way have concerned Joshua Thornhill if his grandson Billy were to turn his attention to Sophie: the less Robert's issue wanted to control the business at Blue Grace Farm, possibly the less likely Robert Thornhill was to stand in Neville's way. So it was not long before Errington, his daughter-in-law and Joshua Thornhill between them were all creating opportunities to bring the two young people together. Whilst Billy at least may have experienced it as fate, it was a fate carefully manipulated. And one not predicted on the night of the Tenants' Dinner, which ended in good humour on very full stomachs.

*

The early afternoon of that day had been a trifle stressful for Vincent Crane. The journey from London to the Black Horse in Waterton had been entirely uneventful. Izzy Yamani had done the driving and for once had kept within the speed limit. Cornwallis Jones was not a man to be arrested for speeding when he had so many other things to worry about on that score. Corn sat in the front of the car and Vince sat in the back. The briefcase with the gold in it was seat belted into the back seat next to Vincent. All of them enjoyed being out of London for a change and the green they drove through was a relaxing contrast to the world they normally inhabited. Cornwallis Jones had a secret smile on his face most of the way, lost in private reflection. The car made good time, though Yamani, who felt greatly favoured to be chosen as driver, frequently checked the clock dial on the dashboard. They had a special appointment with the Angel.

Cornwallis supposed that every young blood would be troublesome about the Angel until the sense of it was driven home. He remembered his own incredulity at what he had been told about Gracie Shallcombe so he had some sympathy with Vince, who wanted to impress with his toughness the likes of Izzy Yamani. Their special appointment was for half past four so at 4.25 that Tuesday afternoon Cornwallis Jones, as the senior member of the party, pressed the buzzer by the side of the iron-studded locked door of the Black Horse.

'Hello?' A voice came from within.

'Its me, Corn.'

'OK.'

The door swung open of its own accord. All three of them stepped inside the inner porch as the door clanged shut behind them. Ahead lay a second, glass, door that remained closed. Cornwallis was in front and had already placed his handgun on the shelf to the right of the main door. The shelf automatically swung round, removing the gun from sight and presenting again an empty shelf.

'Deposit your hardware and come through,' Cornwallis said as he moved through the opening glass doors ahead, taking with him the briefcase and a bunch of flowers. But the two young men hesitated. Izzy Yamani was not carrying a gun anyway so he simply held his hands out in front of him at shoulder height and walked through the doors, which opened again. Vincent, by contrast, looked suspiciously around the porch area, making no move towards depositing his weapon. Again a quiet voice was heard within the porch:

'Could you please deposit your weapon on the shelf?'

Vince could not see where the voice was coming from but, beyond the glass doors, he could see Corn and Izzy sitting at a table talking to a very, very attractive dark haired girl with an unbelievably low-cut blouse. In a matter of seconds a voice, a woman's voice, said again:

'I am very sorry but I must ask you once more to deposit your weapon, dear.'

Vincent saw the girl look towards him. He decided to make a stand. After all, it was just a bleeding village pub.

Nothing happened. A fat lady with lots of dyed blond hair and a really upsettingly low-cut blouse walked across from somewhere out of vision to the right, straight past, to chat with Corn and Izzy. He banged his fist against the glass doors. Still nothing happened. It was getting surprisingly hot between these doors. He decided it might be a good idea to get back into the car. He tried the main door but that was locked as well. This was not good. Through the glass he could see Corn and Izzy were having a pint. Suddenly he felt very thirsty and very hot. He stripped off his black leather jacket and loosened his black tie. The gun was in his rear trouser pocket and he was not handing it over to please anybody. Still nothing happened but it was getting really hot now. He opened his damp shirt down to the waistband. He was sweating badly. If only he hadn't given Corn the briefcase to take in he could have used it to try and smash open the glass. But kicking the glass doors made no impact on them at all. He considered trying to shoot his way out but this was a bit over the top in the circumstances. How long were they going to keep him here? Nobody was taking any notice of him at all. When Corn had finished his drink the fat lady disappeared from view again.

'I'm very sorry, dear, but it is a rule here that no guns are allowed inside. Please put your gun on the shelf.'

Not a sodding chance, thought Vince to himself. The fat lady served Izzy and Corn again. Izzy was eating a pie but Corn was having another pint of beer. Vince felt annoyed and began kicking the glass door as hard as he could. It made no impact at all. The people at the table appeared to be having a good laugh. They did not look at him but he knew what was going on. So in the end, although by this time he felt as though he were baking in an oven and his hands were so slippery with sweat that he could hardly hold it, he took the gun and fired it downwards into the lower corner of the glass door. The door was unmarked but the bullet ricocheted back into Vince's foot. He screamed with pain and sat down. There was no way he was giving up that gun. The fat lady disappeared from view again.

'All you have to do, dear, is put your gun on the shelf. We'd be very happy to see you and you'll get your gun back afterwards. I'm afraid I can't wait very much longer. I have a few things to do. Would you please leave your gun?'

Vincent then lost his temper. He started to rant and rave, though nobody could hear him. He certainly did not put his gun on the shelf. After three or four minutes the fat lady stood on the opposite side of the glass with her arms folded. Vincent could barely breathe, so hot was it and strangely airless. The fat lady shook her head and shrugged her shoulders. She then fiddled about with her bracelet, as far as Vince could see. But less than a second after that a blinding pain shot through every cell in his body. A series of blue flashes bounced round the porch area from every metal object, including his gun. As soon as the flashes stopped, he rolled over with his legs in the air, stripped off his leather trousers with the gun in the pocket and threw them across onto the shelf. He then hauled himself up onto one leg and began hammering on the glass with both hands shouting, inaudibly, 'Get me out of here!'

Mrs. Shallcombe turned calmly to Cornwallis Jones.

'Do tell Harold it was the lowest possible dose. There won't be any side-effects.'

'What in hell's name was that?'

'Microwave,' Mrs. Shallcombe explained. 'Only a teeny weenie touch, nothing to worry about. And we'll soon sort his foot out upstairs.'

The glass doors opened and the sweat-soaked, wet-haired, semi-naked Vincent fell through them onto the floor, landing badly and rolling onto one side.

'Can I get you a drink, dear? My name is Maddie Shallcombe and you must be Vincent. I've known your father for many years, do take a seat and relax.'

Vincent was temporarily speechless but even if he had said something he would not have been heard over the noise being made by Jones and Yamani who were laughing helplessly. The most beautiful girl he had ever seen returned to the table at that precise moment and said:

'Hello, I'm Rachel.'

Vincent, crouched on three limbs, again said nothing but his jaw might possibly have dropped. Jones and Yamani took one look at his face and started up laughing again. Yamani was wiping his eyes on his shirtsleeves. Jones, howling with mirth, had his head down on the table and was stamping his left foot, pounding his right fist on the table. The noise was incredible.

Vincent tried to get up to walk to the table but the pain of the bullet in his foot made him fall over again with a scream. Somewhere, deep in his memory, something was stirring. It was his father's voice from the day before.

'Son, just remember one thing. Never, ever, underestimate the Angel. She ain't what she looks.'

Chapter 9: Bitter fruit

The last day of June was a glorious Sunday. Joshua and Rhiannon Thornhill had enjoyed a long lazy breakfast in the back garden. Little Neville was one day short of two months old. Already he could survey the world nosily from his baby deckchair. He was a sturdy, dark haired child, quite unlike his father. At birth he had been just a little under ten pounds, a good size for a first baby, especially when the mother was approaching thirty-five years old. Joshua, who already had four children by his first marriage, had no recollection of any of them growing as quickly as Neville seemed to be doing. Admittedly it was all a very long time ago and he had been busy on the farm in those days. Now he took great delight in watching the daily changes that Neville underwent. Joshua fancied that, unlike his four siblings, Neville was showing signs of intelligence. How he deduced this with so small a baby is hard to say. His own view, expressed only once to Rhiannon and greeted with some disapproval, was that intelligence passed through the mother's line and Meg had not had a lot of it. He had formed this theory through a close interest in the pedigree lines of cattle but, as Rhiannon pointed out, it was all supposition because cattle were not bred for intelligence. At any rate, the birth of little Neville marked a significant turn in the direction of Joshua's life. Even more so, perhaps surprisingly, than the acquisition of his new wife.

Rhiannon had been trespassing in the lower meadow field when one of the men had reported her presence to him. In the ordinary way that sort of thing would have been relayed back to Robert but he was not there on that particular morning. It had been a cold October day but, for some reason, Joshua Thornhill had been in the mood to walk the dogs and so he decided to ward off the trespasser himself. He had not been told that it was a woman or what she was doing. So he came upon her at the bottom of the field where she had set up her easel and paints. The light had the peculiar sharpness of that time of year and the old man had been simply enthralled by the woman's beauty. It was the effect that he experienced, not the individual component parts, for they were somewhat odd. The reverie of his initial glimpse of Rhiannon was almost immediately broken by the fact that the two large Alsatians he had with him raced out in a threatening way towards her. She saw them coming, growling and panting and, quick as a flash, she had tossed the canvass to the ground, upturned the easel, and swung it fiercely at them to defend herself. Joshua was some way behind the dogs, shouting at them to come back. As he approached he heard the woman address the dogs in no uncertain terms, and in a tone of voice sufficient to keep them at bay for the time required for him to catch them up.

'Get back you stinking son of a bitch,' she ordered Noddy. 'Back, back or your mother eats your balls!' Noddy and Nipper advanced no further but continued to growl. Joshua had never seen anyone, man or woman, stop the dogs like this. Both beautiful and tough but with a harsh American voice and no inhibitions about using it.

What Joshua saw in Rhiannon was energy and intelligence. What Rhiannon saw in Joshua was cunning, which she expected of a man, and the kind of courtesy and loyalty she had only ever before experienced from her father's business colleagues in the Mafia. Joshua had apologised immediately for the dogs' behaviour and insisted she return to the farmhouse for a cup of tea. What they shared was a love of art and nature that rapidly developed into a love for each other.

Two months after Neville's birth was still too soon for Rhiannon to be feeling completely back to normal. She was naturally very tired as she was breastfeeding Neville and hoped to do so for several months. Kathleen was paid extra to make and clear a family breakfast for them on Sundays as a special treat before Rhiannon went off to the late Mass at the Church of the Blessed Virgin in Gloucester. It was not that Rhiannon was particularly religious but she had decided to experience for a while at any rate English, or more accurately Irish, forms of Catholicism. It was a totally different experience from what she was used to back home. Kathleen took Neville that morning to her cottage, wheeling him down the path in his high black pram that seemed to be used for very little apart from the journey between the farmhouse and Kathleen's cottage. Joshua watched them go. He waved Kathleen from the front door and retreated into the house. He had finished his business in the study the previous afternoon. Douglas Dale had rearranged Joshua's will as instructed. He advised Joshua to set out in writing and put in a safe place all the things that might otherwise be difficult to trace were anything to happen to him. Routine advice, Douglas insisted. And it made perfect sense to Joshua to identify his insurance policies, his pensions and where his money was. The envelope had been placed in his mahogany desk against that unknown day when someone else would read it. Joshua looked around the house with a satisfied smile on his face. Everywhere were the traces of his wife and child. He did not mind the untidiness as out of it grew wonderful things – striking abstract canvasses, curious arrangements of flowers and twisted metal, mosaics of glass and tiling, hand-woven embroidered hangings. Neville's toys had been picked up and placed in a box in the middle of the floor. Neville, of course, was far too young to play with them himself but Rhiannon did. She was intrigued by the colours and Neville's reactions to them. She loved the different textures of the animals.

Through the French windows Joshua saw the table and chairs on the lawn and, beyond them, the three remaining fruit trees at the end of the garden. They were the last of what had been an orchard planted in the 1920s by his own grandfather. These trees were well kept and still produced a good crop of apples each year. But behind them had sprung up a rogue plum tree. It could not have been part of the original orchard and would not have been planted deliberately in the position it had since it overshadowed the apple trees so as to deprive them of light. The tree had often annoyed Joshua because when the plums fell it was too big a job to collect them all and the insects, particularly wasps, were drawn to the spoiled fruit. It could take anything up to three or four days before the wasps would demolish a plum. Joshua had intended the previous year to give the tree a vicious pruning but had never got round to it. He did not want to have the tree removed as it did screen Rhiannon's compost corner. She had often complained about squelching the fruit by accident as she had been taking things out to the compost corner.

Joshua decided to do something. Perhaps if he pruned at the wrong time of year the tree would not fruit this year. At worst his efforts would take down quite a lot of branches that would otherwise be carrying fruit. The tree needed discipline and anyway the apples needed more light.

Stuck on the end of the eastern extension to the back of the house was a waterproof implement cupboard and out of it Joshua pulled a stepladder and a hacksaw. Had it not been the day of the World Cup Final this Sunday he might have got Dave Merchant to help him or even do it himself. But Dave had other plans that day. Joshua had seen him through the window that morning walking into the village, half his face painted green and the other half yellow. He surely wouldn't be leaving the TV screen in the pub until the game was over in the early afternoon and would then be unlikely to be in a state fit to climb a ladder safely. Joshua felt impatient on such a fine day to get on with the task.

He placed the ladder securely against the plum tree and climbed carefully up. He was used to high-level work of a kind that someone else might think was dangerous. After half an hour he had made considerable progress on the tree but there was still quite a lot to do. Branches lay where they had fallen and by now it was getting on for one o'clock. Joshua paused. It was very warm. He wore no hat but wiped his face with his left forearm. His grip on the saw was hard to maintain as he was sweating profusely and the veins on his forehead were throbbing uncomfortably. It was a still, heavy time almost completely silent apart from the sound of the flies in the tree. For a second he forgot what he was doing up the ladder. He started and looked around, puzzled. The sun had bathed the whole scene in a warm, deep red, light. Then it strangely began to dim and grow dark to his vision. What was happening? He no longer felt like doing any more and the saw seemed to have grown heavier than he had ever remembered it being before. He closed his eyes momentarily and tried to take a deep breath. How warm and peaceful it had become. A few seconds after stopping work the old man's dizziness got the better of him and he let go both tree and saw. The ladder, though still standing, was now lurched at a precarious angle.

It was early evening before Rhiannon finally found him. He still had not moved.

*

Howard Morgan was an angry man. A hundred thousand pounds bail was quite out of his reach. His ex-wife would not put it up, and his employers certainly would not put it up and he himself had no hope that the meagre possessions salvaged from the wreck of his second marriage, now lying in his rented flat in Bristol, would make any significant contribution to the required figure, even he did sell them. Not that he intended to run away but the police requirement for financial security was of a very conventional kind. So Howard stayed in prison. After three weeks' remand the stipendiary magistrate finally told him that he could go home, pending his trial on a charge of dangerous driving.

The three weeks in question had not been idly spent but were a frenzy of enraged activity. First, he had to formulate a plan for revenge on Freddie Pinker, not only the cause of the problem but also a man who walked free without so much as experiencing breakfast in the police station. Secondly, having a perfect plan, he had to secure the means of executing it. This was no simple task but his present circumstances offered unusual opportunities for progress on that front. At the end of his first week inside, he met a fat safe breaker with severe halitosis and an urgent need to get rid of Semtex. Dangerous stuff, thought Morgan, but good enough if it can be handled. Morgan had heard the prison rumours about Freddie Pinker, suddenly famous as a result of the accident following Paulette selling an exclusive to the Western Mail in which, clad in a black bikini, fishnet tights and a single red rose, she had taken the press round the Pinkers' establishment and been photographed on the pink couch surrounded by teddies. The article was a huge success, combining as it did the account of the accident, the titillation of the photographs and the unusual nature of the business. Eric was delighted with the publicity but the effect on Morgan of reading the article was decidedly negative. He had heard from another inmate that a copy of the newspaper in the prison library might be of interest. When he read it, he decided that Freddie Pinker had to go. With mounting rage he read in the paper about Freddie's friendship with Madame Seraglio, about his new diamond rings and, by far the worst, his sudden success in the deceased pets disposal business. Morgan had always hated both Pinkers but most of all Freddie. It was a loathing that could be more or less controlled so long as he, Morgan, was the most successful of the three, but not otherwise. After three weeks of incessant brooding on the perfect revenge Morgan set about achieving it. But first he made sure, absolutely sure, that he knew how to use the Semtex that he purchased in prison.

Chapter 10: The best-laid plans

The tenth of July was Rachel Shallcombe's birthday. She had not intended to spend it in London, but intentions often go out of the window when important business is at hand. The previous night she had stayed at a luxurious and beautiful hotel in central London. It was not really Rachel's idea of fun but it was necessary in order to meet discreetly with two very different people. She had enjoyed dinner in the company of a charming bespectacled man who came from New York but lived in Chicago; breakfast had been taken with an equally charming lady who had been educated in Athens but now worked in Chicago. Both dinner and breakfast had been eaten in the same corner of the Orangerie where a quiet discussion in the recesses would go entirely unnoticed. In the centre of the great marble floored courtyard was a magnificent display of porcelain and flowers. Around this, small fountains played as numerous waiters stood quietly by, sensitive to the slightest movement that might indicate a need for attention. This was a location where business deals of many kinds were concluded and it was one of the few hotels considered safe enough for the biggest Hollywood stars to stay without needing to import private bodyguards.

Once these discussions were completed, Rachel felt the desire to check out from the hotel and take a walk. She had brought nothing with her other than a tiny overnight bag containing a toothbrush, a few cosmetics, and a change of clothes. This weighed very little and offered no hindrance to a stroll through Hyde Park that cloudy morning. There was a lot to think about strategically but more mundane matters were pressing in upon her. Eventually she turned back on to a road and decided to flag down a cab to take her to the Docklands. London seemed fairly quiet, compared to her recollection of it. But she knew that her impressions were misleading as this was the beginning of the school holiday season. She had spent three years on and off in London as a student and remembered it fondly. There really was no substitute for working there to get a true feel for what a city was all about. This particular afternoon she had investments to make and needed meanwhile to check that no unexpected problems had materialised involving the Americans. Her short visit should suffice: she shared her mother's concern about telephones and the general lack of security or privacy that they offered. A face-to-face meeting was always better if it could be managed.

She paid the taxi and walked some distance from the point at which she had been dropped before turning abruptly to the door of the building that displayed the sign for Protect Limited. This had been one of her mother's most successful enterprises offering, as it did, access to all manner of otherwise highly secure places. It was also an extremely profitable business, and there seemed to be no limit to the number and kind of people who required personal protection in a country that prohibited the handling of guns by the ordinary citizens. Even the use of a convincing-looking chocolate replica gun to threaten a shopkeeper merited serious judicial attention in England. No wonder American celebrities, both legal and illegal, felt naked in the United Kingdom. Equally little wonder that so many of them settled there rather than return to an environment where one demented fan or disappointed client could result in a bullet through the head.

Although Rachel had enjoyed her time at Harvard, and certainly learned a lot there, she had never been tempted to any career other than following in her mother's footsteps. It was a very special business that her mother ran and one which had the highest possible standards. For Rachel this secret career was one she had longed to fulfil. She knew that there were now no more than three surviving Angels in the whole of Europe, one in South America, and one in Canada. That was it. One of Rachel's favourite games as a child had been to ask her mother about the items in what her mother called the Old Things Cupboard. Maddie Shallcombe had many cupboards, most of which Rachel had never looked into, and a few of which even now she would not be allowed to look into. But the Old Things Cupboard had always been available. In it were photographs or miniature paintings of her grandmother, her great grandmother, her great great grandmother and her great great great grandmother. Rachel had learned who these people were and what they had done.

The cupboard held a number of souvenirs collected over the centuries. Her favourite was a plain oak box containing twenty-one gold coins each in pristine condition. They had been sent as a personal gift from King Henry VII to thank Mary Shallcombe for her part in persuading the exhausted houses of York and Lancaster to accept the official line that their bitter dynastic quarrel was over. She also had a special fondness for a large but rather strange looking early medieval ring, clearly too big for the finger of any woman. The metal was gold and the design in the shape of a cross. The centre stone was a carved cameo of a woman's head and the bars of the cross were formed from deep green emeralds cabochon set. On the inside of the ring the sign of a fish had been imprinted. The ring was said to have belonged to an abbot of Glastonbury who paid it to Kate Shallcombe for her services in bringing to a satisfactory end the litigation that for fifteen years the monks had been conducting against the Bishop of Bath and Wells regarding control over the Abbey. The ring itself was thought to be much older yet, possibly being a ninth century item but made up from a horde of Roman jewels. There were parchments and old glass bottles. And a handful of tiny gold African figurines. There were two or three parcels of folded tissue paper inside which ancient and fragile silks were to be found. The silks were said to date from the time of the First Crusade and to represent part payment to Matilda Shallcombe for resolving a quarrel between a pair of Frankish knights who each fell in love with the same woman. All of these things gave Rachel a sense of her place in the world.

'We have a visitor, son.' Harold Crane looked up into his number one security camera. Vincent did not look up. He was sitting sprawled out on a plastic four-legged chair with his feet on the desk reading a newspaper. Harold Crane immediately left the room and went personally to the front of the office to greet his guest.

'Welcome, Rachel, you are always welcome here. Let me show you into my office.'

'Thanks.'

'Come in. Corn can't be here today. I have his report. No problems that he can see.' He ushered her into the private office and closed the door firmly behind her. Vincent did not move, his nose still in the newspaper.

'I have had discussions, detailed discussions, with both sides. If this goes ahead security will have to be the best we have ever had. It will be a big operation, especially for the final phase.'

On hearing her voice Vincent dropped the newspaper. Ever since his humiliating entrance at the Black Horse Vince had dreamed that one day Rachel would come to the London office. Various witty remarks had been planned and memorised against that fateful time when he would be able to impress her with his sophistication and charm. However he had no idea that a visit might happen so soon. He wasn't even wearing the designer shirt he had bought or the special deodorant that was supposed to reduce women to instant swooning compliance. Instead, the balance he had maintained by keeping his two feet on his father's desk to stop his upturned chair, which was already balanced on only two legs, from overturning completely disappeared as he tried to spring to his feet to greet Rachel. There was the most extraordinary row: the screech of the rear legs of the chair across the floor, the shout of surprise from Vince as he was flung into the air backwards, the crash of the chairback on the floor hitting it with full force accompanied by Vince's weight, the bang as his right foot hit the table leg on landing, the judder of the table, the cry of pain as his overturned coffee mug hit him depositing its hot contents on his upper leg, the crash of the mug shattering on the floor and finally, and loudest, the outraged yowl of his father's cat suddenly woken from its sleep in the basket under the table by a shard of pot smacking it on the nose. Rachel raised her eyebrows and waited for the cat to stop its noise.

'Hallo, Vince. How are you doing?'

'Good. Yeap, good,' Vincent managed in a slightly strangled voice whilst he tried to get up from the floor using his better, unbandaged, foot and at the same time hold the hot patch on his trousers away from his leg. His father was grinning from ear to ear.

'Corn is working on the travel arrangements for the Counsellors. I will get him to come up and report to Maddie personally. The cars are being prepared now.' Harold Crane was proud of the efficiency of his organisation.

'She'll be glad to know that. I will be back this evening. Is there anything that you want me to tell her beyond that?'

'Just tell her we'll be ready. Just like she wants it.'

'Good. Well, I'll be off in that case. I have a few things still to do.' She smiled at Vincent who rushed forward, as fast as his limp would allow, to show her out of the building. He interposed himself between the two of them.

'I'll see you out.' Vince stepped back on to his father's foot, then jumped forwards and stood on Rachel's foot

'Ow!' They complained in unison.

Vince was wringing his hands together and looked at Rachel with an agonised expression.

'I'm really sorry. Are you hurt? Do you need to, er, take off your shoe or something.'

Rachel frowned at Vince, saying in an extremely serious voice:

'I don't think anything is broken, but I can't be sure.'

'Oh no. This is terrible. Maybe we should go to the hospital or something. I don't know how it could have happened. I'm so, so sorry!' He ran the fingers of both hands through his Mohican hair in agitation. It was a style originally designed for surviving the rigours of a sports field but not a direct assault by wet hands. The top of the Mohican collapsed on both sides, leaving him with a gigantic fringe that obscured his view of her.

Harold Crane, barely able to control his laughter, turned away from the sight of his son and examined his fingernails in detail. Vince had only just recovered from his first encounter with Rachel. She managed temporarily better than his father. Vince pulled back his ruined fringe and stood speechlessly staring into her eyes.

'Well, shall I see myself out, then?'

'No, no, not at all,' said Vince hurriedly with a start. He automatically stepped backwards again, this time onto the paw of the unfortunate cat, which shot screeching through the open door. Behind him his father had begun to snigger. Vince stumbled out after the cat, holding the door open for her on the other side. Rachel turned to wave cheerily to Harold as she left the room. He was already laughing into his handkerchief to keep the noise down and he waved back with his free hand.

*

Howard Morgan was known far and wide to be an evil bastard. It had always been that way, even when he was an age that most people would have taken for a time of innocence. Mrs Lightfoot found him a valuable employee (but not a hundred thousand pounds' worth of value): he had an eerie pride in completing his work perfectly and greater pride in supervising the other drivers in Mrs Lightfoot's fleet. Even his rather sinister air was not necessarily out of keeping in the type of business she ran. She could manage without him, but much better with him. Morgan was always up to something and had various hobbies which, when enjoyed by other people, could be described at best as educational and at worst as harmless. But Howard Morgan's pastimes of entomology and taxidermy were undertaken in a brooding malevolent spirit. After the break-up of his marriage he had moved his collection of stuffed or petrified creatures into a small terraced house in Bristol. He had also moved in his collection of knives and jars full of formaldehyde. Bristol was a forgiving, unseeing kind of place. After all it was not far from Gloucester where the Wests had managed to murder a substantial number of people without remark. Howard Morgan only intended to murder one and in a city very much bigger than Gloucester.

A couple of weeks after being released from prison Morgan received a visitor, a visitor with bad breath. He brought with him a large parcel tied up with brown paper and string. The parcel was placed very carefully on the kitchen table and the instructions for use repeated very slowly for the last time. Morgan was a careful man and accustomed to handling volatile and dangerous things. Once he had the Semtex, all he needed was a cat.

The capture of a cat was easy enough but killing it was more difficult. He emerged from the experience scratched and angry. He decided to let the first cat go whilst he planned a better exit for the next one. Then he had a much better idea. What was the point of killing your own cat when they were lying dead in Waterton for the taking? Sure enough, since Morgan's search for a dead cat was not tied to a radius of thirty yards from Carlton Corshall, he was able to locate one within a couple of days. Clean, freshly dead. It was just what he wanted.

And so it was that on the evening of Thursday the eighteenth of July Howard Morgan was able to relax with a glass of cold lager having put the finishing stitches into the cat. It lay on his kitchen table apparently sleeping peacefully. Inside it, instead of bones and innards, lay the Semtex recently provided by his obliging acquaintance. The perfect plan was perfectly simple. He would wait until midnight and place the cat on the front steps of the Pinkers' establishment. Freddie was always first up in the morning as he had to get down to the butchers by 7am. So goodbye Freddie. Nothing like a lager, served at just the right temperature, in just the right shape of glass.

Like many obsessed with perfection, Morgan had little time to study human nature. For one thing, his horizons were limited by his own preference for routine above all things. Part of the annoyance of being in prison was not so much the attendant discomfort as the interruption to the plans he had already made in his, as it were, 'real' life. Re-entering his abandoned normality was not without its own new experiences. Experiences which other people take as common place and put down to better foresight next time never happened to Howard Morgan in his ordinary existence precisely because he prided himself on thinking of everything. So, after three weeks absence, it had been a wholly novel experience to enter his house only to be greeted by the smell of decaying food. Accustomed as he was to difficult odours, nothing had quite prepared him for the contents of his fridge. They had not quite evolved into intelligent life but it took a full two days to clean out and air his accommodation. His bedroom was also exceedingly unpleasant: in the intervening three weeks his pet rat had died of starvation. This, as much as anything, had hardened Morgan's resolve to do away with Pinker.

Freddie Pinker's life, by contrast, was no longer predictable to any degree. The routine that Howard Morgan remembered no longer existed. Freddie's life was now almost completely occupied by the arrangements necessary in connection with the deceased pets' business and in particular by the influx of dead cats. The owners nearly always wanted the animals buried where they had been found. And as nearly all the finders brought them straight to the Pinker establishment, the place was a hive of activity. Paulette, who Freddie had once regarded as an unwarranted extravagance, was now indispensable. Eric still went to the animal centre but rather to get away from the press of business than to encourage it. It was almost a week since Freddie had decided temporarily to close the butchers shop and concentrate on the pets business. Eric had been right all along – there was plenty of money in it. The second surprising feature about Freddie's recent life was that he had acquired a nighttime persona. Having for years never been anywhere more adventurous than the Black Horse of a Saturday night, Freddie now found himself swept up by a most entertaining and gregarious crowd of ladies through Paulette. In that group he had become rather a hero for standing up for Paulette and doing it so manfully. His lack of height was now no disadvantage as his reputation more than made up for it. Paulette, it transpired, was a close friend of

Madame Seraglio, so Freddie found himself most evenings over at Madame Seraglio's club and did not now have the energy to get up and open the butchers shop first thing in the morning anyway. In effect his day began roundabout ten o'clock when he reported to Eric in the shop by the Black Horse. To look at him, Freddie's appearance had also changed considerably. Paulette had advised him to put blond streaks in his hair and, despite being rather dubious about it, he had done so: the effect was quite dramatic. Instead of looking like a man of fifty (which he wasn't) Freddie now looked like a man of thirty (which he also wasn't). Part of the reason was that he tended during the daytime to wear his black hat for the pets' ceremonials and it was only in the evening, in the artificial half-light, that his highlights were most commonly seen. Madame Seraglio had encouraged him to wear a heavy silver bracelet that she gave him as a reward for dealing with some trouble in the upstairs of the club and Paulette suggested that he should buy a heavy silver ring to match it. Thus apparelled, despite Eric's sarcasm, Freddie now found himself both well dressed, if somewhat unusually dressed, and very much at home in the private bar of Madame Seraglio's. Freddie's new life was essentially beyond Howard Morgan's imaginings. So also was the ultimate destination of the cat bomb that he had prepared.

That Thursday night Freddie remained over at Madame Seraglio's, as he often did, until the following morning. Unbeknown to him at shortly before midnight Howard Morgan had, very carefully, deposited his cat bomb in the street by the steps of the Pinker establishment. Eric was long since in bed and the area was deserted. Revellers leaving the Black Horse would not in any case have turned in the direction of the undertakers' establishment but they had all left a good half hour earlier. Morgan was quite confident that he had not been seen and that no one else would be coming that way until first thing in the morning. He could not be more wrong on both counts.

Arthur Smollett was keeping his vigil over Carlton Corshall. The latter lay fast asleep, as usual, in front of the butchers shop just beyond the undertakers' establishment. Thus when Morgan removed the cat from its wrappings and left it there, the concealed Arthur Smollett saw everything. In the dark he did not see who the solitary man with the parcel was and even had it been light he would not immediately have recognised him. But he did rapidly realise what the man was about. This was a completely unexpected turn of events. So convinced was he that Carlton Corshall must be the culprit that he was now quite unprepared to deal with the situation. He panicked. Should he call the police? Should he call his wife on his mobile telephone? Should he try a citizen's arrest of the man? Would the man be armed? Did he have someone with him? He had no answers to any of these questions and so, by default, decided to wait where he was until the man had gone. This gave him a few moments longer to decide what he should do. Obviously he had no intrinsic interest in the cat but only in the question as to whether it had died of an overdose and, possibly, as to why this was all going on in the first place. He must be making some progress since at least he had established that Carlton Corshall was not responsible. This discovery nevertheless opened up greater possibilities than he could currently cope with. The obvious thing to do would be to proceed with his original plan and perform a post mortem on the cat to establish its cause of death before it was embalmed, buried or cremated. All things considered, he did not reckon it likely that the owner of the cat would agree to what he had in mind but the opportunity was unique. He decided that the owner would either agree or disagree. If that person agreed there was no harm done. If that person disagreed, Smollett was acting in the public interest and reckoned he could talk his way out of any difficulties. It was, after all, his job to solve just this sort of problem.

Unsure whether he would be committing theft by temporarily abstracting the cat corpse, Smollett decided to proceed cautiously. He drove the car very slowly round to the shop and put the cat in the boot. He had no special equipment with him so simply placed the animal upon some rugs to keep it still on the way. Then he drove as quietly as he could to the front of the animal centre in Little Waterton and parked. The centre was completely closed and Smollett walked over to the front door. He was about to unlock the building when it occurred to him that he had better lock the boot of the car just in case the smell attracted interest, should anyone pass by. It was a dark night and with the exception of one parked car there seemed to be no one about. But he was not keen to take risks, having come so far. Therefore he got out the remote locking device and aimed it at the vehicle.

Who knows how Morgan had rigged the cat bomb? Whatever he had done was sufficiently sensitive to be triggered almost at once.

The rear of the car suddenly buckled outwards and flames shot out of the interior. Huge metal shards flew out like harpoons randomly in all directions. With a clean inwards bowing movement the glass front of the building first shattered then dropped vertically. The front of the building shuddered and groaned. The petrol tank of the car then went up in a second explosion far greater than the first. At this point the car became a burning heap of debris. Arthur Smollett fell to the ground unconscious, knocked off his feet by the force of the second blast and lucky enough not to have been speared by a metal piece. Between the blazing heap of wreckage and his fallen figure, squarely placed in the way of both blasts, was a car, which rocked twice but remained apparently unaffected. Black clouds of smoke belched from the flames and the heavy stench of burning rubber, metal and plastic hung in the air. Other than the rush of heat and the crackle of fire nothing could be heard above the sound of parrots frantically calling from inside the animal centre and the baying of a pair of terrified dogs in the intensive care recovery section.

All over the village, the lights went on.

Chapter 11 – Heat

'Oh Christ!' said the Reverend Hollis, as the first blast rocked the car and lit the scene with fire.

'Shit!' said Eric Pinker.

'Let me out! Get off!' said Maddie Shallcombe. 'What on earth is going on?'

Then a second blast hit the vehicle throwing the vicar onto the floor of the rear compartment. Eric landed painfully on top of him. Maddie was already in the front checking for damage but finding none.

'It's a judgement upon our wickedness!' panicked the naked vicar, endeavouring to stand up and hold his hands heavenwards.

'Don't be an idiot,' expostulated Mrs Shallcombe. 'Eric, what have you done with his clothes?'

'We both got undressed outside and I put the clothes in the boot.'

'Well you can't get dressed now,' Mrs Shallcombe observed. A dozen or so people had come to watch from a distance. Maddie Shallcombe pulled on her dress, which was a single piece sheath shift. She knew that the windows of her car were opaque and also that the armour on the vehicle had saved them all from being killed. She thought it better not to mention that right now. 'I'm going to have a look, see if we can do anything to help. Teddy,' she said to the vicar, 'see that fur coat you were lying on? Put it on for now. Eric, pull on the car rug for a second and I will get the clothes from the boot.'

She started the engine and carefully drove the car twenty or so yards further from the burning vehicle, which in a short space of time had flared almost down into a smouldering black heap. Then she opened the passenger door and closed it behind her. The village was well and truly awake and Rex Cheeseman, a policeman who lived locally, was already taking charge. The fire had burned itself out and there appeared to be no further damage to property. So far as he could see the only casualty was one man lying in front of the animal centre but in a condition that made Cheeseman reluctant to move him before the emergency services arrived. Maddie Shallcombe went to the boot of her car, which had suffered nothing more than bubbled paintwork, and rummaged about in it. Eric must be mistaken: there was no sign of any clothes in the boot of this car. She returned to the passenger door, opened it again and said in an urgent whisper:

'Eric, the clothes aren't in the boot.'

'I know', said Eric ruefully. I left them on the top of the boot and was going to put them inside. But then we drove round the corner to get somewhere a bit darker. They will be over in the lay-by, I reckon.'

'There's no time for that now. Stay here. It looks as though someone has been hurt. I think we should get him to Gloucester infirmary. It could be ages before an ambulance comes.'

So saying she approached PC Cheeseman for his views about it.

'I'll show you how bad it is Maddie. I think it could be three quarters of an hour before the ambulance gets here and, you know, I think you're probably right. We should get the victim to hospital straight away.'

'Shall we go and have a look at him then?'

It was all happening so quickly. Both of them recognised Arthur Smollett immediately. In next to no time Smollett had been laid on the back seat of Mrs Shallcombe's car, his feet on the vicar's lap.

'The Reverend Hollis has kindly agreed to come with us to the hospital in case he is needed.' Mrs Shallcombe smiled gratefully at the vicar. The latter said nothing but might have changed colour. 'Would you like to come too, Constable Cheeseman? Eric and I were on our way back from a fancy dress ball so it's lucky that I have a driver this evening.'

'Do you really need me?'

'No, not really. It would probably be better if you rang the hospital to let them know what has happened and to tell them to have someone ready to receive us. I know where the Accident and Emergency wing is. I was down at the hospital only recently. And could you give Joyce Smollett a ring? She'll want to catch up with us when she can but I expect she needs to get someone over to keep an eye on the girls.'

'In that case, I'll make those phone calls if you take him there. The fire brigade are supposed to be on their way and I think it would be a good idea for me to be here when they arrive.'

'Thank you, officer. Off we go, Eric. Can you drive like that?' Mrs Shallcombe strapped herself in the car seat. She waited for Eric to do the same, which had the desirable result of pinning his toga more securely in place.

Not very long afterwards Arthur Smollett was removed from the car by emergency staff and placed on a stretcher. No one said anything when the Reverend Hollis climbed out from the back of the car wearing only Mrs Shallcombe's fur coat that hot summer evening. It was, after all the middle of the night.

'I feel I ought to stay in case I can be of some assistance.'

Maddie Shallcombe looked at the vicar's bare feet and legs. This had been Eric's bright idea because Freddie was never around to play nowadays. The Reverend Hollis had his qualities but discretion was clearly not one of them.

'You might borrow some pyjamas from the hospital, if you are going to stay. But I don't think Arthur is going to be capable of listening to you for quite a while.'

'Lets go home, Maddie'. Eric was very tired and knew that he would have to drive back.

'I think we should go home. Could you ring Joyce Smollett and let her know how Arthur is? The number must be in the telephone directory. Then I think we could go back.'

'Agreed.' Eric gathered up his tartan toga and got back in. Driving shoeless was surprisingly uncomfortable. He would just sit quietly for a minute before making the phone calls. Luckily he had left his wallet and mobile phone in the front of the car and not in his pockets.

'Alright. Could you drop me at the Hall?' Hollis had started to shake with delayed shock. He really had thought for one horrible moment when the second blast tossed the car that the eye of the Lord, Who sees everything, had been watching them on the back seat.

By the time Maddie Shallcombe got home Rachel was having a cup of tea upstairs in the pub. She knew where her mother had been: Eric had telephoned from the hospital.

'How's Arthur Smollett?'

'I don't know. He looked pretty bad to me. You know, Rachel, there's too much going on in this village, both villages. This is supposed to be a nice quiet place, a cover. What on earth is going on here? Cars don't explode in Little Waterton and what's all this nonsense about cats? Mickey reckons Madame Seraglio is at the bottom of it, something to do with keeping Eric and Freddie in business.'

'Mickey's obsessed with Madame Seraglio so that doesn't surprise me. But he might be right. Freddie spends his whole time over there nowadays.'

'I think it's time that Mickey and Michael paid an official visit to Madame Seraglio, don't you? I'm not having any more of this. And they can repaint the car before they go anywhere in it.'

Rachel frowned. Her mother must have been very close to the fireworks and an attempt on her life couldn't be ruled out at this stage. If Rachel felt anxious about it, it didn't show in her voice. Her mother would already have thought that one through.

'According to Eric the other car was parked.' Rachel began. 'So not rigged to engine activity?'

'No. Not a professional job. Not vandals either. But definitely not professionals. I reckon from the look of it that the stuff was in the boot. The first bang was what started the fire then the petrol tank went up after it. But I can't be doing with this here, not now, and it's going to stop. It shouldn't be difficult to trace who bought the goods. It's not likely to be something old Arthur Smollett could lay hands on.'

Rachel was satisfied. She returned to fill the kettle by the tap.

'Cup of tea, Mum?'

*

People in Chicago are used to hot summers, when the wind blows hard through the skyscraper canyons. It is a city with roots, some respectable, some not so; it is a city with a certain style, a certain poise all of its own; it is a city where a lot of things happen very quietly because they shouldn't be happening at all. Step back from the waterside and gaze into the stylish glass and concrete forms reflecting the blue and you might be seen by one of the men perpetually watching from above, from the twenty fifth floor of the Saunders Building. Floors 25 through to 36 were occupied by the American Tontine Company, which owned the freehold and sublet the lower floors to its subsidiaries. It was an old family holding, the current

96

chairman, chief executive and principal shareholder being one Paul Maria Santini, a man only addressed as 'Paul' by his wife, his mother, and Cardinal Morelli.

Santini was due back any minute from the airport, so the already heightened security was stepped up another notch. The dozen or so men on the twenty fifth floor had radio contact with every operative covering the armoured BMW every inch of the way. CCTV made it possible to follow the journey on two computer screens deep on the twenty fifth floor, and sat by them, watching, was a thin dark haired man who polished his spectacles and tried them on, then repeated the process. On the desk was a fat briefcase on top of a battered paper street plan of the city. Marvin Bernstein could barely sit still. Unlike everyone else in the room, he was carrying no gun. He began to pace round the table. Santini and his bodyguards were in the lift. The chances of him being murdered now were virtually nil. Bernstein exhaled a sigh of relief. The lift opened and two body-guards got out, blocking the view inside the lift. They stepped rapidly aside as a tall, heavily armed man moved comfortably towards them, ignoring them altogether, and extended a greeting to the man who had been in the centre of the lift and was followed out by two further bodyguards.

'Welcome back, Mr. Santini, good journey, I hope.'

'Thank you,' a deep, throaty South Chicago voice replied.

Santini, a thickset man of fifty or so, unbuttoned his pale coat. He wore an immaculate charcoal silk suit, a black shirt and a gold tie. He wasn't carrying a handgun but it could safely be assumed that his overcoat was bulletproof. Bernstein joined the group, bringing the map and the briefcase.

'Good to see you again, Mr. Santini.'

Bernstein was a New Yorker and, despite ten years of living and working in Chicago, had acquired nothing of the local accent.

'Marvin,' said Santini, 'We need to talk.'

He walked the to middle of the entrance hall, past the computer bank and through two layers of double-reinforced glass partition doors. Bernstein followed, and both men got into another, smaller lift.

'Let's go to the office,' said Santini, pressing the button marked thirty-six.

His home was floors 34 and 35 but he was not yet ready to call it the end of a long day. Bernstein looked at his watch: 7.05pm. The watch itself was an ex-Soviet clockwork model with a plain leather strap, remarkable for its modesty in the circles in which he moved. They got out at the Penthouse and stepped into a landscape of white and gold, a spotless, orderly, exquisite apartment bearing no sign that this might be a place for work. Santini walked over from lift to living room, which overlooked the north side of the city. It was growing dark and down below sounded the wail of police sirens. He found the bar, all glass and mirrors, and took out two cut-crystal goblets. Bernstein had seated himself on a nearby five-seater white sofa and looked curiously at the glasses. It wasn't like Santini to drink with his staff, not even his most senior and trusted counsellor.

'Break with tradition. Meet my secret.' Santini then reached behind the gaudy array of litre liquor bottles and brought up a single slender unlabelled dark green bottle. The contents were obviously a red wine and the stopper had been sealed in place by wax and a fine gold-coloured chain. 'From the finest maker in all Italy, Pietro Toresta.'

He poured out two glasses of deep red liquid and Bernstein accepted one of them.

'Your health,' said Bernstein.

'All our healths.'

They sipped in silence. Bernstein waited. His wife, who knew him as a man who rarely stopped talking, had never seen him in Santini's presence. Santini was not yet ready to speak. The journey from New York had been slow. He hated using scheduled flights, even in First Class, but the security for private jets was becoming burdensome since the events of the previous autumn. Too much attention was never a good thing.

Bernstein could wait no longer.

'What did Nazzura say?'

'Mancini gave me this, for Mrs. Santini.'

Santini held open a small box in the palm of his left hand. Bernstein glanced briefly at the spectacular diamond and ruby spray brooch.

'Nazzura didn't see you himself?' There was panic in his voice.

'He said Mr. Nazzura likes reliability. Likes it a lot.'

'So they know about the 5% shortfall?'

'They know.'

'Do we know what they want to do about the next shipment? We can make it up and pay on top. Did Mancini place any orders beyond August?'

'No.'

'I'll get onto them right away. We can't leave them in doubt about the next delivery. We have it covered this time. We...'

'No. Leave it. You don't end a trading relationship over one short delivery. Sure, we make it up. We better.' Santini sipped his wine again. 'Reliability, that's what he said.'

Bernstein moved uncomfortably on the sofa, loosened his sober blue tie then ran one hand through his hair. Santini sat immobile staring a point in space.

'You know, Marvin, money can buy you a lot of things – love, loyalty, very good service – but there's one thing it can't buy – intelligence. A stupid man tells you what you want to hear: an intelligent man tells what you don't want to hear.' He paused and ran his finger round the edge of the delicate glass.

'How much did our organisation spend on your education, Marvin?'

'A lot, Mr. Santini.'

'Five hundred thousand good US dollars, and they were well spent.'

Bernstein continued to look most uncomfortable.

'So tell me, Marvin, as my counsellor, what do you recommend?'

Bernstein felt almost faint.

'You had my report before you left, Mr. Santini. We went through the figures together. I have given you my reasons.'

'So tell me one more time.'

'Well, see, we've tried everything else but we aren't making any progress. Half the south side of the city has gone over to Papadopolous and we can't force them back. We lost sixteen men in six months including three at the top. The Domingo district is ready to fall, and if it does, we can't be sure of controlling the crucial sector with the shipments. We are losing thirty per cent of our last year's revenue as things stand and to bring in mercenaries from Philadelphia will cost us another twenty five per cent with no guarantee of loyalty or discretion. Papadopolous has pacted with the South Americans and he's pushing to step in. If the Eastern families knew how bad it was, they'd be over here themselves. We can't keep it quiet much longer. Six shipments are due in August 28: if we lose only one of them we're finished. Nazzura will do it himself.'

'You checked it out?'

'Yes. Personally. I spent three weeks in London, interviewing their people. The Angel stopped their war, I don't know how, but they was desperate. Charlie the Turk had his heroin cut by the Black Hat gang. They was killing each other everywhere in East London. Finally the Police had to do something. They arrested nine hundred people in one weekend, both sides. Charlie said only the Angel could draw the boundary. No one else knew how the war ended so suddenly. They didn't even know about the Angel but the Black Hats kept to their side of the line and distribution started up again.' He swallowed and continued. 'Mr. Santini, we cannot go on. The inner city districts are gonna explode. We got our kids shooting their kids, people dying in the cross fire, it's all to hell and they ain't gonna let us operate if it don't stop sometime soon.'

'And the terms?'

'I can not make this decision. I did not draw the terms, they were given me. Very exact, not negotiable.'

'I don't do business this way.'

'Charlie confirmed the terms of the negotiation are not to be discussed. The Black Hat boss was told the same.'

'But twenty per cent of our revenue, one week unarmed in the company of Papadopolous, and accept the Angel's verdict, no questions?'

'And the enforcement, and the hostages.'

'I haven't forgotten, Marvin. You get to kill me if I don't take the verdict, right? And my daughter spends the week in the care of Papadopolous' number one, right, in case I start something, right?'

'The terms are the same for Papadopolous.'   .

'What else you want to tell me?'

'Wherever I went, I think Papadopolous' agents were there before me. Some of these people said they'd been through this all with someone, wouldn't say who. Looks like the South Americans are pressuring them, same as with us.'

'It's in your report.'

'Well then, only this. Mrs. Santini said to tell you she lost two brothers but she don't want to lose you or her sons. That's all.'

'I don't like it.'

'Neither do I. But we have no choice. If we do nothing we'll lose a shipment, only one if we're lucky, but it's enough. The money don't matter now. It's a question of confidence. Nazzura is going to kill us all.'

'Intelligence can be a dangerous thing, Marvin.'

'I know, Mr. Santini.'

Santini had the best deputy a boss could have. There was no better counsellor, and he knew it.

'Then, maybe.' Santini finished his glass and put it down. 'I gotta go home now.'

Chapter 12: Visitors

'Anna. Anna Papadopolous.'

'Marvin. Marvin Bernstein.'

They shook hands with a show of confidence. Outside it was raining but the sealed air-conditioned compartment in the first class section had its own sterile, cool atmosphere. The train had pulled out of Paris on time and was now about half an hour into its journey. At a pre-arranged time they had each left their other seats and walked alone to the central first class compartment. It was what had been agreed and, though each of them was nervous, neither showed it. This was an unarmed, unguarded visit and highly dangerous as rogue elements were sometimes apt to act on their own.

'I hope you are enjoying your journey. Come, our table is waiting for us.'

The woman spoke with an accent that was neither Greek nor American but a mixture of both. She walked to the dining table that had been booked for them. This compartment was full of diners. The woman sat down and waited for Bernstein to say something.

Bernstein took off his spectacles and polished them before observing the menu card.

'Shall we order?'

'Of course. But where are your papers? Are you prepared?'

'Yes, yes.' Bernstein polished his spectacles again. 'I am expendable, in relative terms, but the information is not. We sent it electronically this morning. You had the possibility too'.

'And if the transmission is intercepted?'

'Highly unlikely. Double-encrypted, sent from a high security station through a telecoms operator we own, disguised as a request for a holiday brochure.' He laughed. 'We've been asking for brochures for the last two weeks, and sending some out too.'

'Very good. We are not so nervous. I bring the arguments in my head and write in English when I see the Angel. The figures I bring with no names. I write the names when I arrive.'

'Your hostage is ready?'

'Of course. And yours?'

'Yes.'

Bernstein stared out of the window but could see little beyond the fields the train sped past since the windows were smeared with rain. 'If things were different I guess they would enjoy their holidays.'

'I suppose.' The woman studied the menu card and drummed her beautifully manicured fingernails on the table. She could have been anywhere between thirty and forty-five. Her hair was black and her lipstick dark red. She was thin but not worn, discreetly elegant. Her grey suit was textured in the pattern of roof tiles. She had plain patent leather black shoes and handbag. She wore no jewellery apart from a pair of dark blue topaz earrings, a heart-shaped cut. The outfit did not catch the eye but for those who looked, these were clearly tailor-made clothes with no label and hand-designed accessories that very few would recognise. The waiter arrived to take the order.

'I will have this, the fish.' She pointed on the menu card.

'Good choice. I will have the same.'

'And to drink?'

'Water, no gas.'

'The same.'

'We are expected to arrive on time. I understand this is unusual.' The woman gave a wry smile.

'I don't know. It's too many years since I travelled on the train. Not since I was a student. I never quite got to see all the places in Europe I'd heard of and I don't suppose I will ever do it now.'

'Europe is sometimes over-rated. The United States also has many things to offer. And South America. No doubt you will also travel often to South America.'

'I guess we both made that trip.' Bernstein could not but admire her nerve. 'Are you American?'

'Only until I was ten. Then I go back to Greece for safety reasons. Now my education is complete. I help my father. You are a book-keeper, I hear?'

'Only on the bad days. I do what you would expect, you know. I collect information, try to understand it, give advice, sweat a lot.'

'I know about this.' She was surprised that an organisation so well known for its strong-arm tactics would employ such intelligence so high up.

The waiter shortly arrived with the food and fussed around in serving it. Eventually he left them alone. The dining car was becoming noisier as quite clearly most of the passengers had not chosen water to accompany their meal. They leaned towards each other to be heard and each spoke softly. To the other travellers they would have looked like close colleagues.

'You have met the Angel?' She watched carefully for the answer as she took a little water.

'No. But we made the same enquiries you people did. I was in London and I can tell when the ground has been trodden once in front of me.'

'I hear that our friends in South America also have an Angel. But they feel that the business conditions can better be discussed by a natural English speaking Angel.'

'There's another?' He seemed genuinely surprised.

'Oh yes. Only two, however, are suitable. One we have and one in Canada. We do not like Canada, insufficient security from outside interferences.'

'Have you ever used this kind of service before?'

'That is our business.' She looked at him and relented. 'But no. But we have listened to the recommendations and we consider at this time much trouble can be saved if we can resolve this situation in an agreeable fashion.'

Bernstein took this as a good sign but said nothing. They both ate for a while in silence.

'You know England?' She meant it as light conversation but it was taken differently.

'We have no operation in England. Our territory is Stateside. How do you find the food?'

'Not bad. Better, I think, than we will receive on the other side.'

'Well, for one, I'm gonna eat better than I do at home. I never can relax when I am surrounded by firearms. I'm looking forward to English cakes and Devonshire scones and tea and anything else you don't find in New York or Chicago after 6pm.' At this she smiled. She looked at him again, more closely. He locked curiously un-American. His clothes were too casual and ill fitting for an appointment of this importance. He wore dark trousers and a pale yellow shirt with no tie. Folded next to him was the jacket that matched the trousers. It was folded in such a way that she knew immediately he did not normally carry a handgun or a purse, as many American men did. She knew he must be a very brave man: no one else could explain to Paul Santini the checks and balances built into this arrangement. She was confident her father would go with the deal, whatever it was. If they did not the South Americans would likely realign. The war in Chicago had dented confidence all round. Rumour had it that the Puerto Ricans in New York had opened negotiations to extend into Chicago. Everyone knew what this meant: the old alliances would be wiped out, quite literally. 'I hope these guys recognise us in London. Waterloo Station, I hear, is one hell of a big place.'

'Don't worry. They will.' She lifted her large matching black attaché case and opened it. Inside Bernstein caught a glimpse of a thick wad of paper but on top was a turquoise hat with two long peacock feathers. She pulled it out and placed it on top of the case. 'It is an old trick, but one that works.'

'So far so good. I have to admit I would have been happier flying direct to London but Mr Santini would never have let me go without security. So this way we each leave our friends in Paris and take it alone from there. This is the first time I have been on my own in years. It's a very strange feeling. How about you?'

'I am used to it. It is easy to hide in a place like Greece where many hide and wait. Also in Cyprus one can pass the time quietly and safely. You should try it.'

'Great idea but I don't think Mr Santini would allow it. He likes to protect his investment in me. And besides, I like my family to live a quiet regular life. You can imagine how hard that was to arrange.'

'I can. I look forward to meet this Angel. When my father enquired of Charlie the Turk what he will deal with, the Turk said to remember that the Angel has friends more powerful than all of us.'

'Should be an interesting experience.'

The train had stopped and the announcement was given that they would shortly pull into Waterloo International. Anna Papadopolous, who had sworn on her own life to kill her father if he did not accept the verdict, swiftly put on her extraordinary hat and stood up smartly. 'We go.'

*

It was exactly a week since the explosion at the animal centre. Arthur was out of intensive care and Joyce Smollett was visiting him twice a day. He looked one hell of a mess but the doctors were reasonably confident they could put him back together acceptably. Joyce could not know that his life had been saved by Maddie Shallcombe's vehicle taking the brunt of the blast. The doctors had said it was quite miraculous that he had got off as luckily as he did. Joyce was an optimistic sort of a woman. She had seen animals in the centre recover from near-death and she knew from her visits that Arthur was recuperating extremely well. It was not clear when they would let him out of hospital and she had thought nothing of it when DI Jesmond had rung to make an appointment to visit her at the centre. She supposed he simply wanted to inspect the scene of the crime again and satisfy himself about the detail. Joyce had spent the first two or three days directing the contractors who were doing the cleaning up and she had been arguing ever since with the insurance people about who should pay for the damage. Actually the damage was not particularly expensive because they had already made plans for that autumn to re-do the front part of the centre, removing that terrible exterior and putting in a new plain-glass frontage with proper invalid access for which they had just got planning permission. Jesmond was due any minute and Joyce decided she should see him in Arthur's study at the rear of the building where it was still relatively clean and tidy. The bell rang and she hurried to the front of the building and opened the temporary boarding door.

'Mrs Smollett? I am Detective Inspector Jesmond. I believe you have met my sergeant, Sergeant Davis?'

"Oh, hello. Do come in, Inspector. I am sorry about the mess. We are clearing it up quite well but I think I will show you into Arthur's study, if you wouldn't mind following me this way.'

It was six o'clock and the centre had just closed. The cleaning people were busy in the front part of the building and he followed in, stepping carefully out of the way of a bad tempered looking woman with a mop.

'In here, Inspector. Do take a seat. Would you like a cup of tea?'

'No thank you, Mrs Smollett.' He sat down, looking serious. Joyce became apprehensive. She sat opposite him, in Arthur's chair.

'What can I do for you, Inspector?'

'Mrs Smollett, we have had a report in from our forensic people and I have had it checked.' He paused to study her face. 'According to them the cause of the explosion was a cat packed with Semtex.'

'What? What do you mean? A cat?'

'Mrs Smollett, do you know anyone who would do such a thing?'

'Certainly not. Why would anyone want to blow up the animal centre?'

'The car in which the explosion took place belonged to you, I believe?'

'Yes. Arthur borrowed it for the evening.'

'Were you on good terms with your husband, Mrs Smollett? You can tell me the truth. We are very discreet.'

'Was I on good terms? I am on good terms. I visit him twice a day. What do you mean?'

'So you have no reason to think he might want to, shall we say, injure you?'

'No. Certainly not. What are you suggesting?'

'Murders, Mrs Smollett, can sometimes be the result of domestic tension.'

'Arthur would never do anything to hurt me. Never.' He could tell that this was a truthful answer.

'Apart from yourself, did anyone else have the key to the boot of the car?'

'I think there's only one key. We used to have a spare but I can't remember where we put it. I'm sure no one could have opened the boot apart from Arthur.'

'So can I safely assume that he must have put the cat in the boot?'

'I don't think you can safely assume any such thing. Why would he want to do that? What on earth would he be doing with a dead cat in the car?'

'A cat in a vet's car would not arouse suspicion in itself, Mrs Smollett. But a cat with Semtex inside it is another matter altogether. Do you keep Semtex in the animal centre?'

'You know perfectly well that we don't. The police have searched at the centre at least three times since the explosion. We only keep medicines and things that any ordinary hospital would keep. All our drugs are kept under regulated conditions. We don't keep explosives.'

'Forensic have gone over the car with the greatest care. The only prints on it belong to your family.'

'Well, of course. It's our car.'

'You don't follow me, Mrs Smollett. I am suggesting to you that only yourself or your husband could have put the cat with the Semtex into the car.'

'Well I certainly didn't. And what's more, I don't believe Arthur would do such a thing either.'

'Have you asked your husband about this matter?'

'Yes. But he says he can't remember anything.'

'That's not what he tells us, Mrs Smollett. He informed two of my officers quite clearly yesterday that he had placed the cat in the boot himself.'

'I don't believe you. Why would he tell me that he can't remember anything and tell you something completely different?'

'Is this your husband's signature?' Jesmond produced a typed sheet for her inspection.

'What is this?'

'It is a statement dictated by your husband to two of my officers. You may read it.'

She took the statement and read it, very slowly. Jesmond watched her. His eyes then travelled round the study. It was more or less what he could have predicted. There was nothing unusual about it and, exactly as he had been told, nothing suspicious about it either. On the table in front of him was a green plastic frame with photographs of two little girls in it. Eventually Joyce Smollett looked up.

'Did he know what he was saying?'

'Mrs Smollett, the police are trying to understand what happened. We are not framing him, if that's what you think.'

'I am sorry. I just don't understand what this means.'

'Have you noticed anything unusual in, say, the last couple of weeks about your husband?'

'What sort of thing?'

'Anything at all. Has he, for example, shown any interest in cats? I mean anything outside his normal practice?'

'Well, I'm not sure I can help you really.' She was a loyal woman.

'I should tell you, Mrs Smollett, that your husband came to see me in Bristol not long ago. He was in a highly agitated condition.'

'I know he has been to see the police in Bristol about our cat.' She was suddenly careful.

'I would say that your husband had convinced himself that the police ought to investigate the alleged appearance of animal corpses in Waterton and Little Waterton. He claimed that unusual numbers of dead pets were appearing in these two villages. The police have no record of complaints regarding any such incidents. Do you know anything about this?'

'Inspector, I can only tell you that, according to village gossip, numbers of such animals have been found. I can't tell you where or how many and I certainly can't tell you whether the police have been involved. None of these animals was brought to us for treatment.'

'You had a cat, I believe. Your husband claimed that somebody, and he could not tell me who, had killed it with a heroin overdose. Did he mention this to you?'

'He did tell me of his test results, yes.'

'Do you keep heroin in the centre?'

'You know we don't. The police have searched the place, as I said a moment ago.'

'But your husband could obtain heroin, if he had wanted to.'

'If he had wanted to, yes. But he didn't. Are you suggesting that he murdered his own cat?'

'I have no evidence to suggest that he did, although he might have done. I have no evidence to suggest that anyone murdered his cat, or any other cat.'

'Well, if you've quite finished, Inspector, I must be getting home to the children. Is there anything further?'

'Yes. I would like you to volunteer a statement to my officers tomorrow morning, as we are interested in your husband's movements in the week prior to the explosion. Are you willing to assist us?'

'I'm not volunteering anything. If I come to the police station, it will be with my solicitor. Arthur hasn't done anything and neither have I.' She was angry.

'Have you made an insurance claim for the damage?'

'Of course we have. But I hardly think a person making a fraudulent insurance claim would place himself directly between the bomb and the target, do you?'

'Possibly not. Not unless he'd been drinking.'

'Arthur hadn't been drinking. He never drinks when he is driving. I'm sure you will have had his blood tested for that when he was first brought in to the hospital.'

'The evidence so far suggests your husband was guilty of criminal damage.'

'Nonsense. Only our property got damaged. I must say I had expected more sympathy from the police.'

'You must understand we are under some pressure to get to the bottom of this. A great deal of police resources have been deployed in this investigation. Unauthorised use of explosives is something we take very seriously.' Jesmond was floundering but he was an experienced officer. Something about her defensive manner made him think she knew more than she was prepared to admit. So he tried again. 'Did your husband make a habit of being out late at night on his own?'

'I think you'd better be going, Inspector.'

'I will take that as your confirmation.'

'Lots of people are out late at night. It's not against the law, you know.'

'But what was he doing?'

'I have no idea.' She instantly regretted this answer.

'I must tell you, Mrs Smollett, that the circumstances of this situation lead me to believe that your husband deliberately placed a cat in the boot of his car and drove to the animal centre for some purpose which is not known to me. I know of no person who would place Semtex inside a dead cat and give it or sell it to your husband. I therefore conclude that he put the Semtex in the cat, for purposes unknown, himself. I can conceive of no possible purpose served by this activity. It is likely that I shall be recommending in due course in my report that your husband be assessed by a psychiatrist with a view to his being placed in secure accommodation.'

'How dare you suggest any such thing? Arthur is as sane as you or me.'

'Regrettably, Mrs Smollett, I am unable at this stage in my investigations to agree with you. Has your husband been receiving any help with depression or other mental condition?'

'No. There's nothing wrong with him and I insist on having my solicitor present if you are going to continue to question me about him. I'm not going to talk to you any further. If you'll excuse me, please.' She stood up to go but Jesmond did not move.

'There's no need to cloud the issues with lawyers, Mrs Smollett. We can deal with this between ourselves.'

'No. I've already said I want my solicitor present. Now please go.'

Still he made remained seated. He picked up the photo on the desk and looked for several seconds into the faces of the children. Joyce found this insidious behaviour too much.

'We do rely on cooperation from the public for our work. Failing to assist the police is taken seriously because it raises suspicion.'

'Out. Get out of this centre and don't come back.'

'As you wish, madam.' Jesmond finally picked up his coat and followed her back to the front door. He cast one last look round the centre before walking out. Personally he was of the opinion that Arthur Smollett was completely round the bend. But it wasn't his business to say so.

Chapter 13: Aftermath

It was now almost a month since Joshua Thornhill's funeral. Rhiannon and little Neville were both asleep on the downstairs couch, enjoying the peace of a wet Sunday morning. Rhiannon had insisted that Joshua be cremated but also had also insisted that there be quite a showy funeral for him at St George's. The Reverend Hollis was not entirely happy with the timing, coming as it did immediately before his planned vigil. He very much felt that his energies were divided between preparing something for Joshua's ceremony and the Prayathon that he secretly hoped would receive some media publicity for the church and perhaps encourage more people to attend. Of course it didn't, but he was not to know that. Rhiannon had spent two days decking the church in flowers of every colour, despite the fact that she was still quite obviously exhausted from caring for Neville. The rings under her eyes were deeper than ever. Kathleen had stopped coming to the house and had become markedly cooler towards her stepmother since Joshua had been found. Rhiannon did not have the energy to attempt housework as well as trying to learn what the farm business consisted of and feed Neville and look after him. Equally, until the probate documents came through, she felt no one was in a position to engage paid help to keep the farmhouse in order. At first, Rhiannon had been too upset to notice the attitude of Joshua's children towards her changing. Lillian, who lived just outside Dallas, came over not for the funeral but after it. Kathleen was convinced that her sister was bent on overturning the will (whatever it consisted of) in her own favour and the other children generally kept well away from Rhiannon, hardly knowing what to say to a woman averagely over a decade and a half younger than them, a woman who had married their own father. They had no interest in Neville. The family was waiting to see how Joshua had disposed of his money.

The only exception to this generally cold response that Rhiannon experienced was with Robert Thornhill. It was obvious that he expected his uncle to have disinherited him altogether and he did not show any overt interest in acquiring the farm. The freehold parts of it would be left presumably to Neville: Robert Thornhill himself was the only possible candidate for a legal succession to the tenanted farm but he could not work it separate from the freehold land, even had Lord Errington been willing to countenance the grant of a new tenancy to him. All the rest of the family would have been unacceptable to Errington whose land agent, John Gilbert, knew perfectly well what the skills of the various Thornhill relatives were. To have inherited the freehold would have secured an empire: without the freehold land, the high rental Errington would undoubtedly want on the tenanted part was unappetising. There would be no capital for expansion or diversification and nothing to borrow against. Robert, for all his anger at being cheated by his uncle, decided to make his own plans and for that purpose had sold his four prize racehorses to Maddie Shallcombe for £500,000 only recently. He was not a man to struggle on under the constraints of a tenancy agreement just so as to keep the cottages for his cousins. He reckoned he might be able to buy a medium sized farm and kit it out well enough without wasting any more emotional energy on the ties that Blue Grace Farm had for him. He saw no reason why he should stay on for years to run the farm for Neville. But he did nothing. It was as though the heavy summer and the humid afternoons had robbed him of any positive plans. He spent his time attending to the business as normal and would not have it put about that the Thornhills were easy to cheat just because Joshua was dead. Errington's view of Joshua as a lazy man was predicated on the assumption that Joshua was still working. Whereas in reality, though the business was in his sole name or of companies he technically controlled, he had in practice retired and left Robert in charge, only insisting that from time to time he be kept informed as to what was going on. He had seen nothing wrong with paying his nephew a pittance; more fool Robert had been his view.

Rhiannon went over to Bristol regularly twice a week to look at the horses, knowing them to be Maddie Shallcombe's but not knowing that they had previously belonged to Robert. He saw no reason to tell her since it would automatically let her know what he had in the bank. The risk of Kathleen and the others finding out and coming round to scrounge it off him was not worth taking. He had enough on his hands trying to deal with his wife, now almost insane with jealousy. Why she should be so bothered about the supposed affair with Rhiannon when he had openly had many affairs with various girls from the processing plant or the villages he had no idea. Thinking about it after Joshua's death, Robert realised, quite suddenly, that he knew virtually nothing about Rhiannon and in particular had no idea why she was so expert with the horses. She was very reluctant to discuss anything about her past life and always changed the subject if he ever drew close to enquiry. Also, to his surprise, he saw how devoted she had been to Joshua and how genuinely upset she was at losing him. For Robert his uncle had always been a cunning old bastard whose better side was almost entirely hidden from his close relatives. What Rhiannon had seen in him remained mysterious but he could easily see, on closer inspection, what his uncle had seen in Rhiannon.

Her looks were more striking than beautiful and her dress and general presentation were odd by the standards of the conservative village in which she had chosen to live. Most of the time she wore one of a collection of black kaftans, hand-embroidered by herself in the quiet afternoons of her pregnancy and later in the less quiet breaks between Neville waking up screaming and then falling asleep again after a feed. Only once had Robert asked directly about Rhiannon's family: he thought it curious that no grandparents had been to visit Neville and no mention was ever made of them. If you want to know, Rhiannon had said, Poppa will be killed by his work but we're not in touch anymore. Aside from her magnificent mastery of the horses, Robert remained ignorant about her. So he willingly obliged Maddie Shallcombe in taking Rhiannon to the stables, where he watched her work with the horses and listened to her talking about them.

That particular Sunday Robert knocked at the farmhouse door to enquire if Rhiannon wanted any help with the housework. He had noticed that the place was not as it should be: he could see no reason why a girl could not be hired in the meantime if his cousin Kathleen would not oblige anymore. Rhiannon answered the door, putting her finger to her mouth and pointing at the baby who was obviously fast asleep. Robert tiptoed inside. It was late morning but the curtains were still drawn to keep the sunlight away from the child. On the floor several of the large canvasses that Rhiannon had been painting lay cut and ripped, he assumed, by the knife that she carried in her right hand as she opened the door. Even he could see what had been going on: she was destroying the things which had previously made her happy, perhaps, who knows, as a prelude to leaving the area altogether. He held out his right hand.

'Give me that, Rhiannon.'

'Mind your own damn business.'

'What are you doing?'

'Thinking.'

'I came to see if you would, well, like me to arrange some help for the house. The place is too big for one person to look after.'

Neville was stirring in the corner. Rhiannon put the knife on the mantelpiece and began to stack the half dozen or so unfinished canvasses against the wall.

'I'm a lazy bitch, I guess. I just don't have the energy to do this. I'm not really cut out to be a home body.'

'It doesn't matter. This is a difficult time. I'll get somebody in on Monday. You don't have to depend on Kathleen.'

'Robert, why do they hate me? I'm the only one who loved him.'

No straightforward answer to this was possible. So he attempted something a little more indirect.

'They won't be settled until the will is read. They don't have very much, none of us do. I think they just don't have a lot to say.'

'Why in hell does it take so long to read the will? Why can't we get this over with? I gotta get away from this place.'

Rhiannon moved to the nearest window and began to draw back the blinds. As she did so the morning sun fell on her young, tired face. Robert Thornhill watched her, intending to say something else completely. Without warning, without thinking, he suddenly felt sorry for her. He knew he had to get away before she said anything else that might cause him to react without thinking at all.

'Try to get some sleep. I'll send a girl down on Monday afternoon. If you want anything, ring down.' He turned on his heel and walked out.

*

Sunday lunchtime was a good time at the Black Horse. The village had quieted down considerably since the explosion at the animal centre some ten days previously. And in the meantime no further dead animals had been found in the streets around the Pinkers' shop. The Pinkers in any case did not need these unheralded arrivals, mainly because they were doing a steady trade as a result of assorted publicity that came to surround Freddie Pinker. In his own way he had become something of a celebrity and Paulette had taken to calling herself Freddie's P.A. Eric regarded Freddie's new style of dress as rather outlandish but he had to admit that Paulette was right in saying that it drew the customers in. Freddie, on Paulette's suggestion, had taken to wearing a dark blue sequinned jacket in the evenings at Madame Seraglio's. Word was going around in certain circles that the Pinkers were sympathetic people to deal with. Both brothers were equally sure that they did not wish to return to competition with Mrs Lightfoot. Nowadays they referred people on to her when they felt it would be helpful. Although they did do a certain trade in dealing with pets, it was on the flowers that the money was really being made. Increasingly Eric, who had become adept at sourcing cheap and beautiful flowers, was trying to push the florist business at the expense of the rest. Soon the pets' funerals were a showcase for what could be done with the flowers. To Eric's astonishment, Freddie had a genuine talent for gathering clients and, effortlessly, persuading them to spend very large amounts of money on flowers, decorations and, if need be, catering. Having started out not three months previously as pet undertakers, a new incarnation for the business was almost fully formed. The name Pinker had become an expensive by-word amongst the wealthy and occasionally famous for organising private parties and decorating the villas. Freddie got to know his clientele at the club. The sweetest phone call that Eric had ever had in his entire life came on the day when Mrs Lightfoot rang up to ask if Eric would be prepared to supply her with flowers. She had been very impressed with what she had heard and wanted to know what prices he could offer her.

So this particular Sunday, Eric and Freddie were enjoying a quiet pint and Mrs Shallcombe's excellent pies in the bar, discussing between themselves whether or not they should continue with the pets' business or go exclusively into flowers. Freddie was convinced that there was no need to get rid of the old undertakers' stock, which he felt could largely be adapted for the special features required at some of the more unusual parties. Eric was unclear how Freddie could possibly, at a party, use two dozen rolls of black ribbon, a racehorse-sized coffin and the eerie purple padding that went with it. But before Freddie could go into any further detail Robert Thornhill walked into the pub. Eric waved him over.

'Robert, why don't you join us? These pies are excellent. Have you eaten?'

'They do look good. Let me buy you a drink.' Thornhill looked at the brothers but each of them shook their heads. Their glasses had only recently been filled. Robert Thornhill walked over to the bar, looking for Rachel. He knew that Maddie was not there this morning. She had gone over to see the horses herself. Rachel greeted him with her usual smile, but it froze on her lips as she looked beyond him towards the door.

'The two Michaels are with my mother today.' She said this quietly to Thornhill. 'Would you mind giving me a hand with one of the customers? I think he's not feeling very well.'

Thornhill's gaze followed her as she walked swiftly to the entrance porch, where the figure of a man had barely crossed the threshold. Thornhill did not know him to speak to, though he had seen him often enough drinking alone at the bar, nor did he hear what Rachel said to him when she took the visitor by the hand. The man began to stagger about unsteadily before sinking slowly to the ground, out of sight of the other guests in the pub but directly in Thornhill's view. He turned quickly to help her.

'What shall I do?' Thornhill started to look around for a place to lay the man, somewhere he would not so easily be trampled by incoming customers unable to see him until it was too late.

'Just pick him up and follow me. We have a room downstairs where he can rest away from the crowd.'

Thornhill was a strong man and he put his arms under the visitor's armpits and effectively dragged him behind the bar and then down the stairs.

'Where would you like him, Rachel?'

'Could you put him in this chair?' So saying, Rachel opened a small door into a tiny back room on the lower floor. In that room, which was quite dark, he saw a large armchair with high metal arms. She pointed at it and smiled gratefully.

'He'll be fine here. Thanks. I'll deal with him now. What can I get you?'

Thornhill went back up the stairs and Rachel gave him a long lemonade and a pie, refusing any payment and thanking him profusely for his help. She then locked the till, pulled the half shutter around it and put up a sign that said 'Back shortly.'

The man woke up a ten or so minutes later to find himself sitting alone in a small, darkened room. He was held by metal rings at ankle and at wrist into a large armchair. He had no idea where he was, although he did remember walking into the Black Horse and Rachel saying: 'You're banned.' He was not feeling very good. Gradually his eyes focussed and in the corner of the room he saw Rachel sitting, waiting quietly for him to come round. The door of the room was closed. The only lighting seemed to be coming from a source behind him. He rattled the metal rings and tried to squeeze or pull them off. After a few attempts he yelled 'Let me go!' at the top of his lungs. Rachel watched him then walked behind the chair imprisoning him and, out of his sight, sat down on a bench in the corner by the lamp. It bothered him a lot that he could not see her but it was no use trying any further. The armchair had a high back and was bolted onto the floor. So he carried on shouting and swearing for several minutes more. Still Rachel did nothing.

A wave of fear passed over Howard Morgan and he stopped making a noise. It finally dawned on him that he had been drugged and captured and locked in a specially adapted chamber. Wherever he was, he was totally in her power and from the look of the little place he sat in, she must have done this before. How long had he been out cold? His wristwatch was missing. This as much as anything else made him fear for his safety. This didn't feel like a robbery. The only thing Morgan had in his head at first, and he tried to get it out but it wouldn't go, was the story he knew from childhood: Sweeney Todd, the demon barber of Fleet Street. Surely the delicious Shallcombe pies didn't contain human flesh? The tale came back to him in all its Victorian grisly detail. First the customer goes to the barber's shop, next the barber puts the cloth round him, then once the customer is relaxing with the soap on his chin, the barber cuts his throat with a cut-throat razor, presses a switch and tips the body into the downstairs cellar to be cut up for the meat pies that were sold upstairs. How he had loved that story as a child and acted it out with his pets and those of his neighbours, drowning the rabbits and other small animals first in an old shopping bag so that he didn't get scratched or bitten when pretending to shave them. And how he had enjoyed the power of cutting them up with his penknife and secretly burying them. He had had a den in a hidden part of the densest hedgerow where these delights were enacted, and no one ever found him out. Morgan broke out into a cold sweat, hearing in his head the desperate cries of the last cat he had drowned when he was ten. He had never been very good at killing cats. Surely this couldn't be happening to him. He fell silent, quivering with terror. So vivid were his imaginings that he jumped when Rachel finally said something.

'This room is sound proofed. My mother told you before that you are banned from this house.'

'What do you want?' He croaked out.

'Information. I think you need to stay here for a while, or at least until we can have a civil discussion.'

'Let me out of here, you bitch. What do you want?'

'Just a truthful answer, to start with.'

'Let me out.'

'Tell me, what do you know about Semtex?'

'I don't know anything.'

'I thought you might say that.' She walked over to him again and he shrank back nervously. She remained out of reach, just. He stared at the lethal rings she had on her fingers. Twice now he had been rendered unconscious by contact with them. He remembered the terrible scratch on his back that he had had for several days as a souvenir of the fight with Freddie Pinker. He could see a similar wound on his hands where Rachel had grabbed him. But last time they had let him go. Freddie Pinker. Whenever that name came to mind rage filled him. Even here. He roared and shouted, shouted and roared, raved and kicked. Then the Sweeney Todd that haunted his head came back. He shivered again with fear and fell silent. Rachel carried on as though nothing had happened.

'There will be no more dead cats in Waterton or Little Waterton, my mother has seen to that. But there is no information as to where exactly the Semtex came from when the car exploded. We've been told you had Semtex just before the explosion took place. Is that correct?'

'So what if it is.' Morgan couldn't see what any of that had to do with him being captured like this. The Shallcombes were better informed than he could have guessed. Why would they protect Pinker? He could see why they might not like him fighting in the bar.

'Just this. You are banned from this house. You are banned from doing anything to Freddie Pinker. You will be staying here until your bags have been packed for you. After that you will be leaving this area and not coming back. Mrs Lightfoot will be finding a new driver and if you return to this area there will be no second chances.'

Morgan listened to the girl in disbelief, but considerable relief. So he wasn't going to end up in a bar pie! He calmed down a bit. What had he stumbled upon? Then it all became clear to him. They weren't protecting Freddie but Eric. He'd left the bomb outside Eric's shop and it had gone off at the centre where Eric worked. Maybe Maddie was having a fling with Eric, right under the noses of the Michaels. That way it all made sense.

'My mother will be returning later to attend to the details. There is no cause to be afraid of the dark but you will be staying here for a couple of hours. And don't waste your time shouting. Noone can hear you down here.'

She left the room and closed the door behind her. Not a sound came out of it after she locked it, using a small badger-shaped charm on her bracelet. She'd been away from the bar for half an hour: she checked Morgan's wristwatch.

Rachel sped up the stairs, grabbed an oven cloth hanging by the cooker then pulled a tray of pies out of the oven. Several of the customers cheered as the smell of fresh meat pies pervaded the front part of the pub. She turned the pies onto the cooling tray.

'Sorry about that. Now who wants hot pies?' She turned smartly round, removed the 'Back shortly' sign and brought up a pile of plates from beneath the counter. Luckily for his blood pressure, Howard Morgan did not know that ten feet above him Freddie Pinker was enjoying a hot meat pie and a pint of bitter.

Chapter 14: Reading in

And that is how it came about that Howard Morgan woke up with a headache at ten o'clock that night to find himself lying in a half-open coffin in the back of his own hearse, parked in a lay-by some-where outside Swindon. The nightmare he was having about Freddie Pinker sawing his head off to put in a meat pie evaporated as he came to. The car keys were in his trouser pockets and the only valuables he had, together with a few clothes, were neatly packed in two new suitcases piled up on the passenger seat. In prison he had heard the odd rumour about the Black Horse but nobody seemed to know anything too precise. He did not like what had happened to him but he had the sense to see that when two women have the boldness and capacity to do what they had done to him there must be more to it than he could see on the surface. He raised himself stiffly from the coffin, causing a passing car almost to swerve into a ditch as the driver saw his shadowy figure emerge from the box. After all that, thought Morgan, they let me go. So instead of try-ing to drive back to what had been his home and his old life, Morgan decided that the time had come to head off and see if he could make a living elsewhere. If the worst came to the worst, he supposed that he could sleep in the coffin overnight. Time to plan, watch and plan. Freddie Pinker was his for the taking but he needed a better plan.

Having sorted out which of Howard Morgan's possessions were worth his keeping, Maddie Shallcombe prepared a letter, enclosing the keys, for the Housing Officer of the Local Authority that was Morgan's landlord. Everything else was removed by the two Michaels and taken to the dump. This was not how she had planned to spend the day and Maddie was feeling very tired. Her American visitors had spent a couple of nights in two of the apartments underneath the Black Horse, checking out the security and generally satisfying themselves with the arrangements. They had been returned by Harold Crane to Waterloo International the same way they had come, that is to say, in his armoured white stretch limousine with the metal shutters down. Rachel, bless her, was still on duty at ten and had agreed to work through to closing time. Maddie was downstairs in the first basement below pub level reading. All around her were neat piles of typed A4 paper. She did not make notes but had a pack of self-adhesive paper slips that from time to time she inserted into the papers as she went along. The room was inside the main apartment on that floor and had been so designed that one would scarcely know that it was underground. It even had false windows with fake daylight on the other side to light it. The style of the apartment was not English. It vaguely resembled what one might think of as Spanish or Greek. Essentially it was Mediterranean in appearance but of a sophisticated kind, the style in which expensive hotels are sometimes modelled. The floor was brick-coloured terracotta and the walls were white painted plaster. Two walls had frescos on them that tricked the eye into seeing perspective and distance. In the hallway were recessed alcoves. On each alcove wall was an extremely large terracotta plaque imprinted with the shape of an urn filled with flowers and underneath each plaque was a second plaque, again unpainted terracotta, in the shape of a plate filled with oranges and grapes. On the left hand side of the main room, where in the pub two floors above there was a fireplace, down here was a small fountain splashing gently against an intricately mosaic tiled wall piece on either side of which a large white urn similar to that in the hallway plaques stood. Each urn was filled with real flowers. The ceiling was yellow as were the cushions upon the cane sofa and chairs that Mrs Shallcombe was using as her office. Opposite her a beautifully carved olive wood screen covered a large part of the wall between the fake windows.

This flat had its own kitchen. After working an hour or so in this fashion Mrs Shallcombe went over to the tiny kitchen to put the kettle on. As she did so Rachel tapped on the door of the flat and let herself in.

'Mum, where are you?'

'Kitchen. Coffee?'

'Please.'

Rachel walked into the kitchen area and yawned. 'They've gone.

The place is bedded down for the night. No point in carrying on if the place is empty. How's it going?'

'Alright. I'm catching you up now. I want to be quite clear I've understood the figures for the Domingo district. So I'm going through that bit again. Our friends in South America have asked Mr Nazzura to show a little patience with the short deliveries. There's a ceasefire until August twenty-eighth and I expect we'll see soon enough whether or not they accept my views about it all. I will tell them what I think a couple of days before that and I heard this morning that the dates of the visit are now settled.'

So they've both agreed to stay here? Papadopolous and Santini?'

'Of course. Except that they don't know where 'here' is. Their counsellors were both in touch with Harold this morning so we are working on the basis that it is the week commencing seventeenth August.'

'That doesn't give us a lot of time to arrange the security around here.'

'It can be done. The Wings have called in favours for this. This is a much bigger operation that last time. But I'm quite interested to see how Harold thinks he's going to cut the village off from the rest of the world for a week.'

'Not your problem, Mum. It's up to him and he's had plenty of practice.'

'Quite right, dear.'

'Are the gypsies coming again?'

'I suppose they might, but I haven't really gone in to it. Rhiannon Thornhill is in charge at Blue Grace Farm nowadays and I think she might agree to a week's worth of gypsies if we pay her well enough.'

'You'd think she would do it for old time's sake.'

'I don't like to impose on her too far. She has already agreed to act as a passport.' Rachel looked incredulous.

'But why?'

'It's a way of coming out of hiding without coming out of hiding. Her father won't bother her here, not so near to us. But now she has the child it's possible she might be allowed to have her mother come over and see him, at least in London.'

'Your coffee is going cold.' Rachel poured out two black coffees into two differently coloured small porcelain cups. She reached up to a shelf at eye level and brought down a dark box. Out of it she took two tiny chocolate teddies and put one on each saucer. 'Shall we go and sit down?'

'Good idea.'

'Shall I shut the place completely for the night?'

'Probably a good idea in case our Mr Howard Morgan comes back. What can have been going through his mind?'

Rachel said nothing, having serious doubts herself whether Howard Morgan had a mind at all. The information about him they had got in the last few days was very peculiar. She pulled out of her apron a control panel about the size and shape of a remote control for a television. When she pressed a touchpad by the light switch on the wall, one of the fake windows started to whirr. A flat television screen the full size of the window dropped into place. Rachel pointed the control at it and the screen split into sixteen smaller views of different parts of the upper part of the Black Horse. First she enlarged the view of the upstairs bar and pressed a couple more buttons on the screen. The curtains closed, one set after the other, all the way around the property. Then steel shutters dropped and closed over each of the apertures on the inside. Next she pressed further buttons to set the external alarms and finally she turned out the indoor lights and flooded the outside garden with security lights. Mrs Shallcombe took no notice of her daughter whilst this went on. The process took only a few minutes and she was lost in her own thoughts. When Rachel was done, her mother looked up.

'Why don't you use your bracelet?'

'Force of habit, I suppose. I keep meaning to test everything out but it's a lot to learn on top of everything else right now.'

'I fancy another teddy. What about you?'

'No thanks. I'll go and get my laptop. I think we need to model some projections on the Domingo figures. They should match up on both sides but they don't. We need to understand where the gap is.'

'Agreed. We need to get Nazzura to look over a couple of things for us as well. I've only seen it once before but it is possible that there's a hole in the shipments that neither of them knows about. I think there could be an independent operator here playing them off against each other. Neither set of figures shows the gap but put them together and you see it.'

'If that's going on Nazzura will thank us anyway. He may not know if he's been dealing with a freelance supplier.' So saying, Rachel disappeared, returning ten minutes or so later. She had her computer in a small bag over her shoulder and in front of her on a metal tray were two brandy glasses each with a metal teaspoon in it. She put the tray on the marble coffee table in front of the sofa, pushing aside the nearest pile of paper.

'Careful, dear. Oh, that is kind. Warm brandy!'

'The low alcohol answer to coffee.' Rachel grinned. 'How big is the gap, do you think?'

'It must be pretty big because Terry Nazzura is getting uneasy. He claims he has four teams stamping out a rival retail outfit in New York, as well as getting short deliveries and having to make the shortfall from suppliers who don't show their face. This is potentially dangerous for him if it turns out the supplier is not authorised to deal. The South Americans weigh what leaves them but there's never time to weigh properly on the receiving end. They suspect that the problems in Chicago have been set off because some one else wants to come in on distribution up and down the chain. But they won't do business like that if they can help it. They don't like to deal with other Latins anyway. Apparently it causes security problems internally for them.'

'The figures don't make the Domingo district anything special. Why are they fighting over it like this?'

'There's no obvious reason. You could say neither side wants to give up territory. But that's too simple. The cost of defending it is very high. That's why I think there's something funny going on and to my mind there's probably a connection with the gaps in the other figures. At least we need to check it out. Could be the independent is somewhere in the Domingo district pretending to be something else.'

Rachel handed her mother one of the glasses.

'Cheers.' They clinked glasses. Each of them looked thoughtful. A mischievous look came over Rachel's face.

'You haven't seen the Reverend Hollis in the last couple of weeks have you?'

'Eric tells me he's asked the Bishop for permission to go on retreat for a month.'

'Oh really?'

'Poor man. He seems to have been feeling rather tired lately.'

Rachel shook her head good-naturedly. 'Right then. Where shall I start?'

Her mother handed her a sheaf of papers half an inch thick. 'Off you go.'

Maddie stood up and stretched. She slowly straightened her back then sat down again. The television screen was still in place. She pointed at it and pressed a pear shaped charm on her right hand bracelet. The television was tuned to what seemed to be a news channel and at once Maddie became absorbed in listening to it. Rachel looked up.

'I thought the Russians didn't broadcast at this time of night?'

'It's from this afternoon. I thought I'd better record it whilst I sorted out at Morgan's house.'

'Ah.' Rachel carried on transferring figures from one of the papers into her computer calculations. 'When are you going over again?'

'Probably on Tuesday. Sergei is an important client. I need to speak to him again face to face. Can you manage?'

'Of course I can, Mum. Are we still going to see Mr Dale on Wednesday?'

'Yes. But I don't think it will take very long. Well, dear, I think I'd better be going to bed now. I'll leave you to carry on. I know you're a night bird.'

'Good night, Mum.'

'Good night, Rachel. See you in the morning.'

It was four o'clock that morning before Rachel finally turned her computer off and called it a day.

*

The coming week was indeed a busy one for the offices of Dale, Dale & Ogden. Traditionally August was quiet time but in the last couple of years this had no longer proved to be true. Staff holidays, however, were still targeted on August, which meant that the firm was somewhat shorthanded in that particular week. Mr Clifford Dale's secretary had taken over from the normal receptionist and by Friday morning was still not at full efficiency. There was an appointment made for eleven o'clock for Mr Douglas Dale for the executors and beneficiaries under Joshua Thornhill's will and the reception area was almost full. All five of the old man's children were there plus his widow and Robert and his twenty year old daughter Linda. Linda was at University in Durham and had recently become engaged to an army officer serving in Northern Ireland. She rarely came to the farm but had been asked to attend that morning, together with her brother Billy. Billy did not come. He was too concerned about his mother to leave her alone in the house for any length of time in the company of her vodka bottles. Her behaviour in the last month had become completely erratic whenever Robert Thornhill was around. It was obvious that she was convinced Robert was having an affair with Rhiannon and she constantly taunted him about it. Whilst never appearing to be drunk she now seemed almost to have given up food and to be sustaining herself entirely on spirits. Billy was not sure how the bottles were smuggled into the house but he had a feeling that his mother was paying one of the girls from the milk processing plant to drop by in the late afternoon to deliver a couple of litres each evening. Nor did he know where his mother hid it all and he was not inclined to ransack her room whilst she was asleep. Whenever he tried to broach the subject with his father, the response was always the same. There's nothing you can do, his father always said. I've felt sorry for her too in my time but she won't change now. He had tried to persuade his father no longer to see Rhiannon Thornhill but it was clear that he was wasting his time and that his father had no intention at all of spending his life indoors being shouted at by his wife.

Rhiannon sat regally in the large armchair in the solicitors' reception and breastfed Neville who had been purple faced and screaming for some minutes. Joe and William were playing cards in the corner and Kathleen sat opposite Lillian, each glaring at the other. Robert stood with his hands in his pockets staring out of the window whilst Linda sat by him in the window seat reading an old copy of Country Life that belonged to the reception area. Normally, clients would have been offered a cup of coffee but there were so many people that Mrs Tippett could not cope because it would have meant too long away from the front desk. Uncharacteristically, and very inconveniently, Mr Douglas Dale was late. He had been that morning to take his ailing spaniel to the animal centre and ought to have been back by at least ten o'clock. There were no signs of him and he had not sent word. Mrs Tippett was becoming agitated. Presumably the chaos at the animal centre was slowing things down. Eventually, at eleven, Douglas Dale and the spaniel appeared in reception.

'Joan, would you mind terribly just looking after Bobbie for moment? I'll have the meeting in the Partners' Room, if that's alright.' Joan Tippett did not think it was alright and she had already laid out pencils and paper in Douglas Dale's office. But she said nothing to Mr Dale. Bobbie was a very lethargic dog, prior to his illness much given to chewing the furniture in the office. But he was quiet enough now.

'Sorry to be late, everybody. Do come in. We can go through to the Partners' Room. Joan will show you the way.'

Joan then ushered the assembled company into the largest room in the building and closed the door once everyone was seated. She knew that Douglas Dale was in his own office extracting the relevant will from the box that he had assigned to Joshua Thornhill. When Joshua had first visited Mr Douglas Dale in his office he had inquired why it was that the back of the room from floor to ceiling was completely full of identical green boxes with different names on them. Douglas Dale explained how, as a probate practitioner, he had found it necessary to keep a separate box for each deceased's estate he dealt with, and not to mix the papers for one with the papers of another. He was eerily delighted to have a living client as opposed to a dead one to deal with. Joshua, a stickler for order, would no doubt have found it only fitting that his own papers should be moved from the filing cabinet by the desk into its own new green box.

Douglas Dale went into the Partners' Room.

'Good morning. I'm very sorry to have kept you waiting. Thank you all for coming here. I thought that the best thing we could do, now that the probate is through and Rhiannon and Robert are officially the executors, would be for us all to consider the will together. There should not be any secret as to what Mr Joshua Thornhill did. I should also point out the obvious regarding Blue Grace Farm. As you know, the executors have received notice to quit from Lord Errington consequent on Joshua's death. Although close relatives sometimes have the opportunity to insist on a new tenancy, it does not seem that circumstances here permit this. For those of you who are currently living on the tenanted farm you may be required to leave when the notice to quit runs out on the twenty-ninth of September next year. Once we have worked through the will, I suggest that if anybody would like to instruct me to look out their own residential situation I would be perfectly happy to do that.

First of all, before anything else, I would just like to express my deep regret at Mr Thornhill's death. I am sure that you are all aware that the relationship between this firm and Mr Thornhill was one of very long standing and we would like to extend our sympathy to all members of the family at this time.'

He stopped speaking for a few seconds' respectful silence. No one said anything. The room was getting stuffy with so many people and Linda kept coughing and blowing her nose. She constantly complained that the climate up North didn't agree with her. With the exception of Rhiannon and Mrs Huxter, everyone else was in his or her best Sunday clothes. Joe and William were especially uncomfortable, having both put on a lot of weight in the twenty years since purchasing their best jacket and trousers. Lillian Huxter, easily as heavily built as her two brothers, sat comfortably enough in her lilac leisure sportswear outfit and green cotton blouse. Her only concession to occasion was the pair of black stringed dancing shoes she had crammed on over her swollen feet.

'The terms of the will have already been read to the executors on the telephone and I have to tell you that I, as a lawyer, am satisfied that I understand what the will directs and pleased be assured that I will do my best to assist the executors in completing Mr Thornhill's instructions. I shall now read the will in full and then explain it. If there are any questions I will deal with them now and also confirm to you all later in writing the terms of any advice which it is necessary for me to give.'

At this he pulled from his left coat pocket a photocopy of the will which he read, as he had promised, from beginning to end. He could tell that certain members of the family had not fully understood it and that other members of the family were very angry indeed. There was a short uneasy silence. Apart from small legacies to his children, Joshua had left everything to Rhiannon.

Robert Thornhill, who had received nothing, said nothing. He considered the will to be nothing more than a form of sharp practice on the part of his uncle but now he was dead there was not a thing he could do about it. He was bitterly disappointed by his uncle's failure to leave him anything in recognition of all the time and effort he had spent in building up the business. The farm had been his whole world. He had been born there, just like his cousins, and worked there all his life. He had spent his time living in hope of inheriting the work of those many years and could not bear the thought of having to start again somewhere else. The woods and fields of the area were almost part of him. He had hoped to die there like all his ancestors as far back as anyone could trace his father's family, and like his own parents. It was impossible to avoid the terrible truth any longer. The visit to the lawyers' offices had forced them to confront the reality and the anger each of them had for Joshua. Robert had no intention of staying on the farm indefinitely but knew that he would face great problems in moving his wife to a new home. Once Robert had told her what was going to happen, she had thrown herself, weeping, on the floor and begged him to do something, as though he could do anything now. What did Joshua think would be achieved? Apart from the impact on himself, three of his cousins would be rendered homeless unless they did something. It might be possible to persuade Lord Errington to sell the individual cottages, but he would not do it for any kind of discount and it was highly doubtful whether mortgages would be forthcoming on the sort of wages that his cousins had been earning. There were ways out, but it needed Rhiannon to make her mind up what she wanted to do. All the money was now concentrated in her hands. But he didn't know what to make of her behaviour in the last few days, even allowing for the shock of finding herself widowed. She could not have thought the old man was immortal.

Luckily, once he had been fed, Neville slept through the entire appointment with the lawyers and was only beginning to wake. Everyone seemed shell-shocked. Mr Dale continued to drone on but no one was listening.

'....so there are these uncertainties with regard to, shall we say family provision. It maybe that some of you will wish to investigate whether...'

Rhiannon was evidently as agitated as the others and just as angry. Neville suddenly began to scream. A sickening organic smell wafted up from his bedding.

'I'll go and change him.' Kathleen suddenly stood up, picked up Neville's carry bed and marched out.

'Yes, I think I'll be going now.' Before anyone could say anything Lillian had also got up. 'Goodbye, Mr Dale. It's been a pleasure meeting you. You know where I am when you need to contact me.' She stopped Mr Dale mid-sentence, energetically shook his hand, crushing his fingers in her fearsome grip, and clapped him on the back with her other hand. 'And don't forget, if you ever come out to Dallas, you must look us up.' She then left as rapidly as Kathleen had done.

Almost at once Joe and William decided to leave. They were not staying when their sisters were away. Each of them smiled and waved but said nothing to Mr Dale, who was still waiting to finish his sentence. Linda stood up as well.

'Come on, Dad. We should be going.'

'Just wait outside for a minute, will you?'

'Goodbye, Mr Dale. Dad, I'll wait for you in reception.'

'I did have a bit more to say.' Mr Dale was rather miffed.

Thornhill didn't think he should point out that Mr Dale had kept them all by being late, so he said: 'Don't mind them. They've had enough, that's all, and it's lunchtime. We were going to go down to the Black Horse for a pie. If you get down there too late all the meat ones have gone.' At this Rhiannon grimaced, recognising exactly how the Thornhill family operated. She turned to Mr Dale.

'I don't want it, any of it. I'm not interested in money and I don't need it. Give it to them. I've thought about it and I don't want it, do you hear. I don't want his stinking money, I told him that when I met him.' Robert looked thunderstruck. He had spent most of his adult life scheming to get what had been left to her. 'We're going away. Neville and I are going away. And I'm not taking that money.'

Mr Dale also looked rather surprised. This was not a usual reaction in a farming family to the sudden acquisition of money and land. 'What do you mean, going away? We have to complete the executorship and wind things up. What about Neville's future?'

'Mr Dale, believe me, Neville has money coming out of his ass and I don't want it.'

Because Mr Dale was there Robert felt he would not be misunderstood. He went to Rhiannon and put his arm around her. 'Don't decide yet. Don't take Neville from the farm yet. He's a Thornhill too. Wait till the end of the year and you can think about it a bit more.'

Rhiannon began to look as though she would explode with anger. So he withdrew his arm.

'Poppa's got wall to wall attorneys. And they don't tell him what to do. I said I wanted out of here but I'll wait til Christmas, that's all. I only ever stayed for Joshua, and I'm telling you, you'd better think of something else to do with the money, 'cos I ain't taking it.' So saying, she stormed out of the room.

Douglas Dale and Robert Thornhill looked at each other. Neither had expected this.

'This is really rather serious, Mr Thornhill.'

'I know. Joshua's business is a big one, seventy-five full time employees at the last count. Rhiannon needs to find a manager because I'm leaving as well.'

'Mr Thornhill, this is unprecedented. I must speak with my partner and discuss it with him. I take it you have no objection as this has no impact on relations with Lord Errington.'

'No. I don't mind.'

'I shall also ring Mrs Thornhill and secure her permission. Later, I think, when she has had the opportunity to recover.'

It was perfectly possible that the businesses could be sold as a going concern but there were difficulties. Part of the enterprise was conducted on the tenanted land. It would be very complicated to unpick it all and they needed time to think.

'Mr Thornhill, one last thing if you don't mind. Do you happen to know whether it is correct that Mrs Thornhill has private resources? Have you ever met her family?'

'I have never seen them. I only know her father lives in New York.'

Chapter 15: Escapes

Joyce Smollett did not know what to make of any of it. Her life seemed to have become more bizarre by the minute. No sooner had she managed to tidy up the damage from the explosion than she was notified that she would be required to attend at the mental hospital outside Gloucester to which her husband had been transferred. There was some sort of assessment going on and it did not look as though anybody was getting through to Arthur in a sensible way. She felt herself it had been quite hard to understand what he was on about. He was obsessed with the idea that the police were persecuting him for no reason and he simply could not explain away the police evidence so as to convince Joyce that the police were wrong. She knew he had spent the fortnight prior to the explosion mostly away from home every evening. She had no idea where he had gone and he had resolutely refused to say. What was all this nonsense about dead cats? And why did it matter? She knew that Arthur, as a vet, had had a strong sympathetic streak for the animals that he dealt with but this was completely beyond any reason. That morning she had received official notification that Arthur was to be kept for ongoing assessment and that he had been told she could visit him twice a day, without the girls, for so long as she wished. She had also been asked to pack anything she felt that Arthur might particularly like to have with him but that his belongings would have to be checked by the staff before he could have them. She was sitting in Arthur's study, with her elbows on his white table, wondering what to take and what she could possibly say to him to cheer him up. She supposed that nervous breakdowns came in many different forms and, frankly, there seemed no other explanation for any of this. The big question that no one had so far answered was how he had got the explosive. That part of the police theory, that he bought it from

the criminal underworld, made no sense to her. Yes, he hated offi-
cialdom in all its manifestations and he was plainly worked up on
the subject of cats and, yes, he probably did fall out with the police
in Bristol. They were pretty annoying, come to think of it. If anything
deserved to be blown up it was them, not the animal surgery. Surely
he can't have had an accomplice? Maybe the centre wasn't the real
target and there had been an accident. But why Semtex and what
awful sort of people had it? The phone rang.

'Animal hospital, Little Waterton. Joyce Smollett speaking.'

Outside the noise of the drill could be heard as the workmen proceeded with the reinstatement process. She put her right hand over
her ear to listen better through the row.

'Escaped? When? Where has he gone? Have you any idea?'

The decorators would be in the animal centre the following day.
The other vets had been very sympathetic and rallied round.
Arthur's income was being replaced by the insurance company anyway as a contribution to partnership profits. Hopefully the situation
was to have been temporary.

'No, of course I haven't seen him. When did this happen?'

The clients had been understanding and not made any fuss when
they were transferred to one of the more junior partners until such
time as Arthur could come back. The biggest contract was with the
Ministry in the aftermath of the foot and mouth disease in the previous year. The department had not been over-concerned about
switching to other individuals within the same practice. There was
an irony in this somewhere: considering he had been their biggest
fee earner, Arthur Smollett had become totally expendable.

'Yes. I'll be there in about an hour. Have you checked the gardens thoroughly? I can't imagine where he would go if he didn't
come home. I will warn our cleaning lady to let him in if he knocks
at the door.'

Joyce put the telephone down. The last trace of normality had
just disappeared, together with all trace of her husband. She did not
know what to feel, let alone think. She racked her brains for some
explanation. He had only had three visitors whilst he was at the hospital. One was Tony Shea, his partner, who was re-arranging
appointments and needed to talk about individual cases. Tony said
afterwards Arthur seemed perfectly lucid but kept going on about
how he was being kept a prisoner without a trial. The second visitor was Mr Douglas Dale who Arthur had sent for from the police

station. Douglas Dale had written later to Joyce giving a full account of the meeting and expressing the view that they ought to retain an independent doctor to help with the assessment, in due course. Mr Dale subscribed to the nervous breakdown theory and had evidently had problems in getting Arthur to follow the difference between imprisonment and medical treatment. There had been much mention of the former Soviet hospitals and the drugging of political dissidents. The third visitor was Rhiannon Thornhill who had written to Joyce claiming that Arthur was in the process of treating a pair of race horses over Bristol way and that she needed to discuss it with him. Joyce frowned. Maybe there were some racehorses but that didn't explain why, when she later visited, Arthur flatly denied that she had been there. Joyce checked with the nurses whether a purple haired woman had been round and was told that she had. At the time she had put his failing memory down to stress or drugs or both. He'd had plenty of time to get home by now. Where was he? Where do you go without a change of clothes or a lawyer if you're not going home?

All of a sudden she asked herself a very silly question. Was Arthur having an affair with Rhiannon Thornhill? Was that what he had been up to after Joshua died and before the explosion in the pub? Joyce's heart almost stopped beating. Was Arthur having a nervous breakdown because of it? Or had the explosion been part of a plan to fake his own death so that she and the children could claim on the insurance whilst he started a new life? And where on earth was he? Was it beyond possibility that he would have gone up to Blue Grace farmhouse to hide out? There was only one way to find out. A ridiculous idea, perhaps. She picked up her handbag and switched off the office light. It was almost lunchtime so there was no harm in popping out.

'Tony,' she said, knocking on his door.

'Joyce. What can I do for you?' He stopped trying to force a medicine dropper down the throat of a racing pigeon and the bird pecked him hard. 'Ow! Have you got a hanky?' He began to wipe a trail of blood from his finger down his white overall. There were a dozen boxes on the table and floor, each containing an increasingly agitated racing pigeon. Joyce raised her voice over the squawking and the hammering of the workmen.

'I'm just going out for an hour over lunchtime. Can you deal with any calls for Arthur or me?'

'What? Sorry?'

'The phone. Can you pick up the phone while I'm away?'

'Yes. OK. Fine. I'm having a sandwich here anyway.'

Joyce walked rapidly to the car and drove to Blue Grace Farmhouse. The farmhouse appeared to be deserted. Arthur had escaped in the early hours of the morning. If he had been coming home he would have gone straight to the centre that morning, where he knew she would be. He might have persuaded someone to give him a lift. No. Surely not: he would be in his pyjamas and no one picks up a hitchhiker in their nightwear. It would be asking for trouble. Rhiannon Thornhill probably had a car. People with a baby need one. But there were no cars in the vicinity and the curtains of the farmhouse were drawn. Joyce did not know whether there were domestic staff and so she knocked on the door, in the hope of an answer. It was very quiet. She waited, trying to think of something sensible to say should Rhiannon open the door.

Rhiannon was not at home but the sight of his wife through the lace curtains of the ground floor almost caused Arthur Smollett to have a coronary on the spot. He flattened himself on the floor behind the sofa. Was Joyce telepathic? How could she have possibly known that Rhiannon Thornhill had decided to rescue him, once the long tale of police harassment had been explained to her? Arthur was sweating profusely. He was wearing Joshua Thornhill's casual clothing. He knew Rhiannon would not have said anything and in any case she had not come back from her meeting at the solicitor's office. He had no intention of showing himself to his wife as yet. He knew that she would try to persuade him to give himself up and, when he refused, would give him up anyway so that he could be medicated again. Arthur shuddered. He was definitely not going back into the mental hospital, whatever happened.

After five minutes or so a note was pushed under the front door. Arthur lay completely still. He then heard the sound of his own car pulling away from the outside of the house. He went over to the note and read it.

'Dear Mrs Thornhill,

I would like to speak to you regarding my husband Arthur. He has disappeared from the hospital this morning.

Yours sincerely,

Joyce Smollett.'

At the bottom of the page Joyce had put her telephone number at the centre.

Arthur had spent the morning in the guest bedroom, as instructed. He put the note in his pocket and returned to his bedroom. This was unexpected, the most unexpected thing being his strong desire to hide from Joyce rather than run to her. Trust your instincts, he told himself. Hard to do though, when you are doing what I am doing, he replied. Don't talk to yourself. Don't talk to yourself. Remember those two patients who both thought they were Margaret Thatcher and forced a nurse to play mini-golf with them as Dennis? They were always talking to themselves. The effect of the drugs had not completely worn off and he was periodically overcome with a wave of sleep. So he lay down and decided for the moment to give in.

Smollett woke some time later. At first he was hard-pressed to recall where he was. The room was unfamiliar and he had no watch. Then he heard a voice in the hallway outside and the approach of rapid footsteps.

'Hey, you awake in there yet?'

Rhiannon Thornhill hammered on the door. 'Want a piece of pizza? I brought one back from the village for you.' Smollett had not eaten since suppertime the day before. He was almost faint with hunger. She came into the room bearing a couple of plastic shopping bags and a flat pizza box.

'Yes, please,' he gasped. 'Very kind of you.'

'No shit. Here, this side's mushroom and that side's chicken. Want a coke?'

Normally he would never have touched such a beverage, much loved as it was by his girls, but his old life seemed so far away that he automatically nodded. He took a mouthful and instantly felt sickened. Christ, how did kids drink this stuff?

'Thanks.' A lot of eating was done in a very short space of time. Rhiannon sat patiently in an armchair.

'So how did you get out of that hellhole?'

'Not terribly difficult really. I found the janitor's cupboard, put on his overall and walked out. They opened the doors at 5am for the milk and juice deliveries so I just waited to slip out. Joyce had given me a fiver for the papers in the hospital so I got the bus here. I must say I am very grateful to you, Mrs Thornhill.'

'Those idiots never pick the right guy. You're as sane as any hood I ever met.'

'But I don't understand why you're taking such risks on my behalf?'

'Risks? What risks?'

'Well, in case they come to find me.'

'Ha! You think anyone is going to send out the cops after some harmless guy who has a history with cats? Besides, I owe you one. Two maybe. Didn't you just save my life or something back in that shed?'

Arthur Smollett finished his meal on the bed and put the pizza box and the empty coke tin on the bedside table.

'What should I do next, do you think?'

Rhiannon looked at his day-old stubble. 'Want to clean up? Or are you gonna woo me with the smell?'

'I, er, I...' Smollett did not know what to say.

'Only kidding. Look, there's towels in the cupboard here and a big collection of Joshua's things to wear. You're not that different in size. I told Kathleen not to come in tomorrow so we have a while to think it through. I'm going to feed Neville now. Did you find your bathroom? It's on the left through that door.'

She went back into the living room where Neville was shrieking for sustenance. It was dark.

An hour later, feeling quite distinctly better, Smollett entered the living room.

'Fresh out the waves?'

'Mrs Thornhill, how can I ever thank you for your help?'

'I'll think of something. Here, you can start by patting his back. I'm going to fix us a coffee.' She dumped Neville in Smollett's lap and walked out. The closeness of the tiny child brought on a wave of homesickness. Shortly afterwards she returned with the coffee and a bottle of whisky.

'You need a drink, to relax a bit. Being on the run doesn't mean you have to go anyplace. It's like a game, see. Mostly people in your, let's say, situation do something really dumb like call their wife and kids. Easy policing, simple phone tap and pick up your man. But if you don't call home, cops have to work, see, and they got better things to do than oblige the nut house. They figure if you can disappear long enough you ain't mad enough to be in there anyhow. So all you have to do now is get drunk and sleep off the need to make that phone call.'

'Mrs Thornhill, you...'

'Call me Rhiannon.'

'Yes. Rhiannon, how is it you know all this?'

She laughed loudly, causing Neville to screw up his face. 'I guess I watch a lot of bad TV. You going to pour me a drink too?'

'Sorry. Of course. I just thought, well, the baby...'

'I'm only having the one shot. Couple hours from now it will all be gone and Neville won't know the difference' She held up the glass in Smollett's direction. 'Bottoms up, as you people say.'

Two drinks later Smollett was feeling far less anxious about Joyce and the girls. He knew they would be financially in no trouble and Joyce was a very capable woman.

'How long?' Smollett asked.

'How long what?'

'How long am I, er hiding out?'

'Six months maybe.'

'Six months!!!'

'Have another drink, Mr Smollett.'

'Arthur,' he sighed. 'Call me Arthur.'

'Well, Arthur, your wife can't move away from here until things quiet down and then you can go up to Scotland or something. Just appear quietly and let the boys in Little Waterton carry on as they did. After a year outside they got grounds to let you out legally and I'll make sure we find a good doctor to sign you off. But right now you'd better stay low. I heard the news tonight. You didn't make it. Be happy.'

'Mrs, I mean Rhiannon, I surely can't stay here indefinitely.'

'Indefinitely, no. But for now, yes. Anyhow, do you have a better place to go? No clothes, no ID and no money.'

'Well, I suppose not.'

'No one comes here only Kathleen and she ain't my flavour right now. Only one thing I ask you is don't be dumb and ring home. There's stuff going on here for the next month or so that doesn't want people nosing round it.'

'Stuff?'

'Yeah. Don't ask me. I can't tell you.' She filled his glass again. 'Just tell me again about that time in Cambridge you and Joyce were making out in that boat and some guy peed over the bridge onto you. I really enjoyed that whole story.'

'Ah, you remember?' Oh dear.

'Sure. I remember every word. Your whole life, right, Cambridge and the med school and that funny place in Yorkshire you and Joyce started out and...'

'Yes. Yes.' Smollett stopped her. He had told her far far too much. Even about his wedding night. Oh dear. Joyce would never forgive him. So he tried to change the subject. 'How was the appointment at Dale, Dale & Ogden? It's years since I went down to the offices. I believe it's quite smart there now.'

'OK. But tell you what, we had one hell of an afternoon. Young Billy, you know, Robert's son, he came down the pub, said his mom had disappeared, just walked off.'

'I don't understand.'

'She hits the bottle kinda hard and she went out the house when he thought she was asleep. So we looked for her. I mean the whole family. Lillian, Kathleen, the men. It wasn't a whole pile of fun. But no sign. I was kinda glad I didn't see her. I hear she thinks I have a thing with Robert. Billy said I should watch out in case she comes round tonight to set fire to the house.' Smollett looked alarmed. 'It's OK. No chance. I let the dogs out and they ask no questions.'

'So you could say I'm a prisoner once more.'

'Not really, Arthur. You're my guest.'

Smollett suddenly remembered the note from Joyce. He fumbled in his pocket and put it on the table in front of Rhiannon.

'Joyce put this through the door this morning.'

'You didn't speak to her?'

'No. No. I hid.'

Rhiannon cast her eye over the memo.

'I already got the one wife gunning for me. What do you think Joyce will say when I ring her tomorrow? Must be only whores in this country have purple hair.' Smollett looked shocked. 'Only kidding, Arthur.'

'Why do you wear your hair purple? I mean, it looks very nice, of course, but it's, er, it's an unusual choice of colour.'

'It's a statement. It says I exist, I am living quietly but I'm not hiding and I don't do Gucci shoes and have painted nails and a perfect face. Not anymore.'

Smollett was mystified. He lay back in the armchair and thought how wonderful it was to be free. Rhiannon began to hum to the baby.

'Yes, yes, yes.' She tickled Neville's chin with one finger. 'And you ain't never wore a fancy jacket.'

The curtains were drawn and the outside world didn't trouble Arthur Smollett anymore.

'Say, Arthur, I'm gonna turn in now. Young Neville here likes to feed round the clock so don't worry if you hear us. Worst thing about being on the run, I hear, is the irregular hours. Never know what time of day it is, body clock all wrong 'cos you sleep when you can. Here, take this.'

She pulled her wristwatch off and held it out.

'That's very kind.'

'Do it. Believe me, you'll be glad.'

'Well, thank you, Rhiannon. I'll look after it.'

The watch was a man's watch with a white metal strap. It looked like the sort they sold in garages. Midnight. Where had the day gone?

'One other thing, Arthur. I don't like a gun in the home. So if you're figuring on getting one you gotta find some place else to stash it.'

'Gun?? What on earth for? I assure you I wouldn't dream of acquiring such an item.'

*

Rhiannon had indeed let the dogs out. She was now the only person on the farm, apart from Dave Merchant, who could control the two Alsatian guard dogs. Since he disposed of their mother the dogs wouldn't obey Robert unless he brought his stick. They had been trained to scare anyone approaching the farmhouse at night into standing absolutely still and they would certainly bite the ankles of anyone who wouldn't stay put. Joshua had had a paranoia that he would be robbed as he slept in his bed, and Rhiannon said herself now she was alone it made sense to keep the dogs. But they were not allowed anywhere near Neville at all. Mostly now they slept outside in their own kennel by the front entrance at night. If Cathy Thornhill had showed up the sleepers in the farmhouse would have soon known about it.

In fact the dogs did encounter her. Neither dog was tethered, precisely because both had been trained to stay near the main house. No one ever checked to see where they went, but then again, they were always by the house in the morning. Blue Grace Woods was the place they sometimes went to at night, perhaps to chase smaller animals, perhaps to be in the place where the smell of old Tess lingered. And that night, like many others, they had ventured out to the woods and begun to bark there. No one would have heard them in such an isolated spot and it wasn't until the next morning that anyone realised that they were trying to attract attention to something they had found. Dave Merchant was the one they in the end persuaded to go with them. It was a long walk, but he had had a lot of experience with dogs and reckoned something was up. They barked and jumped restlessly in front of him, seemingly looking back every few seconds to see if he was still there. After forty minutes he had followed them to the place deep in Blue Grace Woods where Cathy Thornhill's lifeless body lay.

Chapter 16: Double trouble

'Surprise!!!'

The Reverend Hollis was indeed surprised. His heart gave a violent lurch and began to beat wildly in his ribcage. It was the last possible encounter he would have predicted that, upon opening the door of the Quiet Room, on retreat amongst a silent Anglican Order of nuns, twenty minutes before the Bishop's guest dinner, he should be sprung upon by Eric Pinker and Maddie Shallcombe, both in their underwear.

'What are you doing here?' he hissed.

'Just dropped by for a bit of fun, you know, thought we'd pay you a surprise visit. Lovely place this, isn't it? I used to do the accounts for the nuns...'

'Shhh! Keep your voice down. The Order is silent.'

'It's alright, dear. They can't hear us in here. Come on, you naughty vicar, lend me a hand.' Maddie beamed at him.

'Not here, not here,' whispered the distracted cleric.

'Oh, don't worry, old man. I told you, I know this place. They're getting ready downstairs for the dinner, I bet. Half of them will be in the kitchens.'

'Shhh! Keep your voice down, Eric. Where are your clothes?'

'We don't need them, only a coat. Its warm outside.'

'I can't go outside now.' A hint of stress had entered the vicar's whisper. 'I've got to be ready for the Bishop's speech. He.....' Then he saw Mrs. Shallcombe had taken out of her large handbag a black corset-like contraption, clearly two sizes too small. 'You'll never get into that.'

'Well, not without help. Obviously.'

Eric rubbed his hands gleefully.

'Allow me.'

Eric began to struggle heroically with the garment. The Reverend Hollis decided that the effect of his recent meditations was wearing off. Mrs. Shallcombe began to giggle.

'Oh, wait a minute. We forgot the picnic.' She reached into the bag again, brought forth a small plastic pot of chocolate mousse, opened it and spread it enthusiastically over her chest. This was too much for Hollis.

'You can't, not here. Anyway, I've got to be at the dinner at 7. You'll have to hide.'

'Great idea,' said Eric. 'I know just the place. There's a big cupboard next to the men's room opposite the dining room door. Twice I've walked into it by mistake trying to find the men's. We can warm up in there. Tell you what, you come out after the dinner and before the old boy gives his speech. No one will say anything. We'll be ready for you!'

'Ooh! Cupboards! I love cupboards,' said Mrs Shallcombe happily.

Hollis quickly considered his options but couldn't see a way out. Eric did not seem to be listening.

'Shh! Look, alright. But for goodness sake keep quiet. Wait, wait.'

But it was too late. Eric had opened the door and was peeking out.

'What are you doing?'

Eric shut the door suddenly and put his finger to his lips. He then opened the door a second time and stuck his head round. Maddie huddled up, egging him on.

'Wait, wait. What about your coats?'

But it was no use. Eric was taking no notice at all.

'Coast's clear this time. Narrow shave there. Come on you two!'

'Oh, isn't this fun!' Maddie giggled again.

'Shh!'

They tiptoed at speed down the corridor to the top of the stairs, Eric in front, Maddie close behind him and, struggling to catch up, the Reverend Hollis carrying their coats. Almost at once Eric began frantically to signal they should hide round the corner, which they did. Hollis rushed behind them, keeping as close as he could. He was sweating with stress. What if the nuns found them? What if they bumped into the mother superior? What if the Bishop came up to plan his speech in the Quiet Room library? And what could he possibly say? And how had they got in? And how had they found him?

After a couple of minutes Eric set off again and they this time reached the downstairs floor where Eric and Maddie made a dash for the cupboard.

'Knock when you're ready.'

Hollis groaned inwardly as they disappeared inside. Then he opened the cupboard door again.

'I say, don't forget your coats. Are you really sure about this?'

Maddie began to giggle, pulled in the coats and slammed the door. Hollis cringed: had anyone heard it?

By now it was more or less seven. He somehow had to get through an hour of silent dinner in the adjoining room with twelve elderly nuns. As Eric had said, half of the entire complement of twenty-four nuns did the cooking on any given night whilst the other twelve sat at the table. He could hardly have chosen a more severe, and unsuccessful, environment in which to meditate and distance himself from recent events. Not that there was anything wrong with the convent. It was very nice, having been erected as a miniature copy of Hampton Court sometime in the 1930's. The original occupiers were contemplative nuns and there were almost three hundred of them, but nowadays even the older generation of nuns were not contemplatives. They were teachers and social workers and, although they still wore the traditional habits, their black and white clothing was only knee length rather than to the floor. They maintained a regime of silence in the convent itself to keep a balance with their vigorous lives outside. It had been very kind of them, regarded objectively, to accept the Reverend Hollis, at the Bishop's request, as a temporary visitor for the purposes of his retreat. Nevertheless, Hollis had felt awkward even before Eric and Maddie had appeared on the scene and had become jumpy and nervous following his recent experiences in the back of Maddie's car. He was trying to decide whether divine retribution would strike him down or whether it was just that his ability to cope with everyday life had temporarily deserted him after the two bomb blasts went off.

The nuns' cuisine left a great deal to be desired. It was not intended to be bad as a form of self-punishment but for Hollis the effect was much the same. He surveyed with dread the heavy plates lined up at the top end of the table and wondered how long it would be before he had to go back to the cupboard and its inmates. He had no idea how long the meal would take, as he was not allowed to wear a wristwatch. The stately progress of the meal seemed to have slowed time itself. Off hand he would have said that six hours must have elapsed between the plate of cold cucumber soup and the arrival of the over-cooked boiled chicken, boiled peas and boiled potatoes. But this could only be a deception of the senses and silence, or near silence. He forced himself to drink down at least one glass of the over-sweet elderflower water that was served with the meal because he could see that his neighbour, Sister Audrey, had almost choked on the boiled chicken. He assumed that this was dehydration but on reflection it might have been the fact that her dentures did not fit properly. On his far side he heard Sister Matilda-Margaret wheezing heavily: she had hay-fever and the noise of sneezing and wheezing was distracting him from putting together any plan that would get Eric and Maddie safely out of the convent without their being discovered. What was the cupboard for? Would anyone need to open it? Would they be heard? He knew for a fact that neither of them was exactly quiet in these situations.

Fortunately the clanging of pots and pans from the kitchen area behind the dining hall was probably masking anything going on in the cupboard. Predictably, Hollis became afflicted with super-acute hearing. He was not finding it easy to relax, not least because the Bishop, a florid-faced man in his fifties, kept smiling knowingly at him. This was in truth Hollis' own fault. Hollis had never engaged in doctrinal controversy, considering ethereal matters incapable of proof unsuitable material to distract the ministrations daily required in his life as vicar of Waterton. At the same time he had kept himself sufficiently up to date to know the church politics of those above him in the local hierarchy: who was in favour of the ordination of women, which men were happy-clappy evangelicals, and which ministers subscribed to a form of church worship so ornate that it could comfortably have blended with the high Catholicism of the Counter-Reformation, a form long since abandoned even amongst English Roman Catholics. And so it was that when he had felt it imperative to confess to someone, not for absolution but in order to relieve his conscience, he decided that a Catholic-leaning Bishop was likely to be sympathetic. Or at any rate less likely to show his astonishment than the aromatherapist practising in Upper Waterton, who was the only other person he had thought could possibly be chosen without fear of a breach of confidentiality. Under cover of giving spiritual guidance, the Bishop was treated to a number of interesting revelations, about recent events in the vicarage, the churchyard and the back of a car involving a man, a woman, a vicar, a stuffed tiger, a roll of masking tape, half a kilo of overripe plums, a feather duster and an exploding car. Whether the Bishop believed what he was told or whether he put the whole thing down to stress, Hollis could not say. At points he had had the district impression that the beady-eyed Bishop, whilst appearing to be listening intently, simply did not credit a word of it.

Sister Audrey was working her way slowly through a second slice of boiled chicken and he knew that the meal would last for so long as anybody was eating. He tried not to watch her but it was difficult not, at least in his head, to urge on her clacking dentures. He had finished eating ages ago, as had everyone else. How much longer could she go on? He looked up and saw that the Bishop had left the table. He did not give it a second thought.

The Bishop had not been drinking elderflower water but considerable quantities of a special homemade fortified elderflower wine reserved apparently for him. He marched resolutely towards the men's room, glancing briefly at its badly placed sign and breathing heavily. As he fumbled with the handle, the cupboard door sprang open and in a trice the strong arm of Eric Pinker shot out from the pitch-dark interior, grabbed him, and pulled him in.

Back in the dining hall a desert of tinned peaches and almonds was being served. Hollis had never tasted anything so disgusting in his life, not even in boarding school, but evidently Sister Audrey was enjoying it. She must have spent at least twenty-five minutes on the sickly, perfumed, soggy almonds. People were nodding mutely at him in welcome and encouragement, little suspecting what an appalling abuse of their innocent hospitality he was committing. A great wave of guilt and despair swept over him, terrified as he was that the occupants of the cupboard might lose patience and come out looking for him before the meal was over, assuming it ever would be. Eventually, screwing up all his courage, Hollis felt he could slip out. He stood up clumsily, scraping the chair against the floor and tripping against the corner of the nearest table leg. Forbidden from speaking, there seemed no obvious way to excuse the noise so he was reduced to bowing and grinning to his neighbours, who nodded back at him with artificially exaggerated smiles. The exit door seemed to be half a mile away but he was determined to leave the room now he had got this far. Every eye was upon him, or so it felt. Could he really have an assignation in a cupboard? Or had he imagined the whole thing after all?

At last the door swung shut behind him. He turned into the ill-lit corridor, just in time to witness the Bishop closing the cupboard door. Hollis stood, open-mouthed, rooted to the spot. As he passed by, the Bishop gave him a bland smile. But Hollis could see that there was chocolate mousse on the end of his nose.

*

Rachel knew her mother was out having fun, probably for the last time in a long while. She had already seen her mother's most recent, priceless acquisition. Perhaps not priceless exactly, more like 25,000,000 used US dollars delivered to sixteen bank accounts worldwide. It was in real terms unique, irreplaceable and exactly the sort of investment her mother liked to get. Rachel wanted to see it again, scarcely believing the casual way in which her mother had brought it back from Moscow in her hand luggage. This was not a package for couriers to be trusted with, the risk of breakage being far greater than the risk of theft or discovery. It was only seven o'clock and she knew her mother would not be back that evening and, furthermore, that she herself had to be ready in a couple of hours for the arrival of the two American gangsters who had been due to land that afternoon. This island of peace and quiet was the ideal time to touch again her mother's delicate secret purchase. Friday night the sixteenth of August was a warm, windy evening. Rachel now had help in the upstairs bars and she had fully trained two part time barmen to stand in with her or for her on the karaoke nights. Will ran the karaoke upstairs and Pascal did the downstairs bars. These bars were normally pretty quiet once the karaoke had started up. So by 7.30 Rachel felt a little trip downstairs to the strong room might be managed for half an hour or so. She let Pascal know that she would be downstairs and was not to be contacted. She then walked carefully down the rough staircase to the pub cellar. Below that were a further four floors deep underground, the deepest of all being the impregnable strong room in the fourth cellar basement. It was easiest accessible from the secondary lifts to be found in the pub basement. There were two of these: one formed part of the main lift shaft that ran from the ground floor bar. The second was concealed in one of the many cupboards in the pub cellar and it was to this that Rachel swiftly moved, opening the door with a charm from the bracelet on her right hand. She summoned the electronic lift, locked the door behind herself then dropped down a further four floors in it. Getting out of the enclosure on the fourth floor required not only use of another charm on the bracelet but an electronic keypad into which Rachel tapped her access code. The lower door opened and as she entered the sensors switched on the basement lights.

The strong room was the most heavily fortified part of the Black Horse and was rarely visited, even by Maddie and Rachel. No one else apart from supervised technicians had ever been there, not since Grace's death. Three further doors had to be opened before the central area could be reached. The first was opened by the combined use of another charm from the bracelet and an iris scan of Rachel's eyes. The second door was opened with an electronic code whilst the third was simply a delaying mechanism, which protected the visitor from a too-sudden entry into the central core. The third sequence of doors was glass and would not open for ten minutes, until oxygen had been put back behind them so that the visitor could breathe. Inside were a metal table and four chairs. On the table lay a desktop calculator, a pad of paper with a pencil on it and an open cardboard box with five or six different jewellers' magnifying pieces in it. Underneath the table, stowed away, were a refractometer and a set of scientific scales.

Rachel ignored these things. She simply wanted to look again at her mother's reward for resolving the gang war in London the previous year. She and Maddie had carefully melted away its outer wax covering in the oven, waiting for the top layer and the bright red paint to drain away. They had not been disappointed with what they found. Rachel pulled down a cardboard box roughly two feet by three feet and six inches deep. It was made of a crude, textured cardboard and advertised itself as containing a child's tea set. The outer packaging had indeed once been used for a child's tea set and Maddie Shallcombe's Russian contacts had repacked her goods, which looked exactly like a child's tea set, straight into it. She had brought it back herself ostensibly as a gift. It had been routinely scanned and was actually opened by the security people on her way through. But what they found was what they expected to find: a bright red plastic tea set made and apparently packaged in China.

Rachel had difficulty in believing that her mother could have found such a treasure. How was it that the Russians could bear to part with it? She reached down for the box and put it on the metal table, sat down herself and expectantly lifted the lid. Inside were five large plates, five small plates and five deep drinking vessels. They were enamelled glaze ware, creamy in colour and on the outside decorated in Arabic. On the inside of each item were figures: not Chinese, not Moslem, not Persian. The figures had Chinese faces, Moslem dress and Persian hairstyles. Rachel slowly shook her head, scarcely believing that she saw before her the faces of Genghis Khan and his four eldest sons.

It was known that the great Khan had died in 1227, in the mountainous region Burkhan Khaldun in Mongolia and contemporary chroniclers recorded that a thousand horsemen had trampled the place of the great Khan's burial so that no one should disturb his grave. In the West it was still believed that the grave had never been found. But this was not so. In 1941, in times as troubled as those that the great Khan himself knew, a part of the treasures were plundered and found their way across the traditional land routes to Samarkand in Uzbekistan. In another time, perhaps in another place, the finding would have been a sensation. Then and there the clouds over the Soviet Union and the terror of Stalin's Russia made the great discovery a cause for great fear. What would the Russian leader do with the treasure? The fearful owners of the hands into which the treasure fell dared not ask. They knew that their leader was a suspicious man, a man with a long memory and a sharp sense of nationality and of his own non-Russian identity. He would certainly know, for the memory had never died amongst the survivors or their families: in 1236, according to the curator of the museum in Samarkand, the Mongols had conquered Georgia and had its inhabitants put to the sword. The entire region had been devastated, no prisoners being taken. Stalin, the greatest power in that war-torn time, the controller of all the Republics, was a Georgian. The perpetual problem of the Russian territories was which direction to face. For so long as Russia ruled the USSR, the pride of the eastern regions in the Great Mongol Empire could never be expressed openly. But no non-Russian state would tolerate the destruction of its own eastern heritage. It had been an appalling dilemma. In the end the directors of the Samarkand museum had placed the first few items to be found into anonymous storage and ordered word to be sent back that the grave itself should be covered and forgotten. For decades the secret of the museum had been passed by word of mouth from deputy director to deputy, bypassing the upper layers of centrally imposed Russian directors.

Modern Uzbekistan was a poor country, faction-ridden and insecure. The new rulers were not Asiatic and felt neither the desire for revenge on the Mongols nor any pride in their conquests. Twenty-five million US dollars was a welcome exchange, even less commission from middlemen, for an unmarked box in a forgotten part of a semi-closed museum. What Rachel held in her left hand, and examined closely with the jeweller's glass in her right, was none other than Genghis Khan's personal drinking vessel, inscribed with his name and bearing his own portrait. It had been executed by Persian craftsmen in a figurative style almost completely suppressed by the later influence of Islam. A few isolated pieces in this style survived in a tiny handful of places, but none with an identifiable origin or provenance. Rachel glanced at the square of paper packed with the treasure: she could not read the foreign hand but she knew enough to recognise that it contained a sketch of a map. Her mother had bought knowledge and not just physical objects. The great Khan had few earthly goods, despite ruling virtually the whole of the world he knew. He had many wives and horses but no fixed abode. He was famous for wearing simple clothes and eating simple food. The carpets in his rough tent were made of wool, not silk. He wore no jewellery, only his tested and beaten armour. The only possession that he valued and personally ordered to be buried with him was here, in the box, in the strong room, in the possession of Maddie Shallcombe. Unique. Beyond priceless. Powerful men sold their souls to possess objects like this. Rachel turned the cup carefully in her hand. It had survived for over seven hundred years, crossing from one continent to another. No one had cherished these artefacts since their original, terrible, owner had died. Rachel looked into the painted face of the Khan and into the face of each of his sons, the destroyers of their time, the scourges of all nations, dreaded by all. The world had changed: men with the temperament of Genghis Khan rarely surfaced as political leaders anymore. Yet in the dark world of crime they were everywhere. They dealt in surprise, in wealth, in death. Their stage had shrunk to the margins and the shadows but they too survived as a type. She fingered one of the plates and again examined it using the jeweller's glass. After twenty minutes or so she decided it was time to go back. It would be an easy matter, if ever it became necessary to leave in a hurry, to re-coat these delicate items in wax and paint them over again. They were lightweight, portable and obviously genuine. And the information on the piece of paper was in itself sufficient to buy the clemency or favour of any government in the world. There were many things that Rachel still needed to learn and top of list was her mother's skill for investment.

Returning to the upstairs bar put Rachel in a sombre frame of mind. She knew that maybe an hour's journey away the armoured stretch white limousine was heading over. It would park on the outskirts of the village and its occupants be transferred into Mrs Shallcombe's vehicle and driven by Little Mickey back to the Black Horse. She was not looking forward to it but she knew the Wings had sealed the village against outsiders. The apartments in the cellars had been prepared for Santini and Papadopolous but she was alert to trouble and respected her mother's decision to stay out of the way for twenty-four hours whilst they settled in. They had been forced, unwillingly, into each other's company and required to leave behind them all the security that normally made their lives predictable and as safe as they could be.

Papadopolous was known to be Greek through and through. He had appeared, quite suddenly, twenty years ago in Cincinnati, Ohio, moving rapidly to take over a dozen legitimate businesses in Cleveland, together with a number of not so legitimate businesses both in Cleveland and latterly in Chicago. His wife had been American Irish; a woman cut off from the rest of her family, driven out by an alcoholic mother and older brother. By all accounts, George Papadopolous was in the way of significant business before his wife had been shot dead four years ago in the abortive attempt to kill him. Since that time, using his Irish contacts as much as his Greek ones, he had forced his way into the already crowded but very lucrative Chicago scene and survived over fifteen months of warfare against Santini and his crew. All Rachel knew about him was exemplified by what she had seen in his daughter Anna – harsh, calculating, highly intelligent, smooth and cruel.

Rachel wondered idly what on earth Santini and Papadopolous would say to each other in the back of the limousine. Would they say anything at all? She guessed that they would listen to the music on the tape and try to sleep. With the rear shutters down she knew that nothing could be seen of the countryside and Harold Crane was not a man given to chatting with his passengers. Cornwallis Jones was detailed to ride shotgun in the front and without doubt they would have been driving very warily, at a legal speed, all the way from Heathrow. Half a dozen motorcycles cleared the way ahead and rode discreetly with them for protection but no one would breathe easy until the cavalcade arrived in Waterton, which had been fortified and isolated for the purpose. She knew Papadopolous had put a huge price on Santini's head and it was always possible a stray bounty hunter would try to take him even though there was an official ceasefire between the gangs.

She felt less curious about Santini: the profile details her mother had received fitted pretty much with a dozen other gangsters she had already met. Maybe Santini was as important in the great scheme of things as he thought he was but his temperament and background were of a familiar type. He was Italian American, poor Italian American, and had barged his way up the rackets in Detroit and later Chicago. What made him different from the others, if anything did, was his willingness to plan his moves rather than simply respond to the ebb and flow of honour quarrels and turf wars within the gangster world. That, and the fact that he had invested for his future by training rather than importing key skilled staff. Bernstein, who Rachel had enjoyed meeting, was one of a half dozen loyal and skilled backroom boys educated at Santini's cost to help him grow his empire.

Desperation was what drove men like Santini and Papadopolous to the services of an Angel. To pay what they had to pay, up front as they had, was a sure sign that the war had ground itself to a standstill. It was not her mother's practice to keep Rachel fully informed of her detailed plans for resolving individual cases. Rachel's part was at this point a simple one. She was to help, as directed, and learn whatever she could. Everything was ready. Little Mickey was to bring the visitors through the main entranceway into the little room and she would take them down personally to their apartments. They had been told to bring no luggage of any description. The seconds in command had already been and stipulated what clothes and shoe sizes should be provided for. Rachel had prepared the 'English' wardrobes these men would need to blend into the background and personally acquired the toiletries that they each liked to have with them. The spacious underground apartments had fresh sheets and fresh flowers laid in them. She wondered whether either of them would notice the care that had gone into making them feel at home.

They each had satellite TV and their own supplies of cold beer and ice cream and other American delicacies. Best of all, it seemed to Rachel, if they chose to close the apartment door, it would withstand any kind of weaponry, including mortar fire. Only she and her mother could open those doors from the outside, using the latest personalised technology. So long as they stayed within these apartments, each of them was safe, but coming to England was not about safety or staying alone. The patience of the South Americans was running out, had almost run out, and both Papadopolous and Santini were in deep trouble.

Chapter 17: Lying low

Arthur Smollett, who was a big man, was trying to make himself very small. If possible he would have liked to have disappeared entirely, but it wasn't. He sat, pretending he was somewhere else altogether, on a small stool with his right foot resting upon a purple upholstered footstool. The footstool itself rested upon a deep pink carpet that bore the repeated pattern of tiny gold lions rampaging across it. The room could only be described politely as intimate. Fortunately pink, purple and white striped curtains obscured the interior from the outside shop front. Three other customers were browsing the indoor display along the left hand wall of the shop and Smollett had turned his stool away from them so that, hopefully, he would not be recognised. At first the other customers showed no interest in him whatsoever. One of them, a statuesque figure in a gold beehive wig and wearing powder blue skinny ribbed sweater and powder blue leather slacks was running her fingers across an open-toed high-heeled sandal on display that had straps made of what looked like dark brown fur. The second customer, a very fat lady in a beige overcoat was encouraging the first customer to look at a pair of yellow stilettos in fake crocodile skin with an eye-catching diamante buckle on the front. The first customer appeared to be indecisive and the two of them were giggling quietly in the corner. The third customer was wandering up and down viewing the entire set of racks, making Arthur Smollett increasingly nervous as she moved up towards him.

'Ooh!! I haven't seen you here before. Lovely place, isn't it?'

Smollett pretended not to hear, but it was no use. This customer was a lady of indeterminate age somewhere between forty and sixty who might easily have completed a career as a successful Sumo wrestler. By her own standards she was conservatively dressed in a low cut dark green calf length cocktail frock. She picked up a size fourteen shoe of a design that made Smollett cringe and thrust it under his nose.

'What do you think of this one?' The woman caressed the heel and arched her back. Controlling his urge to bolt for the door and give himself up to the authorities, Smollett glanced surreptitiously again at the object she was carrying. It was a beautifully crafted shoe, black with silver stitched stars on the front and a crystal, perfectly cut, inserted into the shaft of the heel. But the design was such as to throw the entire weight of the wearer upon the big toe, and the spike at the end of the heel looked positively lethal. Smollett could not imagine anybody wearing such an item, at least not to walk in.

'I have a wonderful collection of these. But of course I only show it to my friends.' The lady then pulled out from beneath the shelf racks on the other side of the room a sturdy looking stool and drew it up to Smollett. He began to panic and reached inside the pocket of the overcoat he was wearing to fish out Rhiannon Thornhill's handkerchief. He felt that an extensive nose blowing session might deter further conversation.

'Hay fever, hay fever,' Smollett muttered, trying to turn himself away from his companion.

'Oohh!! What an awful affliction it is. I used to have it years ago but I started to eat honey. It's very effective but you need to do it all year round. Have you ever used honey for anything else?' The lady then nudged her generous backside suggestively into Smollett's generous but not quite so large backside sitting on the adjoining stool. He dared not turn round.

'Shy, aren't we?' The woman then, using both giant hands, fished deep into her cleavage and pulled out a slightly warm business card. 'I'm Anastasia but you can call me Nasty.' She simpered coyly and slipped the card between Smollett's frozen fingers and squeezed his knee. Her companions were ready to go.

'You hoo! Hallo there!' They cooed noisily.

'I have to go now, but you can always give me a ring.' So saying, Madame Seraglio swept off.

The shop bell tinkled as the three of them left.

Where in God's name was Rhiannon? It was bad enough that the only way to get out of the house and have any fresh air was to wear her maternity clothes but this was intolerable. He realised, of course, that he needed women's shoes to match his disguise. He also realised that she was right in saying no normal shop would sell women's shoes in size twelve. What could she possibly be doing down there for this length of time? He did not so much mind putting on the wig or the fortified bra but he very much minded the low character of the shopping establishment in which he was now sitting. Rhiannon had gone downstairs with the proprietress in order to inspect the less exciting stock, which was kept out of sight. He soon worked out that most of the customers were only interested in evening and party wear but there was an entirely different, rather more modest, stock downstairs. Smollett would in other circumstances, if only to get out of a lone appearance in the upstairs shop, have gone downstairs with the other two. But the downstairs steps looked uncomfortably steep and the proprietress of the establishment had taken to stroking his hand to calm his nerves. Goodness only knows what she would do if Smollett were to stumble on the steps. Staying upstairs had seemed like the lesser of two evils, until he encountered the brazen friendliness of the customers. Couldn't these people keep their hands to themselves for goodness sake? He had begun to wonder if he had made the right decision in leaving it to Rhiannon to investigate the less exciting possibilities in the footwear department, assuming that she would be gone only a few minutes. What he had reckoned without was the inordinate time it took to make such a delicate purchase.

Smollett had never gone shoe shopping with Joyce. He had never needed to. He had three excellent pairs of Church's shoes, two black and one brown, which he had purchased twenty-five years ago in London and had re-soled from time to time as need be. His feet, being large, were therefore never the subject of his wife's improvement schemes, which over the years had transformed his appearance from trendy student to up and coming professional and finally to would-be country gent. Like a number of men of his generation he was to all intents and purposes clothes-blind, a condition similar to being colour blind but apt to produce more unpredictable results when the sufferer made his own choices about what to wear. In his own environment he had never seen any reason to throw out or change items of clothing just because they had reached the falling apart level of comfort. What did it matter? Only his family ever saw him at the weekend. It therefore came as a not very welcome revelation that the choice of a person's clothing could act as a bold beacon of invitation for Madame Seraglio and others similarly inclined.

How he missed his home and wife and children. He longed to catch a glimpse of them but had resolved to be guided by Rhiannon in this matter completely. Quite how he could not say, but she knew what she was doing and every day she reiterated that he was not to contact his family. She promised most faithfully that she would keep an eye on them herself and so he got occasional reports of what Joyce was doing and, because Joyce was very chatty, of what the children were up to. In a sort of a way part of him was glad that Joyce did not know what had become of him right that very minute. Profound changes were going on in Arthur Smollett's approach to life and he did not really know what to make of it. One thing that surprised him was how difficult it was to remain indoors and do nothing. Smollett's normal weekends were, when he was not working, pretty idle. He had never seen much point in doing things around the house and never previously noticed what needed doing anyway. But in Rhiannon's home it was different. Rhiannon had told Kathleen Thornhill not to come round to do the housework anymore as she had found a new housekeeper, i.e. Arthur Smollett, who had not yet been introduced to anybody and who had not yet chosen a name for his new identity. However, he was doing the housework in a very real sense. He did everything that a housekeeper would normally do – hoovering, cooking, dusting, washing the clothes, ironing, tidying, polishing silver, waxing furniture, changing the baby, watering the plants and generally making himself indispensable about the home. He had had a lot to learn. For example, using the vacuum cleaner was much more complicated that he had ever suspected, if you wanted reasonable results, that is. And cooking for Rhiannon was also not very easy: she was herself an experienced cook and was determined not to put up with the spaghetti bolognaise that for years had sustained Smollett before he had met Joyce. He also learned, to his surprise, that Rhiannon was not sick to the boots whenever Neville emptied his bowels into a nappy. The struggle with his guts that ensued every time he had to clean Neville up was evidently something that Neville's mother did not experience. But on the other hand she was not inclined to put Smollett out of his misery either. As she rightly said, stowaways had to earn their passage. And Smollett would have had it no other way. After all, he was not a beggar, more a refugee.

Sometimes he imagined how life would have been had he not had a cat, or at least not had a cat stupid enough to get caught by whatever maniac had pumped it full of heroin and dumped it in Waterton. The whole affair was completely mysterious to him. He was also horrified to discover that, once he had been apprehended, no further dead animal incidents occurred. This he simply could not account for and he was most concerned that Joyce might put two and two together and make five, allocating to him responsibility for the plague of dead cats. Only a year ago life had seemed so smooth and predictable. He remembered how in August last year he had sat down with his financial adviser and planned an orderly progress towards his retirement at the age of sixty. How easy it had all seemed: regular contributions, gradual build up of interest, the purchase of an annuity and sensible provision for school and university fees for the children. He was beginning to feel maudlin.

A brief smile flitted across his face as he remembered the day after when the pensions adviser had ill advisedly volunteered to participate in the annual village football match. Arthur supposed that Reggie Redman thought he would encourage a bit of publicity for his services or somehow inspire his clients with confidence. But it had been a ghastly error. Obviously Redman's office in Abbots Stukeley knew nothing about the nature of village football or its customary levels of physical commitment. The game had only two rules. First, it was not permitted to strike any player until he had touched the ball. Second, the game was only over when somebody scored. These rules made for simplicity but also for unparalleled levels of violence. The contest was the perfect vehicle for settling old scores and new annoyances because there was no rule requiring anyone to stop hitting a player even after the ball was elsewhere. The only thing that mattered was that nobody should score. Normally the local hospital had two or three teams on duty during the match. Last year it had been won by Little Waterton after a two-hour scrum resulting in six people being hospitalised and eight others treated for injury. Waterton would no doubt be thirsting for revenge this year and Smollett deeply regretted that he would not be there to defend the honour of Little Waterton. He wondered which of his partners would be on the pitch this year and whether Joyce would succeed in talking any volunteers out of it. The teams were unlimited in number and both men and women could play. But no one over the age of sixty was allowed on the pitch as in the 1990's several veteran players had dropped dead shortly after the game was concluded. The game was invariably refereed by Lord Errington who was notoriously lenient: in forty years he had been recorded as intervening only once, on an occasion when Grace Shallcombe, sitting astride the fallen figure of a defaulting customer, had twisted her belt around his throat to the point where his face had gone completely purple. Smollett had always been a keen rugger player but the village football match was the most exciting game he could ever imagine. Joyce, needless to say, was very unhappy at his enthusiastic participation but she had to admit that two or three farmers who had not responded to written requests for payment paid up promptly shortly after the game each year. So deep in his reminiscences was Smollett that he perceptibly jumped when Rhiannon and the proprietress reappeared at the top of the stairs.

Rhiannon was carrying five shoes, all for the right foot.

'Try these, Mrs S,' the owner said.

'How are you, dearie? I do hope that you haven't been lonely up here?' Rhiannon was grinning from ear to ear, knowing perfectly well from the creaking of the floorboards that could be heard from below that several customers had been in, and she had a pretty fair idea what they would have made of Smollett's disguise.

Smollett gritted his teeth. He folded his arms and stuck out his right foot petulantly, saying nothing. Rhiannon was responsible for everything at this point. It was her bright idea to put him in a brown wig that she had bought from the hairdresser and her idea to make up his jowled face with dark red lipstick. He was not in a very good mood.

'Poor old Mrs S, I think she's still too upset to speak. Terrible shock it is when your health goes suddenly like that.' Arthur Smollett had no idea what this woman was talking about but he assumed that Rhiannon had told her some cock and bull story.

'Not bad, not bad.' Rhiannon had slipped onto his foot a plain black walking shoe with a half-inch heel. He did not look at it but stared determinedly at his knees.

'I think we should try this one as well.' Rhiannon then tried a different shoe on his foot. This time it was a ladies' brown suede tie-up shoe with a half inch squared heel. 'Oh yes, much better.'

The proprietress was nodding vigorously. 'I'll just go and get the other one. Very comfortable shoes, these. All leather, handmade in Italy. Just a minute.'

She disappeared again down the steps. Rhiannon could not help smirking just a little.

'Seen anything else you like?'

Smollett scowled. Seconds later the proprietress reappeared.

'Here we are, just the thing. Very good price on these, you know. Such a comfy shoe, you'll never want to take them off.'

Smollett suffered Rhiannon to put on the left shoe.

'Well, walk about a bit.' Rhiannon was still grinning, but tried to concentrate her grin on Smollett's feet. He marched heel-first very uncomfortably up to the mirror and back again. His knees hurt. How on earth did women walk in heeled shoes? These ones barely had any heel and yet they were impossible. Rhiannon would have to carry him back to the car unless he was allowed to put on Joshua's gardening shoes back on.

'Great. We'll take them.'

'Very good choice, if I may say so. But you may find that you need other shoes, for social occasions. We have some very nice shoes in this size, very unusual. Would you like me to show you our party range?'

Rhiannon was quite tempted to say yes but knew this would be going too far.

'No thanks, not right now. I expect we'll be back another day.'

'Would you like to wear them now or shall I pack them in a box?'

'I'll take the box with the old shoes and my friend will wear the new ones now.'

The proprietress smiled brightly and bounced over to the front cash desk to pack up the old shoes before Rhiannon came over to pay for the new ones. Rhiannon leaned in close to Smollett and said, under her breath, 'Keep your knees straight when you walk.'

'I can't!' Smollett hissed.

'Sure you can. Walk from the hips.'

'What?? Never!!'

'Is everything alright?' The proprietress came over to see whether her customers were having second thoughts.

'Everything's just fine. I was just saying we don't have time right now to look at the party range. My friend was a little disappointed.'

Smollett made a mental note to get his revenge for this. The proprietress came over to sit on Smollett's other side. She stroked his arm solicitously and whispered into his ear, 'don't worry; there's plenty of time for everything. Next time you come you can try everything in the shop if you like.'

'It's such a shame we have to go. It's been a real pleasure to meet you. Can I pay with Visa?'

'However you like, is fine for us.'

Rhiannon stood up and drew the owner back over to the desk and away from the horrified Smollett.

To his great relief, ten minutes later Arthur Smollett was walking, toe-first from the hips, rapidly away from the shop in Abbots Stukeley and heading for Rhiannon's car. They needed to get back anyway. Rhiannon had promised to pick up Neville in twenty minutes time. Saturday shopping was always such a rush.

*

'More bacon, Mr Santini?'

Maddie Shallcombe was standing at the table of the pub cellar kitchen ready to ladle out seconds to her guests. Seated around the table were the two Michaels, Paul Santini and George Papadopolous. Rachel was upstairs in the pub, polishing glasses. It must have been ten o'clock and breakfast had been in full swing for over half an hour. Maddie had herself eaten at seven o'clock that morning but she believed in a hearty breakfast on Sundays for all her guests and the Americans, to their astonishment, found that the smell of the bacon reminded them forcibly of just how hungry they were. This was their second morning in the UK, wherever exactly they might be in it. So far neither of them had been contacted by the Angel and they were both, separately, puzzled. They had hardly spoken to each other although it must be said that the ice had been broken the previous evening when, having spent much of the day asleep on Mrs Shallcombe's recommendation after their first hearty breakfast, they had decided there was not much else to do but go upstairs for a drink, quietly, on Saturday evening. It seemed rather stupid to sit at separate tables so they had sat in the corner opposite the two Michaels and taken out a second chess set. Neither had played particularly well but they had at least exchanged a few words. It was an eerie sensation: no bodyguards, no word from the Angel and no weaponry anywhere. The previous day when Santini had asked Mrs Shallcombe when they would be meeting the Angel, she had replied that she doubted whether there would be any business appointments until everybody had recovered from their jet lag. Santini had not felt like arguing about it. He was, quite truthfully, exhausted. In the two nights before setting off for London he had not slept at all: neither had he slept on the plane or on the interminable journey from Heathrow to wherever he was. Papadopolous was in much the same position, he assumed, as the latter had not insisted on speaking with the Angel either. Or perhaps it was simply pride that he had not wished to be the one to kick up a fuss. Was this some form of psychological warfare? Surely they could not have been taken for a ride, not after so many careful enquiries had been made. Who knows?

'Yes, thank you.' Santini held out his plate for some bacon. Papadopolous was sat quietly drinking coffee and looking thoughtfully round the kitchen area. It was a big kitchen with an old-style grate and a sizeable Aga cooker running across the side of the room. The two Michaels were on very good form and had been telling amusing stories between them for about ten minutes. Mrs Shallcombe had interrupted Michael Riley.

'Well now, as I was saying, the last we heard he went down the hole with the drill to dig up the cable. But, you know, he musta cut through it somehow cos Little Mickey here tells me his friend Patrick saw your man thrown clear outa the hole by the force of the power. Then, they say, he jumped back in shouting 'I'll get you, you bastard!' Course, it killed him.'

The other Michael, who had heard this story innumerable times, laughed uproariously. The two Americans, just about able to follow it, smiled.

'Tell me,' said Santini, 'What do you gentlemen do for a living?'

'Oh, this and that,' replied Michael O'Dare. 'We help about the place and Maddie here keeps us busy, you know.'

'Oh yes, it's not a bad life,' the other Michael agreed.

Santini was no wiser but decided not to pursue it. Papadopolous was sitting with his legs crossed and one elbow on the table. He looked considerably more relaxed than he had the previous day and with one hand was twirling the miniature moustache that he sported.

'Good food, very good food,' said Papadopolous slowly. He spoke with a thick Greek accent and looked very un-English despite Mrs Shallcombe's choice of tweed trousers and brown jacket for him. Possibly this was because of the two gold teeth which replaced his natural canines. They flashed every time he opened his mouth. Little Mickey was studying Papadopolous' face out of the corner of his eye.

'You like my teeth, eh? Ha! Where I come from, in Thessaloniki, every man has these teeth when he is twenty-one. Gift from his family. Left tooth, gift from his father's family. Right tooth, gift from his mother's family. If you fall on hard times, you sell left tooth to pay for wedding and when you die you sell right tooth to pay for funeral.' He grimaced. 'I married but I keep both teeth. Cost of living United States very high. Maybe I need both teeth when I die.'

Neither Michael could see that this was a joke but Santini obviously found it very funny. Mrs Shallcombe meanwhile was tidying up the cooker and opened the dishwasher in the corner by the sink. She returned to the table with a third pot of tea and a cafetiere of fresh coffee for Papadopolous.

'Well, gentlemen, are we all happy? Mickey, would it be possible for you to check if Rachel needs anything doing?' Little Mickey instantly went upstairs.

' I'll be getting ready for this afternoon, Maddie, if I may.' Michael Riley withdrew, sensing that Mrs Shallcombe wished to have a word alone with her guests.

'Well, now, I suggest when you've both had enough to eat, you might like to go upstairs to the little room. Rachel will show you where it is. We'll have the Sunday papers there and you might like to read them. I'll bring up some tea in an hour or so.'

Santini looked at Papadopolous and it was clear that they were both very puzzled.

'What do you mean?' Santini asked.

'Well, it is usual for people to read the Sunday papers on a Sunday morning. It normally takes all morning, you know. Of course, you don't have to. You are free to do whatever you like. My house is at your disposal.'

Santini still looked as though he had not yet had a satisfactory answer. Papadopolous finally said something.

'Good. I read papers. And wait.' He picked up his coffee cup went up the steps.

'I guess I do the same.' Santini followed him upstairs.

Mrs Shallcombe watched them go, then picked up the plates and packed them in the dishwasher.

Neither of her visitors knew how far Waterton had been cut off by the Wings from the outside world. On a Sunday, the situation was not so obvious and in any case her guests had not set foot outdoors as yet. Waterton was now so isolated from Little Waterton that the two villages might as well have been on different continents. Unusually, it might be thought, diversion signs had been placed all the way round Waterton with borrowed police bollards. Several of the roads had been marked and cordoned off for road digging on the Monday morning and; mysteriously since there was no storm, all the telephone lines serving the village had gone down. Satellite TV was still operative but moving out of Waterton other than on a bicycle or by foot had become quite impossible. There were only two ways out of the village on foot and one bridle way. The entire length of the bridle way and the common over which it passed was surveyed and in the case of the common occupied by an intimidating group of Romany gypsies. They were a terrifying crew in almost thirty caravans, some horse drawn and others vehicle-drawn. The gypsies had unmuzzled, vicious-looking dogs that wandered about freely in packs, and no walker or cyclist would try their luck in passing by. This left the road access. A temporary police hut had been placed at three separate points along the road into Waterton and each was manned by a pair of men claiming to be plain-clothes policemen. They took it upon themselves to stop anybody who was not known to them as resident in Waterton or Little Waterton from going into Waterton during the whole of Saturday and Sunday. They claimed that there was a serious viral infection in the village and that it would be better if people did not go in.This level of fuss was sufficient to dissuade everybody from even trying. The irrepressible Howard Morgan, who firmly intended to return to Waterton that week for the purpose of assaulting Freddie Pinker, decided to wait until the football match scheduled for the Monday that week before trying to get in. He had not forgotten the warning he had received from Mrs Shallcombe and was of the view that only the chaos and excitement of the game could possibly cover his entry into the village. Once the game had started, he knew that everyone within shouting distance would be swept up by the noisy confusion and buffeted by the crowd. He also knew that the chances were high that the people he needed to avoid would be busy during the game. So he put his illegal metal knuckledusters in his pocket and bided his time in the coffin.

Three o'clock saw Mrs Shallcombe and her two guests pulling up to the entrance of Blue Grace farmhouse in her car, driven by Little Mickey with Michael Riley in the passenger seat. They parked quite close to the house, and in the paddock by it a magnificent black racehorse was being led around on reins by Rhiannon Thornhill. She was expecting her visitors for tea and knew full well what Mrs

Shallcombe intended. It was a horse to excite the imagination of any race-goer. Santini and Papadopolous were both students of the art of racing and loved the sight of the magnificent creature they glimpsed through the window. They could see that the woman handling it was expert. They could not see her face.

'Do come out and say hello. I'm sure Rhiannon would like you to have a closer look at Bananas. It's a long time since we've seen such a promising animal in this country.' Mrs Shallcombe was unusually cheerful.

The two Michaels got out and each opened a door on the opposite side of the car, allowing the passengers to get out. Mrs Shallcombe got out on the side closest to Rhiannon, together with Papadopolous.

'Shall we say hello then?' She started to walk towards Rhiannon, whose back was still turned.

Mrs Shallcombe's American guests decided, after brief hesitation, to follow her. There appeared to be no one around and, to their quiet amazement, there did not seem to be any security problems. As they approached the railing dividing the paddock from the road, Rhiannon turned round to greet them. They both stopped dead in their tracks and looked at each other. Santini was wide-eyed.

'Excuse me. Did you say this lady's name was Rhiannon?' Santini whispered to Mrs Shallcombe.

'That's right, Rhiannon. Of course, she chose the name herself once she'd settled down here.'

'Is Rhiannon English?' Papadopolous asked, cautiously.

'No, American. I believe her family live in New York.'

The effect of this statement upon the two men was electrifying. Papadopolous drew in breath through his teeth. Santini screwed up his eyes and stared at Rhiannon. They each had seen her face, younger, thinner, two years ago when agents had scoured every major city in the eastern United States looking for her. They had both been visited by high-ranking members of the Nazzura organisation enquiring, not very politely, whether anybody had seen the lady in the photo or done anything to her. But the enquiries were not known to have produced any result. In the end even the boys on the West Coast were looking too. Then, all of a sudden, the search ended.

'I know this face,' said Papadopolous almost under his breath to Santini.

Santini nodded. 'This information can save a man's life.'

'Yes.' Papadopolous replied. 'Jennifer Angelina Nazzura.'

It was their first conversation.

Chapter 18: Anticipation

Not everyone that Sunday morning had been sat reading the newspapers until lunchtime. Billy Thornhill, for instance, had been up early visiting his mother's fresh grave. She had been laid to rest in the eastern corner of the back graveyard of St. George's Church in Waterton. Mrs. Lightfoot had been very kind to everyone and the funeral proceeded without delay. The family doctor had certified that death was expected so there was no need for an inquest. Although he had never been particularly close to his mother, he was understandably sad at her passing and he blamed his father in no uncertain terms as the cause of her incessant drinking.

He had never known his mother without a glass in her hand or, latterly, a mug. As a small boy he had played hide and seek around her feet when she had fallen asleep with her head on the kitchen table. It was following such an incident, when he had been discovered by Joshua Thornhill, that the decision was taken to let his Aunt Kathleen take the primary responsibility for making sure that he got up and went to school in the morning. As he grew older, more and more of the normal contact between child and parent was diverted into other channels for administration. But all the same, he missed her. Her death had made him realise for the first time how few ties he had to his old home and the world of the Blue Grace Farm that had once seemed to be a universe. Perhaps because he felt as guilty as he did, Billy gradually learned to hate his father. Robert Thornhill had done nothing directly to provoke this state of affairs but had spent very little time with his son. When the boy had been young, he was always working and the discipline he administered, when he thought it required, was of a harsh and old-fashioned kind: Billy would never forget the time he was slow in giving his father a copy of the newspaper that he had wanted to read himself- Robert had soaked the nine year-old boy, who was stood in the garden at the time, with a stream of ice-cold water from the garden hose. In the summer holidays when Billy came back from boarding school, he found his irritable father at the busiest time of the farming year. Robert would frequently be up before six and rarely appeared home much before nine. He was not a man that had any particular interest in his son's stories of public school and he left Kathleen to deal with the boy until it was his bedtime.

Since his mother's death Billy had not exchanged a single word with his father and had taken care not to be in a situation where it was necessary. Part of his meditation this very morning was to try and think of his mother without remembering the state he had last seen her in before her death. How could he ever forgive himself for believing her to have gone to bed that day, without checking? Billy placed a small bouquet of red and pink roses on her grave and wandered to the front of the church to sit in peace and quiet. Why wasn't his father here? Had he ever bothered to see the grave once the service was over? Did he even care? Kathleen had sorted things out with Mrs Lightfoot and tried to put together a ceremony that managed to avoid all reference to the horror of the life his mother had led. Billy focussed on the flowers nearest to him and detected that things didn't look quite right. The Reverend Hollis was still away somewhere or other and in his absence the gardener was taking it easy. The grass along the path to the little church was starting to get overgrown and there were a few pieces of litter that had blown through the church gate into the front garden. This sort of thing annoyed Billy, as it did his father. He picked up some discarded sweet wrappers and put them in the litterbin by the gate. It was time to go.

By 10.30am he was stood outside the upstairs library at Hamset Manor waiting to be announced to Lord Errington. He had no idea what was in store and certainly had not the faintest clue that for the last month Lord Errington had spent his time with a powerful pair of binoculars watching Billy and his granddaughter from the battlements on the roof. Dancer knocked on the library door.

'Mr. William Thornhill, your Lordship.'

Dancer gave a creaky half-bow and withdrew, leaving Billy on the far side of the library that spanned the full length of the first floor. The room incorporated a section of what had been an Elizabethan dancing hall but the present structure had been created in the late eighteenth century by amalgamating two adjoining rooms and remodelling the whole to let light and space into the upper floor. To Billy's right were surviving Jacobean windows matching those on the floor below but further into the room were plain floor-to-ceiling Georgian windows that the fourth Lord Errington had furnished with curtains on swinging brasses so that smaller rooms could be created by moving the curtain rods. Behind, on the far opposite side of the room was a galleried bookshelved area with a panelled workspace and desk beneath it. This morning Lord Errington had placed the curtain around the middle window so as to create one of his favourite little rooms. He stepped out and beckoned to Billy.

'Billy, come in, won't you?'

Billy walked uncertainly to Lord Errington. The old man appeared to be particularly animated that morning.

'Take a seat, take a seat.'

Billy walked around the side of the curtain to join Lord Errington in the alcove and sat down on one of the yellow-upholstered heavy chairs. Lord Errington sat down opposite him.

'Just a minute, young man. Need to get this adjusted. Want to hear what you've got to say.' Lord Errington began to fiddle about with his hearing aid, now and again tapping his finger on the chair arm to test whether the machine was working properly. The old man looked up and fixed him with a disconcertingly penetrating stare.

'Corky.'

'I beg your pardon, your Lordship.'

'Call me Corky.'

'Er, yes. Thank you.' More fiddling with the equipment ensued. Billy coughed uncomfortably.

'Ahh. Hear you perfectly.'

Underneath the window a large piece of parchment lay rolled up and in front of it a slender fake-Japanese wood table stood between Errington and Billy Thornhill. Billy glanced out of the window and wondered what Sophie was up to. He had hoped to see her but there was no sign of her at all. How ironic that the one person he always wanted to be with had to live in a mausoleum inhabited by his grandfather's mortal enemy. The feud between the two of them was as traditional as it was fierce. Whatever their individual good qualities, there could be no doubt that they hated the sight of each other and made no bones about it. There were a number of these feuds on the Estate but this was the bitterest, pushed to new depths when his grandfather had managed to cause the death of Sophie's father.

'Very sorry about your mother, Billy. Two funerals in one year, bad show.'

Billy couldn't think of anything to say so he just nodded. Surely Lord Errington hadn't called him in to pay his respects? He had already done what was required by attending Joshua Thornhill's funeral. This again was traditional: no matter how bad their personal relations were, Errington, as owner of the Estate, was obliged to put in an appearance at the funeral of each of his tenants, though it must have been questioned whether there would be another that he would look forward to so much. It was more a case of not giving offence to the immediate family, one member of which was usually the next tenant. Quite often one might rightly have observed on the Estate that if only friends were allowed to attend, no one would be there at all. Billy was beginning to find Lord Errington's unblinking stare too unnerving so he fixed his gaze on the old man's stick.

'Thornhills been on the land for centuries. Same as us.' Errington picked up with his left hand the silver-topped dark wood walking stick that he kept by his chair and with it poked the parchment scroll on the floor. 'Going to need this now.'

Billy got up, manhandled the scroll to an upright position and stood next to Lord Errington expectantly.

'Where would you like it, sir?'

'Corky, Corky.' He tapped the floor impatiently with his stick. 'Unroll it. Over there.'

Errington poked at the curtain separating the alcove from the main room with such energy that Billy decided it was a veiled request to pull the curtain aside to make space, so he did. He next unrolled the parchment. It was easy to do, despite the fact that it was over six foot by five foot long. Wooden handles at either end and brass weights along the top and bottom edges meant it stayed open without difficulty. The great map lay open and flat for inspection. There were numbers of such maps, covering the centuries of Errington control of the Estate. The Estate office had at least forty of them and they were periodically reissued when the changes that had taken place became so marked that a new version was needed. The present Lord Errington had made considerable management changes since his grandfather's stewardship and the version of the plan on the floor in front of Billy was the seventh or eighth to be drawn up by the office in his time. For a moment the old man regarded his handiwork of decades as revealed on the scroll. He scratched his head twice, as though not knowing where to begin. Then he banged his stick on the wooden floor to attract the attention of his listener and began to point at things on the map.

'See that? That's the Manor House. See the green? That's the estate in hand. See the orange there? Those are the let farms. The red, that's industrial land. Twelve thousand acres round here. There's another sixteen thousand in Scotland. We've got a couple of thousand acres up in Newcastle. And a shopping centre.'

Billy knew that the Corshalls had money. But he had assumed that most of it was in the brickworks business and the chemical company which the present Lord Errington's deceased wife, Millicent Toggenburg, had brought in on her marriage. It was well known that the Toggenburgs owned half of the biggest chemical company in Switzerland. He looked in dismay at the map. He had nothing to offer his beloved Sophie. He had spent years acquiring an education only to find that by the time he had graduated there were no easy jobs to find and the professions were so competitive and crowded that he considered himself lucky to have found part-time work in a City bank. He would never be able to compete with the wealthy suitors a girl like Sophie must have. If ever he had wished for money, it was now. What use was it to love her if he was penniless?

Errington began to fumble about in his waistcoat pocket and eventually pulled out a scarlet silk handkerchief. He put it on the table under the window and unfolded it jerkily to reveal a ring. This was no ordinary-looking ring.

'Know what that is, Billy?' Errington put his elbows on his knees and crouched down to look at it glint in the light. Billy looked at it too, but his heart sank with despair. A jewel of this importance belonged in a safe. In the centre of the ring was a flat cut emerald an inch and a half long and half an inch wide. Around it had been set a triple layer of high quality diamonds. The surrounding metal was white and must have been white gold or platinum. He had once or twice admired a similar design of ring, but with a ruby in the middle, on Lady Vivienne's hand. The chances were that the emerald ring was worth more than Billy would earn in twenty years.

'Mother had it reset. Stone in the middle, that's the one that matters. Claremont Emerald.'

Errington waited for the impact of his words to sink in. Billy, of course, knew the story of Lady Claremont Corshall who had been married to the terrifying Sir Placet Corshall. According to the story Sir Placet gave his wife two identical pendant necklaces. Identical, that is, except that each one had a differently coloured central stone. Sir Placet was a man desirous of promotion in the army and insisted that his wife entertain superior officers, to his direction, in the most generous manner possible. On the days when Lady Claremont was deemed to be available she was commanded by her husband to attend supper downstairs wearing the emerald. On all other days, when he required her sexual services himself, she was to wear the ruby pendant. Lady Claremont had been a buxom peasant girl that Sir Placet had selected as his bride with this very idea in mind: no woman of quality would have put up with the demands he made without shooting him herself, as his great aunt had shot his great uncle some ten or so years prior to his own marriage. The lesson was not lost on their young nephew. Sir Placet's had been a brilliant strategy, eventually resulting in Sir Placet, latterly the toast of the regimental officers' mess, being promoted to third or fourth in command under Sir Arthur Wellesley himself. Lady Claremont had ten children, whose portraits hung over part of the first floor staircase. Not one of them bore any physical resemblance to Sir Placet and it troubled him not a jot. They're all legitimate, he was wont to say, and I'll fight any man who says otherwise. The long-suffering Lady Claremont, no doubt having developed an acute empathy with the truly miserable of this world, had built two rows of alms houses in Little Waterton for elderly or sick villagers and she was well remembered to the present day in the Watertons for her efforts to mitigate the cruelty of her husband. Billy had heard the story about the Claremont Emerald and the Claremont Ruby but hadn't realised that the jewels were still in the family and currently in use. He was again unable to think of anything to say.

'I hear you're fond of Sophie.'

A rush of adrenalin went through Billy. Was Lord Errington to stop him visiting? The Corshalls were unpredictable. The present Lord Errington's sister, Constance, had starved herself to death when her own father refused to let her marry Lord Redwall, who at the time was inconveniently married to somebody else. Billy might be a pauper but he had never done anything to be ashamed of and had treated Sophie with the greatest of respect at all times. She was the one who seemed to try to snuggle up to him now and again but fear of the wrath of old Lord Errington was enough to stop the slightest step towards romance. Errington was perfectly capable of taking revenge for his son himself.

'Carlton.' The old man shook his head. 'You've met him?'

'I've seen him but not spoken with him.' Billy was careful what he said. What could anyone say about Carlton?

'Useless. No good at all. He'll not have a penny from me.'

This was getting all rather personal and Billy was keen to get away without hearing anything embarrassing or being prevented from seeing Sophie. He had no idea why he had been called in and he could see serious disadvantages in letting the old man say anything that gave him cause for regret. He was as sharp as a knife: Billy presumed he was working his way towards finding out something about Robert's intentions for the farm, though why he didn't just ask his father directly he couldn't imagine.

'Pick it up, pick it up. Have a look.' The old man gesticulated towards the ring. Billy did as he was told. He held it up towards the window. How beautiful it was. What a pity that Sophie hadn't been an ordinary girl. He sighed and held out the ring to its owner. But Errington was starting to get impatient, as though his listener was particularly obtuse or troublesome. He smacked the floor again with the stick. Billy jumped.

'Me granddaughter. Take the ring to her. Middle of the rose garden, eleven o'clock.' He pulled out his watch, which hung from a chain in his waistcoat pocket. It was five minutes to eleven. Billy frowned. He did not follow. What was all this about? Errington could stand it no longer. It was a long time since he had had this sort of conversation.

'Marry her, damn it.'

Billy sat stunned. What??? Unable to believe his ears, he stood up and shook hands with the old man several times. He could not think of anything at all to say except 'thank you, thank you.'

'Well, go on then. Don't keep the gal waiting. She'll be thinking you don't want her.'

Billy leaped to his feet before the old man could change his mind and walked as quickly as he possibly could in the direction of the rose garden. Seconds later Dancer appeared in the library and made his way over to his master.

'Would your lordship be needing anything?'

'Yes. Thank you. Bring out the Islay.'

Dancer realised that the news must be good for his master to depart from his favourite Burgundy. Lord Errington only drank whisky when he was going to share it with his butler. Minutes later found the two old men sitting opposite each other. Errington was chuckling and rubbing together his bony old hands.

'Is your lordship celebrating?'

'We need an heir, Dancer. But first a marriage. Old Porker can read the banns. Next Sunday.'

By this Dancer understood that arrangements were to be made for His Grace, the Bishop of Ribchester, Lord Errington's second cousin, to announce the intending nuptials the following Sunday.

'Very good, your lordship. Excellent whisky.'

'Bottoms up, Dancer. Let's hope for a boy.'

*

All over the area preparations were being made for the village football match the following day. For the Watertons, the Wakes Week began on the Monday of the football match and ended so as to include the Bank Holiday Monday exactly one week later. The three Watertons all lay within a five- mile radius of one another. Waterton and Little Waterton were closer to each other but Higher Waterton was not far to the east of Little Waterton. Since time immemorial they had all enjoyed the same Wakes Week holiday when all the local businesses closed down and the fun fair came to the big field outside Higher Waterton. Traditionally there was a handicraft market in Little Waterton and the week always began with the children of the Watertons competing in the annual flower queen contest. The winner would be a girl from the local school and she had six smaller girls to be the trainbearers for her. All of the contestants would process, with their trainbearers, along the old field road from Little Waterton into Waterton, where the winner was chosen. The Reverend Hollis, as vicar of Waterton, crowned the winner and the children of the local primary school sang songs around her. All of this took place on the Monday morning but the real highlight of the day was the traditional football match that began at two o'clock prompt on the village green at Waterton.

Relations between Waterton and Little Waterton displayed many manifestations of the intense rivalry one sometimes encounters between close and otherwise confusingly similar organisations. Just as the tension between Spurs and Arsenal or between Manchester City and Manchester United is never fully appreciated by outsiders, so the sporting fixtures of various kinds between Waterton and Little Waterton attracted a spirit of fierce competitiveness at times barely distinguishable from savagery. Village darts matches were serious affairs, pub quizzes could result in fisticuffs and even the whist drives between the Mothers Union from St George's and the Women's Institute in Little Waterton had to be handled carefully lest they disintegrate in mutual accusations of cheating. The sole exception to this generally hostile climate was the flower queen contest. This was unquestionably due to the fact that the only two schools in the area were in Higher Waterton and in consequence the flower queens and their entourages did not divide along village lines because younger sisters of their friends tended to be chosen as their trainbearers by the would-be queens.

The origins of the football match were lost in the mists of time but certain features of it suggested beginnings in a cult of human sacrifice: thus, the severed heads that formed a decorative chain in stone around the twelfth century arch of St George's main entrance were framed by a pair of stone feet at either end and what looked unmistakeably like a knife in the middle of the design. And, possibly, experts might theorise that the flower queen had originally been a powerful female figure supervising the ceremonies. The Erringtons' role in all of this was historically difficult to place. They fulfilled the thankless task of refereeing the game and they owned the old field road and had centuries ago owned all three villages. There were no team colours, as everyone was presumed to know who played for which village and the ball was an odd-shaped leather ball upon which a face appeared, freshly painted before the beginning of each match by the Reverend Hollis. The sheer weight of the ball in wet conditions was such that heading it was out of the question. Contestants might kick it or run with it but to hold it for any length of time was a highly dangerous operation, not least because anything up to thirty team members on either side might tackle. The winning village was entitled to display the ball over the bar of its village pub for the ensuing year and by long tradition, partly in order to medicate the participants, the Shallcombes would open a crate of Special and serve it to anyone who played. The person scoring the goal was entitled to a year's free drinks in both the Green Man in

Little Waterton and the Black Horse in Waterton. For that reason alone the game was played with considerable enthusiasm.

That was not the reason why Howard Morgan intended to play, which he did. The misfortunes that had beset him in recent times he laid entirely at the door of Freddie Pinker. Morgan had become a solitary figure, almost unhinged by his desire for revenge. He was now quite incapable of restraining his annoyance over the slightest thing and resorted to threats of violence almost without provocation. Early efforts at job-hunting were hindered by his fit of rage at the clerical worker who filled in a form on his behalf at the Job Centre with the words 'of no fixed abode', which Morgan took to be insulting. It was not that she minded the foul language (she was well acclimatised to that professional hazard), but when he later returned to the Centre and tried to throw an incensed mastiff dog over the glass partition to attack her, and failed, he had to disappear from the area for several days. Eventually he managed to find a job, through an advert in the paper, as a night watchman for a factory outside Gloucester. During the day he parked the hearse in a lay by somewhere and slept in the coffin. The hearse was fitted with curtains all the way round and the arrangement was more comfortable than might be supposed. Nor did the absence of bathroom facilities trouble him unduly: he shaved in the toilets in the local supermarket car park and found the increasingly pungent aroma of his clothing and person no cause for concern. Luckily for Morgan it was summer time and he was not as yet inconvenienced by the cold. Morgan's plan for the football match was straightforward: he knew that too many people would be there for attention to be caused by his appearance and he planned to park the hearse over in Little Waterton, where Mrs Lightfoot normally kept her fleet, before walking down into Waterton. He would wait until Freddie Pinker touched the ball and then lay into him with all his strength. That afternoon as he lay in the coffin before going to work he imagined with great delight the look of horror then pain on Freddie Pinker's face. If he could kill Pinker outright, so much the better, but if he aimed for the liver or spleen he reckoned the chances of internal bleeding were good enough maybe to do it slowly. That would be much more enjoyable. He indeed enjoyed the vision of it at leisure whenever he was alone.

Others were also planning for the match. This did not include the two Michaels, who would very much liked to have taken part but had been ordered by Mrs Shallcombe to remain off the pitch to keep an eye on Santini and Papadopolous. Eric and Freddie Pinker currently owed them in excess of £30,000 and they felt like issuing a reminder. Spectating at the match was also a hugely popular pastime, despite the risk of the game spilling over the boundary of the village green. The rowdy singing of chants and the hurling of beer bottles, eggs and rotten fruit were regular features of the occasion. This year, as last year, there were signs that Waterton would be difficult to reach except by foot.

The apparently chaotic occasion was in reality heavily controlled by Mrs Shallcombe's Wings and their allies. Harold Crane had mounted an extensive security operation, calling in every favour he was owed. By Sunday evening he knew that there was no risk of armed intruders. He had rented two adjoining rooms in the Merlin Inn in Higher Waterton and was controlling operations from there. Since the arrival of the American visitors he had made no move to contact Mrs Shallcombe and was fully engaged with his own logistical problems. And in distracting the police with a bold series of armed robberies in Bristol upon banks, building societies and fast food stores. A wave of violent crime broke over that unsuspecting city, and Jesmond and his colleagues would certainly not have had the manpower to bother with anticipated disturbances in public order in two small villages so far from their more urgent investigations.

Arthur Smollett was pining to attend the Monday celebrations in Waterton. Although he realised he could not possibly take part in the football match, he knew his daughters would be flower girls and he wanted to see them. This was not something Rhiannon Thornhill would countenance and, with great difficulty, she talked him out of making a guest appearance the following day. In exchange, she promised that if he kept an eye on little Neville she would go down to the village for the duration of the football match and report back on what happened. It was a sort of compromise and it had to be admitted that Smollett would not have wished his wife to spot him in the garb necessary to maintain his cover. Ironically, owing to the sheer inconvenience of changing in and out of different sets of clothes, Smollett had taken to wearing the female outfit most of the time simply because the danger was constantly there that someone would peer through the farmhouse windows and see him. The men working in the sheds would from time to time knock at the door and several of them quite liked to eye Rhiannon Thornhill, who they knew was now a single woman, if they possibly could. All of this made Smollett's already precarious position the more so.

By the time that Mrs Shallcombe and her visitors returned from their afternoon with Rhiannon Thornhill (during which time Arthur Smollett kept himself to himself in the guest bedroom) Waterton was fully decked out for the following day. All the red and white England flags and posters that had been used for the World Cup and Queen's Jubilee that year were out again. The parish council had paid for six rows of bunting to straddle the high street. The wooden benches and tables for the little girls to sit at the following morning were already in place in the car park at the Black Horse and every shop front, apart from that of Pinker & Pinker (which was irreversibly pink) had been decked out in the black and white colours adopted, in defiance of the rules, by Waterton. Needless to say, Little Waterton retaliated by adopting green and white. In each case the choice of colour was dictated by the name of the village pub. Lord Errington, by contrast, was known to be against the development of team colours on the grounds that it was not traditional and he was apt to penalise any player sporting anything that looked too much like team colours by excluding them from the game for periods of up to ten minutes.

The Reverend Hollis was also in a state of high excitement. Not that the cause of it was the prospect of his duties the following day. Rather it was the fear that, despite his resignation from it, he would be drawn back into the traumatic triangular set up generated by Eric Pinker and Maddie Shallcombe. Whatever his private suspicions, Hollis had found the Bishop remarkably understanding on the subject. It was getting late. Hollis went to the front windows and drew the curtains shut. He did not see, as it was out of his line of vision, the pathetic figure of Carlton Corshall sitting disconsolately on the pavement on the other side of the hedge. The latter had been waiting in excess of two hours for his usual supplier to appear. The black BMW and its swarthy young driver had been stopped by the Wings on the approach to Little Waterton. After a polite request to turn back was refused, rather less politely, the Wings had, distinctly impolitely, confiscated the driver's weaponry and car keys, leaving him to find his own way back to wherever he came from. Harold Crane personally wrote on a piece of paper and handed to the driver the location in Cardiff where he would find the car, together with its cargo, at noon on Monday.

That night both the Green Man and the Black Horse were closed. Extensive preparations for the following day were going on. It was almost midnight before Rachel had finished baking the last batch of pies and cakes. Papadopolous and Santini, who still had not been introduced to the Angel, were becoming impatient.

Chapter 19: A difficult game

It would be idle to pretend that Papadopolous and Santini were fully satisfied with arrangements. They were comfortable, well cared for and barely able to control their annoyance that so far, three days into their seven in England, they still had not met the Angel or started to deal business. Equally they could not understand why their lives had been guaranteed safe from Terry Nazzura: this could be the only explanation for the Sunday visit to see the horses. They had much in common, in their joint annoyance. Eventually Santini felt he had to say something. It was breakfast time on Monday and Mrs. Shallcombe for once was sat down having a cup of tea at the table. The two Michaels were upstairs. Rachel was doing something in the back kitchen area so only the three of them were left together.

'Tell me, Maddie, when do we get to see the Angel?' Santini began.

'Yeah. It's time we see him, make discussions.' Papadopolous continued.

'I feel sure that you won't be kept waiting, gentlemen. But today is hardly the day for business discussions.'

'Do you have his number?' Santini persisted.

'This is crazy. Why I sit here every day to wait?' Papadopolous joined in.

'Gentlemen, I feel sure there must be a reason. But I'm not very good at answering questions. Is there anything you would like me to get for you? More tea? Or coffee?'

'Maddie, we have everything. Do you know what this Angel looks like?' Santini was still unsure if he had been conned.

'Oh yes, definitely.'

'What do you think we do today? Does he come?' Papadopolous was no longer able to hide his impatience.

'It's up to you, really. Whatever you feel like, I'm sure, will be alright. The two Michaels will look after you. I did think that possibly tomorrow you might both be engaged in some sort of business discussions but I doubt whether anything would happen today.'

'Why you say that? Today is what?'

'Some village feast, I hear.' Papadopolous' question was answered by Santini.

'Not a feast exactly. Ancient ceremonies. And, naturally, the football match this afternoon.' Maddie replaced her favourite cup on her favourite saucer.

'Soccer? There is a game here?' Papadopolous was plainly interested by this prospect.

'European soccer? Like in Italy?' Santini asked.

'No, no. This is village soccer. Very dangerous, not like soccer at all.' There was a warning tone to their hostess' voice.

'How not? You tell us how is different.'

Mrs. Shallcombe smiled brightly. 'Well, I should tell you, I suppose. There will be a lot of noise and, hopefully, some celebrations here this evening. The game starts at two o'clock on the green outside in the village square. Our team always tries to score a goal in the direction of our pub and the other team tries to score in the opposite direction. The referee is the only one who wears a uniform. You'll see him in black and green stripes. He's easy to spot because he's in a wheelchair – his gardener has to push him nowadays to keep up with the game.'

Papadopolous and Santini looked at each other in astonishment.

'Your referee is in a wheelchair?' Santini said.

'Oh yes. It's an appointment for life. His grandfather was the last referee. Now the game goes on until one side or the other scores.'

Santini seemed unimpressed. 'That's it?'

'You said 'dangerous'. Why dangerous?' Papadopolous was intrigued.

'It's the nature of the rules. There aren't any really, well, very few. You're not allowed to touch a player until he touches the ball. And everybody uses any part of their body they like. And you're not allowed to play off the pitch or after the game is over.'

'This is dangerous?' Papadopolous didn't understand.

'Oh yes, very. A lot of people play and because you're not allowed to play off the pitch, you're safe if you manage to get off it.'

Santini looked very confused. 'Seems simple.'

'Yes, you might say that. It's just that rather a lot seems to happen all at once. The referee doesn't see everything, of course. So sometimes the other players start to enforce the rules.'

'I thought you said there weren't any exact rules?'

'There are a few, mostly things you're not supposed to do. For instance, you are not allowed to carry weapons on the pitch. And if the referee orders time out for a player then everyone has to enforce his ruling.'

Santini shrugged his shoulders. Papadopolous still looked quite interested.

'And if I want to watch? You allow this?'

'Mr Papadopolous, you are free to do anything you like. But please remember not to step on the pitch and if you do, please, please, don't touch the ball. No one will hurt you if you don't touch the ball.'

'Hurt me?'

'As I say, you are free to watch, if you like. You won't get the best view from the upstairs of this building but it is certainly the safest place to watch from.'

'Ah! I do not hide in building any longer. This afternoon I watch directly the game. I want fresh air and stop always thinking where is this Angel.'

Santini was not to be outdone in this fashion.

'Sure. We both go. I wanna see the action too. We go together, unless you are afraid.'

'Afraid? Ha!' Papadopolous exuded contempt at this idea.

Mrs Shallcombe smiled quietly to herself. 'Very well, gentlemen. I will ask the two Michaels to look for you in the upstairs bar at five minutes to two and they will take you to a good viewing spot. I'll be playing.'

The two men stared at her. Mrs Shallcombe swept upstairs, leaving them to their own devices. Each of them descended to their separate apartments and reappeared at ten minutes to two in the upstairs bar.

When they re-appeared, they found each other easily enough on the bar side of the main salon but they could not see the two Michaels at all. The bar was absolutely packed. Rachel and two other women that they had not seen previously were serving drinks at a furious pace. Maddie Shallcombe had disappeared altogether. Most of the people in the mass of customers appeared to be women, firemen or ambulance workers with armbands. A few moments later Little Mickey appeared, almost as from nowhere.

'Follow me, please.'

Little Mickey was forging a way through the crowd and they kept as close to him as possible. He walked outside the pub and glanced at his watch. 'It'll be alright now. Just follow me and we'll cut across the ground. The teams are not ready yet. But be smart about it.'

Little Mickey marched at a brisk pace to cut across the bottom left side of the pitch, ending up about twenty-five yards from the goal at the Black Horse end. The Americans followed him, grumbling about the speed he was doing. Michael Riley was already at the spot and had marked it out by placing two empty barrels of Mrs Shallcombe's to demarcate a zone for the visitors. Around the barrels was a piece of string and, with the Michaels at each end of this makeshift structure, spectators knew to stay away as the area was needed for 'official' purposes. They were right on the touchline.

It was almost two o'clock. The goal posts at either end had been borrowed from a local school and were therefore slightly below the full adult size. It made the game more difficult for the players, particularly as anyone could act as goalkeeper at any time. The players were not able to come onto the pitch until Lord Errington, as referee, had completed his inspection.

'Say, what is the old guy doing?' Santini wanted to know.

'Just checking the pitch, making sure that everything is in order. That'll be his gardener with him. If anybody tries to tamper with the pitch, lay down a booby trap or anything like that, the gardener will spot it. The referee's wheeled over the whole pitch before the game begins.' Little Mickey explained this as though it were the most normal proceeding in the world.

'So how do you get to play on the team?' Papadopolous still couldn't see any players and was wondering where they were.

'Oh, that's not hard.' Little Mickey winked at the two of them. 'All you have to do is get on the pitch or touch the ball. It's up to you which side you play for.'

'Have you ever played?' Santini asked.

'Oh yes. We regularly play, Michael and meself. We was going to play this year but Maddie told us to stay with you both. We had a few items of business to attend to. But we, we'll be staying at the touchline. Excepting, of course, if you would decide to play the game too.'

All three of them laughed.

'So I guess women play in the team too?' It was Santini again.

'Men, women, yes. But not old people, not nowadays.'

'Does the referee order penalties?' Santini was trying to understand.

'No. Not exactly. Sometimes he'll tell a player to stand out for bad behaviour. But the game will carry on anyway. The present Lord Errington almost never orders time out. His grandfather was the same. Do you know in 1929 the third Lord Errington didn't even stop the game when his own son was killed in an unfortunate clash on the pitch.'

Santini turned to Papadopolous and said: 'I guess this is an unarmed community.'

Papadopolous shrugged his shoulders and screwed up his eyes in an endeavour to see what the referee was up to. The person pushing the wheel chair appeared to have a pointed stick in his hand, rather like the wooden spike of a cricket wicket. He was poking about in the ground, apparently checking for holes. The wheelchair had gone over the entire pitch and nothing untoward had been revealed so far.

'Does he get to keep the stick?' Santini, despite his initial reluctance, had become quite interested.

'Yes, yes, he'll be needing the stick. He's testing the pitch right now. When that's done he'll need the stick to make his way through the players when the game starts. He's entitled to hit anyone who won't get out of the way. There'll be testing the ball round about now, it's the last thing before the game starts.'

All around the pitch stood the inhabitants of the two villages and a number of visitors from Higher Waterton and the surrounding farms. Visitors from any areas more distant than that, unless vouched for by villagers, were turned away from the village on the basis that they might represent a security threat. The Wings had the whole thing pretty much under control. Freddie Pinker had personally vouched for Madame Seraglio, who had wished to watch. As he owed her various favours, it seemed prudent to comply. She and Paulette were standing not far from the two Michaels. Madame Seraglio waved in an animated fashion, trying to catch the attention of Little Mickey, but failing.

'Gee! That's one weird-looking dame.' Santini could not stop himself.

Papadopolous nodded vigorously. 'She looks like hell.'

The spectators were becoming excited and, at the opposite side of the pitch, the Little Waterton supporters were singing and chanting 'Little, Little, Little Waterton! Big, big, big, Waterton!' Green flags, banners and scarves were being waved in a decidedly hostile fashion towards the pub end of the pitch. There were two brass bands in attendance, one on either side of the pitch, vying with each other to create as much noise as possible. The Little Waterton band belonged to the local fire brigade, which was based in Higher Waterton but which, for reasons now forgotten, had a long-standing allegiance to the Little Waterton team. Its rival was the Waterton Gardeners' Association band and its musicians and members were to be seen in black WGA sweatshirts. A great gaggle of the WGA supporters had collected immediately behind Little Mickey and the group included a number of children of varying sizes wearing huge black triffid-like hats. The innocent onlooker might at first have supposed this was the most threatening gardening-related image the club could come up with. But it wasn't by any means: the fathers of a couple of these children had transferred the design to adorn their beer-stomachs in black lipstick, where it was much more disturbing.

'Which side are we?' Said Santini.

'Well, if you don't want to be torn apart by an angry mob, I suggest you should shout for Waterton.' Little Mickey thought this was very funny and laughed to himself for several seconds.

Behind them the supporters of Waterton were shouting back with equal fervour. Both camps had accumulated piles of suitable missiles to launch at the enemy team once it set foot on the pitch. There was a very limited opportunity for this at the outset because, once the game began, both sets of players were inextricably intermixed. Targeting individual players during the game was doubly dangerous, since in recent years the practice had not positively been disallowed of dragging the thrower of a missile onto the pitch to join the game. Let us say only that Lord Errington normally reckoned not to see such things, taking the line that certain supporters were too cowardly to play and it would do them good to join in. The missiles in question had to be intrinsically harmless owing to the rule against weapons. Enforcement of this policy was imposed by the ambulance crews who went round confiscating things they thought over the limit and dealing with resistance by pushing recalcitrant offenders onto the pitch, where any injured or struck player would have his revenge. As a result the favoured object of the Waterton supporters was the rotten tomato: easy to aim and throw and sure to burst. The Little Watertonians rarely used that type of missile, preferring eggs, which were easy to carry over from their own village but which needed to be thrown much harder before they made any mess.

Lord Errington was wheeled back to the centre of the pitch by Roberts, who was now carrying the stick across the back of the wheel chair. Errington had the ball in his lap, and the face that the vicar had painted on the ball's surface could clearly be seen from both sides of the pitch. Lord Errington fished inside his jersey and pulled out a large silver whistle and blew it hard. A cheer went up from all spectators, this being a signal to those out of sight to appear. At once the doors of the Black Horse were flung open and the Waterton team jogged onto the pitch, to cries of encouragement from their supporters and under a hail of eggs. They had been penalised the previous year by the temporary removal of several players who were wearing black. So this year they were wearing every possible combination of colours. Thirty people jogged out on the Waterton side and, from the opposite direction, roughly another thirty jogged on to meet them. The far end of the pitch immediately became covered in tomatoes, as did several novice players who, instead of heading to their own positions as previously given by their captain, started arguing with and threatening the audience. They couldn't be heard over the booing but did get well pasted before play even started. The Little Waterton team had been bussed down together at Mrs Lightfoot's expense. She was a keen player in this particular match as quite a number of people owed her money. The two teams were not distinguishable from the sidelines unless one recognised the individual players. But with the best part of sixty people on the pitch, all acting independently, it was only the connoisseur who got the full flavour of the game. Mrs Lightfoot captained the Little Waterton team and the Reverend Hollis was back to captain the Waterton side. Mrs Lightfoot's team was normally pretty well organised but easily distracted. The Waterton side was completely disorganised, despite Hollis' best efforts, but was occasionally the subject of individual brilliance.

'Now remember, gentlemen, don't touch the ball, whatever you do.'

It was questionable whether either of the Americans heard Little

Mickey or, if they had, would have appreciated the seriousness of the warning.

Mrs Lightfoot raised both arms in the air to signify her team were in position: the vicar did the same for his side. Lord Errington gave two sharp blasts on his whistle and Roberts threw the ball high into the air and pushed Lord Errington out of the way as fast as he could.

'Get on with it, then, you bastards!' shouted Roberts as he fled.

An even greater row now came from the crowds as both bands made as much noise as they possibly could. The WGA band totally lost form and some players broke away from their designated area to get right to the edge of the pitch as an intimidatory move.

Clifford Dale (a keen rugby player in his youth) dashed to pick up the ball. In a trice he was hit by a powerful jet of water aimed at him by a fireman from a parked engine. The Dales played for Waterton. It was an obvious foul that made the ball too heavy to throw or handle easily. Dale dropped the ball under the pressure of the water and Lord Errington pointed at the fireman. Hundreds of hands pushed the unwilling fireman on to the pitch. He had fouled for Little Waterton and his punishment was to play. Instantly six or seven Waterton players jumped on top of him and started kicking and hitting him.

'Classic move.' Little Mickey observed.

One of the Fowler boys, playing for Little Waterton, grabbed the ball and began to run with it but he didn't get very far. A wall of fifteen or so Waterton players blocked him. No one took the ball: they were waiting for the Reverend Hollis to catch up and take it. He carried the fewest grudges in either village and was probably the only one able to move round the pitch safely, or more or less safely, when he wasn't carrying the ball. But the Little Waterton team were not prepared to wait. Tom Bennett, who was a big man, grabbed the ball from his teammate and tried to run down the side of the pitch. Douglas Dale tackled his legs shouting:

'Freeze Bennett, you owe us our fees!'

Clifford Dale was not far behind his brother and roughly pushed Bennett, who had almost got away from the older man, back to the ground shouting:

'And that's the interest on them.'

Two or three men on the Waterton side had been thrown out of the Green Man in humiliating circumstances and now that Bennett, the publican, had touched the ball they were ready to have it out with him. Robert Thornhill played for Little Waterton but was too busy defending Tom Bennett to take any notice of the ball. At this point the Dales were in the middle of a heap of struggling bodies. Billy Thornhill came running in, almost unopposed, and bravely scooped up the ball, heading towards the goal. But he was too inexperienced, despite his speed, to avoid Casey Redthorne, the burly café owner from Waterton, who roughly shoved both Billy and the ball in the direction of the Reverend Hollis. Hollis thumped the ball and ran briefly with it. He passed it to Peter Ogden who naturally played on the same team as his partners, but Ogden was too weedy to withstand the onslaught that followed. Six of the Little Waterton men seized him at once. Four of them held him down whilst the other two fought amongst themselves as to which of them was to have the ball. Discipline was breaking down on the Little Waterton side. Mrs Lightfoot ran up and punched both players in the head herself.

'Wesley! You take it!'

Mrs Lightfoot had been careful not to touch the ball. A disappointed murmur ran round the crowd. They knew that when Mrs Lightfoot touched the ball there would be an explosion of remonstrance against her charging rates. She was a brave woman to play at all.

Santini and Papadopolous had never seen anything like it. They stared transfixed by the ebb and flow of the play. Every now and then they were able to discern the rules at work but it was difficult to follow when the players did not wear colours.

'There's Maddie Shallcombe.' Santini pointed towards Mrs Shallcombe who was at the bottom corner of the pitch close to the goal post that Waterton would have to score through. She appeared to be facing outward towards the crowd. Santini was mystified.

'What's she doing, Mickey?'

'Oh, she'll be bad-mouthing people in the crowd. They owe her money.'

'What for?' It didn't make any sense.

'To tempt them. To tempt them onto the pitch. Once they are on, you are entitled to hold them there until the ball arrives.'

Santini deduced the rest for himself.

Meanwhile Eric and Freddie Pinker were running vigorously around the pitch making sure neither of them touched the ball until it was necessary. Eric in particular was most reluctant to touch the ball, as he owed lots of people money. A few of those were on the pitch and he had no doubt that several others were waiting to join the game later. He looked very uncomfortable but he was an important member of the Waterton team. He reckoned he could talk his way out of trouble, whatever happened.

Trevor Pickering, Robert Thornhill's farm foreman, played for Little Waterton. He was not a man who owed money or for that reason need have fear on the pitch, but unluckily for him as he ran towards the target goal with the ball he was tripped up and pushed to the ground by his apprentice Ralph, whose family had always played for Waterton. Ralph punched him hard in the stomach and he fell to the floor, winded.

'That's for calling me 'lad' and telling the men I'm thick.'

Ralph kicked the ball up field and carried on fighting.

All this time Howard Morgan had been standing quietly by the side of the pitch, following Freddie Pinker with his tense gaze and muttering to himself. He was determined to take his opportunity and fix Pinker for once and for all. He could see that Eric was never close enough to Freddie at any one time to be able to intervene. Besides that, Eric was distracted by his need constantly to keep an eye out for his numerous creditors. Morgan had played in previous years and he knew what the Pinkers were supposed to do on the pitch. Quite a few of the Waterton side had rugby experience but they were only any good in a defensive role: several were quite portly and used their extra weight to good effect in stopping the opposition. But only Freddie and Eric were capable of putting on a burst of speed if required and strong enough to withstand a two-man tackle long enough to throw the ball on. He knew exactly where in the chaos he was likely to find the Pinkers. It was their normal strategy, and quite a successful one, to keep a low profile until the heavies on both sides were so exhausted by the diversionary fighting that they could use their speed to weave the ball through the centre or side of the pitch. They tried to run as a pair separated by, at most, one player who would decoy any chasing player into a fight en route. This plan had worked for two years but not last year, when Mrs Lightfoot, in her pre-match training meeting, had detailed Morgan and one of the other drivers to break up the formation. Morgan could see the Pinkers had not come up meanwhile with a new plan, and he followed keenly what they were up to. His knuckledusters were now on his hands, hidden by a pair of gloves and he was itching to lay into Freddie Pinker's soft organ tissue with them.

After three quarters of an hour's play, the game was well and truly blooded. Emergency personnel dared not step on the pitch, for obvious reasons, and waited until players pulled out the injured who could not walk themselves away from the pitch. Two men were already in the back of ambulances, one from either side. The initial surge of energy in the game had abated and it was usually in this part of the game that the chances of a fast runner trying to score were at their best. The last thing Morgan wanted was for the game to end without him having his go at Freddie and so, knowing he could not wait indefinitely on the sidelines, he decided the time had come to step on the pitch. The ball was still some distance away, more or less in the middle of the ground: this was always a game where it was difficult for either side to make progress towards a target goal. But the Pinkers had begun to circle closer and closer to the pockets of fighting men and women, calculating the odds each time the ball moved whether the time to grab it had come. As soon as Morgan showed himself, a murmur went round the Little Waterton side. They began to lose shape at once. Several players pointed at him and one of them tugged Mrs Lightfoot's hair to attract her attention without being mistaken for an enemy player. Morgan was assumed to be playing for them again, as he had the previous years, but it was known that Mrs Lightfoot was a hearse short and not very happy about it. Three of her regular pallbearers were playing in the team. Mrs Lightfoot was no fool and had suspected that, whatever he was up to, Morgan would do what he could to join this game. She knew that his highly controlled sadism made this an exquisite sporting event for him. Morgan seemed oblivious to the danger he was in, so consumed with hatred was he for Freddie Pinker.

'What's the matter?' Papadopolous turned to Little Mickey.

A great roar had gone up from the crowd at the far side of the pitch.

'Ah, that'll be Maddie. I expect she'll have persuaded one of them onto the pitch.'

Sure enough, and perfectly within the rules, Mrs Shallcombe had her hands in the long hair of a youth aged somewhere in his mid twenties. She had dragged him backwards onto the ground and was sat astride his back, holding his face down on the grass bellowing:

'Where's the ball? Get the ball! I need the ball!'

Rhiannon Thornhill, struggling through the excited crowd,

tapped Little Mickey on the elbow and nodded at the Americans.

'Mickey, mind if I stand by you for a minute or two?'

Before he could give any answer Billy Thornhill came running towards them, with the ball clutched round his middle. His father was running close behind but the unprepossessing Mr Ogden, who made up in intelligence what he lacked in size, had positioned himself cleverly: as Billy Thornhill sped towards Ogden he was intercepted and the ball burst out of his grasp towards the crowd. It was very heavy, in parts stained with blood and had one tooth stuck in the stitching. Purely on reflex Santini stuck his foot out to stop the ball escaping into the crowd, it rolled at speed back towards the players. A great roar went up again from the spectators, this time people were clapping in appreciation of Santini's bravery. He had no idea what was going on when two of the players seized him and dragged him over the line.

'Oh no!' Little Mickey frantically signalled to Michael Riley to keep an eye on Papadopolous. Little Mickey then saw Papadopolous rush on to the pitch after Santini and try to drag him back, lashing out at the two foul-mouthed farm hands who were pulling.

'Which side are you on?' One of them demanded to know.

They didn't get an answer as Santini swung a vicious right hook into the jaw of the nearest assailant. He fell to the floor screaming with pain.

'Oy!' The second man was after revenge. Papadopolous punched him heavily in the gut. In about two minutes ten players were involved in the brawl. Papadopolous had not actually touched the ball but neither had the man he'd struck. The Little Waterton men were definitely getting the worse in that particular corner as both Michaels now joined in to protect Papadopolous and Santini, and the Michaels were known to be Waterton men. Suddenly, from behind, they were hit by a high-pressure jet of water. Presumably Lord Errington had pointed the finger at the fireman because seconds later he was being pushed onto the pitch in the same way his predecessor had been.

The Little Waterton team was again becoming distracted and Mrs Lightfoot was running round punching her own team members as hard as she could, trying to get some discipline into them. The noise was absolutely deafening all round the edge of the pitch. Maddie Shallcombe jogged up to Michael Riley, who was staggering, soaking wet, away from the melee. Santini and Papadopolous were sitting on the ground off the pitch, back between the two barrels.

'Thank God for that,' gasped Mrs Shallcombe. 'Get back and see to them. And don't you lay a finger on Eric. You are on duty. You too,' she said, pointing at Little Mickey.

They did as she said but they were clearly not happy about it. Maddie by now was very dishevelled and her clothes were torn and blood stained. For once she was not wearing either her bracelets or her rings. It was almost an hour and a quarter since the game had started. Neither side was making much progress and all the bigger men were showing signs of fatigue.

Then it happened.

A wall of sound rose on the far side of the pitch. No one at Mrs Shallcombe's end could see properly and both teams headed off towards the source of the excitement. Eric Pinker had seized the ball and darted fast towards the goal, making more than half the distance in a matter of seconds. It was a cool move and he narrowly avoided being captured by the needlework shop lady in Little Waterton, who had been supplying him with fancy ribbon and had received no response to her invoices. Behind him the Reverend Hollis easily held her down. She was a newcomer to the Little Waterton team and was not expecting an attack from behind to follow so quickly. Eric saw Freddie and also Tony Shea from the animal centre, where he owed rent, and decided it would be safer to toss Freddie the ball and outrun Shea into open ground. Freddie was ready and within clear sight of the goal. The crowd were screaming dementedly. This was it. Howard Morgan decided to attack.

Freddie Pinker cradled the ball and began to pelt towards the goal. He was some distance from a group of figures rolling on the ground when Morgan overtook him from behind, diving for his legs and hitting hard on his back with the knuckledusters. Freddie was an exceptionally strong man and still had the ball as he rolled over, trying to kick off his assailant. Morgan struggled over on top of him, uninterested in the ball except insofar as it was blocking his ability to slug Pinker in the abdomen and for that very reason Freddie wasn't letting go. The two of them rolled over a second time, this time Morgan coming directly into full body contact with the ball. A swarm of players had gathered.

It was as though a roll of thunder had been heard. Every member of the Little Waterton team cheered. Mrs Lightfoot, their popular captain, had given orders that she wanted revenge for her lost hearse and mourning suits. Twenty-eight members of the Little Waterton team streamed out towards Howard Morgan, lifting him from Freddie Pinker into the air and throwing him from man to man until Mrs Lightfoot gave him the first heavy kick on the backside. The pallbearers and drivers, who in previous years had been restrained by Mrs Lightfoot's control from paying Morgan back for a year's worth of foul language and petty viciousness, now had their chance. The swirl of blows and insults around Morgan grew all the time.

Freddie had no idea what was going on but he still had the ball and was not too far from the goal. He realised his attacker was Morgan, but in the heat of the game it didn't strike him as anything unusual. He was totally focussed on one thing only: the goal. It felt like slow motion but in reality he threw himself towards it at serious speed. Had they wanted to, the men in the Little Waterton defence could never have caught up with him now. Almost there. Almost. Yes!!! He ran between the goal posts, kicked the ball into the net, pulled off his tee shirt and punched the air.

A second mighty roar went up, this time from the Waterton supporters and team. Mrs Shallcombe was running round in circles with her arms in the air screaming:

'We've won! We've won! We've won!'

Lord Errington blew his whistle three times and the game was officially over. Six hundred people immediately invaded the pitch. The last, horrible, thing that Howard Morgan saw through a forest of legs before he blacked out was Freddie Pinker being carried by a wave of cheering team members towards the Black Horse to claim his reward.

Both teams jogged, ran or staggered into the Black Horse, Morgan's captors dumping his unconscious bleeding body on an ambulance stretcher on their way to the pub. Rachel and her helpers had already opened a crate of Special, with more stocks waiting. They had cleared the bar for the team players to come in. All conscious players got one drink before, if they needed to, going off to hospital. It was said that a glass of Special took the pain away for weeks. Each player who was given a drink had his hand stamped by Rachel with a non-washable dye print of a Black Horse. That way they could not get two drinks. Mrs. Shallcombe, breathless and in tatters but still very much in charge, herself ushered Santini and Papadopolous to the bar.

'Get them a Special each, Rachel. They've earned it.'

Rachel seized the right hand of each man and stamped the back of it. One of the other ladies then handed over the Special. The two exhausted gangsters looked at each other.

'I guess we did.' Santini led the way to the table in the corner, and they sat down together.

Chapter 20: Hidden enemy

Other people might have suggested that Robert Thornhill was sweet on his uncle's widow, notwithstanding that his own wife had only just died. He, naturally, would have denied such a suggestion with the utmost vigour.

Whilst his understanding of the world of business was acute, Robert Thornhill's understanding of the workings of the emotions was rudimentary. In the early period of estrangement from his wife there had been many casual affairs, with which he became bored, and which made him morose. In recent years his contact with the fair sex had been restricted to the combined operations of avoiding his wife and chatting to his sister Kathleen about ways in which the men might be chiselling unlawful benefits out of the farm business. Indeed, his contact with his equals was also curtailed by a combination of long hours and general disinclination. His usual recreation was occasional shooting with Norman Tidmarsh, a pensions salesman who lived in Abbotts Stukeley. For whatever reason, Tidmarsh preferred to spend his leisure time in relative silence and, apart from the sound of shots and footsteps through grass, peaceful afternoons with Tidmarsh involved the minimum social intercourse. Rhiannon, in any case, was still in the process of evaluating her relationship with Joshua Thornhill. She was not a sentimental woman but had, as she put it, things to work through (whatever that meant) and seemed to spend a lot of time sitting in the front room next to Neville's cot. Perhaps she was reading, perhaps watching television – occasionally he would pass by trying to catch a glimpse of her, simply to satisfy his curiosity. Very recently it had been difficult to do this as new heavy curtains had been fitted and for much of the day the interior of the house was either dark or obscured by lace. Robert assumed that these had been the idea of the new housekeeper but he had never met her. Neither, for that matter, had Kathleen or anyone else on the farm. Rhiannon said that she was too busy with Neville and the housework and that she would get round to introductions later.

The day after the football match was cloudy but fine. Wakes Week in the Watertons was a time when very little work of any description was done in those three villages. Much of the workforce on the farm had either used their holidays or taken urgent sick leave. Robert was not deceived by any of this but in a certain sense he was not averse to letting everyone party at once, provided they buckle down the following week and caught up with lost time. The factory operations were easily kept going by labour from outside the villages. Besides, it was traditional for Wakes Week to be a time of enjoyment, and Robert Thornhill was in favour of tradition.

At eleven o'clock he decided that the various jobs he had set himself were all successfully completed. His mind turned to whether Bananas could yet be driven back to the stable in Bristol where she was being trained. He had more or less recovered from the game the day before although there was considerable bruising over his face and torso. Trevor and Ralph had a broken leg each and were laid off for the next six weeks. This was bad news but, given the fight between them, hardly surprising. As he made his way up to Blue Grace farmhouse, Robert Thornhill wondered what proportion of his workforce would show up on the following Tuesday after the celebrations of the Bank Holiday the day before. One of the things he had not yet done was to discuss with Rhiannon how the executors' accounts should be drawn and he decided to raise it that morning as well as planning out when to move the horse. Naturally it would be wrong to think that he was looking for excuses to see Rhiannon Thornhill, although he had noticed that she was at the football match and seemed to be enjoying it. Perhaps he would ask what she thought of it. He knew for a fact that she had not been there the two previous years.

Standing before the farmhouse door his eye settled upon the brass pig. The world after Joshua Thornhill's death was a difficult one. No one really knew who was in charge anymore. Although Robert continued to give orders there had previously been a sense that he was acting as the heir apparent and was invested with an authority of ownership even though he owned nothing. Now it was all different and the real owner was known to be Rhiannon

Thornhill, though the titles and papers were temporarily vested in her and Robert Thornhill. Psychologically it seemed to make a difference to the men and they had lately been slower in obeying his requests. It was evident that the lack of interest of the new owner in what went on was somehow something that the workers could feel. He didn't think it was anything to do with Kathleen, who continued to be as surly as ever. But it had to be admitted that the era of the executorship was in every sense an interregnum. Moreover, because the landlord had served notice to quit, great uncertainty hung over the main farm which on the face of it would have to be vacated by the twenty-ninth of September the following year.

He seized the brass pig and hammered on the door. There was no sound from inside. So he hammered again. Rhiannon was not at home. She had taken the baby, in his own little forward-facing rucksack, for a walk. None of the men were working on the farm so it seemed an ideal time to take the baby for a bit of fresh air and pick a few wild flowers from the fields that were set aside and not sprayed with weed killer. Wonderful wild flowers had suddenly sprung into life, multiple varieties that Rhiannon had never seen before and she was hoping that something in there could be rare and beautiful. Possibly Robert had not missed her by very long because she had only finished breakfast half an hour previously. At any rate there was no sign of her when he knocked.

Though Thornhill couldn't see it, the front room of the farmhouse was beautifully tidy. The carpet had been hoovered and the breakfast things cleared away. There were even fresh flowers around the shelves and the smell of incense was periodically lessened by Smollett opening the windows for a breath of air. When he heard the knocking at the door, he naturally assumed that it was Rhiannon who had forgotten her keys. No one else ever came without making an appointment.

It is hard to say, as Smollett opened the farmhouse door, which of them was the more surprised.

'Ah!' Smollett tried to shut the door but Thornhill stuck his booted foot in the way.

'You!!' Roared Thornhill.

Smollett was still trying to force the door in Thornhill's face but it was no good. Thornhill was younger and fitter and was not having it.

'What do you want?' Smollett eventually demanded.

For a moment Thornhill said nothing. He could think of nothing useful to say but he certainly wanted to have a good look. There he was, the escaped village vet, dressed as a middle-aged charlady and wearing a brown wig. What could one say? What was he doing there? Suddenly it all made sense.

'Rhiannon isn't here. Do you want to leave a message?' Smollett felt it somehow safer to stick to the mundane.

'You bastard! You left Joyce and the girls to move in with her. The baby's not Joshua's at all: it's yours! That's why you came up to the house that night when Neville was born! You've been carrying on with her for months!'

Thornhill gave Smollett a violent push backwards into the room. He fell to the floor but was more shaken than hurt. The breeze slammed the door shut behind them.

'No! No! You've got it all wrong!'

'You pervert. Look at yourself!'

'No. This is all wrong.'

'All wrong? What is a grown man doing dressed as a woman? Why else would you have moved in with her? You bastard!'

Thornhill was a very strong man and he sprang to haul Smollett off the floor by the scruff of his neck. Luckily for Smollett, at that precise moment a key was heard to rattle in the front door lock. Rhiannon had decided to come back. Neville's nappy needing changing and the ghastly stench was distracting her from the flower-hunt.

'Hello!!' Rhiannon shouted cheerily from the front door and closed it behind herself. She strolled into the front room then stopped suddenly, taking in the scene before her.

'How could you?' Robert rounded on her furiously.

'How could I what?'

'Pretend that Neville was Joshua's son.'

The effect of this statement caused something akin to an explosion in the room.

'What? What did you say?'

'Pretending when all the time it was his, that pervert's?'

'It? What it? My son it? Pervert? Get out of here, you lousy rat!' Her voice rose higher and higher as she thought about it the more.

Thornhill was unwise enough not to obey her.

'Did he even know? Or has it always been your dirty little secret?'

It was one question too far. Rhiannon dashed to the side of the room and started to grab items off the shelves, hurling them at Thornhill and shouting at the top of her voice. 'You stinking son of a bitch! How dare you suggest such a thing? Get the hell out of my house or I'll kill you with my bare hands. Who asked you in here anyway? What right have you to ask about my business? Out! Out! Don't you dare come back into this house or our lives again!'

Several breakable items hit the wall and broke. Thornhill retreated, not knowing quite what to do. He was not a man to hit a woman, although he frequently hit men. Smollett had taken refuge behind the sofa and had no intention of coming out.

'Out of here or I call the cops!'

Another piece of Rhiannon's homemade pottery hit the wall, narrowly missing Thornhill en route. He decided it would probably be a better idea to leave before she broke his skull.

'You hussy!' Thornhill intended to hurl his last insult and leave. But the effect of this was not as he had expected. It did not provide a cover for his dignified exit.

'Hussy? I'll hussy you hussy! I do as I damn well please. I have nothing to hide. If I want to be here with anyone I like, that's my business. You know what? I'm going to the fair. And I'm going to take Arthur here. So up yours, you tight-assed Brit! And get out of my house right now!'

Clearly she was now twice as annoyed. The attack on her honour was far more graciously received than the attack on her freedom. She was picking up furniture and hurling it in his direction. This was getting too much. A small table smashed against the side of the sofa and the mirror on the wall fell off and broke.

'Do as you like!' Thornhill shouted over his shoulder as he opened the door. He went out and slammed the front door shut. For good measure he kicked the garden gate on his way past.

In the farmhouse it was then relatively quiet. Neville appeared quite unperturbed by the upheaval. Rhiannon was wandering round the living room kicking things and muttering 'Bastard!' under her breath. Smollett was still hiding behind the sofa but he had stopped shaking.

Robert Thornhill stamped his way back to Blue Grace cottage. His heart was black with fury. If his assumption had been correct, he might have challenged the paternity of the child and asked his solicitor as to ways of upsetting the will. But this was the last thing on his mind. Mostly he was suffering from a condition that others, but not he, might have described as jealousy. After all, what business of his was it?

*

That Tuesday morning neither Papadopolous nor Santini had showed up before lunchtime and, when they did appear, they were each sporting still the bruises and cuts caused the previous day. Nevertheless they did not complain and no longer asked Maddie Shallcombe when the Angel would be appearing. For all they knew, the Angel had been murdered on the way over. The security they were enjoying seemed perfectly satisfactory and they had no complaints about the accommodation, the food or the company. They were both quite comfortable in sitting in the upstairs bar that lunchtime and, for the second time, chose to be in each other's company. The pub was very quiet and, when Santini remarked upon it, he was informed that everybody in the area was in Higher Waterton or, to be more exact, in a pair of fields outside it where the annual fun fair was being held. Most of the businesses in Waterton were closed partly because the owners wanted to go to the fair and partly because everyone was exhausted following the celebrations for Freddie Pinker's victorious goal. Mrs Shallcombe had spent about half an hour over the lunch (which Rachel had cooked) trying to persuade an amateur photographer, who happened to have a good shot of it, to part with a photograph of the jubilant Pinker being carried shoulder high across the pitch. Maddie was prepared to pay an outrageous price, but not a totally outrageous price. In the end she sealed the bargain with a drink of Special and she had ordered an enlarged copy of the photo to be delivered, framed, in a week's time. At three o'clock Mrs Shallcombe called time and the pub closed.

Santini and Papadopolous were sitting quietly in the corner at the table that they appeared to have adopted. Mrs Shallcombe went over, first nodding at Rachel to lock up.

'Now, gentlemen, I would like to show you one of my upstairs rooms.'

They had come to regard Mrs Shallcombe as a source of entertainment and, though neither of them knew what she had in mind, they assumed it was something to keep them busy.

'OK, we come.'

201

'Sure thing, Maddie.'

'Mr Santini, you come up with me and, if you wouldn't mind, Mr Papadopolous, I would like you to come up with Rachel in a moment. We can go up by foot but it is quite a long way up to the second floor and I think we ought to use the lift.'

Santini followed her, although he wondered where the lift was. He certainly hadn't seen one. He and Papadopolous had been using stairs, admittedly concealed stairs, running into the pub cellar. Santini was in the apartment in the first cellar, that is, the floor below the pub cellar. Papadopolous was one floor below that.

Maddie walked over to the spot by the coat rack and waited.

'You'll need to stand close and keep your hands by your side. Nothing to worry about.'

She was talking to Santini and guiding him into position by her side. Papadopolous stood a couple of yards back, keeping near Rachel. Once Santini was in the right spot Maddie activated the lift walls using her charm bracelet. The expression on Papadopolous' face as he watched the walls of the lift click into place around Mrs Shallcombe and Santini was one of utter astonishment. A minute later the tiny red light on the exterior side panel of the lift turned green. Rachel looked at Papadopolous and gestured him to move forwards. Into a hole underneath the light she inserted a charm from her bracelet, which caused a small section of the lift wall to fold back and admit the pair of them. Once inside she put the charm in the panel in the rear wall, just as her mother had done. Seconds later the two of them arrived at their destination and got out.

The second floor was internally quite different from any of the other areas in the establishment. On the left side of the upper floor, right the way along, were full-length glass windows through which one could see across the river at the rear of the pub. On the right hand side of the second storey were equivalent windows looking out over the village green. Santini made it his habit to take detailed mental notes of the appearance of buildings, particularly those he had slept in, and he had remarked the previous day that it was quite impossible to see anything through the windows of the second floor. They looked completely reflective of external light and he had assumed that special glass had been fitted. From the outside the windows seemed to have a slight golden haze about them. On the opposite side of the room a blank white-painted wall could be seen. Some six feet from it a computer stood on a small table and in the middle of the room was a projection unit. The room looked almost as though it had been set up for some sort of conference or presentation but instead of rows of desks for delegates four large comfy armchairs, each in grey leather, had been placed so as to face towards the blank wall. The second storey seemed remarkably big. Between the lift area and the armchairs was a circular glass table some eight feet in diameter. The surface of it was frosted and bore in the middle an etched horse rearing its legs in the air. The horse was painted black. Four folders lay on the table, each full of papers. There were four chairs around the table.

As Rachel and Papadopolous stepped out, Mrs Shallcombe was already pouring coffee for Paul Santini. She handed out another two coffees and then took one herself. At first no one said anything.

'Now, if I remember, you two gentlemen were keen to have discussions with the Angel. Please take a seat for a moment by the table.' Mrs Shallcombe folded her arms.

Santini looked expectantly towards the lift. But it had completely disappeared as the walls had receded once more into an area up beyond the second floor.

'Possibly,' she continued, 'you may feel that your time in our little community has not yet been used. But I would not agree. On Friday night when each of you arrived I would say that you were very tired, tense and, how can I put it delicately, unhappy with each other. Today I feel we are ready to sit down together and think about the problem which has been referred to me.' The two Americans looked at each other in bewilderment. 'That's right. I'm the Angel. You will find that appearances can be deceiving. Now Rachel here, for instance, is not just an excellent barmaid. She is also an outstanding economist.' They stared at Rachel in disbelief. This was unlike any corporate meeting that either of them had attended. 'Rachel is going to make a presentation which she and I have put together using the information supplied. It will take about half an hour and afterwards I am going to put to you some of my ideas for you to think about and give me your impressions. Tomorrow we will have visitors to help us. Alright, Rachel. I think we're ready.'

Mrs Shallcombe walked over to one of the armchairs and ushered her guests to take their comfy seats. It was clear to her that her guests were still adjusting their minds to this turn of events. They were watching, each other and Mrs Shallcombe.

Rachel had the computer ready to go and commenced her carefully prepared thesis.

'My mother needs to decide how the districts of Chicago should be organised and we have both spent a very long time reading the materials that we received. My specific input has been to compare the figures, particularly for turnover and importation, to check whether there are any anomalies. I believe that this is the first time that figures have been compared across the board. I have figures not just from both of you gentlemen but also from our South American colleagues. Additionally I have information from Mr Nazzura in New York City, and I believe you both know him, as well as a third party, a contact of our South American friends, that you will meet tomorrow'

At the mention of Nazzura both Santini and Papadopolous drew in breath. They hadn't realised that Nazzura was in contact with the Angel and knew about what was going on in England.

'The results,' Rachel continued, 'were not as I had expected. In fact, what we have discovered may come as a surprise to both of you. If we decide that my analysis is correct my mother will deliver the verdict personally, which she is not obligated to do, but will do it in New York in order to have a face to face discussion with Mr Nazzura, who may well be an affected party.'

This was certainly not going the way they had expected. Mrs Shallcombe sat quietly at the back watching their reactions with her experienced eye.

'I'm going to show you some overlays and graphics to demonstrate the figures that are given in detail in the folders waiting for you on the table. I promise you I have not manipulated the graphics for my own purposes. This is what we found and, when we come to look at the detail, I will take you to the critical parts and you can see for yourself on the figures. But the broad picture is like this. First of all, these blocks show three years of delivery figures from the South Americans' point of view. You can see that the amounts are constant. For convenience I'm going to call them 100% and they are represented by the blue line. This second frame shows in addition the amounts recorded as delivered by you two gentlemen. The Santini results are shown by yellow block and the Papadopolous results are shown by yellow hatching. As there is no third operator known to the South Americans to be taking delivery, the two added together should also be 100%'

This frame caused a sensation.

'This cannot be right.' Santini turned from the screen to stare at Rachel.

'What's going on?' Papadopolous banged his fist on the chair arm.

'Gentlemen, if you let Rachel finish we can give you the detail in a moment. I think you both have the point.' Mrs Shallcombe restored quiet for Rachel to proceed.

'Now this frame traces the gap between the blue and the combined yellow figures. You can see it starts approximately two and a half years ago, stayed constant at around 2%, climbs in a very slow curve to 4% and then shoots up to 15%. We tried to understand the figures against the time frame to see why it is that this interference was not picked up. This next frame shows the gap growing along the red dotted line of the graph and at the bottom I have marked the time frame and certain events against the time frame. Point one shows the unfortunate death of Mr Romano. I see that in the paperwork Mr Papadopolous claims no responsibility for this killing.'

'This one we didn't do.'

'Mr Papadopolous, please let Rachel go on. We will have plenty of time to discuss her presentation in a moment.'

'The second point marks the death of Mr Constantinidi. Responsibility for this death is claimed by the operatives of Mr Santini, but acting on their own without warning him.'

'Larry the Latin did this. He tells me they found Constantinidi's men hijacking their shipment. They wouldn't give up so he had no alternative.'

'Please, Mr Santini. Let Rachel finish.' Mrs Shallcombe sounded slightly impatient.

'There are many other deaths I could record on the chart but what you see is that from the point of the Constantinidi killing the missing element stands at 15% and this coincides with the hostilities between your two groupings. The next frame shows figures that Mr Nazzura has kindly supplied. Over the last three years this shows the shortfall in goods remitted to him from Chicago to New York. Both your organisations failed to make full delivery. The fluctuations, again, coincide with the period following the death of Mr Constantinidi. There is a maximum of 10% deficit from Mr Santini and...'

'Never! Never! It was five not ten per cent. We sweated over that five per cent. He...'

'Mr Santini.'

'Yes, I know. Wait.' Santini stopped himself with difficulty.

'The figures show a 10% shortfall at the receiving end. And the Papadopolous delivery figures show a 5% delivery deficit. I am aware that this does not correspond with what either Mr Santini or Mr Papadopolous believes should have been received. Mr Nazzura's figures also show a third party importer...'

There was absolute silence.

...'whose identity is not known to Mr Nazzura. The amounts the third party supplied in actual figures come to more than the combined volumes missing from all the deficits previously identified. The quality of goods, I am told, is identical to those supplied by our South American colleagues and they have no trace of these amounts being sent by any other means although they admit that the origin must be their supply chain. It follows, logically, that there is an independent at work who is shall we say helping himself to goods belonging to the South Americans both at or following delivery to Chicago, inside the supply procedures of both Mr Santini and Mr Papadopolous and who also has a separate ability to purchase within the South American organisation which they do not know about. One of the things that we need to understand better is the progress of the war and what sparked it off, bearing in mind that the various other businesses had co-existed geographically for a number of years. Aside from importation, I understand from this paperwork that each of your organisations specialises in different areas of work and for a long time would operate in the same neighbourhoods. It appears that when Mr Constantinidi died another gentleman, a Mr Hidalgo, was also killed. We understand that Hidalgo was a frequent visitor to both your organisations and that he was a high-ranking checker working for the South Americans. It is my theory that the independent stood more to gain from the death of Mr Hildago than any other single event in the war.'

Rachel shut down her computer. Mrs Shallcombe then stood up.

'Gentlemen I suggest we now return to the table and look at the detailed figures. We would like to spend this afternoon going through the detail of the figures and considering the flow through the Domingo district, which is the key to the importation. I would like each of you to tell me how you see the activities of Larry the Latin. I have a special reason for asking which we will go into tomorrow.'

They moved to the table and each picked up a folder.
'Thank you, Rachel.'

Chapter 21: Lifting disguises

'But I'll be recognised!'

'Maybe, maybe not.'

'Look, can't I stay at home?'

'No way. We can go together. He can't tell me what to do.'

It was clear to Arthur Smollett that Rhiannon Thornhill was not to be deflected from her plan to go to the fair. It was Wednesday morning and she was still hopping mad at Robert Thornhill. Arthur could not see why it was so important to prove a point to Thornhill, who probably wouldn't be there anyway. But he was a practical man and had never been able to communicate with people who took points of principle.

'Rhiannon, don't you have a hat or scarf or something I can wear over my head? I was very easily recognised when Rob...'

'Don't mention that man's name to me ever again.'

'Yes, alright, but have you got a scarf or something?'

'Sure I do. I have a hat only God Himself would recognise you under it.' She marched off and returned a couple of minutes later carrying an enormous orange sombrero with plastic flowers and fruit on the top. 'Joshua gave me this last summer for when I would paint in the fields.'

'Thank you. Shall I carry Neville, then?' Smollett, in the extraordinary hat, knew full well that he was now effectively invisible. The brim of the hat was a foot on each side and unless somebody was prepared to stare directly up into his face at point blank range, there was no chance he would be recognised. This sort of staring simply wasn't done in England and he was quite confident about this disguise.

'No, wait, I need to fix my hair.' She walked swiftly back to her bedroom, leaving Smollett with little Neville who was already tucked up in his car seat and obviously on the verge of falling asleep. Neville was a far quieter child than his own girls had been. Goodness, the noise they had made between them even as small children. He winced at the recollection, thinking in retrospect how remarkable it was that Joyce had been able to stand it all day. Dealing with Neville had given him a completely new understanding of what his wife must have been through whilst he was away at the practice. Where on earth was Rhiannon? He looked at the wristwatch she had given him. She had been gone almost half an hour. At this rate Neville would be ready to feed almost as soon as they arrived. What on earth was she doing? Admittedly she couldn't simply leave her hair on the chair overnight as Arthur did but still, this was ridiculous. Nevertheless he realised that Rhiannon was not, shall we say, in a very good mood and that to chide her along would probably be counterproductive. At least that was his experience with Joyce when she was in a bad mood. Another five minutes went by and at last Rhiannon returned. She had changed her clothes again and this time was wearing a long sleeved red cotton blouse and white jeans. She had put big plastic daisy earrings on and smeared glitter in her purple hair. Her lipstick was mulberry and she had black eye liner to enhance her eyes. The result was dramatic but hardly harmonious. Smollett decided it would be safer to lie.

'You look nice.'

This was obviously the wrong thing to say.

'I don't want to look nice, I want to look angry. Red is the colour of anger.'

This didn't explain the face makeup, which was normally not something she wore but Smollett was already in retreat. It was actually quite hard to quarrel with him, though Rhiannon did her best as she was in the right frame of mind for it.

'Righty-ho, come on, Neville.' Smollett picked up the baby still in his carrier and headed off to the car before Rhiannon could change her clothes for a third time.

Fifteen minutes later they were parking in the field behind the fair ground near Higher Waterton. They got out of the car, Smollett removing little Neville who carried on sleeping in the car seat and Rhiannon hauling Neville's changing bag from the back. Fortunately it was a dry day otherwise the field containing the cars would have become sea of mud. There must have been several hundred cars, probably more, and it did cross Arthur's mind that he was at risk of ruining his only pair of ladies' shoes. But there was no time to worry about it as Rhiannon was already striding along in the direction of the music and he was hard pushed to keep up with her. It was almost midday and he was hungry.

The fair was a much-loved annual event in the Watertons. The fair ground people were all Irish, not gypsies. Their arrival in the village was always greeted with excitement by the village children who knew that there would be lots of toffee apples and candyfloss and striped lollypops before long. It was always laid out in the same way: the carousels and rides for the younger children were near the entrance together with the coconut shies and the floating turtle stall. Arthur remembered that particular stall: one year he had to spend a full two hours there whilst the girls, having spent their money trying, insisted on watching everybody else try to hook plastic turtles out of a big tank of water. The turtles carried numbers and some of the numbers (not all of them) corresponded with prizes in the middle of the stall. Arthur wanted to go home. But he dutifully followed Rhiannon, hoping against hope that she did not encounter Robert Thornhill.

The second section of the fair consisted of rides for teenagers and adults. Naturally there was a waltzer, a dodgems arena (Smollett would not have minded going on that but Rhiannon insisted that it would wake the baby), a big wheel and various other contraptions that to Smollett looked far too dangerous for anyone to be on. The screams of those who were strapped on board only justified his suspicions. He did not like to stand too close to them in case somebody was thrown off or the machines broke apart. Something of this anxiety must have been visible despite the fact that his face could not be seen.

'No need to be scared, madam. They never come off. We'd be out of business if they did.' One of the artificially happy fare-takers bellowed in his direction. Unfortunately for Smollett, Rhiannon assumed (since she was the only woman there) that this remark was aimed at her.

'We ain't scared,' she bristled, ' you mind the baby.' To Arthur Smollett's absolute horror she then seized Neville's baby seat and thrust it into the man's arms.

'Right, madam, two tickets, £3.00 apiece. I'll be listening for your screams.'

Rhiannon handed over the fare and hustled the petrified Smollett up the metal steps so that he could climb on. It all happened too quickly and by the time he had thought of an objection both he and Rhiannon were standing side by side in the wall of death.

'Take off the hat.' Rhiannon grabbed it and handed it to the man giving the instructions to the passengers. Arthur was feeling extremely nervous: he had seen this ride in operation before and had not the slightest inclination to try it.

'Hold my hand and, whatever way this thing moves, turn your head the other direction. Don't look forwards, whatever you do.'

This wise advice had not been heard by Arthur Smollett who was upwind, a foot taller and in any case terrified out of his wits. Lots of people seemed to want to get on and in no time at all the cage was full and the music blaring. At least fifty people had come over to watch and there was a temporary metal grandstand where people could wait and view from the top what was going on inside.

The machine began to turn, slowly at first but fast enough for Smollett's wig to be ripped away into the face of some one on the opposite side of the contraption. Smollett barely noticed, so bad did he feel. He instinctively faced in the direction of the movement, which was now increasing at a cracking pace. Within seconds it was impossible to move and he was immobilised by the force of gravity as the wall spun at top gear. Rhiannon, who was next to him, had faced away from the movement and he could hear her making noises next to him, obviously enjoying the weird sensation of the movement. It was as much as he could do to close his eyes against the pull of the force: this was the worst he had ever felt in his entire life, comparable only to the feeling he had on downing his tenth pint on his stag night. He expected to die any minute. Then something happened which the onlookers were obviously aware of but the people on the ride were not – the machine had now reached full speed and the floor was pulled away leaving the riders hanging on the wall only by the force of the movement.

In the unreal lighting that the machine splashed over the riders at random intervals they appeared, even in daylight, to be fast asleep. Their positions were exactly those of a person lying in bed, despite the fact that they were bolt upright. Perhaps something in his posture drew Joyce's eye to Smollett, for she hadn't seen the wig hit the other side of the machine.

Joyce Smollett was high up, with the other spectators, having at last found a place where she could sit in a prominent position, should the girls want to find her. The girls, who had promised to stick together but refused to be seen with their mother, only returned every quarter of an hour or so to get some more cash off her. Wendy was now fifteen and was in charge of her nine-year-old sister. They both felt very grown up and after an hour of fighting off requests for tattoos and belly-button piercing Joyce felt quite relieved to be able to sit down at a pre-designated spot and wait for them to come back. She was unperturbed by the extraordinary figure her husband now cut and automatically assumed his clothes were some sort of disguise. Nor was she the least surprised to find that he must have managed to hide himself within a five-mile radius of his home. Arthur is not daft, she thought. The only puzzle was who he had been with, but the reclining figure of Rhiannon Thornhill beside him explained everything.

In the period since Arthur's disappearance, Joyce had drawn up a list of people likely to hide her husband: it wasn't very long. No matter how grateful a person might be for a decent operation done on a pet, the chances of that gratitude extending to full-scale concealment of a stowaway were slim. Arthur had a good appetite and it cost a lot to feed him. So it had to be someone who owed him a big favour or a lot of money. At this stage in her analysis her thoughts turned for the second time to Rhiannon Thornhill, who had been conciliatory but evasive on the occasion Joyce had first questioned her on the subject of Arthur's disappearance. She remained on the list of suspects, together with the Reverend Hollis, Arthur's sister Enid and a strange man known only as Ginger, a tattooed gypsy who lived somewhere off the Chippenham by-pass. Ginger dropped by about once every three months to thank Arthur for saving the life of his horse and he always brought good luck heather sprigs with him for Arthur's surgery. Ginger was quite capable of going looking for Arthur if he heard he was being kept indoors anywhere against his will.

Once the mystery had been solved, Joyce felt both relief at locating her spouse and a certain satisfaction at having done better than the authorities: at least Rhiannon Thornhill had been on the list of suspects. She had never subscribed to the theory propounded by that awful woman from the asylum, Mrs Bong, that Arthur must have committed suicide in remorse for the bombing that so narrowly missed his loved ones. Joyce had refused to report him deceased and told Mrs Bong to clear off her property before she called the police. The mention of the police had been suspiciously effective in causing her to leave. So had Rhiannon really been having an affair with Arthur? She had to admit that at one time this explanation had held its attraction for Joyce, given Rhiannon's known interest in older men. But Joyce had been making inquiries in the village and of the men who worked on Blue Grace Farm: it was the universal view that if Robert Thornhill ever found her having an affair with anyone apart from himself there would be big trouble. Arthur was not a man for big trouble, that much she did know. She missed him terribly, as did the girls, and had begun to have serious suspicions about care offered by the mental institution once she had met Mrs Bong, who reminded her of nothing so much as a vampire, if a rather chubby one.

After what seemed to Smollett like hours the dreadful machine eventually began to slow, the floor returning as the music became less frenetic. At long last it stopped. The machine may have stopped, but it was still going round in Smollett's head.

'Wow! That was great!' Rhiannon walked shakily off the steps towards the man with Neville in his arms. 'Thanks for holding him.'

'Glad you liked it. I think your friend is not very well.' Rhiannon took the baby and the hat and with her eyes followed Smollett's zigzag movement away from the main pathways between the rides. He leaned with both hands against the side of a hot dog stand and breathed very deeply several times. Then he walked off a few yards out of the way where it was quiet and spent several minutes kneeling on the ground being sick.

It was then that Joyce put her hand on Arthur's shoulder and said quietly into his left ear:

'Arthur? Arthur, would you like to come home now?'

Even if it meant being arrested and locked up for a hundred years Arthur Smollett decided to go home.

'Joyce, wait for me. Please wait.' He was then sick again.

Joyce moved back a few paces, keeping one eye out for the girls. Someone had handed her Arthur's wig, assuming she was with him. Rhiannon Thornhill walked briskly over.

'It'll be OK to take him home by now. Shall I drop him off?'

'Have you been looking after him, Mrs. Thornhill?'

'Kinda.'

'Oh, thank you. I don't know what to say.'

'He's really keen to go home. I told him to wait until they gave up looking. You'll have to keep him indoors. He can't go out as a man.'

'Yes, I see. Is he wearing maternity clothes?'

'I got a cupboard full he can use. I'll bring them over tomorrow if you like.'

Joyce took the orange sombrero from Rhiannon and gave her a happy smile. She then nodded and walked along to collect the debilitated Smollett.

Rhiannon decided it would be a good time to go home and give Neville a feed. She had quite forgotten in the excitement why she had intended to go to the fair in the first place, namely to show Robert Thornhill what for. Alas, Robert Thornhill had the misfortune at that very moment to walk along between the stalls past her very nose. He didn't quite know what to do so he said, gruffly:

'Morning.'

'It's afternoon.' She deliberately turned away from him and watched Joyce and Arthur disappear into the crowd.

'Got to be going.' But he showed no signs of going anywhere.

'Well, go then. I'm not stopping you. I can do exactly as I want. You can do the same, that's the way it works. Goodbye, then.'

Robert Thornhill still showed no signs of moving. On the other hand he didn't apologise either. He had the uncertain face of a man who had just seen Arthur Smollett led away by his wife.

'The Blue Grace boys got a shooting contest going on. You should watch.'

'What for?' This was a sign of weakness and of slight interest. Robert pressed on.

'You're their employer. Shows interest. I'm shooting too. Coming?'

He didn't wait for an answer but trudged off towards the far side of the fairground. For unknown reasons, Rhiannon decided to follow.

The shooting booth had four rifles along the range and in front of them, at a short distance, were various moving targets. The idea was that each shot would be shown on the card covering the target. The speed of movement could be adjusted and the movement itself was irregular, an irregularity that could be enhanced by speed. Standing by the booth was a group of five men – Rhiannon knew them all and they waved as they saw her approaching.

'The loser buys the drinks!' Trevor Pickering addressed himself to Rhiannon. 'Serious contest, this. Ralph and me reckon we can win. He wants that CD of Madonna.'

Trevor pointed to one of the prizes in a glass case by the side of the stand.

'Afternoon, Mrs. Thornhill.' Dave Merchant was there with his brother Sam.

Rhiannon smiled at them, noting the fact that three of them were wearing a plaster cast on one leg. Three crutches were leaning against the side of the booth. Dave Merchant had two black eyes and an enormous plaster on the top of his head. But everybody seemed quite cheerful, that is, everybody except Robert Thornhill, who scowled at the rifle range.

'Right. Let's get started. Three then two.' Robert Thornhill, as always, gave the orders.

The man in charge of the booth had obviously been told what to expect. Ralph, Trevor and Sam went first. Trevor hit the target three times and was the clear winner in the round. Ralph only hit the target once but seemed quite pleased with this performance. Sam, who failed to hit anything, said nothing but clapped his brother on the shoulder and announced that he'd like to see Dave do better. Dave did. Both he and Robert Thornhill had full scores bar one shot.

'It's between us, then.' Dave looked at Robert Thornhill.'Come on, boys. You've got to support me this time.'

In the second round the stallkeeper increased the speed somewhat and the targets started to move more jerkily. Dave only hit the target twice out of five shots but Robert Thornhill managed to hit it three times. The men clapped politely.

'First round is mine.' Ralph announced. They were about to leave without a prize.

'You didn't win a prize for Neville. I want to have a go!' Rhiannon turned to Trevor and pushed the babyseat into his arms. 'Just hold him for a minute. He'll be fine.'

The stallkeeper looked expectantly at her. She handed him four pound coins, marched to the middle rifle and said, very loudly:

'Show me your full speed.'

At this, the stallkeeper reset the target, which began to spin and jerk fast around its circular course. Rhiannon aimed and fired five times. Every one was a hit. The men, apart from Robert Thornhill, cheered.

'I'll have that teddy out the case. Ralph, you take this.' She pulled £20 out of her purse and put it in his hand. 'The first drink is to celebrate the teddy.'

The men cheered again.

'Can I help you with this?' Trevor said. 'I'll meet you all back at the Boss' car in a minute.'

'You go with the boys back to the car. I'll take this. You've only got one leg. Here, take the keys.' Robert Thornhill insisted on taking the babyseat.

'Thanks.' Trevor led the others slowly off back to Thornhill's car.

Thornhill himself followed Rhiannon back to the car, put Neville in the back seat and closed the door. She wound down the window in order to reverse out of the spot. Robert Thornhill was still standing by the car but had walked over to her side of it. She pointedly took no notice of him at all.

'Where did you learn to shoot like that?'

She didn't answer but drove very slowly along the exit route then stuck her head out of the window and yelled:

'New York City!'

*

Mrs. Shallcombe and her American guests did not go to the funfair. Having first wondered when work would ever begin, her guests were now wondering when it would ever end. They had remained working on the figures and arguing as to their meanings through the remainder of Tuesday and Wednesday with only brief breaks for food and sleep. There was a lot of detail and the possible interpretations were narrowing rapidly down. By seven o'clock Wednesday evening, when all four of them were exhausted, the clear consensus was that the Domingo district, in which Larry the Latin operated, mandated by Paul Santini, was regarded as unstable by both sides. It seemed to all of them likely that an unnamed agent with whom Papadoplous occasionally dealt was in fact Larry the Latin. As the revelation gradually dawned on Santini he became quieter and more thoughtful. The information on the figures was impossible to deny and, worse, the dealing chain identified by Nazzura was one that led straight back through Larry the Latin's associates to him.

At 7.10pm Mrs. Shallcombe received a phone call from Little Mickey down in the bar. She listened for a moment or two then said:

'Give us five minutes. We'll see them on the third floor.'

She nodded at Rachel who retreated upstairs.

216

'Gentlemen, I did say yesterday that I had visitors who I feel you should meet and then we can come back to this.'

'Why?' Santini felt very much under threat as it looked like his operative had gone independent and run the war as a cover. He was feeling vulnerable.

'You'll see. I think you'll find, both of you, that this will be a worthwhile meeting. These gentlemen are my reliable associates.'

'I am ready for a break.' Papadopolous threw down his pencil and stood up.

'Yeah, I guess you're right.' Santini could not deny that he was tired too.

Mrs. Shallcombe walked to the far corner of the room and pulled back a sliding door. Because it was decorated in the same scheme as the wall itself, neither of them had noticed it before. To be fair they had been very busy.

'This way.' Mrs. Shallcombe said. 'It's not very far up here. Just a bit more pleasant.'

They followed her upstairs, taking their time. As they reached the top of the stairs, each of them gasped at the unbelievably beautiful glass windows that came into view.

'Lovely, aren't they? My great grandmother had them made as copies of those in the Sainte Chapelle in Paris. You'd never get planning permission for it nowadays, of course.'

The upper floor was bathed in brilliant ocean blue. When Grace Shallcombe had set fire to the Black Horse, all the valuables, including fixtures and fittings, had been safely packed away elsewhere first.

'I've never seen anything like this.' It took a lot to impress Paul Santini.

'You know, it was even more beautiful before we put the armoured glass on the outside. But you can't have everything. Can we offer you gentlemen a relaxing drink now?'

The top floor of the building was considerably smaller than the floor beneath. The full extent of it was perhaps two thirds of the floor space of the remainder of the building and, once again, the entire floor was taken with a single room. This floor was obviously adapted for entertaining. It was furnished with soft black upholstered window seats all the way round the windows, which stretched from top to bottom of three walls. In the middle of the room a marble fountain splashed, the bowl of the fountain being roughly six feet in diameter. The central figure was a white marble sculpture, neither quite abstract nor quite a female figure. Papadopolous was more interested in the fountain than in the reproduction windows.

'Have I seen this shape before?'

'Possibly.' Mrs. Shallcombe beamed. 'It was an experiment. The artist made it for my grandmother. We have his letter saying how much he hoped she would enjoy it. She was quite a fan of Picasso and there are not many sculptures from the period before the First World War. Please,' she gestured towards a boomerang-shaped glass table on the far side of the fountain, 'do take a seat and Rachel will fix us a drink.'

Papadopolous and Santini followed her round and each sat on comfortable but curiously shaped blocks of what seemed to be perspex. There were six of these seats around the boomerang. Rachel came over from a small standalone perspex bar in the middle of the floor behind them to serve drinks.

Meanwhile her mother disappeared. The lift opened on three people, somewhat squashed together. Mrs. Shallcombe got out first and behind her two men followed. They could not have been more different. One was a small man in his early thirties with blond hair and blue eyes, casually dressed in white trousers and a black designer teeshirt. On his feet were expensive-looking French loafers and he carried a small black leather handbag like the ones Italians carried. Round his neck was a single silver chain. The other man was middling in height, very thickset and Asiatic in appearance. He had black hair and a stern face but he could have been anywhere over forty years of age. He wore black trousers, black leather boots and a bright red quilted waistcoat with a high, embroidered collar. There were no buttons but a series of cloth fastenings that all pulled together on the right hand side. The jacket had square shoulders and reached down to his knees. Considering it was mid-summer, the getup had to be some form of traditional dress, otherwise one could not imagine anyone choosing it.

Mrs. Shallcombe seemed very pleased. She immediately set about introducing her guests and visitors to each other by their real names. It turned out that the blond-haired man was called Peter Russov and the other man Islam Abdullayev. After shaking hands with the Americans and sitting down Abdullayev said something to Mrs. Shallcombe in what sounded to Papadopolous like Russian, and she replied in the same language. Then she said:

'Shall we use English? First of all, thank you for delivering personally and honouring my house by your visit. These gentlemen are distinguished business guests from the United States. I know that you had particularly wanted to speak with Mr. Santini on one matter. I am confident he would not mind if that discussion took place with all of us present. But first, may I show my guests what you have brought me?'

'With very great pleasure, Maddie.' It was Russov who spoke.

'Here is our most valuable doll, export quality.' His eyes twinkled as he handed over a six-inch long parcel wrapped in gold coloured paper.

'Thank you so much.' Mrs. Shallcombe took the parcel and opened it immediately. Rachel, behind her, was pouring a glass of red wine for Russov and an elderflower water for Abdullayev. Inside the box was a costume doll. The female figure had a pottery face, dark hair and red glass eyes. Mrs. Shallcombe took it out of the box and reached into her dress pocket, pulling out a tiny penknife and a jeweller's microscope. She walked over to the bar and turned on the light immediately over it. She scraped at the eye of the doll, and stared down at the red iris through the jeweller's glass.

'Perfect. I will look closely at these overnight but they seem to be, as you promised me, perfect.' The two newcomers nodded knowingly at each other and each seemed in his turn to be pleased. 'I'm sure our American friends would like to see what all the fuss is about. You see this lovely costumed dolly. Well the upper layer of her eyes is candlewax. I will replace it later, of course, for security reasons. But underneath you can see that she has two matching ten-carat eyes. I'm showing you these so that you know what I did with some of my advance fees and to acknowledge payment, gentlemen.'

'What are these stones?' Santini, who owned several chains of jewellery outlets, was consumed with curiosity.

'But this cannot be. There are only ten in the world and all accounted for.' Papadopolous recognised the items.

'Twelve, not ten.' Russov interjected.

'I see you have heard of red diamonds.' Mrs. Shallcombe smiled to herself.

'On the open market £2.7m. minimum per carat.' Papadopolous breathed tensely, talking almost to himself. 'Fifty-four million pounds sterling, two stones together. More than eighty million US dollars.'

'Like I said, gentlemen, I acknowledge receipt of your fees. I believe my suppliers to be very reliable.'

She smiled at Russov and Abdullayev. 'Rachel, dear, would you like to put our charming doll into the strongroom?'

Rachel stepped forward, took the doll and called the lift. Until the lift shaft closed around it neither American could take his eyes off the doll. Neither of them had ever seen such a valuable object before.

Mrs. Shallcombe returned to her seat around the table. She extended an arm to Russov and turned to Santini. 'It is not the custom, I believe, in Mr. Russov's country to punish a lower crew member without giving his superiors the chance to give reparation. Mr. Russov has something to say to Mr. Santini which probably Mr. Papadopolous ought to hear as well.'

It was obvious from the look on Santini's face that he had no idea at all what was coming. And this from a man who had spent years successfully playing poker in the back rooms of Chicago.

'Mr. Santini, I was led to believe, and now I hear it was not true, that an operator in Chicago was working as part of your organisation. One year three months ago Mr. Abdullayev and I visited him and made successful arrangements for a consignment of high quality diamonds to be placed with him for investment on our behalf, with very generous fee terms attached. No investments were made and we now have information that our property was used to further his own activities, not your's. From information we have received in particular in South America we believe he used our assets to purchase cocaine for supply to New York. Our custom requires that we offer you the opportunity to purchase this man's life. We have extended his time for repayment by one month. That time is now over. What do you wish?'

'Who is it and how much?'

'Twenty five million US dollars.' Abdullayev interposed. 'I only know this man as Bitchov.' He slapped his thigh and laughed.

'I don't...'

'It's a joke, Mr. Santini. He always calls my friend here 'son of a bitch' so we call him Bitchov. To you he is Amadino. Larry Amadino.'

'Larry the Latin?' It was Papadopolous who said this.

Santini at first said nothing. Was this believeable? If it were, it explained how the direct purchases through the South Americans had been funded. Did the dates tally? Who were these men? Two days ago Santini would have bargained over the twenty five million. He could not have afforded another high-ranking loss.

'How long do I have to think about this?'

'We stay here until tomorrow morning. Maddie has a good place for us to be. This village is very well protected at present. Ha!'

'Ha!' Abdullayev thought this was funny as well and he slapped his thigh again. The Americans, who were unaware that the village was under day and night surveillance from over three thousand British gangsters in one disguise or another, couldn't see what the joke was.

'My men are protected too.'

'Ha!' Russov smiled and winked at Abdullayev.

'Ha!' Abdullayev responded and slapped his thighs again.

It appeared they were unconcerned on these matters of detail.

'Then you will tell me tomorrow morning. I come at breakfast time and you will tell me if you pay us 25 million US dollars or no.' Russov stood up.

'How do I know you're telling the truth?' Santini said carefully.

'We do not lie. We do not steal. We do not cheat. Maddie obtained clean references for us from Israel Malek and we have handled two very delicate purchases for her. Twenty-five million dollars is nothing to us. Bitchov did not know it yet but we have two billion dollars for investment. We tested him, for his good faith, and he failed. We have tried to deal with small organisations but discipline is fragile. Who can handle two billion dollars? We search for partners and find nobody. Bitchov we chose because we want investment in secondary cities. Not New York, not Washington, not Los Angeles but nice quiet places inland, investments scattered quietly.'

'You are Russians?'

'No. Shurtan. Smallest former Soviet State. Shurtan Republic. We speak Russian and I am Russian stock. My friend Mr. Abdullayev is Kasimin.'

Mrs. Shallcombe intervened to explain:

'The Shurtan Republic is extremely wealthy in mineral deposits. The big organisations in the banking world fund big electricity projects but they require repayment in US dollars. The value of gold, which Shurtan produces in vast quantities, is falling all the time.

They have learned that to sell on the open market floods it and causes the price to drop. So with the diamonds they prefer to invest very quietly in dollar economies.'

'So you have Government backing?' Papadopolous probed.

'No.' Abdullayev said 'I have two billion dollars' worth high quality diamonds and I need business partner. Our esteemed President Hashimov does not need to own the diamonds. He owns me, and my family, and the land we have lived on for two thousand years. I will serve him the best I can.'

'So why do you choose to deal with Amadino? You could sell in the open.' Santini remained suspicious.

'It is the need for secrecy and for delay. In the market a rush of diamonds would be traced at once to Shurtan. Our Republic has promised never to break the producer countries' cartel agreement. Second, we believe the criminal organisations of North America, we intend no offence, use diamonds as currency and for long term investment.'

'So now you look for new partner?' Papadopolous said sharply.

'Sure. Not drug producers. Not retail drug sellers. This removes many possible partners. What our President permits is only that we deal with importation level. He has many times stated he will execute members of drugs trade. He will not allow investment direct through drugs trade. This is why we pick Amadino. He promised us he could handle this business and he promised us that he did not retail directly any drugs, but the diamonds stick to his fingers.' Abdullayev shook his head. 'We deal with Amadino because we have to put two feet into one boot.'

'Chicago is your preferred location?' This time Santini had spoken.

'Of course. Before the war, your organisation was very attractive to us. It is the war and Mr. Amadino that have caused us difficulties. But your organisation is not as strong as it was two years ago.' Santini's face darkened. 'We have another saying.' Abdullayev's eyes glittered as he watched Santini's reaction. 'Measure seven times before you cut.'

'So if there is no war,' Papadopolous persisted, 'and you could deal with people who do not retail drugs, many hands, many feet, you still choose Chicago?'

Russov and Abdullayev appeared to have anticipated this question. Both of them answered at once.

'Perhaps.'

Chapter 22: Caution.

If he had been a more cautious man or a more nervous one he would have known better than to open the door when Eric had knocked and whispered:

'You busy in there?'

The man who opened the door was not by disposition cautious, no more than the Reverend Hollis had once been. But some people, as Hollis could have told him, become cautious only with experience. Eric beamed and stuck his head round the vestry door. Still in a whisper, but louder, Eric turned to address someone behind him:

'It's alright. Come on, we've got plenty of time.'

It was half past ten in the morning and the service was not due to start until eleven. Eric entered the small musty room with an exaggerated tiptoe and looked around for a place to put down the big basket he was carrying. The room had no windows, and only a pair of dark wood chairs as furniture. In the door was a curtained glass panel. The electric lights were on and, though it was the height of summer, the room was cool.

Eric put the basket down and took his spectacles off then pulled a roast chicken wrapped in a plastic bag from his pocket. The smell was unmistakeable.

'What?'

Maddie Shallcombe bounced in behind Eric and removed her long beige summer coat, turning to hang it on the hooks on the back of the now closed vestry door. She then reopened the heavy mahogany door, extracted the sizeable iron key and put it into the opening on the inside and locked the door.

'Hello, again!' She said. Her clothes consisted of nothing more than a formidable beige satin bra and matching G-string. There was a lot of Maddie Shallcombe and not very much of the G-string.

'Perfect, perfect.' Eric said. 'This looks like fun, but better take your specs off.'

'But…'

'Yes. Good idea,' Mrs. Shallcombe joined in, 'better safe than sorry.'

She confiscated the spectacles and gave them to Eric to put somewhere where they wouldn't get broken.

'Tee hee!' Eric rubbed his hands gleefully. 'I'm going to help to start with. Got it all planned out. You'll need to sit down.' He pulled over one of the chairs.

'And undo these.' Maddie in one movement unzipped his trousers, pushed him onto the chair and sat astride him. Pinned down in this fashion there was no prospect of escape, had that been his wish.

'I….'

'Don't worry, plenty of time.' Maddie began to wriggle to get where she wanted to be. Not that there was any sign of resistance. Only some muffled grunting.

'Good, very good.' Eric was inspecting progress excitedly. 'I don't need a lot of space.'

'We've brought a friend.' Maddie arched her back. 'Are you ready?'

From the other side of Mrs. Shallcombe Eric said:

'Ready, steady, GO!'

Whatever the Bishop had expected, it was not a boa constrictor.

'Not afraid of him, are you?'

'No, oh no,' the Bishop gasped.

'I love snakes,' cooed Eric, 'always wanted one this big.'

Eric then lifted the middle coils of the fifteen-foot reptile and confidently wound it round the interlocked figures on the chair.

'Ohhh!' Maddie sighed. 'Nice and tight.'

The Bishop was now completely submerged.

'Better not move too much,' said Eric, 'in case you frighten Pickles. Tell you what, I think I will put on the handcuffs after all.'

He pulled out four pairs of cuffs and dropped them on the other chair.

'No need to…'

'You heard the lady. Better safe than sorry. Don't worry they don't hurt. I'll leave you one hand free to keep his head off Maddie's neck. Just pat it back, see. Like this.'

The snake was quick but the Bishop was quicker. Apart from his right hand he was locked in position.

'Naughty, Pickles. Careful or you're not having that chicken.' Maddie scolded.

'Doctor Eric comes to town!' Eric pulled out from his coat pocket a pair of blue plastic gloves with ribbed fingers. Maddie began to giggle.

At that precise moment someone tried the door handle but the occupants of the vestry were so busy they failed to notice. The Reverend Hollis recognised the giggle and went pale. They must have come for him. How to get away? There was no sign of the Bishop yet but if he stayed in a private area of the church, there was no telling what might happen to him. He still hadn't recovered from the shock of the car bomb. He looked at his watch and frowned. Ten minutes to go but he couldn't afford to wait back here. There was nothing for it: he'd have to sit in the front of the church without waiting for the Bishop's arrival. This classified as an emergency and the Bishop would understand. If need be he could deliver an extra long sermon at the beginning to give the Bishop time to get over to read the banns. Hollis, his heart pounding with terror, went to find the organist. The nervous tick under his right eye started up again as he looked over his shoulder for the third time.

Three minutes later the organist struck up in the main church. The Reverend Hollis was relieved to be sitting in full view of the congregation. Villagers were still shuffling down the pews and coming in at the back. Quite a lot of the men were wearing bandages or casts and he himself had one enormous black eye and a slight limp. Three or four children were crying and two women in the overspill pews were breastfeeding babies. Lord Errington, clad in his now laundered referee's outfit, and Lady Vivienne always put in an appearance at this service. Generally Errington had his hearing aid on and was given to shouting 'Hear, hear!' if Hollis said something during the sermon that he agreed with. They sat in private box pews at the very front, visible during the service only to the vicar and anyone else in the raised area of choir-stalls and altar. The choir was shuffling about, and two of the boys were kicking each other on the far side, thinking the vicar couldn't see them. He would deal with them later. This year Lord Errington's granddaughter and Billy Thornhill were also sat in the box, holding hands surreptitiously. The church was almost full. Hollis began to breathe more slowly as the organ for the fourth time belted out the tune of 'Fight the Good Fight!' It was a great favourite with the villagers.

'But they're early,' Eric complained. 'Better luck next time, eh? Just when we'd got off to such a good start. Come on, Pickles, back you go.'

He stroked the monster, eased it off and heaved it back into the basket, which he closed firmly.

'What a shame,' said Maddie, 'but best be off for now. Ta, ta.'

They grabbed their coats, unlocked the door and disappeared as quickly as they had appeared. Half way down the outside path Maddie tugged Eric's coat.

'Did you untie him?'

'Oops!' Said Eric. 'I'll just go back.'

But it was too late. The verger had gone in to get his robes.

Eric, with a cheery smile on his face, listened for a few seconds at the door. He wondered what explanation the Bishop would offer. Eric had great respect for the ingenuity of the clergy.

'Your Grace! What on earth has happened to you?'

'Give me a hand, man. Thieves have overpowered me. They were looking for the Treasury.'

Eric would love to have stayed but couldn't. Maddie would already be sat at the back of the church between the two Michaels on a pew opposite Tom Bennett and his wife, the proprietors of the Green Man. The Watertonians were always on the north side of the aisle and the Little Watertonians on the south. Freddie had to sit at the front as he was to be mentioned by name in the thanksgiving service following the football match. The service was not only traditional but was likely to produce an especially valuable collection as the villagers thanked their Maker for a match without fatalities.

*

Almost exactly twenty-four hours later Maddie Shallcombe found herself in church again.

'Should be any time now.' Terry Nazzura looked at his flashy gem-studded watch and paced uneasily up and down between the seats. He was a small, overweight man in his early sixties, tanned with black hair. The whole force of his face lay in the eyes, black and tense, practically unblinking, reminiscent of a lizard or a bird of prey.

In front of him Paul Santini and Marvin Bernstein stood together, Bernstein leaning against the plain, whitewashed wall of the crypt. Next to the door on the left hand side stood four of Santini's heavies, all of them with their arms folded, as instructed. On the right hand side of the door were four of Papadoplous' heavies, also with their arms folded. This was a place of God, not fighting. Just a little bit of respect for the place was enough to keep order and hold their voices low.

The Catholic Arch-Diocese of New York had done its best over the years to help the needy and stop trouble before it started. Nazzura's own father remembered Bishop Malloy, and spoke of him with great respect. Malloy had been the one to open the crypt of this nineteenth century church to serve as a private chapel where immigrant families could offer prayer in their own languages, long before it was acceptable generally in the Church. It had become known as the Church of the Tongues for that reason, though officially it was known as the Church of Saint Dominic and Saint Joseph. Not that more than one living tongue was ever used at once. The neighbourhood moved from Irish to German to Polish to Spanish, and each time the character of the church changed with it, rather than carrying several traditions of worship at once. Thus, Saint Dominic had been added to the tally in 1960 when most of the surrounding parish had become Spanish speakers, and the switch to Spanish had been marked by the acquisition of an intercessor with a special affinity for Spain and its former colonial empire.

This church was a natural choice for the South American Consortium as a meeting place that morning. It was strategically surrounded still by Spanish-speaking districts: Nazzura, Papadopolous and Santini all felt uncomfortable and very exposed in going there. They could cope with Brooklyn, but only the parts they chose themselves. Their men were unlikely to blend in the background and they didn't know the area or the codes of behaviour that made a district safe if you knew them. The crypt was quite deep underground and could not be attacked from the rear or sides, not with ordinary firearms. The only way in was through the door, which was covered by eight armed men. Nazzura had left his operation upstairs and outside. He had only a single bodyguard who stood discreetly by the altar, never taking his eyes off the men by the door. Papadopolous and his daughter, Anna, were sat together on the back row of seats closest to their bodyguards.

No one said anything in response to Nazzura's remark. He continued to pace up and down, glancing as he went at the plain brass crucifix on the altar table and the flowers beneath it. The crypt was a remarkable contrast to the opulence and display in the church upstairs. If Brooklyn had been anything of a tourist destination, for sure the main church would have been on a list of things to visit in New York. Local Indian craftsmen had created the Stations of the Cross in inlaid stonework over a period of thirty years. New York had always been a city of mixed nationalities, and the German and Irish founders of the building had no trouble in locating craftsman of the highest quality. Benefactions by wealthy Germans who had made it big in the meat markets of Chicago had paid for a lot of the decoration. This was the church that they and their parents had been helped by when they first arrived on Ellis Island. Upstairs the style of the Counter-Reformation was in full swing. The floor was black marble and every alcove carried its own Saint and tiny forest of candles. Whereas the upstairs church was rich and dark, the crypt was a place to relieve the senses of overload. It was cold, and stark. Anna Papadopolous started to shiver then stopped herself – it looked too much like nerves.

Nazzura didn't know this parish but he was happy enough to see August twenty-sixth, the long awaited day when the Angel would deliver verdict on the war. Nazzura knew the South Americans must be in the immediate vicinity, probably checking security. But they were not due in until 11am and there were now two and half minutes to go. In his whole life he had never been in such a dangerous gathering. No one had told him directly anything about what had been going on but he knew that both Santini and Papadoplous had paid fortunes to reach settlement. They figured, and he didn't blame them, that it was time to cheat the Philadelphia mercenaries who were waiting for calls from both sides. He hated the Philadelphians. Kranz would fight for anyone and change sides without warning. He remembered how his father Tony had been caught in the Philadelphia wars when three mercenary groups got involved in their business. He hated them all. Nazzura cooperated by releasing his figures because the cost of suppressing the rogue supplier was crippling him. The rogue had begun by supplying Nazzura but ended by competing directly on the street. Whoever it was played a bold game: supply Nazzura when others failed to deliver, cut him from his usual allies, run up a dependence on the rogue, then insist on sharing the street territory. Nazzura in the end saw what must have been planned some time ago. He owed Santini and Papadopolous no favours but he didn't like the way he was being forced to make up the shortfall and buy from unreliables, people he couldn't see. Or therefore threaten.

Maddie Shallcombe, by contrast, was sitting quietly reading a little booklet she had found at the entrance to the church. It was a short history of the parish and explained about the building and some of the priests who had worked there over the years. She was wearing a white linen suit, a pale blue blouse and a blue flowered headscarf, out of respect for the location. On either side of her the two Michaels sat with folded arms, looking alertly around. She crossed, and then uncomfortably uncrossed her legs. It was pleasantly cool down here and she had managed to find a pair of comfy white shoes before setting off. Still at her age she loved the hustle and bustle of last minute journeys, though she had to endure the irritation of the two Michaels at her choice of transportation. They, naturally, would have preferred to travel First Class, or even business class and they knew perfectly well she could afford it. But it did not suit her. It was always the same for these high-tension trips. Mrs. Shallcombe sat at the very back of the plane in the cheapest economy seats with Little Mickey beside her in the aisle seat and Michael Riley was told to travel in business class and sleep. There was big trouble if he didn't sleep because he was on duty next to Maddie on the way home. The Michaels did not like being drugged but they had to accept it when it was their turn to sit in business class.

Maddie figured the safest place was the least likely, and she had certainly picked it. She invariably chatted amiably to whoever was in the window seat. The turbulence on these transatlantic flights in the tail section of the plane was intolerable. Neither of the Michaels was a good traveller and, whilst one of them was lying in business class in a drugged sleep, the other was invariably throwing up into the airline sick bag. It never bothered Maddie in the least and she knew full well that, however bad they might feel, the Michaels were always one hundred per cent on alert. After a trip like this it would be a case of another week's holiday in Ireland. Little Mickey knew the route from Waterton to Heathrow almost inch by inch. He had done it on Wednesday picking up the Shurtans, on Thursday dropping them back and on Friday returning the Americans. Then again on Sunday for the purposes of this trip. The Sunday flight had been a late one, security problems made worse by the fact that Mrs. Shallcombe insisted on shopping at Heathrow. He supposed it was another of her bizarre precautions, along with standing for two hours in the check-in queue amongst a heaving mass of passengers. She never seemed to stand still or be in a crowd of less than two hundred people. It had taken a long time for the Michaels to get used to this but she was a quite exceptional employer.

At 11 am precisely there was a knock on the heavy wooden door of the crypt. Nazzura nodded at one of Papadopolous' men to open it. Mrs. Shallcombe looked over the seated figure of Anna Papadopolous and saw behind her the two young men who came in. She doubted whether either of them could have been much over thirty. One of them, who she knew as Carillo, was the higher in rank and he came in first. He walked confidently, almost with a swagger, towards Nazzura and shook his hand. Carillo was dressed in an American style. He had black trousers, black trainers and a plain black teeshirt with an enormous gold cross on a chain round his neck. His shoulder length hair was tied in a ponytail at the back but he did not wear any kind of headgear, which presumably marked him out as not belonging to anyone in the neighbourhood. Carillo had important political connections and was an intelligent operator who ruled in alliance with others of his kind: he was not a man to repeat the mistakes of twenty years ago when the generation of suppliers before him had tried to enforce a monopoly with arms rather than persuasion. The covers he used were so convincing that for much of the time he was on good terms with the unsuspecting US agencies in his own country. His companion Maddie also knew, but only from one encounter. He was Ortiz and was a US citizen, though his parents were Colombian. Ortiz was big, probably as big as the Michaels but he was clearly not a man who went running at five o'clock every morning as they did. Ortiz was wearing a crumpled linen suit with a striped teeshirt under it. Mrs. Shallcombe assumed the jacket was to conceal his weapons. Ortiz lumbered along behind Carillo with his hands folded across his beer belly, as instructed. Ortiz was stupid, which meant he was reliable so long as nothing happened to Carillo.

'Please, please come forward.' Nazzura was standing by Carillo and beckoned both Papadopolous and his daughter, Santini and Bernstein towards him. They gathered at the altar end of the church close to where Mrs. Shallcombe had been biding her time. She stood up and briefly shook hands with each of them. Only Santini and Papadopolous knew what the verdict was likely to contain but nothing in this world is less certain than the outcome of a mobsters' war.

'Thank you for coming personally, all of you. I appreciate that the security situation means you have put a lot of effort into getting here. First I would like confirmation from Mr. Santini and Mr. Papadopolous that the hostages have now been returned on each side.' Maddie Shallcombe paused and each of them nodded. 'Very well. I will read my decision to you and I have here seven identical signed copies of it. I will keep one. One copy is for Mr. Carillo and his organisation. One is for Mr. Nazzura and his organisation. One is for Mr. Santini and one for Mr. Bernstein. One is for Mr. Papadopolous and one for his daughter Anna. I will distribute the copies now before reading so we can all follow it together. If anybody wants to say anything afterwards it must only be to request clarification. I will allow five minutes for that then we will leave this building in the order previously agreed.' From out of the folds of the little booklet about the church she extracted an A4 size manila envelope. From that a single sheet of paper was pulled for each of the six designated recipients and from the seventh sheet she began to read aloud:

'1. The war between Paul Santini and George Papadopolous ends as of 11am Eastern Standard Time Monday 26th August 2002.

2. The districts known as 16, 27, 14, 52, and 12 will be officially ceded to Mr. Papadopolous and his organisation.

3. District 72, also known as the Domingo district, is to be handed to the organisation of Mr. Papadopolous at noon Eastern Standard Time on Tuesday, 27th August 2002. For that purpose all operatives of Mr. Santini shall withdraw from that district with their own personal chattels only, causing no unnecessary damage. Necessary damage includes dismantling security and computer systems.

4. All remaining districts in the Chicago system shall remain in the control of Mr. Santini. Specifically the operatives of Mr. Papadopolous shall forthwith withdraw from district 63 and all construction works currently going on there.

5. There shall be no reprisals for casualties suffered by either side prior to the giving of this verdict.

6. In the event that Lorenzo Amadino, also known as Larry the

Latin, should meet an untimely end within six months of this verdict, neither Mr. Santini, Mr. Papadopolous, Mr.Nazzura nor the South American Consortium shall take any action in respect of that death.

7. Observance of the above terms is guaranteed by Mr. Terry Nazzura of New York City and by the South American Consortium now represented by Mr. Luis Carillo. The Consortium is authorised to hold up to two million dollars from the trading account of each of the organisations of Mr. Santini and Mr. Papadopolous pending confirmation from the other party that no financial breach of these terms has been sustained.

8. Should either Mr. Papadopolous or Mr. Santini refuse to accept this verdict, Anna Papadopolous and Marvin Bernstein will do so in their stead.'

Mrs. Shallcombe looked up and around the small group. The bodyguards, including the two Michaels, were too far away to make out what was being said. She saw at once that only Santini and Papadopolous understood the reference to Larry the Latin. To every one else the name meant only a Santini gatekeeper with a reputation for keeping dubious company, until the recent cycle of the war only a small name in a very big game. It didn't matter. Maddie Shallcombe also knew that these terms could be accepted.

'I have no questions.' Santini said.

'It is clear.' Papadopolous folded the paper and put it in his breast pocket.

Terry Nazzura nodded at them and they turned to leave. Santini left first, his bodyguards exiting the door ahead of him and Bernstein scurrying behind. Anna Papadopolous smiled a cold smile in the general direction of Maddie Shallcombe and followed her father and his men out. Terry Nazzura was a cautious man: it was his strength not his weakness. It made him quick to strike and thorough in his planning. He was equal parts greed and nerves. He had the usual ulcers that afflicted his profession. It was his turn to leave and he was to take Maddie Shallcombe with him. She walked over to Luis Carillo and held her hand out to shake his. At first he hesitated but then took it.

'Thank you for your support during this process. I would very much like you to convey my good wishes and respect to Mrs. Maria Bastilla.'

At this Carillo's face lit with a quiet smile. He should have guessed that the South American Angel, currently operating from Venezuela, would be known to her European counterparts.

'My pleasure. Safe journey.'

Nazzura forced a smile and shook Carillo's hand. They stood at opposite ends of the supply chain and were uneasy in each other's company. Neither directly dealt with the other under normal circumstances. Nazzura was one of the three most feared gangsters on the East Coast but perspiration stood out on his forehead, in spite of the cold of the crypt. He walked rapidly towards the exit, knowing that his most dangerous moment was now. He had, after all, been dealing with the thieving independent. Nazzura's stomach was grinding hard and his ulcers told him to run. He told them to go to hell. Ortiz was watching him walk away towards the door, studying the way he moved and listening to his breath. But nothing happened. When Nazzura reached the door, he beckoned to his bodyguard to follow and Maddie Shallcombe walked after them. She had never thought they would disrupt her meeting with a murder: without her the traitor within would not have been found. Nazzura came up into the steaming Brooklyn air. Maddie joined him a moment later, back into the noise of the street and the din of the traffic. The two Michaels waited for Nazzura's limousine to pull up. They stood back to back directly in front of Maddie Shallcombe, leaving four of Nazzura's footmen to cover the other side and the nearby roofs. The vehicle was a six seater and Nazzura felt a lot better with his own men in front and the two Michaels behind him. His six shipments were due August twenty-eighth, the verdict's biggest test.

Chapter 23: Off the straight and narrow

Neither high-ranking police officers nor hospital personnel necessarily enjoy the full comforts of a Bank Holiday. As Mrs. Shallcombe and the two Michaels were somewhere over the Atlantic, a decidedly uneasy conversation was going on between DI Jesmond and Mrs. Jamie Bong. The late afternoon sunshine filtered through the dirty Venetian blinds of Mrs. Bong's office, part of a pre-fabricated block in the grounds of the very institution from which Arthur Smollett had recently, and untraceably, absented himself.

'Why weren't we told before, Mrs. Bong?'

'I'm terribly sorry, Inspector,' she simpered, 'but people quite often return to us without our needing to trouble the police.'

'But this man is a dangerous suspect. We believe him to have been in possession of explosives and to have caused considerable damage to a rural community. I must ask again, Madam, why we were not informed at once?'

He pulled out his notebook, threateningly. Mrs. Bong coyly flicked back a wisp of hair that had once formed part of a fringe and now fell over her forehead at inconvenient times. She was a woman in her late thirties who perhaps had once looked quite presentable. Both from her flirtatious behaviour and from the fact that her pink suit with its pencil skirt could only have been purchased by someone a stone lighter, it could be assumed that Mrs. Bong had not noticed what fifteen years of chocolate biscuits can do if left unchecked. Jesmond was exasperated.

'I am waiting for an answer.'

'I'm so terribly sorry, Inspector,' she lisped breathlessly, pursing her baby pink lips in his direction, 'we really didn't want to trouble the police unnecessarily.'

'Madam, you are in serious breach of your responsibilities which require you immediately to report the absence of any person reasonably believed by the police to be a danger to himself or others.'

Mrs. Bong stood up. She had been sat behind her utilitarian office desk with the policeman sat on an equally utilitarian hospital chair opposite. He was not comfortable and was not pleased. Mrs. Bong wiggled her bottom and snuggled suggestively against the wall behind her. Her mousy brown hair was beginning to go grey and her conversation was running distinctly thin. Alas, the policeman did not look up but started to write in his notebook. He was keen to conclude matters: there was no ventilation in the office and he did not like the overpowering smell of Mrs. Bong's flowery perfume. Nor did he want the smell of it impregnating his clothes when he returned home that evening. The room was surprisingly cramped considering Mrs. Bong was the chief administrator with final say over virtually everything, including medical treatment, that took place here. Perhaps the five enormous pale brown metal filing cabinets on the right hand wall had something to do with this impression.

Mrs. Bong walked round to the policeman's side of her desk and pulled over, rather too close for his liking, a second metal chair. She crossed her podgy legs and leaned across towards him.

'Oh, please don't write anything horrid about us.'

'My report will conclude that no explanation was offered for this lapse and that a review of your procedures is recommended.'

'How very unfortunate, Inspector.' Mrs. Bong sighed and unbuttoned the top two buttons of her over-filled blouse. She stroked her neck with her left hand and drew the chair closer. The policeman moved his back.

'It would be a great misfortune if a report like that were filed. You see, we've had this trouble recently before.'

'I am aware of that, Madam. Is there anything else which you would wish to say?'

Mrs. Bong flicked the hair out of her face once more and gave a half-wriggle on the chair. She unbuttoned a third button and began to play with the tiny pearl pendant hanging from a fine gold chain round her short pink and white neck.

'I do feel, Inspector, that the services we provide are not always appreciated. We are, after all, here for the benefit of the community. And we have the interests of the patients and the public at heart.'

Jesmond said nothing but continued to write.

'I intend to make a report, Mrs. Bong, but before I do so I will read back to you what I have written and will then ask you to sign each page by way of confirmation.' His flat tone told her that her womanly charms were not appreciated either.

'Dear Inspector, you must realise how difficult it is sometimes for our doctors to make these clinical decisions. Sometimes patients appear to require only limited medication. It is a sensitive area for their professional judgment as to whether individual patients require significant medication.' Her voice was insinuating and annoying.

'Are you suggesting that for highly disturbed patients at risk of harming themselves or others the allegedly secure ward in this establishment depends entirely on medication? If so, I must refer you...'

'No. Oh no. I am simply trying to explain how disappointing it will be for our doctors if you should file a report which is or perhaps which might seem critical of them.'

'To the best of my information, Madam, there are no resident doctors in this facility. You have a full complement of nursing staff and you are personally responsible for the supervision of hospital administration. Which doctor...'

'I'm afraid I never name names. It does so affect the morale of my staff, including my highly esteemed visiting consultant.'

'Very well. I will now request you to wait one moment whilst I complete my report so that I may read it back to you this afternoon. Forgive me, Madam.'

Mrs. Bong retreated behind her desk.

'Inspector,' she whispered, leaning forwards across her desk and stretching both arms out towards a glass paperweight containing a red plastic flower, 'I do feel the police and we have so many interests in common, it would be rather unfortunate if our happy relationship were to be disturbed.'

Jesmond looked up.

'What do you mean?'

There was near complete silence. Outside the clanking of the janitor's bucket could be heard through the door. Jesmond eyed her warily. The chief constable played golf with a lot of people.

'Have you never wondered, Inspector, how nice it would be to have your very own parking space? I mean, how awful it must be for you never to know if there will be space for you at the station.'

Jesmond had stopped writing.

'Naturally I wouldn't dream of suggesting anything improper but it so happens that we do have rather a lot of space in our Bristol office car parking area. We hardly use the reception facility there and, after all, it is only a very short walk from your own police station. You see, what I need is just a little bit of time. I feel very confident that quite soon our missing friend from Little Waterton will reappear and save you so much paperwork. There's really no need to rush things. After all, he's been away for a little while now and he doesn't seem to have misbehaved.'

'I suppose you mean he hasn't blown anything up yet?'

'What I'm trying to say, Inspector, is that it could very easily be that we could make available to the police, to any officers you care to choose, the benefit of three parking spaces starting, say, tomorrow. We would have to charge for it, of course, so that nothing improper would be thought to be going on. But our charges would be comparable to our internal charges and they are extremely reasonable. I myself only pay £1 a month and I find it so much more convenient, as I am sure your police officers would. Still, I expect you wouldn't be interested in a private parking space when you already have your pool at the station. A little time, Inspector is all I need. A couple of weeks at most. I can't see it would make any difference and, after all, nobody would ever know. I'm not writing anything down, am I? Are you?'

The telephone rang like a high-pitched drill. Both of them jumped. Mrs. Bong picked up the receiver and placed her pink painted nail over the connection, severing it. Her eyes never left his face.

'Tell me, Inspector, do you really need to file the report quite so urgently? It is your decision, naturally.'

Jesmond looked again at the closed Venetian blinds behind Mrs. Bong's desk. This place gave him the creeps. On the other hand, he and his sergeant were completely fed up with trying to get a parking spot where their own cars wouldn't get bashed or scratched in the police car parking pool. It was a losing battle. Scrapes and shunts were endemic in the area and sometimes he felt almost as though there must be some sort of competition to see how close to his car the junior policemen could park without actually scraping it. Several times he had tried to get home and had to wait because the officer with the keys was doing something else. Then again, a lot of the visitors to the police station were not there on a voluntary basis and when they went home quite often decorated the police vehicles by scratching them with coins in revenge. Three spaces would enable him to offer one to his own boss and the other to his sergeant. They all had the same problem and he reckoned that this could be a very popular, possibly promotional, move. So, rather against his instincts to hound this corrupt and horrible woman, he replied:

'I feel that the Police Authority would most likely be interested in renting any surplus car space which you may have. If this were the case, it would take me at least two weeks to process the relevant paperwork, even if, as you say, the spaces were available tomorrow. As I presume you need to hear quickly on this issue I could, of course, and without any impropriety, give it priority over the filing of the draft report which is as yet unsigned.'

Mrs. Bong didn't want to appear too grateful.

'How very sensible, Inspector. We all know how busy the police are nowadays. I will personally see to it that the forms are posted to you this very afternoon. I will complete them for you and all you need to do is sign at the bottom. But we are not in any hurry to receive the signature. In fact, we would probably not be able to process it for a couple of weeks even if it were received the following day. We also have quite a lot of things to do here.'

She fluttered the mascared eyelashes over her watery blue eyes. 'I feel sure our understanding will be of no concern to anyone else.'

Inspector Jesmond looked at his watch. He was not looking forward to coming off duty because his wife had invited the neighbours round so they could paint the front room together. The idea was that the Jesmond household got done first and then they moved next door to paint the neighbour's house. Did he need this? Why couldn't they get a normal decorator?

'I must be going now, Mrs. Bong. I can see myself out, thank you.'

'Goodbye, Inspector.' She raised her left hand and twiddled the fingers in the air. 'Always such a pleasure to see a police officer.'

Jesmond fled into the fresh air. As he headed out along the path back towards his slightly bashed car, he walked by a dishevelled woman in hospital pyjamas sitting on the grass nearby, sobbing her heart out. I must get home, away from this place, he thought.

*

Vincent Crane was in heaven, or as close to it as he was ever likely to get. He sat in his underpants, smiling beatifically, his left foot immersed in a bowl of fragrant warm water and kneeling on the floor attending to it was Rachel Shallcombe. It was almost worth the horrendous pain he had experienced. He dreaded to think what his father would say about the whole thing and wondered vaguely if he should tell the truth, but the truth wouldn't be very palatable and, anyway, he had to explain why he had been knife throwing when he was supposed to have been inside the Black Horse standing in the for the two Michaels who were still somewhere with Mrs. Shallcombe and weren't due back until the following morning.

'Ahh! Oh, that's better!' Vince let Rachel put more warm water into the bowl.

'Not too hot?'

'Perfect. Everything is just perfect.' He closed his eyes.

'Pity,' said Rachel dourly, 'pity you didn't drop the knife on the other foot where your bandages would have protected you.'

'Doesn't matter,' said Vince, still with his eyes closed.

'It will.'

'What do you mean?'

'Medicine. You need something to clean and heal the wound. Nasty spot to cut yourself right between the big toe and the next one.'

'It'll be alright. I just need to rest it and....'

'We have medicine for this sort of thing, don't worry.'

'No. I mean, no thanks.' He had already heard from Corn, who had no sympathy whatsoever on these occasions, about the formidable, not very comforting, medicine cupboard over at the Black Horse. Serves you right, Corn would say, for being a prat. No one in his right mind bets against Tombstone Phillips.

'Sorry, Vince. I'm on duty too and there'll be trouble if your foot goes septic. Not afraid, are you?'

'Me? No way. It's nothing to me. I mean, knife throwing is dangerous. You expect to get hurt sometimes. I can cope.'

'Good.' Rachel had put his foot up on the table for inspection. Vince was no longer so comfortable. They were upstairs in the lobby between the apartments belonging to the two Michaels, by the medicine cupboard. Vince thought it looked more like a small operating theatre inside than a cupboard but what would he know? He had been in once, he realised, but he could not remember very much. Between the time when Mrs. Shallcombe gave him a drink at the bar to the point, about three hours later, when she finished stitching the bullet wound on his other foot was blank.

'We need to go downstairs first. Can you move?'

'Yes. But why?'

'Can't stay up here all afternoon. You come and sit in the little room and I can get on with my business. I want to talk to Tombstone anyway.'

'Let me lean on your shoulder, Rachel, and I'll manage the stairs easily.'

'No need,' she said, much to his disappointment, 'if you stand over there we can take the lift.'

So they did.

Tombstone Phillips was sat alone in the little room, playing solitaire. He was as much a mystery to his employers as he was to strangers and Harold Crane, who had worked with him for years on various protection assignments, could only warn his son not to argue with Phillips over anything, not to comment on the man's name or handlebar moustache and, above all, not to play any game of any kind with him. His grandmother had been a gypsy so he got called Tombstone, Vince's father had warned, but he tries to live up to his name. Whilst the two Michaels were not around, someone trustworthy had to guard the Black Horse and Phillips was that man. Besides, it was time Vince learned to know more of the people in the business, now that he was nineteen.

Phillips was a skinny man and was wearing a pair of smart new black jeans, faded checked blue shirt and very smart black trainers. This was presumably casual wear because he was not out gambling on cards. For his nightime work he invariably wore his lucky silver suit, high heel boots, Stetson and red waistcoat. He always came into a gambling joint with his left foot first and always picked up the first card of any game with the first finger and thumb of his left hand. His career in cards was legendary. He had started as a cardsharp on a luxury liner, preying on the elderly passengers, but had such talent that ten years later saw him playing at the tables of the Mafia bosses, places where no one in their right minds even thinks of cheating. At the table he was all frowns and rarely said anything. Away from the table, he was the hottest tempered man alive. Any challenge of any kind he was compelled to take up and did not take defeat too kindly. His second great skill, as a knife thrower, was what had got Vince into trouble.

'What's the point,' Vince had said as they crossed the car park behind the pub, 'when you can use guns nowadays?'

At once Phillips pulled a knife from out of his left sleeve and threw it at the pub wall where the point ran head height half an inch deep.

'You hear something, boy?' Phillips had asked. 'She is fast and she is silent.'

'Bet you can't do it again,' Vincent had observed, ignoring his father's advice. Instantly Phillips pulled a second knife from his belt and threw it into the wall virtually into the same spot.

'Bet me what, boy?'

'Well....'

'I'll take your shoes, I like those shoes.'

Vince surrendered them without argument. At least he had remembered one thing his father had said, even if it did mean kissing goodbye to his favourite, very expensive, black trainers.

'You want them back, you do it. And if you don't, I'll have your trousers.'

Vincent began to see why he had been warned not to play anything against Phillips.

'I....'

'Not afraid, boy, are you?'

'OK. Give me a knife.'

Phillips plucked a murderous-looking straight blade from a sheath inside his shirt and threw it to land point down between Vince's bare feet. It was so deeply embedded in the gravel that it was half a minute before Vincent could get it out at all.

'Them's fine-looking trousers,' Phillips whispered in his ear. Vince pretended not to hear and took aim with his knife at the impossible target twenty yards away.

'Point first, boy. You do it point first from this distance.'

'Course,' said Vincent, shifting the knife into his left hand. He didn't quite have the confidence to take the heavy knife point first into his right hand, and it slipped under its own momentum, point first between his toes. Vince let out a great shout.

'Oh God, my toe's off!! Look at the blood!!'

'Don't get them trousers all blooded up, boy. Or I could get real angry.'

Vince was in agony but his urge to survive had not deserted him. He ripped off his black jeans clean as a whistle and continued roaring with pain.

'Another time, boy. I'll get you some help.' Phillips ambled off and two minutes later Rachel came rushing out of the pub towards Vince. Of all the people he had least wanted to see at that precise moment, Rachel Shallcombe had been top of the list. Why was he never ready for her appearances? And what must she have thought? No shoes, no trousers, rolling about on the floor shouting etc. etc. She had not even asked for an explanation but that didn't lessen his embarrassment. Rachel swiftly took off his black sock and inspected.

'Just a little cut,' she commented dryly.

'But the bleeding...'

'Will stop. Come with me.'

Later, when they interrupted Phillips' game of solitaire by going into the little room, it was Rachel who spoke first.

'Tombstone, would you hold Vince down for a second while I put the medicine on?'

'Sure, little lady. You ready, boy?'

'No need at all, Tombstone.'

'I said I'd do it, boy. You arguing with that?'

'No. Not at all. Carry on.'

Tombstone sat Vince down in the straight-backed chair and sat on his lap, his legs either side over Vince's knees and both hands holding the cut foot still for Rachel. 'Ow! I can't breathe.'

'You complaining, boy?'

'No. It's OK.' Vince smiled weakly.

Rachel returned with a small black bottle and some cotton wool.

'This stuff does hurt a bit but it's very good.' She dabbed some on the cotton wool and put it on the wound.

'Aargh!!!'

'Hold still, boy, for the lady.'

'Aargh!!!'

'That's better,' said Rachel. 'Now I'm off to the kitchen. Shout if you need me.'

She disappeared round the corner. Tombstone Phillips stroked his moustache. Vince was about to ask him a question then thought better of it.

'You up for a little game of cards there?' Tombstone Phillips whispered in Vince's ear. He jumped with fright.

'Er....'

'I see you have a good-looking shirt on you right now, boy.'

'No. Er, no thank you. I'm not, er, recovered yet. My foot. I mean, I can't concentrate now. The pain.' Vince pointed downwards and wished Phillips would go back to his cards.

'Hmm. Maybe some other time. Soon, maybe.'

'Not today, Tombstone. I'm just not up to it. In fact I'm thinking of going to bed early. Yes.'

Phillips greeted this with an expression of astonishment. 'You serious there? It's only four o'clock.'

'Yes. Oh yes. Blood loss. Need to recuperate, just resting. Mustn't overdo it now both feet are bandaged.' Vincent then turned his head towards the kitchen and yelled. 'Hello there! Rachel, hello!'

Rachel returned a minute or so later, her apron dusted with flour.

'Yes. What is it, Vince? I'm in the middle of baking.'

'Look, I'm really sorry about this, but you wouldn't by any chance know how I could, er, get some, er, replacement clothes?'

'Meaning what?'

'It's a Bank Holiday and I've, er, well, lost my shoes and trousers.'

'Lost?'

'Er, yes.'

'He bet them fair and square,' Phillips bellowed from the corner, 'and very comfortable they are too.'

Rachel turned to look at Phillips. With a twinkle in her eye, she then looked back at Vince. Vince hung his head low and wished the earth would swallow him up.

'I think,' Rachel volunteered, 'you might borrow something to wear from Michael Riley and just turn the bottoms up. You can use a belt. But shoes, now that's tricky. We're about the same size. You can borrow some flip-flops from me but you're not having my clothes. After all, I don't want to hear you telling anyone you've been inside my trousers!'

'Thanks. Thanks very much,' Vincent stuttered turning puce, and pretending he hadn't heard the joke. Why, whenever she was around, did his mind go blank and everything fall apart? And then it came to him. With a sickening lurch in his stomach he suddenly realised what the problem was: he was in love with Rachel Shallcombe. Oh no. What would his father say to that?

Chapter 24: Stalking prey

Bank Holiday Monday in Hamset Manor saw Lord Errington conducting his annual review of the estate with John Gilbert, the land agent he engaged to keep an eye on the tenants and their needs. Once a year they sat down together and went through management issues not covered by their monthly Estate meetings, but more especially to consider any major changes such as investment in new buildings, any bankruptcies or legal actions. Gilbert was normally very difficult to get hold of because his firm ran the local cattle market, so Errington preferred to see him on the Bank Holiday when his office was closed and his mobile telephone did not disturb them.

The agent was a red-faced giant of a man with a sixty-inch waist and a booming laugh. He invariably wore a brown tweed suit, except for appearances in Court or in London. He might have been forty-five or then again fifty-five and he was as astute and affable as any man on earth. Full of amusing stories, he naturally did not tell any to Lord Errington who, rightly, might have suspected that he himself was the subject of some of them. Gilbert had just arrived at the Manor House, having brought along his various files relating to Blue Grace Farm, the tenancy of which was the major item for discussion that afternoon. He had heard that Sophie was to marry Billy Thornhill but was unclear what impact that would have on Lord Errington's plans. Errington had already had one long discussion with his agent about the farm, shortly after Joshua Thornhill died, as a result of which Gilbert served the notice to quit terminating the tenancy of the farm. This was the routine sort of task that he dealt with himself and rarely if ever thought of calling in the services of Dale, Dale & Ogden owing to the serious holes that their fees made in his Estate management account. Dancer had just shown Gilbert into the library. The agent wandered over to the window and looked out into the distance. Gilbert was early, which he knew would please Lord Errington, and he knew also that Dancer would be downstairs assisting his master to adjust his hearing aid so that Errington would not miss a word of any discussion. A minute or two later Dancer opened the door and Errington walked briskly in, a pair of binoculars hanging by leather thongs round his neck.

'John, good to see you.'

'Congratulations on the impending nuptials.'

'Thank you. Thank you. Jolly pleased. Looking for an heir, you know.'

Errington shook his hand. 'Bring that map, would you?' He prodded it with his stick and waited until the puzzled Gilbert had picked up the big Estate map by its wooden rods. 'Come on, then. Orf we go.'

'Shall I bring the Blue Grace files, Sir?'

'No need. No need. You'll remember. Just the map. Orf we go.'

Gilbert had no idea where Errington was headed. All previous meetings had been held in the library and the files were usually consulted at some point. Dancer meanwhile reappeared so as to open the door and he preceded them slowly down the staircase. Eventually they reached the front entrance to the building. The exertion of coping with these steps cost both Dancer and his master several minutes' recovery time.

'Got to be ready for the villains. You bring the map.' He gesticulated towards Gilbert. 'Alright, Dancer?'

'Yes, thank you, my Lord.' Dancer had his breath back.

'Good show. Now get Roberts and me wheelchair or the blighters will outrun us. And the gun. Don't forget the gun.'

'Very good, my Lord. Will Mr. Gilbert be requiring a firearm, your Lordship.'

'No, no. He will push.'

Gilbert had no idea what this was about but he thought it prudent not to look a fool by asking. Nothing was in season for shooting, so what could be going on? Before his thoughts could develop he was interrupted by the arrival of Roberts with the wheelchair.

'I greased it as you asked, Sir.'

'Good. But put that damn pipe out or the smell will scare 'em orf.'

'If you say so, Sir.' Roberts scowled in a surly way and put out the pipe. Lady Vivienne could never understand why her father-in-law put up with the man's rudeness. He would never have tolerated this from any of his other staff or his tenants. Roberts was a law unto himself: an excellent gardener and very fit. Errington undoubtedly regarded Roberts as some sort of noble savage battling with the elements and nature. In Lady Vivienne's view, Roberts' main claim to employment by the household was his acquisition some five years ago of a charming and efficient wife who had suddenly appeared on the scene following Roberts' annual walking trip to the Highlands.

'Good afternoon, Mr. Roberts,' Gilbert said.

'Not really. It's going to rain later. You'll see,' the Scotsman growled.

'Any signs yet?' Errington asked the gardener.

'Aye. My contact says they're on their way.' At this he held aloft his mobile phone. 'But we're ready for 'em.'

Errington climbed rapidly into the wheelchair, handing Gilbert his stick and instead laying his shotgun across his lap. Roberts began to wheel Errington at considerable speed across the gravelled drive and down the side of the building towards an area of the lawn where a large hole had been made in the adjacent flowerbed. It looked as though a drunken giant had kicked out everything in a fit of spite.

'Ahh! We'll get the varmints this time.' Roberts muttered under his breath, marching on towards the smaller of his two greenhouses.

Gilbert noted the damage to the glasshouse – the whole of one side had been smashed in and practically everything within had been trampled and wrecked. He said nothing. Roberts and Errington had already moved on at a smart pace. Gilbert followed them as quickly as he could but was somewhat hindered by the map and the stick. Three or four minutes later, and a considerable way from the house, Errington signalled for Roberts to stop.

'Right. This'll do,' he whispered, pointing as he spoke, 'you take the map and head 'em towards me. Might bag more than one of 'em.'

'Right you are, Sir.' Roberts relieved Gilbert of the map and hid behind the low stonewall on the other side of the track. Errington had stopped behind an ornamental bush close to the track, and hid himself as well.

'You push the chair and don't panic. Need to take aim.'

Gilbert bent down partly to hear Errington better, as he was still speaking in an almost inaudible whisper, and partly so as to hide behind the bush and join Errington's concealment. He watched Errington's practiced hand load the gun.

'What....'

'Shh!!' Errington whispered back urgently. 'When Roberts raises the map over the wall, prod me in the back. Get me in their path. Can you see him?'

Gilbert lifted his head to spot the gardener leaning low over the wall concentrating with his binoculars on something in the distance.

'Yes,' answered Gilbert.

'Now, John,' the old man continued in his whisper, 'about this Thornhill business. Tricky for us, tricky. Gossip is Thornhill's orf. Not interested. Not staying. Rest of 'em no use at all. Billy's no experience. Got to learn it all. University man.'

Gilbert nodded patiently. He hadn't heard that Robert Thornhill was thinking of going elsewhere, not even applying for a succession to his uncle's tenancy. This was awkward, leaving, as it did, his relatives behind. Gilbert's plan had been to agree a farm business tenancy with Robert at a high rent and give him, say, twenty years on the land but not under the old fashioned legal set up his uncle had enjoyed, and particularly not at his uncle's low rental.

'Always been Thornhills on the land.' Errington raised the gun and eyed an imaginery target down the barrel. 'Robert's the man. Hard worker. Knows what he's doing.'

'Should I discuss it with him? We can offer twenty years and see what he says. Otherwise Blue Grace goes out to tender and we have to deal with his family in the cottages. Some of them might have a legal right to stay, if they were farm workers but we should get a couple of them back. I've got a pretty good idea on the rent we should ask. I recommend....'

'Shh! Can you hear something?' With his hearing aid up at maximum the old man's sensitivity to noise was far sharper than Gilbert's. 'What's Roberts doing?'

Gilbert obediently broke off and peered over the bush again.

'He's waving at me.'

'Good. Very good.' Errington whispered fiercely and turned his hearing aid off. 'Now listen. Offer Robert Thornhill the tenancy. Agree a rent. Go low if you need to. Give him the margins on the milk. Tell him the Estate wants partnership. Go into turf with him. You know, sports turf. Tell him baseball quality. We've the contacts, need a man controlling production. Partnership. 50:50. Get Clifford Dale in. Paper it up.'

It was true that Errington had intimated in the past that the Estate ought to be supplying sports turf, at very high prices to a high quality market, and had even gone as far as costing the exercise. However the production specimens were not high enough in quality. If he had thought about it earlier, Gilbert would have said that only someone of Robert Thornhill's fanatical standards might pull it off.

'John, keep an eye on Roberts now. When the map's in the air, push me out towards 'em.'

'Towards what?'

The answer supplied itself. Seconds later a loud snuffling and grunting could be heard moving swiftly along the track in the direction of Roberts' vegetable garden. Gilbert heard Roberts frantically shouting and saw him waving his arms at the pigs, striking one on the back with the heavy map. The pigs were huge, and fast. They turned and began to stampede towards the bush hiding Gilbert and Errington.

'Now!' Gilbert yelled, prodding Errington in the back and pushing the wheelchair directly out into the path of the oncoming pigs. In what seemed like an eternity Gilbert waited silently, praying that Errington was up to this. If the pigs got to them they would be seriously injured.

Bang! Bang! Bang!

Two of the great creatures lay dead on the track, shot neatly through the head in each case. The third was rushing, terrified and squealing, back along the way it had come.

'Blighter's orf the Estate.'

Gilbert silently agreed with Errington, watching the last pig cross the boundary back into Pig Home Farm. 'Hah! Reggie Fowler's on holiday this week again. That'll teach 'em. Free range pigs. Hah! Too clever they are. Damn pigs wait till he's gone then bolt for it. Very good, Roberts, very good!'

Roberts was standing over one of the pigs. 'Fancy my onions, do ye? Oh yes. Well, they are the kiss of death to youse.'

'Roberts,' Errington cut across his vengeful monologue, 'bring the wheelchair in.' Errington thrust the firearm into Roberts' arms and began walking back to the Manor. He turned his hearing aid back on. 'Now, John, the Thornhill plan. Advise me.'

Gilbert cast an eye over the fear-spoiled carcasses and followed Errington. In the background Roberts continued to lecture the dead pigs.

*

It was exactly a week since the football match and most of the bruising and swelling round Howard Morgan's body had gone down and turned from blue black to yellow. He could now see out of both his eyes again and the gash on his face was held together by two sets of invisible, or almost invisible, sutures. His left forearm was cleanly broken and on it he had a lightweight cast. His arm was in a sling. There was a second big gash on his head. This had been successfully held together with sutures after his head had been shaved. The wound had been left to the fresh air and his head was now covered in dark stubble. His right big toe had also been broken, goodness knows how, and had its own separate cast. So extensive was the bruising that the doctors insisted he remain in hospital for observation in case there was internal bleeding or some other side effect that might manifest over a course of days. Six days had passed in which Morgan had done little but brood on the subject of revenge upon Freddie Pinker. The hospital ward was as busy as a railway station in rush hour. The place was full of noise, day and night. No sooner had he gone to sleep than he was woken up by the sound of coughing or the jangle of the tea trolley or, worse, the screaming of babies brought in by visitors. He probably hadn't slept in the entire six days for more than 20 minutes at a time. What with lack of sleep and the painkillers he was being given, Morgan's ability to plot Pinker's downfall was at an all time low. He was supposed to be seen by his doctor at nine o'clock that morning and cleared to leave the hospital but the doctor hadn't showed up until nearly five o'clock in the afternoon and had simply signed the form without even bothering to inspect him. Morgan didn't care. His clothes had been laundered by the hospital and they had removed the arm of his jacket so that he could wear it with his cast. Mrs. Lightfoot had retrieved the keys to her hearse from his trouser pockets but his two suitcases were waiting for him under his bed. One of them contained exactly what he needed – his collection of taxidermy implements and his jar of chloroform-soaked rags.

His plan was cunningly simple: kidnap Pinker using the chloroform and torture him to death using the implements. He had plenty of hooks and knives, some of them with interesting frilled blades. He had dwelled in loving detail on the pain Pinker would suffer as his internal organs were removed one by one after Morgan had tied him up. Nothing could stop him this time. It was no good trying to capture Pinker in the village. Morgan had no wish to go back to either Waterton or Little Waterton right now and risk another meeting with Mrs. Lightfoot or for that matter with the Shallcombes. But he knew exactly where he would find Pinker – at the club in Bristol where he hung out with his secretary. What could be simpler? All he had to do was work out when Pinker normally left, find out what his habits were and then jump him one night from behind. He could easily hire a car, bundle him in the back and then drive to somewhere nice and quiet. He knew a few places that might do for his purposes. And as for the body, he'd buried enough in his time to handle that. Morgan's eyes gleamed wickedly. He would make that bastard Pinker whimper like a baby. Maybe he should start with the toenails. Or even the toes. Yes, that was a better idea. Work his way up slowly. Break off for a bit and then blind him with a punctured eyeball. He couldn't wait. Morgan had a superhuman urge to do it that gave him a real will to live. Another man might have concluded after Morgan's various recent encounters with Freddie Pinker that the fickle hand of fate was not pointing in a friendly direction, but Morgan did not believe in such nonsense. He had a plan, a good one, and the means and the will to execute it. The sooner the better. First, Operation Spy.

And so it was that as soon as the doctor had signed him out from treatment, Morgan caught the bus from the hospital into the centre of Bristol, taking with him his two suitcases. With great difficulty. One arm was out of action and he could barely manage with the big case and the carpetbag both on or under one arm. But he did. True it is that he cut a rather curious figure and several small children ran away when they saw him coming but he found a little garden square amongst the office blocks where he could sit down without being interrupted. Most of the stuff in the suitcase he didn't need anyway or could replace. His money was still in his wallet, untouched by his attackers, and the only things he needed for Operation Spy were his wallet and the jar of chloroform-soaked cloths. He felt it would be prudent to practice on someone to start with.

Seeing a homeless person lying in a sleeping bag behind a neighbouring bench, Morgan crept up to him with the chloroform cloth and put it over his face. There wasn't much resistance as the man was already half drunk and had been whistling aimlessly to himself.

Immediately he went first pink then purple then stopped struggling. Good, thought Morgan, almost instantaneous. Very efficient. Morgan reckoned the effect of the stuff would last for several hours so he simply abandoned temporarily his two bags by the now "sleeping" figure, intending to return and collect them later. Chances were everyone would assume they belonged to the sleeper and would not take them in case he woke up. Perfect, Morgan sniggered. He put the jar back into his right jacket pocket, which bulged out showing only the shiny metallic top of what looked like, and was, a jam jar. He limped off in the direction of the club, intending to have a pint or two in the area until Pinker arrived.

Seven o'clock came and went. Eight o'clock came and went. By nine Morgan was beginning to think that Freddie Pinker wouldn't turn up at all that night at Madame Seraglio's. But then, shortly after nine, a blue open-topped Golf with a silver go-faster streak down the side roared up to the front of the club. Freddie Pinker, in a white suit and sporting a single gold earring, climbed out of the back. Paulette, modestly dressed as ever, was the driver and she waved animatedly at him as she sped off round the back of the club to park. Freddie Pinker hitched up his trousers, pulled down his silver and blue waistcoat and ran his fingers through his tousled, blond-streaked, hairstyle. He was almost a foot shorter than the lady greeter at the club door. She stood under the purple and gold awning, which had been used to create a fancy entrance at ground floor level, and slightly to one side of a large flashing sign that read 'Madam Seraglio's Lair'. On the front of the building, despite the best efforts of the local Council, alternate pink and purple flashing neon lights had been displayed to depict a bottle pouring champagne into a glass. Underneath that a pair of stiletto sandals flashed in a sequence so that it looked as though the high-heeled shoes were walking along the front of the building. If anyone had any doubt as to the nature of the establishment, the front door carried a large printed sign warning customers that only properly dressed ladies could be allowed inside, except with special permission.

The Bank Holiday trade, Morgan had noticed, was pretty hectic. Certainly from seven o'clock quite a lot of people had gone in, all of them, so far as he could tell from a distance, dressed as ladies. Quite why so many women should congregate in one particular club was a question that did not trouble Morgan, although he could see why Freddie Pinker might find it congenial inside as he would be one of about three men, if you excluded the loincloth-clad young waiters he could see through the ground floor curtains. Quite a number of the women were very beautiful and the rest were of unparalleled ugliness. But that was true of men too, he thought, staring at his reflection in the beer glass.

Freddie Pinker chatted for a moment with the person at the door and then went in. This was Morgan's cue. He let himself carefully down from the bar stool and walked across the street. Looking fairly belligerent, he endeavoured to push past the greeter. This was a mistake. Such an action would be ill- considered under any circumstances but was definitely not designed to get by Gloria, who for a number of years had been highly successful in the world of professional wrestling. They eyed each other with mutual distaste. Gloria noted his battered appearance, stubble and plaster casts, the one on his right toe sticking out of a pair of hospital sandals. Morgan saw a twenty-five stone six foot five inch personage with an additional four inches on her high-heels and a further five inches from her red beehive hairstyle. To say Gloria recognised that Morgan was not one of their regulars would be a considerable understatement. She restrained her urge to throw him off the premises and, instead, blocked his way with her powerful left leg. The red sequinned evening gown she was wearing as a uniform was slit to the waist and, reaching inside the garter on her left thigh, she pulled out a matching red mobile phone.

'Madame Seraglio, we have a new visitor. Can he come in?'

Morgan scowled for all he was worth, standing his ground. Madame Seraglio, meanwhile, had consulted the CCTV screen that pointed over the entrance. There was a pause whilst Madame Seraglio assessed the situation and took in the full charm of Morgan's appearance.

'Yes. Bring him in and tell Annabelle to seat him at table four.'

Madame Seraglio had a fair idea as to what Morgan had in mind. He was, not surprisingly, instantly recognisable. She had been there when he had set about Freddie Pinker during the football game and she had had two separate accounts of attacks, potentially very serious, by Morgan on Freddie Pinker as narrated by Paulette.

'Come with me.' Gloria addressed Morgan who obliged, at a distance. Gloria went into the dark red reception area and snapped her fingers. Instantly two men wearing what looked like office clothes rushed up to help. They liked to be dominated and Gloria was always happy to oblige.

'Get me Annabelle, you worms.' They scurried off. Morgan looked completely disgusted but stood his ground. He could hear the pounding of disco music coming from one side of the building or possibly underneath it, he couldn't tell. Ahead of him was a black door that he couldn't see beyond. On his right was the cloakroom area. Eventually from behind it Annabelle appeared by pulling open a red curtain hanging at the back of the cloakroom section. Gloria leaned forwards and said in her husky voice:

'Madame wishes this gentleman to be seated at her special table.'

Annabelle was a good deal smaller than Gloria but was dressed in the same uniform. The only additional item she sported was a pair of full-length red net gloves over which her meaty forearms bulged.

'My pleasure.'

She beckoned Morgan to follow her and led him through the black door in front of him.

Morgan was taken to a table almost at the front of what appeared to be a nightclub floor. There was a small, slightly raised, stage about six feet ahead of him and on the left hand side were two doors. Behind him were anything up to twenty tables, difficult to make out in the low lighting and cigarette smoke. He could not see Pinker so decided to sit down and order a drink. Annabelle left a drinks card with him. There were only three items on the drinks menu. There was a bottle of champagne at £50, a bottle of pink champagne at £65 and a bottle of dry white wine at £25. Morgan was outraged but knew he had to buy something. He decided on white wine, even though he hated the stuff. Chances were it would take him all night to get down even half a bottle.

In front of him what looked like a Zulu dancing show was in full noisy progress. There was a three-man collection of musicians, mostly on percussion instruments, and three extremely energetic male dancers. Their costumes seemed to consist mainly of beads and feathers but there was no doubt they were extremely skilled. The audience was volubly cheering them on. He looked around, hoping to catch a glimpse of Pinker in the half-light. The man seemed to have disappeared altogether.

After about fifteen minutes Madame Seraglio, enjoying a quiet glass of pink champagne in her studio, pointed to the back of

Howard Morgan's head as it appeared on the CCTV screen of the nightclub zone.

'Freddie, darling, would you do something for me?'

'What's that then?' Freddie Pinker obligingly got up from his seat by the television where he and Paulette were watching the racing highlights from the early afternoon. He was used to running errands for Eric, being the younger brother, and found the transition to being Madame Seraglio's factotum quite painless.

'That dreadful man, your friend Mr. Morgan, is sitting in the nightclub. Would you mind terribly just walking past him without saying anything and going into salon No. 3? You need to go out the back way and then come back here. Is that alright?'

Freddie supposed that Madame Seraglio was up to something but he didn't mind: he had long since stopped trying to understand what Eric was planning from time to time and he was well accustomed to apparently meaningless requests. Besides, he wanted to get back to watch the second half of the programme and it was quicker to get on with it than waste time asking questions.

'Fine. Shall I go now?'

Madame Seraglio nodded and smiled.

Freddie walked right past Howard Morgan and opened the left hand door of the two, which Morgan could see more or less in front of him. The sight of Pinker at such close quarters made Morgan start muttering under his breath and he clutched his glass so hard one might be forgiven for thinking it would break. Morgan patted the jam jar in his pocket and laughed quietly to himself. Then he put down the glass and stroked the jacket pocket where he could feel the knives clinking together. It couldn't be long now. Pinker would soon be squirming alright. Operation Spy was going extremely well. The perfect plan. Nothing could possibly go wrong this time and he was ready for everything. Pinker hadn't the brains to defend himself, if only Morgan could get to him. Brains. Now that raised some interesting torture ideas. Morgan was starting to lose his concentration. All around him the Zulu dancers pranced, making their way through the tables before leaping back onto the stage to cheers from the audience.

A minute or so later Madame Seraglio herself stood behind Morgan's chair, or rather, loomed over it. He was hunched up with one elbow on the table and his cast-carrying foot stuck out in front. She bent over his left shoulder, enveloping him in a cloud of musky smells, and whispered:

'Would you care to join us for a private game of cards?'

She then swept past, swaying as she went, the lights bouncing back from the black sequins on her dark blue dress. She went through the same door as Pinker and closed it behind her. How could Morgan resist? He waited a couple of minutes then put the money for his drink on the table under his glass, got up and limped to the door. Nobody took the slightest notice of him: the floorshow was now at its height.

As Morgan opened the door, he saw at the far side of the room only four chairs and a small table with a lamp lit upon it. There was no apparent sign of anyone in the room, but that would have been a hasty conclusion. Madame Seraglio, who had been waiting behind it, with one foot pushed the door closed behind him. With her left hand held out a glass of blue-coloured champagne. She smiled steadily, fluttering her long false lashes and towering above him.

'Everyone has to drink my health before we play.'

Morgan took the drink and downed it in one.

'Cheers!'

She continued to smile, unblinkingly, at him.

'Do take a seat. I will just let the others know we now have a foursome.'

Whilst Morgan took a seat Madame Seraglio turned to lock the entrance door. But it made no difference to Morgan, who slid gracefully to the floor in a drug-induced sleep.

About an hour later Morgan woke up again. Or at any rate, he presumed he was awake. He came to to find himself lying naked apart from his underpants strapped to a bed, a red leather-covered bed, splay legged and face up. It was not comfortable at all. Then he heard Madame Seraglio at the end of the bed. The lighting was low and he could not see very much but what he saw he did not enjoy. Madame Seraglio was sitting, a mountain of blubber, between his legs. She appeared to be wearing a black leather bikini and both her legs were tattooed with black fishnet tights and suspenders. On her feet were red patent leather stilettos of a kind that the police would classify as an offensive weapon. One of the shoes had its point grazing Morgan's throat.

'Good evening, Mr. Morgan. What an unexpected pleasure! Let me introduce myself. I'm Nasty.'

And Morgan knew she was.

'My dear Mr Morgan, what a wonderful opportunity you have bestowed upon my humble establishment and how thoughtful of you to have brought along some playthings with you.' Madame Seraglio picked up from the bed two of Morgan's implements. 'It's such a delight when our friends try to tease us with surprises.'

Morgan didn't know what was going on but he could neither move nor speak. His two socks had been stuffed in his mouth and his trouser belt had been used as a gag. He shook his head furiously from side to side.

'No need to be so modest, Mr Morgan, I know you are just the man to enjoy the sort of surprises I like to give. I can see you've been trying something out already! Look at these lovely cuts and plasters. But I can help them hurt so much more, darling.'

She wiggled her hand under his nose in delight and pushed the stiletto heel into the flesh under his chin quarter of an inch or so. Morgan would have shaken his head again but the pain of the last time was still fresh in his mind. Madame Seraglio smiled serenely and reached over to the side of the bed, where she put the knives back with their companions. Morgan dared not move his face, although he could feel blood trickling down his chest like a warm snake. Next into his line of vision came a huge hand with a plastic surgical glove on it.

'You see, it's no use trying pain without years of practice. This, for instance, is sold in every gardening shop and is exquisite if you know how to use it. Let me show you.'

Morgan tried to grunt dissent but nothing came out. Madame Seraglio held aloft a large cactus and rubbed it energetically in the cuts on his chin, head and face. At once sharp and dull pain merged into a wall of throbbing fire, as hundreds of tiny barbs seared their way deep into the flesh.

'Lovely, isn't it? And only the beginning. Just think where we can go tonight, all on our own. And if I'm very careful we can make it look like you did it all on your own, so you can show your friends. Now, isn't that a good idea? Or shall I bring in Little Freddie to lend a hand?' Morgan was trying furiously somehow to say 'no'.

'You don't like that idea? No? Oh, then, very well, we'll do it all on our own. What fun we'll have!'

The bed heaved as she reached over for his sharpest knife, holding it an inch or so from his face.

'Sharp is good. Yes, it is good. But it lacks a certain style, I always feel. You know, the same is true of fire. It's too, let us say, direct. No frisson of anticipation at all. But put them together and a little goes a long way. Let me show you what I mean.'

So saying she slowly and deliberately cut his underpants away. The fear that gripped Morgan as the implement approached his privates was convulsive but nothing compared to the pain he experienced as his torturer set fire to his pubic hair with a tiny jewelled cigarette lighter that she had taken from a pocket on the inner side of her bikini pants. Morgan, purple-faced and writhing in agony, made nothing but muffled noises.

'Delicious, isn't it?' Madame Seraglio observed, extinguishing the flame with a red leather duster. 'You see how it is: anticipation sharpens the little something that follows. There are simply so many super things to do. We will have fun. But do let me show you the difference between flesh and bone. Bone is really in a league of its own, and people seem so easily to forget its potential. But I see you must have had a little taste for it already.'

Morgan was again violently shaking his head as she started to stroke his broken arm. His lower body was smoking and his legs were shaking.

'Breaking is such a crude method. You must have been so keen to try it. Poor darling, it's fracturing you need to practice. Hairline fractures are a speciality of mine. Simply marvellous. And so effective. Did you know that nerves in the arm go all the way into the face and teeth? Or perhaps we should work our way down to the face. Start in the eardrum, say? No? You'd rather start with the arm? Oh, have it your way then…'

After four hours of cutting, teasing, inflaming and strategic burning by Madame Seraglio, Morgan had blacked out with fear and pain and exhaustion.

Gloria, on her employer's instructions, drove him early next morning to be dumped, unconscious, at the doors of the mental hospital from which Arthur Smollett had recently escaped. Gloria also had strict instructions to notify the nearest nursing staff member that Morgan had insisted on being left there, and had said the staff were to be told he wanted his medicine otherwise he would do it to himself again unless they took him in. When the nurse searched his pockets she found Morgan's collection of knives and a cactus, which hurt her hand. It was clear from the position of the various wounds that Morgan must have been intending himself serious harm and certainly could not be trusted to keep his property any longer. Gloria explained that she didn't know who he was but funny people did sometimes come to her work to make a nuisance of themselves and the policy was to drop them back home, if the address was known and they were still there the next morning. The nurse on duty decided the easiest thing would be to put him in a wheelchair and let him sleep in reception until Mrs. Bong came in at eight o'clock.

When tidings of the new arrival were relayed to Mrs. Bong she decided the only thing to do was for the duty nurse to wake him up and for his particulars to be taken. It was not long before the staff ascertained not only that Morgan was barking mad, shouting and raving about exploding cats, pink men at football matches, meat pies with human flesh in them, sleeping in coffins, setting fire to himself and gouging out the liver of some enemy he was going to capture with a jam jar. When they asked him where he came from and he responded with Little Waterton, the duty nurse reported the matter immediately to Mrs. Bong, who came down personally. She took in thoughtfully the dishevelled and ruined figure of Howard Morgan, who scrawled his signature on the particulars as correct and was told he could have a bed to rest, if he liked. He did like, though he continued to shout periodically at imaginary figures with whips and knives.

Dr Reekin, her visiting consultant, was called into the office once he had been taken to converse with Morgan and after he had sedated him. Mrs Bong had trusted to Providence and been rewarded. She was not quite sure how to begin, but the situation showed promise: Dr Reekin got £300 just for turning up once a week and another £150 for each piece of paperwork he signed.

'Fancy that,' Mrs. Bong observed casually, handing him a cup of coffee.

'Thanks. Fancy what?' Dr. Reekin asked taking a chocolate biscuit from a tin on Mrs Bong's desk. He was overworked and had four children and a wife who was pregnant.

'Why, don't you see? Little Waterton. We are supposed to have lost someone from Little Waterton. And now, you see, we have someone from Little Waterton again.'

The Doctor, who was new to this particular institution, didn't see at all.

'I need to finish my rounds.' He drank the coffee at speed and put the biscuit in his overall pocket. His Scottish voice carried a hint of annoyance.

'Oh, don't worry yourself with the paperwork. I'll deal with it. But I need you to sign the form here before you go, otherwise I can't process your payment. Just a formality, but you know how it is. We need to do it all properly'

Reekin signed the printed form, which was apart from that blank, and excused himself. The door shut behind him with a bang, closing off the clanging noise of the breakfast trolley being brought round for the patients not requiring secure conditions.

Jamie Bong subscribed to the theory that if you helped life along, it would help you along too. She knew just what to do. How easy it would be to conflate the records of the Little Waterton patient who disappeared with the Little Waterton patient who miraculously and conveniently had just appeared. Or, more accurately, re-appeared. Only she and Inspector Jesmond had cause to know the details and it was most unlikely he would insist on checking the specific identity if she could point to someone being re-admitted. For example, now that Dr Reekin had certified that the new arrival was completely unstable and needed to be kept securely on an indefinite basis, there would be no further cause for direct police intervention at all. Just a full drugs regime and a nice lock and key. After all, he could always be released back into the community after a year or two, when everyone had forgotten about the explosion. She finished writing on the form. Then she searched for a few minutes in one of the filing cabinets that lined the walls. The earlier form relating to Arthur Smollett was not hard to find. How convenient office shredders are when one is in a fix, she thought. When the racket of the shredder had died down she walked back to the telephone and dialled a familiar number.

'Inspector Jesmond, please.'

On her face an evil smile played.

Chapter 25: Expensive thrills

Chicago's nightlife may have had few attractions for Larry Amadino, but its afternoon life certainly did. Normal evenings he was on duty doing the things he needed to do – checking shipments, seeing people, shooting people, keeping an eye on the bars and clubs his managers ran, plotting his next double-cross. Normal afternoons, on the other hand, were a time for relaxation and the ladies. Karl the German and Carlos Estrella were always with him, of course. They had a kind of routine, if you could call it that, although they never liked to think of anything as predictable.

Today was the twenty-seventh of August, a nice quiet day, particularly quiet compared to the chaos of the previous twenty-four hours. For reasons he didn't know Santini had instructed him to pack up operations and move into the adjoining district. Amadino had had to make a show of compliance but, having packed up virtually everything ready for the move that went ahead at midnight, he still hadn't finally worked out whether it was a good time to come out as a solo operator or whether to wait for an opportunity to take out Santini in the next couple of months and use the cash he now had to take over the existing empire and buy the three top men, excluding Bernstein, who was too loyal to Santini and would have to go as well. For now he shelved the problem, more from exhaustion than anything else. Tomorrow goods were due in and Amadino was ready to deal with them. He was not in the mood to do any more worrying and so he did what he always did for relaxation. He went for a cup of Japanese tea in the side bar of the Hotel Kyoto.

The Kyoto was a wonderful place. It was far enough away from the businesses he ran that he could almost forget all about them. Karl and Carlos, his bodyguards, liked it there too. The front lobby was completely open and they had a clear view across from the side bar of anybody who stepped through the revolving door on the opposite end of the building. Amadino ordered his green tea from the waiter, and the men drank coke. They were young and asked no questions. It was rare for a gangster to hire mercenaries rather than promote his ambitious associates from street enforcement. Amadino could have done things the more normal way but his moves right now were ones he didn't want to share with anyone who might understand their implications. Karl didn't interest himself in much besides his wages and his food. Carlos barely spoke English and was only interested in his wages and women. Neither of them spoke much at all, which suited Amadino fine.

The side bar was nice and cool. Beautifully decorated Japanese plates carrying small mouthfuls of food were placed on the table in front of Amadino. The mirrors around him blended into the white marble walls. The waiter smiled and nodded: he didn't speak much English either. They were waiting. Amadino looked at his diamond-studded watch and sipped his tea. He'd picked up a brochure from the bar on the way in and began to read about the tea ceremony in Japan, to pass the time. He was casual but his men weren't. The ceasefire had been operating for only a very short period and there were any number of old scores that got settled under cover of this kind of war. They had understood enough about their employer to realise he was not popular everywhere.

Just when Amadino had been about to give up and move on, a woman walked into the bar and sat down. She made no move in his direction but the men knew that's why they had come. In her late twenties, she was tall and athletic in build, with platinum-white hair and high cheekbones. Her eyes, heavily emphasised by makeup, stood out a brilliant blue. No one said a word. The waiter knew her and brought out a tray of tea for her, and a second cup. A moment later another woman, strikingly beautiful, but dark, came into the bar from the ladies' rest room and joined the first. They chatted idly for a few minutes and Amadino continued to read his brochure, ignoring them. The men looked at each other and, taking care his employer did not see him, Carlos winked at Karl. They were looking forward to a half hour's peace and quiet.

The blonde stood up, paid the waiter and walked gracefully by the reception desk to the lift. Her friend followed, passing by Amadino's table and quietly placing on it a flat electronic keycard and under it a hotel calling card with the number 2901 written on the other side. The number was face down to the table. The two women disappeared into the lift and still Amadino carried on reading his brochure. Five minutes or so later he put it down and pocketed the card.

'I'll be gone maybe a half-hour. Stay here and stay alert. Cover me to the lift.' Carlos grinned. 'Go smirk in the bathroom, dogface son of a bitch.' He could say what he liked. Carlos didn't understand. But Karl did.

'We will do everything as you wish,' said Karl, walking with his boss to the lift and waiting until the white-suited Amadino got in. Amadino was only in his early thirties and still young enough to dress in the flashy way that most of his older colleagues no longer did. Owing to the war he had been promoted young. Amadino pushed the plastic keycard into the lift control to gain access to the upper executive floors and the doors closed behind him as he left his bodyguards in the hotel foyer.

Room 2901 wasn't a room at all. It was a suite of ten rooms with a six-seater dining table and floor-to-ceiling bronzed windows overlooking the city on two sides. He turned the heavy metal handle quickly as soon as the keypad lit up green. He went into the lobby of the room. The girls would be waiting for him inside, just like last time and the time before. He counted himself among the sophisticated when it came to female company and he only paid for skill, not enthusiasm or looks. These girls were pricey but worth every cent. They spoke English, with strong accents, sure, but he remembered enough Russian from his days in class back in Cuba to be able to follow what they sometimes said to each other and occasionally he would break into their conversation with a few Russian words of his own. These were easily the most beautiful girls he'd found and he reckoned they'd be good for a few more visits before anyone recognised his habits.

'Come in,' said the blonde, taking his arm. She was still wearing the dark blue two-piece outfit he'd seen her in. She led him into the main room beyond the first door. It was designed to be both restful and elaborate at the same time. The carpets were pale green, and the walls were papered in pale green silk, patterned to show Japanese characters on top of ocean waves. Two big, low sofas of Western design lay ahead, covered by densely patterned off-white silk. Either side of the window stood a serene arrangement of isolated flowers and tree branches. Amadino could hear the water splashing to fill the Japanese sunken bath in the room beyond. He liked to start with a wet massage.

The dark haired woman must have been in the bathroom because her friend looked towards the inner door.

'Welcome, and please to seat yourself.' The blonde had a deep voice and impeccable courtesy. Amadino was delighted with it, since he had never previously found it with the whores who entertained him. He took a place on the sofa. 'I will make you our relax drink again, if you like.'

'Please,' he replied.

The table in front of them already contained an assortment of miniature bottles, not all of them labelled, and a cocktail glass. He'd tried it last time and it was good, so he leaned forward to watch her measure and mix. It was very precise work. Behind he heard the rustle of the dress belonging to the dark-haired woman as she came into the room. He smelled her perfume, and remembered it.

The blonde took no notice and carried on with her steady progress. She didn't even look up when the dark haired woman, in her padded leather gloves, whipped a flexible steel wire round Amadino's neck from behind and expertly garrotted him. It was over almost without a struggle and virtually in silence.

The dark haired woman laid Amadino out on the sofa. No blood had been spilled. She walked to the outer door of 2901 and knocked twice before opening it. A short man, Asiatic in appearance, and wearing a white overall and cap wheeled in a big laundry basket. The woman said something to him in a language, which was neither English nor Russian. He went to the sofa, removed a few white towels from his basket and hauled Amadino feet first into it. He then replaced the towels to cover him. The blonde meanwhile said something more to the man in the same language. She opened the lid of the basket and found Amadino's head. With her left hand she closed his eyes and with her right she put into his open mouth a small cut diamond, taking care to leave it under his tongue. Then she used both hands to snap his jaws shut. The man put the towels back for the second time and pushed the basket to the outer door. A few seconds later he was trundling it down the corridor.

The blonde had a paper carrier bag and out of it, in the bedroom, the two women each pulled a change of clothes and a wig. Their hotel bill had already been paid and so they walked to the service lift, calling it with a service card normally only available to the staff.

At the basement floor they walked out into the car park where a white European BMW saloon was waiting. They got in the back and were gone.

It was over an hour later before Karl and Carlos began to get concerned that Larry the Latin had not returned. They insisted that the Japanese desk clerk came with them to search for him. However it was a big hotel and neither of them knew which room he had been in. Larry always figured he needed a bit of space. After all, if he didn't tell his bodyguards exactly where he was on these occasions, they couldn't be tortured to reveal it. Karl insisted the best way to search was methodically, starting with the lowest floors and working upwards. Fortunately at that time of day most of the rooms were unoccupied. By the time the three of them reached the twenty-ninth floor, some two hours later, both bodyguards knew Larry the Latin would not be found alive. What neither knew was that he would never be found at all. There was no sign of him, or a struggle, anywhere in the building.

Late that evening, when he received from a breathless Marvin Bernstein the exact news of Latin's disappearance, Paul Santini showed only slight surprise.

'You knew?' Bernstein was genuinely horrified.

'Not exactly,' Santini replied. Latin had been another of Santini's trusted, handpicked, men 'Let's say it was only a question of time.'

'Papadopolous?'

'No.'

'Nazzura?'

'No.'

'The South Americans?'

'No. It doesn't matter who. A lot of people have reason to be impatient with him.'

Bernstein was painfully aware of the Angel's verdict from the previous day and he knew there could be no reprisals. Santini had so far said nothing about the extent of Latin's outside activities, confining himself to an explanation of what the Shallcombes had led him to suspect in relation to the shipments and the war.

'How big is the damage?'

'There is no damage, Marvin. Three hours ago a young boy, a nobody, dropped a letter in on our front door here.'

Santini pulled an opened white envelope from his pocket and placed it on the table between them. Bernstein reached out, curiously, to inspect it. On the front were scrawled the words 'Mr. Paul Santini, Chairman'. Inside Bernstein found a wristwatch, diamond-studded, bearing on its back the legend 'Lorenzo Amadino. Christmas 2001.' Bernstein also had a watch like this. This one had been given to Larry the Latin on his promotion to senior ranks following the recent death of Santini's brother-in-law. He never took it off. Bernstein shivered.

'You didn't tell me.'

'No need to alarm you before we knew what happened. Tomorrow should give us no problems. Promote Tony Urbino or bring Ferrara out of retirement for a couple of weeks. Either one of them can handle our business until the shipments go through and our withdrawals are tidied up. We have new plans, Marvin. But we needed first to see if our partners were as capable we were told.'

'We?'

'From tomorrow night we are in alliance with George Papadopolous. We have a new business. Let me tell you about it later.'

Bernstein's face froze. What was going on? And how many of Santini's deputies would be sacrificed?

'New business?'

'Yeah. Diamonds. Two billion US dollars' worth.'

They were once more in Santini's office. The older man looked out over the City calmly. Bernstein, who had been very agitated at first, sat down. There was effectively nothing he could do anyway. Santini continued talking, but quietly, almost to himself. 'There's no threat here, Marvin. Latin did his own outside security and now I know why. You're safe enough. I gotta admire the speed, the thoroughness, of those operatives. We can do a funeral, memorial service, next week, without a body.'

'Memorial service? You're sure the body won't be found?'

'Yeah. I guess they took it in payment. Just make sure his mother comes out from Havana. Look after her. Make sure she has enough to live. I hear he sent nothing back there.'

'I'll get on to Ferrara first in case we want to move Tony Urbino direct into new operations. I'll do it right now.'

'Wait.' Santini held up one hand. 'I should thank you, Marvin, for looking after the business while I was away.'

'My pleasure, Mr Santini. I'm very glad you're back, believe me.'

Bernstein had seen sudden changes of direction before but never so calm a loss of a senior executive.

'Marvin, you ever heard of the Shurtan Republic?'

'I know where it is.'

'Day after tomorrow, I want you to find out everything there is to know. And find me a couple of reliable people that speak Russian, but aren't Russian. Or Shurtan.'

'When you say not Russian, how about the former Soviet Republics?'

One of the many reasons why Santini trusted Bernstein never to double-cross him or scheme to take over was his lack of desire for dramatic change: the mark of a true boss was a hunger Bernstein simply didn't have. This meticulous attention to detail was his irreplaceable quality. He deserved reassurance.

'Simple refugees or immigrants OK but no one in any kind of racket. Otherwise you decide. And, Marvin, Larry turned out to be a poisonous snake to a lot of people, including to me. But I didn't need to do a thing about it. One day you'll hear the full story but right now we have a lot of work to do to get ready. Believe me, you're not in any kind of threat here.'

*

Diamonds began flooding quietly into Chicago that September. On the third Saturday in October, Paul Santini met Bernstein and his Harvard-educated assistant, Detmold Karajan, to look over the goods and be briefed on progress. In the centre of the Santini vault was a stack of six plastic boxes.

'What are these, Marvin?'

'Diamonds graded according to quality. We have every stone double checked on arrival.'

'Any duds?'

'None, sir,' Karajan answered. He was primarily responsible for that side of the activities. He had just returned from Antwerp and had recruited two specialists on six months contracts. Santini bent over a plastic box, the size of a small rubbish bin and ran his fingers through the contents.

'I ain't never seen goods like this.'

'No, sir. It's very encouraging.' Bernstein replied. 'The only snag is that we've about bought every profitable business that's for sale within a two State radius of here heading west.'

'Then go further west. Have you any new ideas?'

'Yes.' Bernstein was most valuable when most creative. 'There are a lot of companies only profitable at the margins but sitting on valuable real estate. Some of these could easily file for bankruptcy, without suspicion. We set up a supply contract where they owe us money and we pay the owners under the table in diamonds. We then take stock for debt and take over companies. We strip out the properties then sell on or file Chapter 11 bankruptcy for what's left. It's foolproof, and because we'll be doing the parts of the operation you can see across the State, it'll be taken as normal market practice. We put a five-year moratorium on market-ing the diamonds and they won't break the terms. They know who we are.'

'Good. Very good. Do you have any targets?'

'Here's the list.' Bernstein picked a notebook out of another plas-tic bin and handed it to Santini. The record storage method was unusual but convenient, and safe.

'These businesses aren't ones I recognise.'

'We're outside the Mafia tradition. These are legitimate owners, but greedy.'

'Even better. No turf wars outside.'

'I had a meeting two days ago with Anna Papadopolous before she goes back to Antwerp. They have no problems but are running short on investment ideas. Some of their people don't have the edu-cation to deal with the legitimate companies.'

'Then go do it for them. Charge half of one percent on transac-tions under half a million dollars and a quarter of one percent on anything over that.'

'We could charge a lot more.'

'Maybe. But they gotta breathe. Overcharge and they don't get dependent on us. They expand, train their own. Give them the ser-vice and they stay onside. Payment is easy. Take dollars from the market and reroute them to the Shurtans.'

'OK, Mr Santini. I have no problems to report.'

'And you, anything?' Santini looked hard at Karajan.

'None.'

'OK.' Santini said it in a way that told them the discussion was over. As he turned to leave the vault (his heavies were waiting on the other side of the door, only three of them now conditions were peaceful), Santini beckoned Bernstein over again. 'Marvin, one last thing. Send a basket of flowers to Maddie Shallcombe.'

'Any message, sir?'
'Thanks. Best wishes. Paul.'

Chapter 26: Water

'Psst! Quick! Psst!'

The Bishop looked up from reading his sermon for the coming Sunday. It had been a slow day, the last Thursday in October.

'Over here!'

He still couldn't see whereabouts Eric's voice was coming from. The Bishop put his teacup down. The day was drawing to a close and the Palace conservatory was starting to feel chilly. The sun was sinking slowing over the hedges of the garden.

Tap! Tap!

There he was. Eric's face appeared at one of the glass panes of the conservatory door. There was no sign of Maddie. What was he wearing? It might have been a floor length black cloak. Eric was standing in the shadow and gesticulating for the Bishop to come out. Not everyone in his shoes, given the Bishop's previous encounters with Maddie and Eric, would have remained in the conservatory at all.

'Psst! Open up! Quick!'

The Bishop stood up and opened the conservatory door. Eric swooped across and grabbed his arm.

'Come on! She's waiting!'

'But the Archdeacon is due at…What are you wearing?'

'Aha!' Teased Eric. 'Don't worry, we've got one for you. Nice and warm, these. Hurry up, though.'

Eric was chivvying him down the back path towards the Palace again.

'Where are we going? The door's on the other side of the building.'

'Oh no it isn't! Come on, hurry.'

'What do you mean? Of course it…' He stopped talking and stared at a small half-sunken door at semi-basement level previously concealed completely by bushes. Eric was holding aside a swathe of yellowing leaves. 'What's in there?'

'It's perfectly safe. Come on, or it'll be too late. You'll love it. You've got first go.'

Before he could say a word more, Eric had hustled him down three dark steps. Once he was at the bottom, Eric darted back and shut the wooden door with a bang. It was pitch black.

'Where are you, Eric? Where are the lights?'

'Don't need them. Just a tic.' Eric pulled a powerful torch from a pocket on the inside of his cloak. As he held out the beam of light, the Bishop realised Eric was wearing, apart from the cloak, only a pair of black boots and his underpants. This, the Bishop deduced, must be the Palace undercroft, whose entrance had been mislaid some time during the Second World War when a stray bomb intended for Gloucester docks landed on the south wing of the Palace, killing the gardener and one of the Bishop's predecessors in office.

'Better put your costume on quick.'

'But I....'

'No, really, the rats will eat your clothes. We've put rat-deterrent on the cloaks.'

'What!!!'

The Bishop rapidly stripped down to his underpants and shoes, and grabbed a second black cloak, held out by Eric. It did indeed have a faint disinfectant-like smell upon it. But at least it was warm. Eric was forging ahead with the torch, creating a path of light ahead of him but leaving the Bishop in absolute darkness.

'I say! Wait for me!'

It was quite a scramble to keep up with him. Spiders' webs were hanging from the low ceiling and it was impossible to tell what was stored down here. Big boxes covered in black dust lay stacked everywhere. What were they? Ammunition? Food crates? Wines? Old furniture? The smell of damp pervaded everything. The Bishop was listening for the scamper of rats, or anything else for that matter. He heard water dripping and slapping. The Palace moat ran round three sides of the building quite close by, but it was at a much deeper level than the undercroft.

Eric was headed to the wall at the far side, where in the distance the Bishop could see flickering lights. As they picked their way closer, they could see the entire section of this side of a wall of boxes had been lit by dozens of slow burn candles. It was practically dark outside. Almost at once Eric's concealed portable tape machine played several minutes' worth of bats squeaking and fluttering. The Bishop tried to see if there were bats on the ceiling. He knew there'd be a preservation order on them if there were. It was a fatal lapse of concentration. During it Eric completely disappeared.

'Eric? Eric? Where are you?' Some of the candles were starting to falter. There was no point trying to go back: he hadn't the faintest idea how to thread a path through the boxes in the darkness beyond this section. 'Hello? Is anyone there?'

Where had he gone?

'Oooh!'

'Aha!' The Bishop at least knew Maddie was somewhere nearby: but where? Her voice hadn't sounded too far away but the bat noises were distracting. Then he stopped for a second. This was rather fun. Wonder where she is? About twenty yards away he saw a slight movement and dashed towards it. It was a coffin lid dropping shut. He approached it with caution until he felt with his hands that it was clean and new. Undoubtedly stock from Pinker & Pinker. On slowly lifting the lid, he found Maddie Shallcombe wearing only a white cloak (presumably as a fake shroud) pretending to be asleep. Next to her head he found an unlabelled glass jam jar. Maddie began wriggling about. He lifted the white cloak to discover he had been wrong. She was wearing something – a single flail leather whip, maybe twelve feet long. It was the kind used by nineteenth century lion tamers but right now it was being used to bind her hands to her waist with the handle fast between her legs. It must have been fairly tight because no amount of exotic wriggling shifted it in the slightest. This game was quite distinctly improving. He hesitated. Eric always had a plan, but what was it?

Then he considered the jam jar, and opened it extra carefully. No pythons or other animals appeared. Good. In the background Eric switched the tape to shrieking ghosts. Yes, he must on the right track. It crossed his mind that by now the Reverend Hollis would surely be unconscious with fear. Perhaps one was meant to eat the stuff in the jar? Think like Eric. No, better, think like Maddie. He stuck a finger in the dark goo and tasted it. Maddie was watching with one eye, between wiggles.

'Oohh!' she moaned with the shrieking ghosts.

'Mmm! Delicious.' What an excellent taste? A sort of syrup. He knew exactly what this was for. He tipped it over Maddie's breasts and smeared it rapidly over her neck and most of her torso. She didn't seem to be complaining but wasn't keeping still either.

After fifteen minutes or so he'd managed to lick off a fair amount of the goo. Eric must have been up to something in the background: the odd rusty clank could be heard behind the ghosts. The tape switched to drums being beaten very loudly. The Bishop recognised the opening bars of 'Thus Spake Zarathustra.'

'Untie me!' gasped Maddie.

He complied, with difficulty in the general stickiness, but managed in the end.

'Sit here!' she commanded, pushing him onto the coffin lid. There were two metal hooks on the inside of the lid and she tied him to them by the ankle. The Bishop was more concerned as to what the music was leading up to and he strained his eyes to see the area where he deduced Eric must be.

Maddie, in her cloak, was sufficiently goo-covered to make a passable bride, and Eric pulled the lever that was to cause her bridegroom to rise amongst them. It sort of worked, but rather too rapidly. Instead of creaking slowly out of his coffin, the life size metal-framed Count Dracula over by the wall shot out of his constraints and hit the old lead piping above him with the force of an axe blow.

'Oops!' said Eric.

The pipe was ripped. Water began to be pushed out, until the force built up. In a few seconds the pipe had completely severed and water was gushing at high volume onto the floor.

'What's happened, Eric?' Yelled Maddie over the roar of water and the din of the music.

'Not sure. Water pipe.' Eric replied. He had moved over to the area immediately by the burst pipe and could barely hear anything.

'The mains to the Palace, possibly the central heating pipes,' observed the Bishop, trying to undo the bonds on his feet. One was off but the other wouldn't budge. At least the water was warm.

Maddie, soaked to the skin, joined Eric by the wall: they were feeling about for controls for lights. Too late. The water cascaded down across the floor then up over the first layer of boxes, extinguishing the candles. It was totally dark.

'Give me your torch, Eric!' Yelled Maddie. Eric switched it on and held it out for her to shine towards the wall for him.

'Got them!' Shouted Eric in reply.

'No! Don't!' The Bishop tried to be heard over the row. 'Stop! You'll fuse the electrics.'

Too late. Eric flicked a couple of switches up and they heard the snap of the electricity mains going dead.

'Oops!' said Eric again. Count Dracula's coffin was floating round at knee depth. Other boxes were lifting and shifting, banging into one another and splintering. There was a distinct squeal of rats somewhere behind them. The music still hammered on: the tape machine was on top of a high pile of boxes. The Bishop calculated that in a very short space of time all three of them would drown. Until he freed his leg, he couldn't do a thing. 'Come on, Maddie, think of something!' He muttered.

The water was up at waist height. Eric had climbed to the tape machine where his head hit the ceiling. He had run out of ideas. 'Sorry about this. Must have rigged the tension too tight,' he said ruefully.

The Bishop was stood on one leg, the coffin lid floating securely next to him. Maddie had clambered across the scene to the side-wall.

'It's alright,' she shouted unheard. Grace Shallcombe used to play in the undercroft as a girl and Maddie knew from her stories about the place and her own occasional visits that somewhere along this wall there was a lever to open the sluicegate from cellar to moat. She couldn't see the gate but knew it existed, and had herself previously seen the lever but taken no notice of it. The water continued to rise. Chest height and the Bishop was lying over the coffin lid like a surfboard and paddling towards her, more to stay near the beam of light from the torch and away from the rat noises, he hoped. Eric was somewhere behind them, presumably still at high level.

'Got it!' Maddie found the lever and slammed into it with all her force and considerable weight. The lever juddered. At least it hadn't been dismantled. 'Move!' She tried again. This time the lever shifted, and all in one movement the concealed sluicegate swung into action. The entire face of one wall fell outwards and a swell of almost ceiling-high water rushed towards it. The tape machine groaned as it fell into the drink. Maddie, who had not let go of the lever, threw the torch into the water and instead grabbed Eric's foot as he swept by in the current. She pulled him onto a shelf by the lever. 'Where's Porker?' she asked peering about.

Eric pointed towards the distance where against the night sky they could just make out the crouching figure of the Bishop, clad in his underpants, surfing at racing speed out into the Palace moat.

Luckily the gardener and his friend were fishing there. They were unaware of the disasters that had overtaken the Palace water, heating, lighting and electricity. But they had certainly seen the waterfall that erupted from beneath the Palace, propelling the Bishop across their fishing lines and raising water levels in the moat so high as to threaten an overspill! Both men had already jumped to their feet. The gardener recovered first.

'Your Grace! What has happened?'

'Give me a hand, man,' the Bishop spluttered. 'I'm on a survival course. Get blankets for my instructors.'

Not far away Maddie and Eric, hearing this in the now uncannily silent night, looked at each other. A grin reappeared on Eric's face.

'Happy Halloween, Maddie!'

*

There were two letters in Robert Thornhill's hands. In his left, a crumpled one he had taken from his trouser pocket, being a letter to which he had not yet replied. In his right, an unopened fat white envelope bearing in print on the top left hand corner the bold black words 'Dale, Dale & Ogden'. It had arrived that morning by post and he had put it on the mantelpiece to open when he was able to think in peace and quiet. He hadn't seen Rhiannon since last Friday morning and the farmhouse windows were dark in the evenings. No one had seen her. He'd made it his business, casually, to ask. When the will was read, she'd said she'd wait until Christmas before going anywhere. So why would the solicitors be writing to him now? She never went away for the weekend.

A freezing wind howled against the windowpanes of Blue Grace Cottage and down the chimneys. Thornhill was sitting at the kitchen table and looked up. The cottage was in an exposed position and he reckoned the bonfires over at Higher Waterton would not be affected. The field for the annual Bonfire Night celebrations was the same one used for the funfair during Wakes Week, only this time there would be three separate official bonfires, each with its own Guy. In line with recent practice, and in an effort to stop the plethora of Bonfire Night face-burnings and other serious accidents, the local

Parish Councils and the Fire Brigade had banded together to run one big bonfire for each village in the same field. The three Parishes clubbed together to have a single, massive, fireworks display and a single open air potato bake and barbecue. All the Thornhill family, with the exception of Robert, and all the farm workers would be over there that evening, celebrating robustly the failure of Guy Fawkes in his attempt to blow up James I and his Parliament. Robert didn't feel like going. Besides, he needed time to think. He knew what was in the first letter but wasn't sure how to respond. Gilbert, on Lord Errington's behalf, had written offering a long farm business tenancy and proposing a partnership with the Estate in selling turf. Robert would not agree the rent level suggested, but they would not have expected him to. The partnership was very tempting, very. He could have taken it even without Rhiannon's help but he was waiting to hear from her. Under the table Cathy's cat began walking repeatedly over his feet. It was annoying him so he picked it up and threw it out of the front door by the porch. Stupid animal. In the distance the horizon was lit up by a flickering, ghostly, light – it was the reflection of bonfires all over the county, some big, some small. For several days the sound of bangers going off round the villages announced the proximity of today, the fifth of November.

It was a Tuesday. Robert returned to the table and put the recent Errington offer under a cup to weigh it down open. He had finished his supper. Kathleen had left it in the oven for him – roast beef, mashed potatoes and peas. The remnants had been put to the far side of the table so as to leave a clearing where he could study his post. Nowadays he was alone at night in the house. Linda had gone back to Durham weeks ago and Billy was living over at Hamset Manor. Usually Robert would spend the late afternoon at the milk processing plant office and in the early evening on the telephone to agents and people buying and selling various things. He had a pad of paper by the phone and Kathleen collected the slips in the morning, typed the instructions and gave them to the various people for following up. By half past nine of an evening, unless he was going down to the pub with the men, Thornhill would be getting ready for an early night and an early morning next day. He rarely slept beyond 5.30am.

That morning he'd got up at five, having lain awake most of the night. He had no idea where Rhiannon could be. He'd never heard her speak of other friends. He tried to work out where she might be, from fragments of her past conversations. So tonight he returned to the same question and forced himself to go again over the events of last Friday morning. He just couldn't see how it had gone wrong.

Knock!Knock! The brass pig. What do you want? Don't be hostile. Baby crying. Must speak to you. Some other time. Why avoiding me? Leave me alone. Business deal. Baby crying. Go away. Work together. Baby crying louder. Go away. Let me in. Get out, can't force your way in here. Talk to me, business opportunity. Not now, please go away. Don't try to push me out. Rhiannon crying. Baby screaming. Dogs barking. Then he kissed her. Thornhill shied away from the memory and quickly blanked it off.

Where was she? Joshua's car was still at the farmhouse and all her stuff was still to be seen through the windows. Not quite all, a voice in his head corrected him. Her jewellery box is gone. Rhiannon had a pottery box, six inches or so square and three deep. She had made it herself and once had showed it to him for him to admire, how the flowers were painted on. Inside, he had noticed, there wasn't much – a couple of gold neck chains, one with a St. Christopher, and her wedding ring.

The outside temperature had dropped considerably and swirls of leaves were tapping against the window on the other side of the room. Inside it was warm. Probably for most people's taste too warm, but Thornhill was used to the temperature levels his late, sickly, wife had found desirable and Kathleen had simply left everything as it had been.

Thornhill decided to boil the kettle for a cup of tea. He was delaying opening the letter. Had he offered her the half million pounds for the freehold land? No. He didn't think so. But then more bits of that fateful morning were coming back to him again. Things he shouldn't have said but had and other things he should have said but hadn't, and worst of all, things he'd done when he shouldn't and not done when he should. No use thinking about that now, he told himself. He walked back to the table. The kettle had boiled but he didn't bother with the tea.

The tenancy and the freehold land together and the turf partnership, now that would be worthwhile. There was big potential in the turf and he would push the Errington partners hard for control. Gilbert couldn't manage day to day, wouldn't want to. Errington couldn't do it himself. He'd tried and failed. With Rhiannon on the sales side they could try the American market. Had he said that to her? No. He didn't think so. Or had he?

He walked round the table, and sat down. Both letters lay in front of him. Time to do it. He picked up the solicitors' letter and opened it, clumsily.

'Dear Mr. Thornhill,

Re: The Estate of Joshua Thornhill, deceased.

We have received instructions from your fellow Executor, Mrs. Rhiannon Thornhill, as residuary beneficiary of her husband's estate, that she wishes to offer you the opportunity to purchase the freehold land comprising the bulk of the estate property. We have recently secured, on the estate's behalf, a valuation from a reputable local firm, Thomas Evans & Co., of whom you are aware, which is attached for your information. Mrs. Thornhill is aware of their valuation as follows:

(i) £750,000 Freehold land as per attached Schedule, with vacant possession.
(ii) £250,000 Thornhill Dairies, as a going concern.
(iii) Blue Grace farm tenant right claims, live and deadstock.

She has instructed us, subject to contract, nevertheless to offer all land and other items comprised within those valuations to you for the total sum of £450,000 (four hundred and fifty thousand pounds), contracts to be exchanged within 28 days of the date of this letter. If within that period no contract is entered into she will, on completion of the estate accounts (and against our advice), put all the above property into auction for sale without reserve.

We are also instructed that any communications regarding the above must take place through ourselves. Mrs. Thornhill and her son are no longer resident at Blue Grace farmhouse and we have instructions not to disclose her address.

We suggest you may care to take independent advice as to the above offer and we look forward to your early response.'

The letter was typed 'Yours faithfully, Dale, Dale & Ogden' but at the bottom Douglas Dale had signed his own name, 'Douglas'.

Robert Thornhill read the letter a second time. Outside, the cat cowered under his car. All around it the puddles in the rutted track were beginning to freeze. Fireworks crossed the sky randomly and exploded. He read the letter a third time. Then he put his head into the crook of his left arm and cried.

*

Rhiannon was never to be seen in the area again. She had cried in fear for her child when Robert Thornhill raped her, and cried in anger and disgust once he had gone. That his actions were accompanied by pressing requests for her to marry him and work in his business made things worse: she knew she would never be free of him, and that he would force her again. So she did the only thing that she could think of that day and rang Maddie Shallcombe. Maddie immediately drove over with Little Mickey and Rachel.

Rachel was horrified and helped Rhiannon pack her few treasured possessions into a small suitcase. Neville and his mountain of baby equipment filled every spare inch of the car. Rhiannon was heartbroken that her memories of Joshua and his home were now overlaid with loathing for his nephew. She had no fear for herself, only for the child: she had done nothing to encourage Thornhill – indeed she had done everything to discourage him and to assert her own right to do as she wished.

Maddie Shallcombe was not surprised. She knew that Robert was not a man to be thwarted in his desires, and had already warned Rhiannon months ago when Neville was born to watch out for him.

'I have a place you might like to borrow, Rhiannon,' Maddie had said. 'It is some way from here, in Glastonbury. Little Mickey can drive you there today and I think you'll like it. Rachel will go with you. Robert will never find you there. We sometimes hire out the house. It's just by the Tor, in Chilkwell Street. My great-grandmother used to spend a lot of time there.'

Rhiannon, because she was an artist, already knew Glastonbury from a number of visits and was pathetically grateful for this offer. Of all the places in Britain that had a reputation for healing, Glastonbury was the most extraordinary.

'Oh, thank you. Aunt Mad.'

'Everything is ready in the house and there's a cleaning lady who goes in once a week, a nice lady called Irene. She'll help you out with Neville as well, I think you'll find. Her own children – she has four – have all left home now.'

With tears in her eyes Rhiannon had hugged Maddie, who stroked her purple hair and looked over at the sleeping Neville lying happily in his carrycot.

'Rhiannon, dear,' Maddie had begun again thoughtfully, 'I need to know what you think about this situation, for the future. You know that if your father should hear of this, Robert Thornhill will be dead within forty-eight hours.'

Rhiannon dried her tears and nodded. She had still clung to Maddie as she replied. 'I know. I can't go to the police because the risk is then open that Poppa gets to hear. Either we let him know or we don't. But it's like there's no way to punish Robert for this.'

'I'm not so sure,' Maddie had replied. 'I'd say Robert would suffer more by losing you than anything else.'

'Then let him. I don't want him killed. He's Joshua's family. I just want to get away from here. I can't stand it any longer.'

She had started to cry again and had cried and reminisced most of the two-hour drive to Glastonbury. Rachel had gone with her and could see that her distress was such that she ought to stay for a couple of weeks whilst Rhiannon settled into her new surroundings. She really did need help with Neville whilst she calmed down and adjusted to the suddenness of the change in her situation. Rachel was impressed at how her mother had instantly known where best Rhiannon should be in order to recover. Glastonbury, which many would claim had never truly been Christianised, was a special place for all the religions that were centred upon it. Christians revered the Abbey and the legend of a visit by Joseph of Aremathea: the pagans treasured the mighty horoscope said to be laid out in the surrounding field-patterns. Moreover there were not just artists in the town but also significant numbers of white witches who used the place for meditation and danced round the Tor, a great hill towering over the town. All of these persuasions revered the ever-flowing water of the Chalice Well.

The Chalice Well had its own gardens, beautiful even in the wintertime. The iron-rich waters, springing deep from the bowels of the earth, were always the same temperature. In summer the water was cool: in winter it was warm. It was to this well, the splashing waterfall beside it and the big flat stone pool at the springhead that Rhiannon went every day. She stood, barefoot, in the cold winter mornings, listening to the water gurgling down the stonework and waiting for her anger to wash away.

Chapter 27: Wedlock

'Yes! Yes! Yes!' Said in ecstatic tones.

'What do you want?' Vincent Crane looked up crossly from the book he was reading and hastily covered it with a copy of the Evening Standard. Izzy Yamani was hopping round him waiving an envelope in the air.

'Its F-F-F-Friday!!'

'Go away. I'm busy.'

'Look at this, mate. Got the tickets. And the birds – well, no probs there. Cheryl's dead keen to see this band, been hassling me for weeks if we can do it. And her mate Tanya's got her eye on you.'

'Tanya?'

'Yeah, the skinny one.'

Vince frowned. 'Don't know her.'

'You do. Cheryl's mate. Bonfire Night disco, silver hot pants. You know.'

'Oh, yeah. Right.' Vince sounded bored.

'Don't sound so keen then. It's taken me ages to get these tickets. I'd say we are definitely in with a chance here. Cheryl says she wants to go down Smithfield afterwards dancing but we can get a meal and I've got the big car tonight. Play our cards right and they might be tempted to finish the night in the car. Bottle of champagne after the meal, all that. I'm going in white. Black's out. What are you gonna wear? All your stuff's black.'

'Nothing. I'm not going.'

'You what?' Yamani briefly stopped breathing.

'I told you Monday. I'm not going. Don't fancy it. Alright?'

'No. Not alright. This is Total Wipeout. These girls are ours. Tanya's been on for a month about where are you nowadays. And

I'm telling her you'll be there. Cheryl's no way going out without her. What's wrong anyway?'

'Nothing. Just don't fancy it.'

'How can you not fancy it? What's the matter with you, Vincent? You've changed. You never go anywhere no more. We used to have a real good laugh. I can't keep going out on my own like this. You're supposed to be my best mate.'

'I've gone off it, discos and stuff.'

'Stuff? Like clubs and pubs and football and girls and drinking. What's up with up with you since you got back this summer? Space aliens get you in a crop circle?'

'It's my business if I want to stay in.'

'So, OK, Vince. What do you do? I mean, when I'm not looking, what do you do? There you are, indoors, all on your own, no TV. What goes on?'

'Nothing, leave me alone, OK? I just don't fancy going out tonight.'

'Suit yourself.'

Izzy put the tickets in his pockets and began to pace round Harold Crane's office. The staff outside were ready to rush out of the building. It was 5.20pm. Only about half an hour left if he was going to text Cheryl in enough time for her to get down from Stanmore with Tanya. He tried to think of some more arguments, and picked up the newspaper on his way past the desk. Vincent jumped like a rabbit, so Izzy followed the direction of his guilty stare:

'John Donne's Love Poems?? I don't believe it!' Yamani oozed contempt.

'Stick your nose out, OK?'

'Come on, mate. Birds are all the same. Easy come, easy go. Lose one, pick up another. You're not still on about her, are you?'

'I said, shove it.'

'You haven't seen her in three months.'

'Two months two weeks, if you must know.'

'So what's all this poems stuff? Here, I know a poem. Dan the Can down the Slug and Lettuce told it me –

There once was a girl from Morocco
A big fairy caught in a grotto
Just don't make a pass
At that hole in my...'

'Shut up! Shut up! For Christ's sake, go away.'

282

'Look, Vince, you are wasting your time and my tickets. She ain't interested. She's out of your league. She is not for the having. Got it?'

'What do you know about her? Nothing. Nothing at all. You've hardly spoken to her even.'

'Vincent, please listen to your old mate Izzy. See, Rachel is an Older Woman. She's like nearly twenty-six or something. And she's loaded and she already dumped Tommy Patel ages ago. Yes, The Tommy Patel.'

Vincent looked thunderstruck.

'You sure?'

'Yeah. He's supposed to be not very happy about it. He likes the best of everything, that one. My mum's cousin Rochelle knows his mum. They used to run a shop together out in Cape Town years ago.'

'So what does she say?'

'Not a lot. Just that. Patel's gutted. Not given up, like.'

Vincent felt suddenly even more depressed than normal. Patel was a cult hero. Cool clothes, everything. He was supposed to have made millions from some deal with his uncle where Tommy did time for him, took the whole rap, then came out to run the family business with him in South Africa. Tommy had everything – fast clothes, fast girls, style, even a law degree. He was really sharp. Vince couldn't believe his ears. What did he have to offer that Patel didn't? Vince's sagging face said it all. Finally he managed:

'Yeah, OK. She doesn't like Patel.'

'But she does, see. Likes him But Turned Him Down! Anyway, according to Rochelle.'

'Well, so what?'

'Well, let's go down the pub. We can chat there if you like but I got to go. See, all I got to do now is text old Cheryl. It's not a commitment or nothing. Just a little suggestion she might fancy knowing where to find us, like. Seeing we've got the tickets on us. OK. OK. We can always sell them down the pub if we don't want to go. Plenty of time to make our minds up. Why don't you just pack up the office side, like, and I'll text her now. Go on, then. OK?' A pause. 'OK?'

Vincent sighed. He needed to find out more about Tommy Patel. Izzy must know something.

'OK.'

'Good man! You won't regret it.' He rushed over to a chair in the far corner of the Docklands office and furiously started to punch buttons on his mobile phone. Vince began the closure sequence for his station on the computer. It was going to be a long night.

Ten o'clock saw Vince, Izzy, Cheryl, Tanya and Cara, another girl they brought with them, squeezed in a corner of a former warehouse in the East End. Right at the back of the warehouse the band was bashing out a massively noisy number. They couldn't see the band but it didn't matter. They got the atmosphere. The noise was literally deafening. Coloured lights zig zagged across the space. Glitter was falling from the upper levels. Everywhere was cram jam packed with young people, and most especially lots and lots of scantily clad girls dancing for all they were worth. High up on six or seven platforms, above the crowd, couples covered in coloured or metallic paint and metal jewellery simulated sex in time to the music. It was so hot in there that everyone was soaked with sweat. Some of the girls were frenetic. Some of the dancers would drop to the floor and be carried off by staff to recovery rooms out the back. All kinds of stuff was going on around him: Vincent Crane looked fed up.

He felt weird wearing white not black and was too hot and anyway both Cheryl and Tanya had got to the boring legless stage too quickly. Izzy was flirting with three other girls as well as Cara and was slipping his card into their bras. It was his latest thing. The card was in a heart shape and had his phone number printed on it under the words 'Izzy is the one.' It was too noisy to talk.

Vince made hand signals to Izzy that he wanted to go out for some air. Izzy gave him the thumbs up and put his hands down Cara's bra top to put in a card for her. Cheryl pushed Cara out of the way and started dancing aggressively in front of Izzy, who was already looking beyond her and waving and blowing kisses to another girl who hadn't had a card yet. Vince could see what was coming but he didn't want to be there at the next catfight. Why didn't Izzy just stick to a couple of girls for the night? He was the one who claimed they were all the same anyway. Vince always seemed to end up with them afterwards when it was his turn to drive, collecting their clothes and drying their tears and getting them home. Then he couldn't get rid of them afterwards. Tanya had been following him round like a sheep since he took her back. Same as that girl Vera, the one Izzy met in Oxford Street. It was like he couldn't go anywhere without seeing one or the other. And they hated each other and argued if either of them saw him with the other.

Vince stepped out in the fresh air. He wished he hadn't come. But now he had to stay until Izzy was ready to pack it in, most probably at breakfast time. It was bitterly cold outside but that felt good after an hour and a half in the warehouse. He ambled over to the all night café next door. There were several cafes all in a line. This one was full of people getting a break from the noise. There were quite a few drivers in there already. Some were like him and did it when it was their turn. Some, believe it or not, were dads who'd brought their teenage daughters and the daughters' friends to dance but the dads hung around in case there was trouble, and they always drove them back at one o'clock. It was like magic. Clock strikes one, the birds are gone. That left the older birds. Most of them worked in offices in the City and were quite a lot older than Vince and Izzy. Izzy did try hard with them but they were not easy like the teenagers and didn't like it if he fiddled with their clothes without being asked. But most of the people in the café were mini-cab drivers hanging about looking for a fare. Some of them were OK and some of them looked very dodgy. One or two, he supposed, must be plain-clothes police but he couldn't have told you which. And anyway this venue wasn't a problem place. Vince's dad knew exactly where he was and had some strong views about not mixing in other people's parishes.

Vince went to the counter and ordered two cans of soft drinks and a glass. He didn't see why he had to slurp it from the tin just because it was trendy. Besides, it ruined your clothes if there was a spill. He carried the tray over to a table by the door, knowing that Izzy would find him easily enough if he wanted to. Anyway, his mobile was on so it didn't really matter how far away he went, provided Izzy had the car when he needed it.

In a way, Izzy was right: he had to do something. But what? All he wanted to do was hang about with Rachel Shallcombe but she was on the other side of the country, and he was supposed to be working with his dad in London to learn the business. It would have been fine, apart from Rachel being so far away. He liked the work, the things they did. They went to some really interesting places and Izzy was there quite a lot so he never got bored. But he couldn't help brooding on when he was ever going to see her. It was alright for Izzy to say: 'Well, ring her.' But what would he say? And she was always doing stuff for her mum or working in the pub. God, she was beautiful. He stared blankly into space, trying to keep his mind off the writhing bodies in the warehouse. And those fantastic eyes....

All at once, he knew what he had to do. It was staring him in the face. He needed to settle down. Give her a good home. Look after her. This was his one chance. She was between boyfriends. Tommy Patel was in South Africa most of the time. She didn't have anyone reliable around. Vince was very reliable: look at him, stone cold sober on a Friday night. Right, so what was he waiting for?

*

When Vincent Crane set off from London early Saturday afternoon, the wedding celebrations for Billy Thornhill and Sophie Corshall were already in full swing. They had been married in St. George's, Waterton, by the Bishop of Ribchester and the tenants and family on both sides repaired afterwards to Hamset Manor. Maybe two hundred or so people gathered for the reception and outside caterers were called into deal with the food and drink. Sophie herself had insisted that Mrs. Allott the cook be given the day off to enjoy herself whilst someone else did the preparations.

Sophie chose a short pale blue wedding dress overlaid with removable white lace. As she rightly said, it could be reused for parties later. She was not a woman to purchase so expensive an item and use it only once. Lord Errington had his hearing aid switched on for the whole day, so excited was he. It was a cold and brilliant afternoon and the guests enjoyed a hearty hot buffet, seating themselves amongst the tables on both the library and great hall levels. The only point at which they were all in the same place was towards the end when the wedding cake was to be cut and the speeches made. Tim Parsons, Billy's best friend from his college days, gave the usual risqué best man's introduction, followed by a brief speech by Billy in praise of his wife. To the great surprise of the tenants, but not her relatives, Sophie also made a speech welcoming the guests and expressing the wish that one day her own grandchildren would look on her portrait with Billy and remember them well as decent people and worthy custodians of Hamset Manor. Then, unexpectedly, she toasted her grandfather, 'sportsman and gentleman whose upright dealings and love for the Estate will never be forgotten.'

Old Lord Errington was deeply troubled at this observation but he waved his stick modestly in the air and smiled broadly around. He would do nothing until the last moment but that moment could not be far away. Time was moving rapidly against him. An heir, an heir. It had not escaped his attention that Carlton did not turn up for the occasion.

*

Roundabout half past four Vincent knocked at the Black Horse. Mrs. Shallcombe had closed the pub until seven, when Rachel's two trained helpers would be coming in to run everything. Maddie herself was weary and needed a break. She didn't mind in the least that, after all the stress of the summer, Rachel had decided to stay over in Glastonbury longer than originally planned. She had been there a month and was due back on Wednesday. Vincent tried ringing the bell and calling through the intercom. She heaved herself up from her chair in the little room and laid aside her book.

'Come in, come in. What's the rush?'

'Hello, Mrs. Shallcombe. Can I talk to you, please?'

'Yes, Vince. What's the matter? I wasn't expecting you, that's all.'

'I had to come to see you. It's really important. Is she here?'

'Who?'

'Rachel.'

'No. I'm afraid not. Did you want to see her or me?'

'Her. No, you.'

'Vince, do come and sit down. All this pacing about is making me nervous. What's the matter?'

'Nothing. Well, er, when is she back?'

'Vince, please tell me what's wrong and meanwhile sit down.'

'Oh, sorry.'

'Yes?'

'Oh, it's nothing really.'

'Nothing? Have you just come over from London?'

'Sort of.'

'I see. Well, can I offer you a soft drink or a juice?'

'No thanks. Er, well, OK. Thanks.'

Mrs. Shallcombe raised her eyebrows and padded off in her slippers to get a drink from the fridge. When she returned to the little room Vince was pacing about in circles again, looking worried.

'Your juice.'

'Er, thanks.' There was a pause whilst he gulped down the drink then resumed his pacing.

'Vince, come and sit here. Now, what can I do for you?'

'Mrs. Shallcombe, I need to ask you something. I've never, well, I don't know what to say.' Maddie frowned and wondered what he was going to confess. His father hadn't been in touch so it couldn't be that bad. 'Mrs. Shallcombe, I am nearly twenty and I've got a job and may I have Rachel's hand in marriage?'

It all came out at once. Maddie was dumbstruck. Vince added, hastily: 'I'm reliable and everything and I'll look after her, you know.'

There then ensued a longer pause whilst Maddie tried to think of something tactful to say. In the end she managed, very quietly:

'Vince, dear, have you actually discussed any of this with Rachel?'

He shook his head, rather sheepishly.

'I was sort of, well, hoping she'd be here.'

'Rachel makes her own decisions in life, Vince. But I don't think she'll marry you, not you or anyone else.'

'But why not?'

'It's the job, dear. The Shallcombe women never marry. It's too dangerous for an Angel to marry. And we never do. All the Angels stay single and they take the title 'Mistress' when they are in charge of the House. When I die Rachel will be the next Mrs. Shallcombe.'

Vincent looked so sad that Maddie put her arm around him.

'Have they never married, then?'

'No. Vince, your father's family have been the Angel's Wings for nearly three hundred years. There's a place in Rachel's life for you and you will be looking after her until the day you retire. Tell me, has your father told you anything about the Tale of the Angel?'

'He said there's some weird initiation ceremony but wouldn't say what. You know, when the Wings recruits a new proprietor into the business.'

'It's not a ceremony, Vince, exactly. More an explanation, a particularly vivid explanation, of where the Angel came from and it tells you a bit about our history.'

'When is it then?'

'Usually it would be on your twenty-first birthday but there are no hard rules. Your father said you were doing well as a trainee.'

Vince brightened up. 'Yes. I want to go into the business, if I can.'

Maddie had seen how crestfallen he was.

'Wait here.'

She left the room and made a phonecall. Ten minutes later she returned.

'I've just been speaking to your father. He agrees with me that there is no harm in telling you the Tale a little sooner than we normally would. Would you like to do this?

'You're sure Rachel......'

'Absolutely sure, Vince.'

'Then yes. Please.'

He sat to attention waiting for Maddie Shallcombe to begin, but instead she stood up.

'Well then, a few safety precautions.'

'What do you mean?'

'I need to check your blood pressure and just have a quick look at you. We don't want you to come to any harm, do we?'

Vince began to look worried.

'I thought you said it wasn't a ceremony.'

'That's right. Come with me.'

Maddie gestured him to follow her behind the bar area. She walked downstairs and into the small cupboard where the captured Howard Morgan had sat. This time, by contrast, Maddie invited her visitor to sit down in the restraining chair. She took a box from out of a hidden wall-cupboard. Vince turned round to get a better view, feeling distinctly uneasy in the confined space.

'Now let me hear you breath in and out.' Maddie put the stethoscope on his chest and listened intently. Then she took his arm and wrapped a cloth around it and pumped up the hose inside. 'Blood pressure fine.'

'Er, can I ask a question?' Maddie nodded at him. 'Can you tell me what's going on? I thought I was going to listen to a story.'

'That's right, dear. Now just take a seat and I'll explain. I'm going to light this big candle here and fill this bowl with water and you will watch the reflection in the water whilst I'm talking. I'm going to give you a potion to drink, only a little, and it will make everything come alive for you. So real that you may at points need restraining, for your safety. Some of the things you will think about are terrifying and you will experience them, the sights, the sounds, everything, just as they happened.'

'Will I be on drugs?'

'Not exactly. The concoction is not available as a recognised drug. It's called ergot and has been known from earliest times but it is exceedingly dangerous in untrained hands. You will never experience it again.'

'My father?'

'Oh yes, and your grandfather and great-grandfather back for centuries.'

'Will it hurt?'

'Not at all,' she said, strapping his hands and feet before leaving the room. After about quarter of an hour's absence she returned with a tiny phial, that she poured into a glass of another liquid. 'Drink this and wait. When you hear your own breathing, tell me.'

Vincent drank the liquid. It was heavily sugared. They waited.

'Maddie, Maddie, it's so noisy here!'

'Now, Vince, look at me. The rushing you hear is your own breathing. Very soon you will feel prickling on your skin and the room will seem hot for a moment. Yes, now. Whatever I say from now on you will see. Do you understand?'

He nodded and looked at her.

'Look at me and see me as a young woman.' Maddie passed her hands over her face then down over her body. Vince's jaw dropped open. 'What do you see?'

'Wow!! You look like Rachel.'

'Hmmm…Vincent, I am wearing clothes today.'

'Er, oh yes.'

'Now let the image change. Long hair, see? And my hair is fair, not dark. What do you see?'

'Hair down to the waist, long fair hair. Unbelievable !!'

'Now, Vince, look at the water. Try to concentrate on the light and the patterns on it.'

Maddie turned off the sidelight. It was now pitch dark in the room save for the play of candlelight on the surface of the shimmering water. 'Forget who you are, Vince, and watch what happens in the water. You are there. Listen to the Tale of the Angel.'

Chapter 28: The tale of the Angel

Forty-two generations have lived and died since the distant days of the first Angel. The terror from the Northlands is all but forgotten, the burnings and the slayings, the land of forests and wolves that once these Islands were. In the year of our Lord 877, in the bitter cold of November, many weeks' march from their coastal base, a small band of Norsemen travelled overland towards the Irish Sea. Their leader was the bravest of his kin, a young man, tall and well built, a warrior by trade, Anlaf Guthrumsson, youngest son of the King of Denmark and East Anglia. For six years, as long as he could remember, his father's men had fought their way into the English heartlands, moving out from their bases in the East in the summertime and retreating when necessary in the autumn. In the time of his grandfather, the invaders had gone home with booty of every description – gold, silver, jewels – to winter over in Denmark. But England was warmer and the land was good. Many followed to make camps, then settlements on the English coast and the numbers grew until the whole of the North and Eastern England was filled with colonists as well as fighters. The rivers and coastal waters were alive with Viking shipping, and the Vikings settled in the City of Londinia for trade.

Anlaf was no Christian. His shield and weapons, and above all his sword, were dedicated to Odin. Death in battle was his goal, his passage to eternal feasting in the hall of the gods. He had volunteered for this mission, the most dangerous and secret ever undertaken in living memory. He and six companions were to reconnoitre the land and bring information for his father in spring to launch an invasion of Wessex. They would strike the Anglo-Saxon Kingdom in its heart and meet with Viking warships waiting on the western coast. Then the hordes would face north and move across the land taking all they wanted and burning all habitation, clearing a way for the settlers behind them. The ships would capture slaves to sell and the last opposition would end.

The seven men travelled at night, hiding by day. They traced a path by moon and stars through the vast dark forest regions, hearing the wolves howl around them. The army retreated as the cold drew in and the days grew shorter. Anlaf and his men pressed on slowly in increasing cold and hunger. The safest routes would lead to discovery. They would be overwhelmed and killed by the Anglo-Saxons. So they chose to skirt the quiet settlements along the Ridgeway, heading ever west. As they went, so the weather worsened until the great storm that separated Anlaf, who was searching for food, from the others. In the blinding conditions he lost his way, unable to find shelter. Realising he would soon die of cold, he decided to head for the track way. In the distance he saw a single light, and trudged towards it. With his last strength he hid his Viking sword under bushes and crouched up against the back of the wooden enclosure, drawing his cloak around him and trying to stay awake.

Vicious guard dogs barked inside the enclosure at the approach of a stranger, and lucky for Anlaf they had. He was found by the mistress of the house to be lying unconscious, half-covered by falling snow.

He woke up three days later, a sick man. Audrey stood by the bed and waited. At first he said nothing, so she addressed him in his own language:

'Your companions were captured and killed in Beckhampton. You were lucky.'

'Will you kill me?'

'No, but you must hide to live.'

'You speak as I do.'

'It is not difficult. Drink this soup.'

'What is it?'

She laughed. 'If I had wanted to kill you, you would be long dead. You may stay until you are well enough to go but I have taken your sword and I will keep it in payment.'

'You dare take the sword of a Viking prince?'

'You must be very sick to tell me you are worth a ransom. Eat, and stop quarrelling. When you thank me for my help I will teach you enough of the speech hereabouts so that they will not kill you instantly.'

He ate. 'Whose house is this?'

'Mine.'

'But you are a woman.'

'Very observant, my prince. My name is Audrey. I live on the edge of Beckhampton and my house offers lodging, when it pleases me, to travellers. You cannot travel further until the spring, when the mass of traders moves across the Ridgeway. Then you can go on safely, dressed as one of us.'

'And if I will not wait?'

'The sickness in your chest will kill you within two days. I have seen it many times before. You need to rest and there is no other place. No one would dare attack you here.'

'Why not? You are alone.'

'My half-brother is the Lord of this area, and he is greatly in my debt. The help I give him in his alliances is worth killing anyone who looks angrily at me. Sleep now you have eaten. What is your real name?'

He saw no point in lying. 'Anlaf.'

'Anlaf Guthrumsson, the lost prince. Tomorrow I will cut your hair in the style of our serfs. You will pretend to belong to me.'

'Never. Kill me now.'

'Are you afraid of cunning when your gods value it so highly?'

He fell silent. 'Why do you speak our language?'

'I speak many languages and I must understand my guests. I have a servant of your people. She was given to me as a slave when she was very young and before my mother died.'

This was their first meeting. Anlaf grew well and strong and grew to love the woman who had rescued him. Her father was an Irish monk fled from the monastery at Clonmacnoise. Her mother was a noblewoman who later remarried, and left the girl with her own household.

As the winter wore on, Audrey took Anlaf as her lover and in February became pregnant by him. She learned of Anlaf's mission as he pleaded with her to return with him but she knew the Norsemen would separate them and kill the child, selling her as a slave. The Anglo-Saxons amongst whom she lived would kill father and child; of that there was no doubt. In the cold months of the year, rumours of battle preparations were rife in the Kingdom of Wessex. King Alfred was warned by Audrey, through her half-brother, that the target would be in the west – his spies in East Anglia told him a great force was massing. Alfred's men marched into the west to face the Danish horde, seeking the better ground on which to make a stand and hoping to hold their own against superior but less disciplined attackers. Anlaf borrowed his sword back and escaped to fight at the side of his father, leaving Audrey less than a day's march from the battlefields.

It was May and the child inside her would not be noticed, but time was running short. The two armies clashed at Eddington, both sides suffering terrible losses, neither able to claim victory. On the third day following the battle, when the rival armies were camped within smell of one another and were busy burning or burying their dead, Audrey, Mistress of Chalkham, sent word to the two Kings, Arthur and Guthrum. They must know that she had been visited by a supernatural spirit, an Angel or a goddess who had a message for them, that they were to appear at her house, unarmed, leaving their escorts outside the stockade. Neither King could ignore this message, as within hours the men of both armies knew of it. So they appeared as she requested to hear the words of the spirit form:

'The sons of the Danes and the sons of the men of Wessex shall become powerful only if they live in peace. I shall touch this human woman with my strength. Bring forth in all his armour Anlaf Guthrumsson, son of Guthrum the King, and bravest of his kin. If he can kill the unarmed human woman, the Kingdom of Wessex shall perish. But if she shall overcome him then shall she give King Alfred and King Guthrum fair terms of peace. Three days and three nights shall the two Kings then sit in the house of the woman to discuss with her. And they shall accept her verdict. So shall both sides justly claim victory and share the land in peace.'

A cold fear came upon the King of Wessex but he was a Christian and would not defy an Angel. The fearsome Danish King laughed and sent immediately for his youngest son. Anlaf Guthrumsson heard the order from his father and his face paled. He raised his sword but his arm shook and he could not kill the woman who stood before him. 'This sword belongs to the Angel,' he said, and laid it at the woman's feet. Audrey took up the sword and told the Danish King that he must accept Christian baptism lest the Angel blight his men with weakness and curse his people forever. 'Go,' she said, 'and bring me the head of any Lord that shall oppose you. The Angel will strike down your opponent.'

The King went out from the house and poured the water of the stream over his head with his own helmet in front of his horde. He held his great sword over the heads of the army and proclaimed that Odin and Christ were one and Christians must share the land. His first Lord denied it and the great King fought and killed him, spearing his head and holding it aloft as the proof of the Angel's words.

Three days and three nights in the house of the Angel's woman they argued and on the morning of the fourth day the judgment of the Angel was written, the great peace between the Anglo-Saxons and the Vikings, drawing the boundary between them and valuing their lives equally, the Peace of Eddington.

The Angel spoke through the woman once more and told both sides to claim victory and never speak of her intervention lest she be troubled with worthless requests. So both Kings left her presence and peace returned to the land. The life of the child was saved by this cunning and two years later Alfred called upon the woman again to pact for him with the Viking Coelwulf, who held Londinia.

In every age the work of the Angel must continue: Rachel Shallcombe will be the forty-fourth in her line.

Chapter 29: Full circle

The perch on the battlements had proved useful on a number of fronts.

Lord Errington rang Mr. Clifford Dale, insisting that Dancer drive the car down to the village to collect him. Mr. Dale was not given to arguing with this particular client, knowing that it was a waste of his breath. He prepared himself to add yet more codicils to the old man's will. Dancer had strict instructions to collect Dale at 10.30am and to drive along the main Estate road, and return the exact same way. At 10.45am precisely Mr. Dale, carrying his will file, was escorted to the library for an audience.

'Mr. Clifford Dale of Messrs. Dale, Dale & Ogden.'

Dancer bowed and departed.

'Come in, Cliff, come in.'

Errington had his hearing aid switched on. Mr. Dale, however, never noticed such things.

'Good to see you, Corky. Keeping well?'

'Not bad. Not bad.' He made no mention of the latest letter from his consultant telling him that his prostate cancer was now very advanced. Damn quacks. 'Sit down. Coffee?'

'That would be very nice.'

Errington did not ring the bell. Dancer came in immediately, pushing a trolley bearing a small pot of coffee and some biscuits for Mr. Dale together with the glass of water, not Burgundy, that Errington had ordered for himself. Dancer thought this most irregular: Mr. Dale didn't. Lord Errington did not wander off to the window and make a speech, as he usually did, but sat attentively in his chair. The old boy's on good form, thought Clifford Dale.

'Got to make provision,' Errington began. 'Read this.'

He handed over a single piece of poor quality paper. Mr. Dale read aloud:

'Amniocentesis results completed. Male embryo, no abnormalities recorded.'

'That's it. Sophie's.'

'This is excellent news, Corky.'

'Had to tell you meself. Need your advice about the will. Should I change it?'

'As things stand, everything goes to Sophie and in the event of her death to any child she may have. Any additional grandchild of yours should be notified to the Toggenburg lawyers but essentially I need to take instructions for Sophie's will in the circumstances. There seems no need to provide direct for her child unless you think she will not do so. It would only be necessary to think about redoing everything if you decided to alter the main gift to Sophie.'

'No, no. Then leave it as it is.'

Errington resisted the temptation to switch off his hearing aid. He could feel Mr. Dale was about to burden him with a lot of legal advice. A pre-emptive biscuit might head it off. 'Excellent biscuits. Have more.'

He rang for Dancer, who appeared immediately but took some time to cross the room.

'Yes, my Lord.'

'More biscuits for Mr. Dale. Different ones.'

'Very good, my Lord.'

Clifford Dale smiled apologetically. Errington stood up, stared out of the window and turned his hearing aid off. Periodically he turned round to see if the younger man's lips were moving. The old man frowned, as though deep in reflection at the advice being given. There was plenty of time. Carlton never moved before lunchtime but, still, they ought to be making a start. Errington tapped on the window, which he assumed would stop his adviser.

'Damn birds. Can't reseed anything nowadays. Pasture's pecked up again.'

He pointed with his stick at the home grounds round the house. Mr. Dale got up politely and affected interest. 'Got to sign those tenancy papers in your office. Got to see that pasture close to. Damn birds. I'll drive.'

He rang for Dancer before Clifford Dale could say a word. Mr. Dale took this to mean that Lord Errington was ready to sign the engrossment of the Thornhill tenancy and would come to his office for the purpose. If only he had mentioned this, he could have brought them with him. But allowance had to be made for clients of this age. Dancer reappeared at the door just as Errington reached it.

'Ring Gilbert, Dancer. Tell him to come.'

'Very good, my Lord.' Dancer turned to go.

'Car keys. I'll take 'em.' Dancer handed them over without protest. Errington occasionally drove and was anyway a couple of years younger than Dancer. Mr. Dale, anticipating an imminent departure, rapidly ate a couple more biscuits before standing up. 'Follow me.'

It took another ten minutes before they reached the car, parked in the old stable block by the side of the house. Most of the way Errington was muttering about the birds and their ravages. He slammed the door on Mr. Dale sitting in the passenger seat and, very gingerly, lowered himself into the driver's seat. He pushed the central locking down on the driver's side.

'Right, Cliff. Got to keep my eyes on the road but you'd better look out for birds on that pasture. Got to tell Gilbert. Full report.'

Half way along the back Estate drive, as Clifford Dale was in the middle of a running commentary about the number of birds he could see out of the side window, and where they were, the car ran over a log.

'Damn logs! Road's supposed to be clear all year.' The car had run over the log with its front wheels and Errington stared out of the window. 'Hang on,' he yelled, slamming the gear into reverse and hitting the log again with the front wheels. 'Damnation. Never get used to this gear system. Try again, eh, no tyres gone!'

He revved the car furiously and, in first gear, drove over the log a third time, clearing it with front and back wheels. Mr Dale was trying to open the passenger door.

'Better check the damage, Corky.'

'Yes. Quite right. Hang on.'

Errington opened the driver's door, which unlocked Dale's door too. Mr. Dale manoeuvred himself out of the vehicle. Errington remained in the car, fiddling with the rear mirror.

'Oh my God!' cried Mr. Dale. 'It's Carlton.'

Or had been. There are some things best done with a lawyer present. Murdering a close relative is one of them.

*

It was the first of May 2003, Neville Thornhill's first birthday. He was spending the morning, warmly wrapped, running round the great lawn of ruined Glastonbury Abbey. He staggered contentedly towards the ducks, pointing and making faces as he went. Every now and again he fell over and stared about, trying to work out what had happened. Rhiannon strolled behind him with a changing bag and a loaf of bread for the ducks, periodically telling him off for trying to put grass and dirt into his mouth. So much had happened in one year that she did not have the energy to think about it any more. How great it would have been if Joshua could have seen Neville today. She had changed her hair colour from purple to green.

*

Robert Thornhill did an unusual thing that day. Mid-morning he went for a walk, instead of supervising his men. They would have said that there was something wrong with him. Thornhill had it all: the farm, the tenancy, all the businesses and a new deal with the Estate. Yet his temper grew shorter and shorter. Some claimed he had always been a black-hearted bastard. Others said success had gone to his head. Kathleen claimed it was his son's attitude that had spoiled it all. She had even seen the terrible letter he had written, after Robert had hung it on the nail by the toilet. She didn't agree that he had driven his wife to her death or cheated her father's widow. And she certainly didn't think it was right for a Thornhill to take the name Corshall.

Thornhill kept his eyes on the ground and trudged through Blue Grace Woods with the cares of the universe upon his shoulders. He banged the farm gate shut and pulled his overcoat about him. The woods were deserted, and he needed to be on his own. Under one arm he carried a shotgun, loaded.

As he marched along, kicking stones out of his way, he heard a man's voice directly ahead of him shout 'Ow!'

'Hold still, who is it?' Robert Thornhill levelled his shotgun at the man further down the path. 'This is private property.'

'Don't shoot! Don't shoot!' Eric Pinker, who had been rubbing his eye, immediately held his hands up and walked closer. 'What a fantastic stroke of luck, your being here. You must be the new owner.' Thornhill did not lower his gun. 'Eric Pinker. Don't you remember me? I did your dog's funeral last year.'

It was not surprising that Eric hadn't been recognised. He was wearing black and green combat clothes and a black wool balaclava over his face, and had been crouching in a ditch not far from the path. A less self-possessed owner might well have shot him where he stood. Thornhill said nothing.

'Oops!' said Eric, removing the balaclava. 'Lucky you didn't pot me there. Ha! No need to worry though.' Eric grinned cheekily at Thornhill and with the forefinger of his left hand he delicately guided the barrel away from himself towards the nearest tree. Thornhill looked very irritable. He had come out to brood. What was this chap doing on his land?

'Now,' said Eric, taking Thornhill by the elbow and walking alongside him in the direction Thornhill had been going, 'I have a wonderful idea for a business deal, just the thing for a place like this.'

Thornhill eyed him suspiciously. 'You shouldn't be here. This is my land.'

'Terribly sorry. You're absolutely right. But there's a jolly good reason. See this ditch,' and before Thornhill could stop him Eric had propelled him off the path, 'just look at that.'

'What about it?'

'What about it? It's perfect. The most fantastic natural playground you could imagine. Look at my get-up. Look.' He pointed to the camouflage and from the bottom of the ditch produced a military helmet with part of a bush on it. 'Don't worry. They're not your leaves. These are plastic. You need year-round leaves for war games.'

'War games?'

'Of course. It's all the rage. Fantastic business. Lots of people do it. And you can charge fortunes. They play with paint guns. And there's lots of money in the support facilities and costume hire.'

'Support facilities?'

'You know, toilets and refreshments and places to change and souvenirs and photos.'

'Photos?'

'Oh yes. Costumes. People love it. Especially the night battles. Totally scary, totally safe. I reckon there must be £5,000 in one night session and.....'

'£5,000!!'

'Well, gross. You do have a few expenses. Nothing too much because they get written off over a period. But this place is the best

I've surveyed for this. All very top secret, you know. Don't want word to get out.'

'Why not?'

'Competition. Limited market. Drives the prices right down. But, of course, our partner would be protected from that mostly.'

'Why?'

'Well we know the customers' preferences. We don't just cater to a bunch of office managers, you know. My brother Freddie, you remember him, he helps run a club up in Bristol. A very select club, very special games they want to order. Nothing illegal, of course. But they do need a lot of support.'

'What sort of special games?'

'Well, we thought as a taster we'd run an Avengers' evening for the ladies. A sort of night battle. Pink luminous paint and everything. Champagne in the caravan for the ones that get killed early and lots of nice warm leather clothing selling in the car park. I have a super supplier lined up. Sale or return. Cash or visa only. But I don't suppose you'd think about coming in with us on this? We did have a look at Turtleton Manor, and it does have some potential but it would take quite a lot of work to get it to this standard. I mean, this place is a goldmine. Just look at the natural obstacles and nothing dangerous here. What do you think?'

'I.....'

'No. Quite right. Don't decide now. Just think about it for a day or two. I know where you live. The best thing would be if I did a little proposal in writing so we can go through the figures in detail together. Here, have one of my business cards and I'll get right back to you. What a stroke of luck you coming along here just now!'

Eric pulled a small box out of his combat jacket pocket, removed a card and thrust under Thornhill's nose. The card was green and white striped and in big green gothic letters across the front was written 'Pinker & Pinker. Fun with a Gun. Perilous Parties Arranged.' The telephone number and the website address followed. Thornhill took the card, frowning. Eric casually looked at his watch.

'Oops!' he said. 'Got to be going. Terrific bumping into you. Here, do try out the gun. It's a sample. And the paint comes off in the wash. Clever, isn't it?'

He pushed the paint gun into Thornhill's free hand, checked his watch again and set off abruptly in the other direction.

So instead of deciding whether life without Rhiannon was worth having, Robert Thornhill tried out the luminous paint gun on the nearest tree. Not bad, he thought. Not bad at all.

Printed in the United Kingdom
by Lightning Source UK Ltd.
113418UKS00001B/5